Temptation

By Nicole Edwards
The Club Destiny Series:

Conviction

Temptation

Addicted

Seduction

Infatuation

Captivated

Devotion

Perception

Entrusted

The Alluring Indulgence Series:

Kaleb

Zane

Travis

Holidays with the Walker Brothers

Ethan

The Devil's Bend Series:

Chasing Dreams

The Dead Heat Ranch Series:

Boots Optional

Nicole Edwards

Temptation

A *Club Destiny* Novel
Book 2

Published by SL Independent Publishing, LLC
PO Box 806, Hutto, Texas 78634

Copyright © Nicole Edwards, 2012
All rights reserved.
ISBN: 978-0985059149

Cover Image by: © Oleksiy Maksymenko/All Canada Photos/Corbis
Cover Design by: Nicole Edwards Limited

Temptation – *A Club Destiny Novel* is a work of fiction. Names, characters, businesses, places, events and incidents are either the products of the author's imagination or used in a fictitious manner. Any resemblance to actual persons, living or dead, business establishments, events, or locales is entirely coincidental.

Erotic Romance
Contains M/M Interaction
Mature Audiences

Chapter One

"Club Destiny." Luke didn't bother trying to hide the gruff irritation in his voice when he clicked the answer button on his cell phone and all but slammed it against his ear. The damn thing had been ringing nonstop for the last two hours, so he'd stopped bothering to look at the screen before he answered.

"Hey, bro. What's going on?" Logan, Luke's nothing-if-not-persistent twin brother, greeted back, seemingly immune to Luke's umbrage.

Flying under the radar for the last two months had taken some creative manipulation, but Luke had pulled it off, making a full-fledged effort to work on some of his own personal issues. Nonetheless, said personal issues were not resolved, but he found himself right back in the thick of things once again. He shouldn't be surprised that his brother was calling, and he wasn't really, he just wasn't in the mood to talk to him considering the ass chewing he was expecting.

"Not a damn thing. What about you?" he barked back, walking through the main floor of his club on the way to his office.

He'd spent the better part of the morning with Club Destiny's head bar manager, going through their weekly order, and trying his damnedest to get back into the groove. Between that and answering the phone, he hadn't had a minute to himself. Which in his current state was probably not a bad thing.

"Glad you could make it back," Logan said, and Luke heard his brother's sarcasm, as well as his frustration, but at the moment, he didn't give a damn.

"What do you want?" Luke made it to his second floor office and slammed the door behind him.

Thankfully there were only a handful of people at the club that early in the day since they weren't open to the general public yet. Only members were allowed in during the morning hours, and they all knew to give him a wide berth on a good day. Unfortunately for them, today wasn't a good day.

Temptation

Even with the few familiar faces he'd seen that morning, Luke's only desire was to be left alone. Although he'd managed to abandon his responsibilities, as well as any of his personal relationships for the last eight weeks, Luke still wasn't in the mood to be around anyone, and he wasn't keen on the idea of talking to his brother either.

"What the hell's wrong with you?" His brother never did have a problem calling him to the carpet so to speak, and apparently, Logan wasn't in much of a better mood than he was.

Which was surprising with all that had apparently happened to Logan during the time that Luke had been away. The man was a husband now, for Christ sake. That alone should make his brother much more pleasant than he currently was.

With a silent groan, Luke flopped down into the high back executive chair that he managed to occupy for at least a few hours every day. Glancing around the immaculate office, gleaming with hardwood and soft, iridescent lighting, he tried to remember what made him find comfort in the place.

Oh wait. He didn't.

The oversized mahogany desk, a full size, distressed leather sofa, and the intricate, *way* overpriced designer rug had been someone's idea of soothing. Instead, the result was just fucking ugly. And the confined feeling that overcame him when he walked in didn't help either. Without windows, the not so small space seemed more like a broom closet than an office.

Even after spending thousands of dollars on some highly recommended interior designer, Luke hadn't felt comfortable in the space. Which explained why he spent most of his time down in the club or caught up on the mountains of endless paperwork from home.

Despite his discomfort with enclosed spaces, the club as a whole offered him a sense of peace that was absent from his personal life, thanks to his own demons that managed to haunt him day and night like a bad case of the flu. Rational decisions weren't generally on Luke's short list of things to do, so purchasing the club ranked right up there with one of the best he could come up with in quite some time.

Though he often wondered if the club actually intensified those demons.

Remembering that he still held the phone to his ear, and his brother wasn't going to wait patiently for long, Luke answered. "Just trying to get some shit done around here." *And not succeeding worth a damn.*

Luke almost felt guilty for directing his annoyance at his brother, knowing the other man had spent the last two months trying to juggle his own responsibilities, including a full time job and apparently a new wife, along with covering for Luke's absence at the club. Yes, the wife part had been a surprise because when Luke had left town, Logan and Samantha were only dating. When he came back... *Bam!* – New sister-in-law.

For some unexplained reason, just the thought of Samantha had Luke's body going instantly hard. Most likely that was due to the fact that he'd known Sam intimately, on more than one occasion, thanks to the few times Logan had invited him to be the third. The remembered feel of Sam against him, or her hot, sweet mouth on him, had Luke almost longing for another encounter with her. *Almost* being the key word.

Since his personal demons had begun making a daily visit, Luke had sworn off those little sexcapades.

Granted, Luke liked Sam. And as far as Logan went, she was a perfect match for him.

The fact that they had gotten married shouldn't surprise him as much as it did. Or perhaps the fact that his identical twin brother hadn't bothered to mention that little tidbit of information prior to Luke taking some time off was what kept throwing him off. Either way, he tried not to think about it too much. Especially knowing that what they had shared before could never be again, especially after that last night...

Luke brushed off the thought. He didn't have time to dwell on what couldn't be.

"I'm glad you're back, Luke, but we need to talk." Though Logan's tone was slightly less frustrated than before, Luke easily picked up on the insistence his twin had thrown in for good measure. Luke hated when his brother did that shit. He'd much rather face the anger than to have to face the fact that he had let his brother down.

"Then talk," Luke stated, leaning back in his chair, thinking twice about propping his size 15 boots up on the polished wood top.

He could almost predict what Logan wanted to talk about after all their twin bond was strong, and for most of their lives, they could finish each other's sentences, sometimes even knew what the other was going to say before they said anything at all. And now wasn't much different.

"I'll drop by around lunch time. Don't disappear on me," Logan stated flatly before the line disconnected.

"Sonuvabitch," Luke mumbled to no one in particular. He might deserve to have Logan show up on his doorstep and read him the riot act, but it didn't mean he was going to be happy about it.

Luke hit the switch to turn on his computer screen so he could scan through his recent emails. While he had been away, he'd managed to stay on top of things as best he could. He couldn't abandon his responsibilities altogether, though he'd been so fucked up in the head that he had wanted to. Even now he had a hard time keeping his focus. So many things had happened in the last couple of months, Luke wasn't sure he knew which way was up anymore.

As much as he wanted to blame everything on what had happened that last night with Logan and Samantha, Luke knew he couldn't do that. Sam might've come into Logan's life, and in turn Luke's, but the woman hadn't done anything specific that would have thrown Luke's life off course the way it had been. No, he only had himself to blame for that, but his own denial wouldn't allow him to admit that either.

"Fuck," Luke ground out as he pushed out of his chair, nearly sending the damn thing over backward. He had too much shit to do to sit around pondering the reasons why he felt so off kilter lately.

He should just leave again, take another extended vacation and get away by himself. Not that it would do him any good. After all, he'd spent the better part of two months doing exactly that and look where it had gotten him.

Not a damn place.

Resigning himself to staying at the club and attempting to take care of business, Luke grabbed an invoice off of his desk and headed back downstairs to talk to Kane Steele, his bar manager. According to their earlier conversation, it appeared that there were some issues with the deliveries while Luke had been away.

Either that or someone was fucking with him and stealing his inventory. Luke didn't even want to contemplate that happening; Heaven help the asshole who would be brave enough to steal from him in the first place.

~~*~~

Sierra Sellers wasn't all that enthusiastic with the idea of being set up, regardless of how hot and mysterious – her mother's words, not hers – the man might be. Apparently her mother was under the impression that Sierra needed a date, and rather than asking her if she were capable of finding one on her own, Veronica Sellers had chosen to make her own arrangements. Those arrangements had led to Sierra piling into the backseat of Logan McCoy's supercharged Cadillac CTS while he and his wife talked quietly in the front seats.

After a very brief, very one-sided conversation with her mother, Sierra had resigned herself to this outing. Very reluctantly she might add. Veronica's argument consisted of the words "new to Dallas", followed by "essential to network", with a cherry on top of the conversational sundae being "get your business established".

So, no, Sierra hadn't come up with a strong enough excuse not to go along with her mother's logic, though she still didn't understand how a date was going to help her in that regard.

When Veronica had mentioned that XTX – the company her mother worked for – was holding their annual vendors conference in just two days, Sierra hadn't thought anything of it. Why would she? XTX didn't have anything to do with the interior design company that Sierra had yet to even name.

Only when Veronica mentioned that the conference was in Las Vegas had Sierra's ears even perked up. And here she was, on the next leg of this journey that she only hoped would turn out the way her mother intended.

And yes, she was incredibly nervous, despite her reluctance and despite the fact that she felt as though she were being led to an execution. Even armed with a few details about the man she was going to meet, Sierra wasn't feeling all warm and fuzzy about the outcome. The positive side of this endeavor was that she at least knew what the man looked like. Or at least she thought she did.

According to both her mother and Samantha, she was off to meet Logan's identical twin brother. That had immediately piqued her interest because hell, she had to admit, Logan McCoy was smoking hot. Not that she would share that little tidbit of information with anyone, especially the man's wife whom she had become close to over the course of the last few weeks.

But realistically, how similar could the two of them actually be? They were grown men for goodness sake, and surely their personalities would set them worlds apart in appearance. So when Sam and Veronica had reiterated the fact that they were identical, Sierra had mentally rolled her eyes and resigned herself to finding out on her own. Maybe her mother's physical descriptions were accurate. Although Sierra liked Logan enough, she still wasn't all that enthusiastic about the idea of being set up with a man – gorgeous or not. The one positive that she could manage to conjure up from this entire screwed up ordeal was that she and Sam had actually become good friends. Since the woman was the epitome of what Sierra had worked her entire life to become, she knew she would ultimately win in this deal.

At twenty-nine years old, Sierra still had some growing to do when it came to establishing herself in business, but after meeting Sam, she knew she'd found a role model who could undoubtedly teach her some things along the way. And when said role model had ganged up on her with the help of Veronica and another woman they worked with at XTX, insisting that Sierra actually meet Luke McCoy, she had found herself outvoted.

Both Veronica and the other woman, Deanna, had spoken very highly of Luke, but something had set her sensors off when Sam had talked about him. If Sierra wasn't mistaken there was something much more intimate about the way Sam spoke of her brother-in-law. Just in case she was imagining things, Sierra hadn't bothered to ask. Not that it was any of her business anyway.

Now, two days later, she was on her way to meet the man, though she got the impression that he had no idea he was being set up.

"You said we were going to a club?" Sierra asked, interrupting the loving couple holding hands in the front seat. "Isn't it a little early in the day?"

"It's a club, but it isn't what you're thinking," Sam offered. "Well, at least not entirely."

Sierra noticed the subtle way Logan squeezed his wife's hand.

What other kinds of clubs were there? Besides the ones that offered drinks to people who congregated to laugh, drink and have a good time?

Oh!

Her mind struggled with the possibility before shrugging off the comment. Glancing at her watch, Sierra added, "I didn't realize clubs were open this early."

Eleven thirty on a Tuesday and Sierra was on her way to meet the mystery man who, despite the fact that they didn't know each other at all, would likely accompany her to a four day business conference to be held in Las Vegas.

The Entertainment Capital of the World.

Sin City.

And one of Sierra's favorite vacation destinations.

She could certainly get down with going to Las Vegas, no matter whom she was going with. She was quite fond of the city, having gone numerous times for girl's only getaways. Never once had she come back disappointed. Going for business, now that would be the first, but no more so than going with a man. Any man.

What would they do if they didn't get along? How was she supposed to suffer through four long days in the party capital of the world with someone she had nothing in common with?

Granted, she was jumping ahead of herself. She hadn't even met him yet. The one upside to it all, if he looked anything like Logan McCoy, at least she was in for a visual treat.

Logan maneuvered the car into an underground parking garage, and Sierra felt the butterflies take flight in her stomach.

Glancing down, she noticed that she was wringing her hands in her lap, a sheer sign of the tension coursing through her veins. She chalked it up to the fact that she suspected Luke had no idea she was coming or anything else that was in store for him, in the coming days. She'd gathered that from the conversation she'd overheard – ok, more like eavesdropped on – earlier between Logan and Sam. When Logan mentioned that Luke didn't seem to be in the best of moods, she'd momentarily questioned her sanity.

Not that she really cared what kind of mood he was in, as long as he could manage to be polite and courteous for four days, only a few hours at a time while they were in Vegas.

Moments later, Sierra was climbing out of the back seat, coming to join Samantha standing at the side of the car.

"Brace yourself." Sam smiled brightly, looking almost playful.

"Is there something I should know before we go in?" Sierra asked, for the second time questioning what she was walking into.

"Not specifically. Let's just say that Logan's brother is the *darker* twin."

"Darker?" Confusion set in, and Sierra tried to comprehend what Sam was saying.

"You know, mysterious. Ominous." Sam laughed as she took Logan's hand.

Great. Just what Sierra needed. Her mind immediately conjured up a version of Logan McCoy; only this one had a permanent scowl, making him look sinister. She smiled to herself.

With a deep breath, she stood up straighter, adjusted her short skirt, and steeled herself for whatever was to come.

How bad could it be?

Chapter Two

"You find it?" Kane asked, looking both weary and determined as Luke approached.

"Of course I fucking found it," Luke growled, slamming the invoice on the bar top. "Right on my desk. Now you want to tell me how we lost eight cases of our best vodka?" Luke knew he was being an asshole, and he knew that Kane was working his ass off trying to figure out what the hell had happened during the week that the other man had also been on vacation, but Luke didn't need theories, he wanted fucking answers.

Three thousand dollars' worth of vodka didn't just up and walk away, yet no one seemed to know a damn thing.

"Shit, Luke. I don't have any idea." Kane answered, running his fingers through his shaggy, brown hair, a clear sign the man was at a loss.

Sucking in a ragged breath, Luke glanced around the near empty main floor of the club – the equivalent of counting to ten – in an attempt to hold on to the anger that was begging to break free. He only hoped there weren't any customers getting a firsthand glimpse of his tirade.

Since all other areas were limited to their exclusive members by design, he should have thought to have his mental breakdown behind the big double doors that separated the two divisions of the club. However, since Club Destiny saw a large portion of its overall revenue from the public club and bar, Luke spent a lot of his time right in that very spot.

Staring at the empty area now, Luke acknowledged the dim lights above weren't nearly as attractive as the neon glow of blue and red that outlined the walls and the bar when the club was open. The usual mass of bodies that filled Club Destiny from wall to wall was nowhere to be found, nor was the noise that came with so many people occupying one place. To be honest, Luke wasn't sure which way he preferred most.

As he tried to gain his composure, not wanting to beat up on Kane too much, Luke inhaled deeply, took one more look around until his eyes landed on the man sitting at a table near the back.

Shit.

Luke wasn't feeling overly social, and Cole Ackerley was the last person he wanted to talk to. Thankfully, it didn't look like Cole was up for talking either. Instead, Cole sat at an empty table, drinking what appeared to be a soda, rather than a shot of whiskey he normally favored.

For all intents and purposes, Cole looked like he didn't give a damn that Luke was staring his way, but Luke felt the heat of Cole's midnight blue eyes burning a hole into him. They certainly had some things they needed to talk about, but like usual, Luke would put that disaster waiting to happen off for a little while.

Since Cole was one of the main reasons Luke had gone MIA for the last two months, there wasn't much he could say, even if he wanted to. After everything that had happened between them that night…

Not going there.

Those damned demons he'd managed to bury temporarily were not going to show up now. If he weren't careful, Luke would manage to brew up a shit storm of issues he hadn't been able to figure out during those few weeks he'd disappeared. Since he hadn't been able to get to the bottom of them then, he knew for damn sure it wouldn't be happening now.

He didn't give a damn what that said about him, or how much of an asshole that made him look like. Luke was not ready to address that little clusterfuck.

At least not right now.

He'd wallow in the denial for a little while longer, thank you very much.

His reaction to Cole that night had been pulled from deep down inside of him, and Luke knew that was a part of him that he couldn't contain. The part of him that set him apart from the rest. Did it bother him? No, not usually. Until now. He'd always been open to sexual experiences that bordered on the taboo.

When his eyes met Cole's, Luke felt the other man's confusion and for a moment, he thought about confronting him. Clearing the air. Instead, he turned his back, trying to focus on the stack of papers lying on the bar. Despite the fact that Luke had managed to run off for some much needed time alone, he had also heard that Cole opted to keep a low profile for the last few weeks, as well. He wondered if the solitude had helped Cole because it sure as hell hadn't done a damn bit of good for Luke.

A moment later Ava Prescott's sultry voice fluttered through the otherwise quiet club, but Luke didn't turn around. Ava wasn't there to see him. She was obviously there to see Cole, which wasn't at all surprising. Cole's membership with the club was a longstanding one, and his involvement as a third in the relationship with the Prescott's wasn't a secret. Nor was the fact that Cole was open about his sexuality, enjoyed his freedom as a single man, and he would not, no matter what, disclose any information about what went on between him and other members of the club.

Cole was one of the most respected members at Club Destiny, and despite the fact that the man was approached often by other couples, he was downright particular about those he spent his time with.

Luke remembered the first time he and Cole had found themselves in a situation they hadn't expected. The one night when the two of them ended up alone with the very sexy, extremely flirtatious, Susie Mackendrick. That night had been memorable, and so had the few other nights he and Cole had shared Susie's bed. And her kitchen table. And her shower.

Luke found himself smiling for the first time that day. Those memories of Susie still sent a spark of desire bursting through his blood stream.

Maybe that was the key to getting him out of the funk he was in. Calling Susie or better yet, just showing up at her house would definitely distract his overstimulated brain for at least a few hours.

The woman was incredibly creative when it came to sex. She was also a self-proclaimed submissive, which worked well with Luke's darker urges. Although there were times when those dark, dangerous urges to dominate made him realize that Susie probably couldn't handle some of the things he wanted to do to her.

Which led him back to Cole…

Fuck!

He was not going to go down this road again. Not here. Not now.

With an irritated sigh, Luke turned back to the bar, ignoring Ava Prescott's sensual purr of as she greeted Cole. Luke flipped through the pages in front of him though he could have been reading instructions in Chinese for all that he was seeing.

It wasn't that he cared who Cole was with.

He honestly didn't.

Ok, maybe that was a lie. He cared just a little.

Those damn lingering memories of that one night still haunted him, still had him jolting out of a dead sleep, confused and yet... aching.

He tried to tell himself that it was just lust. What he and Cole had done wasn't wrong. At least not in relative terms. When it came to Luke's sex life, there were boundaries he crossed every damn day.

Yet he had never – *never* – crossed that line. He had never thought he was interested. But that night, Cole had managed to give Luke the one thing he'd been longing for. The resistance that had lit Cole's indigo blue gaze still haunted him. Luke had been boiling with a longing so deep, so dark, that he hadn't known how to satisfy it. At least not until he had instructed Cole to go to his knees...

Fuck!

Readjusting himself, Luke couldn't deny the fact that the memories still stoked a fire that he couldn't extinguish. His jeans were past the point of uncomfortable, and he had no choice but to stand there and stare at the damn papers in front of him. No way in hell was he turning around to see Cole sauntering off with the Prescott's.

Pushing the papers aside, Luke planted his hands on the bar top, pressing his head down between his shoulders in an attempt to alleviate some of the tension churning inside of him. Every time he began to think about that night, or Cole, or hell, even Samantha, Luke's brain got more and more fucked up. What had he learned in the two months since that one fateful night?

Too much, and yet not nearly enough.

The one thing he had come to terms with by the time he decided enough was enough and hiding out wasn't the answer was that he wanted Cole. He didn't want emotional bullshit, or strings of any sort, but he damn sure had never met a man who made his body throb the way that Cole did.

Yet here he was. Keeping his back turned, and his expression guarded as Cole prepared himself to be the filling in the Prescott's sex sandwich. The thought had his balls tightening and his dick throbbing. Remembering that night and the way Cole had given himself over to the moment had Luke gritting his teeth. When the man agreed to something, he gave everything he was.

Granted, Luke was discriminatory with his partners, but he had been drawn to Cole from almost the moment he had met him. At the time, it hadn't been in any way related to attraction, just simple admiration. Cole was an admitted bisexual, open to almost anything, trustworthy, honest and beyond discreet. Everything that his members looked for in a partner or a third.

But then it happened. That one damn night at his house when they had invited Cole to be the fourth in a little rendezvous with Luke's twin, Logan, and Logan's then girlfriend, Samantha. That night had sent Luke's mind whirling with uncertainty.

When Ava and Daniel Prescott passed behind him, Luke did turn, this time watching as Cole followed not far behind them. Turning his attention back toward Kane, Luke had the other man walk him through the events of the last two weeks.

He didn't have time to think about Cole, or anyone else. He had a business to run; one that apparently couldn't manage to hang onto a few thousand dollars' worth of liquor, unless someone was paying attention.

Chapter Three

"Who is *that*?" Kane interrupted Luke as he was trying to decipher a handful of receipts that hadn't already been logged.

Luke turned his attention to the three people walking through the back entrance to the main floor of the club, and he immediately understood his bar manager's astonished tone. His first reaction, which he managed to choke back, was to grumble at the sight of his brother and his wife.

Not that he wasn't glad to see them.

The funk he couldn't seem to shake still lingered like a storm cloud threatening to burst open at any second. Seeing Samantha, knowing the previous impression he'd made on her, Luke wasn't so sure he would be able to look her in the eye.

The absolute last thing he expected was for his brother's new wife to walk right up to him and throw her arms around his neck, but that was exactly what she did. Instinctively, Luke's eyes darted to his brother, immediately seeking direction. When Logan merely smiled back, Luke managed to lift his arms – apparently made of lead – and wrap them around Sam, tentatively hugging her back.

And the next thing he did might've damn well changed his life forever.

Having briefly glimpsed the woman who had been beside Sam and Logan as they came through the door, Luke hadn't taken a chance to really look at her. With his arms still wrapped around his brother's wife, Luke's gaze landed on the sexiest, most petite woman he'd ever laid eyes on. A hot flash of lust shocked his system, and he froze where he was standing. Doing his best to keep his cool, Luke let go of Sam and took a step back, his eyes still glued to the woman.

Standing before him, with her back straight, her magnificent breasts thrust high, Luke couldn't stop his gaze from roaming down the full length of her. At barely five feet tall at the most, even in those sexy as hell knee high black boots with at least three inch heels, the woman captivated him. And that was saying something because Luke had never been attracted to tiny, petite women, mainly due to the fact that he was damn near six and a half feet tall.

Had he met her before? She looked somewhat familiar, yet he knew he couldn't have because he would have remembered her. Hell, she would have played a starring role in many of his erotic fantasies, so no, he was certain he hadn't.

Her eyes were an exotic ice blue that glowed with something so intense, so unique, Luke had to remind himself where he was and who else was around. He imagined wrapping his hand in the long, glossy, black hair that hung like a silk curtain down her back, tilting her head back so that he could claim her mouth.

She must have recognized the heat in his eyes because she abruptly stood even straighter than before, gripped the edge of her jacket, slowly closing the expensive leather over her very impressive cleavage. She might've been able to limit his visual feast, but no matter what she did, she couldn't cover up those toned, trim thighs exposed beneath the hem of that little black mini skirt she wore. He let his eyes wander, his mouth watering from the temptation that small body offered, before returning to meet her silvery blue eyes.

"Luke, I'd like you to meet Sierra Sellers. She's Veronica's daughter," Sam introduced him to the beauty standing beside her.

Luke didn't know who the hell Veronica was, or maybe he did, but his brain wasn't functioning at the moment. At least not past wondering whether her panties and bra were silky and black like the halter she'd hidden from his view. He choked on a growl and glanced over at his brother, needing a cold shower if he was expected to have a rational conversation.

"Veronica is Xavier's administrative assistant," Logan clarified, and Luke caught the amusement in his brother's tone. "Sierra is Veronica's daughter."

"Sierra, this is Luke McCoy, my husband's twin brother and the owner of Club Destiny," Sam offered.

To Luke's surprise, Sierra released the edges of her leather jacket, her firm, perky breasts once more daring his eyes before she took a confident step forward. As she held out one delicate hand, her fingers tipped with – no, not a bright fuck-me-red like he expected, but a soft, cotton candy pink – Luke forced his brain to function, willing his hand forward to take hers. Immediately he recognized his mistake because the second their fingers touched, he felt something bright and hot ignite deep in his groin, a spark almost as bright as the blue flame of her eyes burning right through him.

Her hand was tiny; her fingers delicate and soft, her grip firm yet utterly feminine. Luke knew he held on longer than he should have, but for some reason, he'd been struck deaf and dumb from the moment he laid eyes on her.

"Nice to meet you." Sierra smiled, a slight tilt to the corner of those seductively full lips, her bright blue eyes focused intently on him.

Holy hell. He was in a world of hurt. Even the sound of her voice was seductive.

"Why don't you ladies order a drink, while I take a minute to talk to my brother," Logan said, bringing Luke back to the present.

"Kane, get these ladies anything they want. We'll be back in a minute," Luke managed to say when he found his voice, instructing his bar manager as he headed after his brother. The same brother he was going to have to punch for bringing a distraction the likes of one Sierra Sellers into his club.

What the hell was he thinking?

Shit. He needed to get his head in the game, not find another person to lust after. He wasn't quite sure what the hell had just happened, or who the hell the smoking hot woman was, but Luke was pretty sure it wasn't going to matter in a few minutes.

Sierra Sellers, no matter how heart stopping beautiful she was, or how confident she appeared, would never be able to handle a man like him and surely Logan was aware of this before he'd brought her into the club.

"So are you going to tell me what was so damn urgent for you to come down here? Or do I have to follow you around like a dog?" Luke's indignation was back full throttle, and he directed every ounce at his brother.

"Man, you need to relax," Logan stated as they made their way into Luke's office, shutting the heavy wooden door behind them. "I figured that little hiatus of yours would have calmed you down a little."

"Well, you were wrong," Luke huffed as he propped himself on the edge of his desk. "And I'm not in the mood for any shit right now."

"I'm only saying this because you're my brother and I love you, but damn, man. I think you need to get laid," Logan chuckled.

"Fuck you," Luke retorted, hating that Logan enjoyed getting a rise out of him.

Logan glared back, and Luke knew that no matter how many warnings he gave his brother, he wasn't going to back off. With a deep sigh, Luke relocated to the chair behind his desk. "Let me have it."

"What the hell happened to you?" Always direct, Logan was. Luke scrubbed his hands down his face and then stared back at the mirror image sitting across from him. There was no reason to play dumb; it would only prolong the inevitable. Logan wasn't stupid, and Luke knew that he'd been acting like an ass for quite some time now which made Logan's concern only that much more predictable.

"I know something happened that night," Logan said making reference to the night Luke, Cole, Logan, and Sam had all engaged in some overly erotic entertainment at Luke's house.

Before Luke could interrupt, tell Logan exactly what he thought about his brothers interference, Logan held his hand up.

"I'm not asking for details. It's your business, but I'm going to offer some advice, even if you don't want it."

Luke knew Logan, and he knew that arguing with him would just prolong the agony that this conversation had already turned into. Instead, he gave him the attention he sought as he leaned back in his chair, crossing one ankle over the opposite knee. He was proficient at pretending nonchalance, though he felt anything but.

"Look, what happened that night took us all by surprise. Sam especially, but it had nothing to do with what happened between you and Cole. And, you know I don't judge. Ever." Logan leaned forward in his chair, his elbows resting on his knee. "I know that something happened that night between you and Cole, something neither of you wants to acknowledge, but damn it, Luke, you've got to figure this out."

Luke heard the frustration in Logan's voice, and as much as he appreciated the sentiment, Logan was on the wrong track. "Little brother, I appreciate your relationship advice, I really do, but it isn't necessary."

"Bullshit." Logan stood from his chair. Driving his fingers through his hair, he turned to stare back at Luke. "That isn't why I came, but while I'm here, you knew I was going to give you my opinion. Figure it out, Luke."

Temptation

Luke nodded his head, knowing that his acknowledgment was the only thing that would move Logan on to his true reason for being there. After all, Logan wasn't telling him something he hadn't spent the last several weeks thinking about. As a matter of fact, he'd thought of nothing else except that one October night the four of them had been at his house.

What happened had taken him by surprise more than anyone else. Something had shifted deep inside of him, something so unexpected he didn't know how to deal with it.

He knew what he wanted. It didn't mean he was happy about it.

For years, he'd been satisfied, or so he thought, with the various trysts he'd experienced. Just the thought of wanting something more permanent, even more monogamous was enough to make Luke's eyes cross. Where the hell had that come from anyway? Was it the fact that he was getting older?

Shit. He had no idea, but the more he thought about it, the more he came to the realization that he was ready to slow down. Some of those baser urges may never be satisfied, but hell, Luke wasn't sure he would ever find a woman who could handle what he desired anyway.

Maybe he would have to compromise. Maybe he would have to just… settle. Ok, so that definitely wasn't the answer. Luke didn't take kindly to settling for anything less than what he wanted.

And when it came to sex, Luke wanted it all. He wanted his partners to be willing to give in to his every whim. There were lines that would be crossed, and up until the night he had lost all control and taken Cole in a way he had never done with another man, Luke knew there weren't many lines that he *wouldn't* cross.

The problem that he knew he would run into would be to find a woman who could handle that side of him. The side of him that sought to find the sheer pleasure from sex – boundaries be damned.

Despite the anger and frustration that continued to build because Luke didn't believe there was a release for the personal demons that haunted him. The one's that made him feel like a sexual deviant at times for wanting the full and complete submission of a woman, her willingness to give herself over to him, to trust that he would care for her and take her higher than she had ever dreamed possible.

Not that being with Cole had changed any of those wants, but Luke had found a release that night. One he had never known before. And that had scared him beyond measure. To the point that he wondered about his sexual preferences and wondered if he had been looking in the wrong place the entire time.

Then he realized that he hadn't been. He wasn't gay; although that night, the thought had crossed his mind. No, being gay would have been easy to accept, but Luke knew his interest wasn't only in one gender. He liked women and apparently he found just as much sexual satisfaction in men.

Scratch that. *One* man.

That life altering realization had come to him after a week of being holed up in his vacation cabin, forcing himself to think things through. To decide what the hell it was that he wanted. And to stop thinking about the fact that he couldn't change the man that he was, even if he wanted to. Which he didn't.

And no, Luke wasn't in any position to talk about, or even deal with what had happened. At least not now.

"So, why did you come?" Luke asked, suddenly more than willing to get this conversation over with.

"I need a favor," Logan said, this time smiling that mischievous grin that told Luke he wasn't going to like what came next.

Tipping one eyebrow up, urging Logan to get on with it, Luke didn't move, and he didn't say anything.

"XTX has a vendor's conference in Vegas this weekend. I owe someone a favor and she's called me on it."

"A favor?" Where the hell was Logan going with this?

"Sierra is Veronica Sellers' daughter," Logan stated.

"So you've said." Luke's testy response was met with Logan's even broader smile.

"Sierra's an interior designer who just moved to Dallas from Nashville to be closer to her mother. She's looking to build her business here, but she doesn't have many contacts. Veronica seems to think this conference might be just the place to get her daughter's name circulating."

That sounded reasonable enough, but it didn't explain why Logan was there. "So how does this involve me?" Luke asked, trying to tie it all together.

Temptation

"I need you to accompany Sierra to Vegas for the conference," Logan said, taking a step back as though he were already anticipating Luke's reaction.

Luke pushed up from his chair, ran his hand through his hair and then directed a death glare at his brother. "Are you fucking serious?"

Luke didn't quite know what to make of his brother's request. The woman he'd just been introduced to, the one that made his dick stand up and take notice, needed a date. To Vegas.

What the hell was Logan thinking bringing her here?

"Did you completely fucking forget who you're talking to, Logan? That sweet, innocent woman out there doesn't stand a chance around me, and you know it. You know me better than anyone else, and hell, you saw my reaction to her. You bring the two of us together, and you're opening up Pandora's Box."

Surely his brother had gone insane. Logan had his own sexual preferences, a little on the dominant side, but the two of them weren't even in the same league. What Luke wanted, no, what Luke needed, was far darker than any single woman could give him. And that woman, with her sleek black hair, long legs, and tight body was a temptation that Luke wouldn't be able to resist.

"I know what I'm asking, Luke. I wouldn't have come here if I had any doubts." Logan's calm, assertive attitude pissed Luke off.

Fuck.

He was fucked no matter how he looked at it. The part of him that wanted to shield that unsuspecting woman from a man like him was being held back by the part of him that wanted to strip her naked, right in the middle of his club, and fuck her blind.

"Ok," Luke heard himself say, against his better judgment.

"*Ok?* You'll go?" Logan's incredulity was obvious.

"I'll go."

"One more thing," Logan said as he turned toward the door. "Cole Ackerley's attending. He's going as a representative of CISS. Alex can't make it, and Cole has contracted for him before. I just thought you should know."

Sonuvabitch.

Luke watched his brother walk out of the room, but he didn't make a move to follow him. He didn't think his heart could handle the movement. What the hell was he getting himself into? Being around either of them wasn't going to be a hardship, but Luke had a feeling he wouldn't be able to control his baser urges.

Alone with both of them. In Vegas. For a weekend.

What the fuck?

Luke was so totally screwed.

Chapter Four

Sitting at a small table close to the bar, Sierra forced her gaze to the woman sitting across from her. Despite the overwhelming desire to search the room for the sexy, brooding man she had been introduced to only minutes before, she fought to focus.

The man made her skin tingle. Everywhere. The way his eyes had grazed her, the equivalent of a sensual caress, had sent a shiver down her spine. Had he looked closer, and yes, she knew he had tried, he would have seen her nipples pebbled beneath the shiny black halter she wore.

Looking down at her hand, she remembered the feel of his skin on hers, the way heat had spiraled low and fierce in her belly moments before her internal muscles had contracted. She had never had a reaction as all-consuming as the one she had to the feel of Luke McCoy's giant, callused palm on hers.

How was it possible for a man to come across so mysterious, so powerful, that Sierra felt it all the way down to her toes? The way he looked at her, the way his penetrating hazel eyes touched every inch of her overheated skin had Sierra wanting to search the room for him once more.

"So, the flight leaves Dallas on Thursday morning at seven. Logan and I will be glad to give you a ride to the airport if you need one."

Sierra had to process Sam's comment and erase the graphic images of Luke from her brain.

Flight. Airport. Oh, right.

"I'm good, but thanks. I figure my mother will want me to come along with her."

Sam nodded her understanding, taking a sip of her drink. Sierra stared down at the half empty glass of cranberry juice and vodka she'd ordered. Despite her original concern that it was a little too early to be having a drink, she found the combination was just what she needed to calm her rioting nerves. Yes, Luke McCoy was driving her to drink.

And to think, she'd just met the man.

He owned a nightclub, Sierra thought as her eyes drifted around the room, taking in the sleek, modern decor – smoky glass, metal and wood – that decorated the room, giving it a sophisticated feel. Admittedly Sierra had never seen a night club in the harsh light of day; the decision maker lights at two o'clock in the morning notwithstanding.

She glanced toward the grand staircase that led to the second floor, and she wondered what was up there. From where she sat, Sierra could see a set of heavy wooden double doors that were closed, and she had a desire to go up there to find out where Luke had gone.

"Have you been to Vegas before?" Sam asked, interrupting her thoughts once more.

"Several times. Some of my girlfriends and I would try to go out there a couple of times a year." A sudden homesick ache stirred inside of her.

Sierra had only been in Dallas for a couple of weeks and leaving the comfort of the place she had grown up had been difficult to swallow at first. Granted, the opportunities that were presented to her in Dallas were vast, but that didn't make the transition any easier.

"Well, this will be my first time," Sam stated quietly, and Sierra was almost positive the other woman blushed.

"Really? Aside from the conference, I'm sure you'll have a great time." Sierra laughed. "Not that you won't have fun at the conference."

Sam laughed in return. "I hope we get some time to ourselves to enjoy the sights."

"We're in a great location. The hotel we're staying at is one of the nicest in the area, even though it is at the south end of the strip, it's still close to other resorts we can visit."

"So, do you gamble?" Sam asked with a twinkle in her eye. Sierra got the impression her question had a double meaning.

"A little. I like to play blackjack, and of course, drop some quarters in the slot machines." Sierra took a sip of her drink, letting the tart, liquid fire flow down her throat. At this rate, she'd need another, and surely it was too early in the day to actually get drunk.

~~*~~

Cole Ackerley stepped out into the dimly lit hallway, clicking the door shut behind him.

Temptation

He'd just spent the last hour and a half with the Prescott's, succumbing to Ava's every desire, yet the yearning that had consumed him for the last two months hadn't been sated. Which was unusual because Ava and Daniel Prescott could generally scratch that insatiable itch with minimal effort. The woman didn't know the term inhibition when it came to her desires. Between her beloved strap-on, which she used rigorously on her husband, and her desire to direct every movement, Cole could generally get lost in the sensations that the man and woman inspired within him.

Not so much today.

Sure, Cole found his release, but only when he closed his eyes, pretending the man plowing into him from behind was Luke McCoy while Ava used her very skilled mouth to suck him dry. Yep, that had certainly worked, but now, as he walked down the empty corridor to the main doors that would take him back to the main floor, Cole felt... alone.

That was a new emotion for Cole, considering he'd grown accustomed to his solitary life, enjoying it actually. Yet in recent months, Cole had found out some things about himself that he wasn't sure he thoroughly understood.

Taking the stairs down to the main floor, Cole's attention was drawn to two women sitting at one of the tables near the bar. He recognized Samantha McCoy immediately. The other woman, he'd never seen before, but he couldn't seem to tear his gaze away from her. Sitting at the table, talking animatedly with Sam, Cole admired her momentarily. She was exquisitely beautiful, in a very sensual, extraordinarily exotic way.

Damn near tripping over the last step, Cole focused on his feet, slowing his movements because he couldn't tear his eyes away from the black haired beauty. When her gaze landed on him, apparently drawn to his less than graceful entrance, Cole's heart thumped hard in his chest.

Those eyes.

Even from across the room, Cole could see the glimmer of silver in her blue eyes, a color he'd never before seen. When one slight eyebrow arched, Cole tilted his head slightly, trying to read her intent. Oh, he'd seen that look before. Numerous times.

Women were attracted to him physically. He knew that. And without ego, he accepted it. He was a big man, which in general, drew attention, often unwanted, but attention nonetheless. At six feet, four inches, two hundred and seventy pounds of solid muscle, Cole would never be considered average. And thanks to his rigorous training regimen, he kept himself in shape.

He maintained eye contact with the woman until his attention was diverted to Sam, who turned to glance in his direction.

"Cole." When she called out to him, Cole faltered only briefly, wondering whether he should just wave a hand, acknowledging Sam, or take this opportunity to be introduced to this woman.

His brain told him to head out the back door, as was his original intention, but his dick instructed him otherwise. Several steps later, Cole was stepping up to the table, being greeted by Sam with a quick hug.

"Cole, I'd like you to meet Sierra Sellers. Sierra, this is Cole Ackerley."

When Sierra stood from her chair, all five feet of her, Cole nearly took a step back. The woman was tiny. And when she held out her hand, he hesitated briefly before returning the gesture and taking her small, cool fingers within his grasp. A powerful torrent of desire spiked his blood stream at the contact, causing Cole to abruptly pull back.

"Nice to meet you, Cole." Her husky, seductive voice slid over him, making the hair on the nape of his neck stand up.

"You too." *How incredibly eloquent, Ackerley.*

"I hear you're attending the conference in Vegas as a representative of CISS," Sam stated, interrupting his temporary lapse in cognition.

"Yep." *Ok, maybe it wasn't temporary.*

"Sierra's attending, as well. She's new to the Dallas area, establishing her interior design company here, hoping to meet some potential clients at the conference."

Cole couldn't speak, so he nodded his head. Good Lord, he looked like a total idiot, but his vocabulary skills had suddenly been rendered useless.

The sound of footsteps from behind him jolted Cole, making him turn in time to see one of the McCoy brothers walking down the stairs. Logan. That certainly wasn't Luke all decked out in an Armani suit. But it wasn't the suit that was the main difference in the brothers. Logan had a gleam in his eye, an easiness about him that Luke hadn't seemed to inherit, which set the otherwise identical brothers apart.

"Cole," Logan greeted, holding out his hand.

Cole gripped Logan's hand, returning the handshake. "Logan. Good to see you."

"Same here." Logan slid his hands into his pockets. "Alex tells me you're attending the conference this weekend. Hopefully, we'll get a chance to have a beer at some point."

Again, Cole couldn't seem to find his voice, the thought of Sierra's eyes boring into him was a clear distraction, one that he couldn't seem to shake. Just when he realized that he needed to say something, do something, so he didn't look like a clumsy idiot, Luke McCoy descended the steps and Cole's heart damn near plummeted to his toes. His heartbeat increased, and there was a sudden roaring in his ears. It was a visceral reaction, one only Luke managed to instill in Cole.

Well, that was until he'd laid eyes on Sierra Sellers.

"I look forward to seeing you in Vegas," Cole managed to choke out, seconds before he headed in the opposite direction.

He might look like a stammering fool, but that was nothing compared to what would happen if he were within ten feet of Luke. After what had happened between them months before and the fact that Luke had successfully avoided him since, Cole hadn't been able to look the man in the eye. And it had nothing to do with embarrassment and everything to do with the fact that he longed for an instant replay of that night.

Which was another first for Cole.

Hell, the day had been full of them already, and as he walked through the doors leading to the parking garage, Cole wondered just what this weekend had in store for him.

~~*~~

Sierra's attention was drawn to the omnipotent male descending the stairs. As far as appearances went, and the way that both Luke and Logan carried themselves, Sierra was pretty sure she had never seen two men look so much alike, yet so vastly different. There was something intensely masculine, and yes as Sam mentioned, very reticent about Luke.

Though Logan was the mirror image, and sexy as hell in his own right, there was something more demanding about Luke, something darker, more intriguing. She glanced quickly at Sam, who was smiling back at her knowingly.

"Don't worry. You aren't the only woman who has had that reaction." Then she lowered her voice a little. "Like I said earlier, brace yourself."

Sierra watched Luke move toward them, briefly glancing toward Cole who was exiting through the main doors at the same time.

Was it her imagination, or was Cole leaving because of Luke? She hadn't gotten a good read on the incredibly handsome man because he had seemed incredibly nervous, or maybe that had been her.

When their eyes met, Sierra had felt an intrinsic longing reflected in the midnight blue gaze staring back at her. She'd been surprised by the all-consuming heat that rushed over her.

Hadn't she just been thinking about Luke and the way the man seemed to make her libido awaken from a decade-long coma? It seemed ironic that she would have a similar reaction to another man so soon afterward.

Hormones. That's what it was. Luke must have awakened her to the point that she was now flooded with them.

"Let's go next door and get a bite to eat while these two have a few minutes to talk." Logan's deep voice interrupted her thoughts and had her attention returning to the couple standing beside her.

Not to mention the man fast approaching, whose eyes were riveted to the doors that Cole had just exited. Interesting.

Sierra felt the butterflies take flight once more. Just being near Luke was short-circuiting her insides and now she was going to be left alone with him. She took a fortifying breath and then graced him with a smile. She could do this.

Surely she could do this.

When he smiled back at her, a sexy, crooked, mischievous grin, Sierra knew she'd need more than courage to get through the next few minutes.

"I hear you need a date for Vegas," Luke stated as he took the seat that Sam had been sitting in, motioning to the chair across from him. The man clearly didn't have a problem with getting to the point.

"Depends on who you ask," Sierra stated, returning his playful grin and easing into the chair.

"Not that I have any doubt you could find one on your own."

Was he flirting with her?

Sierra took in Luke's rugged features, his midnight black hair and hazel eyes that were more green than brown, thanks to the forest green polo shirt he wore. His thick, well groomed eyebrows were half-cocked while his sexy lips were tilted into a smirk as he waited for her response.

"I won't dispute that, but being I'm new in town, and definitely not looking to find anything more than someone to accompany me to the conference, I decided to take my chances."

"Ever been to one of XTX's vendor conferences?"

Luke's penetrating gaze was directed at her, and Sierra felt the warmth of those radiant green-brown eyes all the way to her toes. She was grateful she was sitting down because she wasn't sure she would be able to hold herself up thanks to the way her knees had turned to jelly.

"No, I haven't. My mother has been to a few, but I didn't get many details from her."

Veronica hadn't been forthcoming with any information; other than that Sierra would want to take someone with her because there were numerous after hours' events that would be couples mostly. No matter how much Sierra protested Veronica hadn't let up.

Sierra was a little shocked at how adamant her mother had been since Veronica was single as well, and wasn't likely to be taking a date. Though she knew Veronica and Xavier usually attended events together, as far as she knew, they weren't actually a couple. Being that Xavier was widowed, and Veronica had been divorced from Sierra's absent father for nearly two decades, Sierra figured they could do whatever they wanted.

"I'm amazed that Logan thought to invite me," Luke said, but Sierra got the impression he didn't mean to say the words out loud.

"Why is that?" Unexplainably intrigued by the man, Sierra wanted to know more about him.

"Tell me a little about you, Sierra." Luke obviously wasn't interested in talking about himself if his deflection of the subject was anything to go by.

"What do you want to know, *Luke?*" Sierra addressed him, using his name the way he had used hers.

She was all for getting to know this man, but based on the vibe she felt coming off of him in waves he was used to things going his way. The slight tilt of his lips into a barely there smile told her that he realized she would be a challenge.

"Kane, bring Sierra another drink," Luke instructed the bartender, but he never took his eyes off of her.

She liked the way he looked at her; the dark passion that swirled just beneath the surface was there for the world to see, but Sierra knew he held something back. Probably a lot of *something*s, if she had to guess.

"You're from Nashville?"

"Born and raised. My mother moved to Dallas right after I graduated from high school. I stayed to go to the University of Tennessee. Until recently, I've been working for a design firm in Nashville. I started there after I graduated, but I've always intended to start my own business."

"Other than your mother, what made you want to come to Texas?" Luke asked as Kane sat her drink on the table, removing the empty glass.

"Nothing, honestly. I love Nashville, and if she hadn't been so far away, I probably would've never left. But, design firms are a dime a dozen here, the clientele desirable, so I figured I could kill two birds, so to speak. Being close to my mother is important to me, more so than where I start my business."

"Do you live with your mother?"

Sierra laughed, trying to imagine how that would even be possible. "Hardly. I think we'd kill each other if we were under the same roof."

Growing up in a house, just her and her mother, had been a challenge. Two of them, both self-sufficient, exceedingly independent, and more than a little bit princesses in their own right meant that neither of them could be under the same roof for long without trying to see who the bigger diva was. They had barely managed to survive Sierra's teenage years.

No, she certainly hadn't moved in with her mother.

"What about you, Luke?" Sierra asked, trying to turn the tables. If she wasn't careful, she got the impression Luke would know everything there was to know about her while she would walk away knowing nothing.

Likely his intention.

"What about me?"

"Do you live with your mother?" Sierra smiled, then took a sip of her drink. Wow. Apparently Kane thought she needed some courage of the liquid variety by the strength of the drink he'd made for her.

Luke's raspy laugh tickled Sierra's insides. A gruff, unpracticed sound. Like his laugh muscles hadn't been used in quite some time.

"No."

Well, hell. Talking to this man was like pulling teeth. Instead of asking anything more, Sierra pierced him with a glare, tilting her head slightly to the side as she waited for him to continue. When Luke leaned back in his chair, crossing his massive arms over his chest, Sierra knew they were at a standstill.

So be it. She wasn't about to give in.

"Can I assume you'll be attending the conference in Vegas?" Sierra finally broke the silence, figuring she needed to get this conversation over with before she lost the little bit of nerve she still had left.

"You can."

Sierra laughed again. If nothing else, this trip was sure to be interesting.

Pushing her chair back from the table, Sierra stood, shocked momentarily when Luke rose abruptly, his enormous size making her feel even smaller than she normally did. She couldn't look him in the eye without tilting her head back. Even with heels she came just barely to the middle of his broad chest, and he was easily twice her weight and width, but she wasn't about to let him intimidate her.

"I'm glad to hear it. I think I should be going. It was very nice to meet you, Luke. I look forward to seeing you in Vegas. I'm sure you'll be able to find me if you're interested." With that, Sierra gave him her brightest smile, turned on her heel and walked straight out the front doors without looking back.

Her heart was racing, her hands were sweating, but Sierra wasn't about to let that man know what he did to her. He was dangerous. She could feel it in her bones. He would want things from her that she wasn't sure she was ready to give.

But, damn was she tempted.

Chapter Five

Luke boarded the plane at DFW International airport, and waited patiently for the other passengers to make their way down the narrow center aisle as they looked for the optimal place to spend the next three hours. Considering patience wasn't his strong suit, Luke mentally patted himself on the back for not running through the crowd to get where he was going.

Glancing through the cabin, he took note of the other passengers, looking for one particular person. The seat wouldn't matter.

As he approached row eight, he noticed a dark haired beauty seated next to an equally dark haired beauty, only the other one was about twenty years older. The woman seated to Sierra's right must have been Veronica Sellers, considering she looked like an older, more refined version of Sierra.

When he approached the row, he caught Sierra's attention and tried to control himself.

"Morning."

The smile beamed at him was bright enough to rival the sun, and Luke was momentarily blinded, his heart instantly kicking into overdrive.

"Good morning, Luke," Sierra offered a prim and proper response. "I'd like you to meet my mother, Veronica."

"Nice to see you again, Veronica. I was hoping I could steal Sierra away from you for the next few hours. If it isn't too inconvenient."

The grin Sierra's mother shot at him mirrored her daughter's initial one, but the twinkle in her eye was just for him. The million watt smile Sierra had flashed him was no longer visible, but her confusion was.

"I don't mind at all," Veronica stated sweetly, giving her daughter a good-natured shove. "Join Mr. McCoy, Sierra. I'll be fine."

Luke watched the emotions play on Sierra's face, confusion, disbelief, and then something else… Determination. Her shoulders went back, and she forced a smile, but Luke could tell she wasn't happy with his request.

For the last twenty four hours, he'd spent his time thinking about this woman, and he vowed the moment he woke up that he wouldn't be kept away from her any longer than he had to be. The idea of hijacking her from her mother hadn't come to him until a few minutes before he boarded the plane, but now as he watched her reluctantly move out of the seat and into the aisle, Luke was glad he'd opted to do so.

"There are empty seats about six rows back," he told her as he followed, a front row view to her perfect ass encased in tight, faded jeans that hugged her hips. So small, yet so incredibly curvy, the black t-shirt molded to her petite frame showcased every slight peak and valley. He'd been so engrossed in taking her in, he almost missed the way her spine straightened at his remark. He grinned to himself.

To his surprise, Sierra moved two additional rows back and to the other side of the plane, purposely ignoring his original instruction. Instantly he knew this trip was going to be more than interesting, it was going to be downright hot.

Luke allowed her to sit by the window while he took the aisle seat, offering them a degree of privacy without a third person in their row. Being that the plane was small and apparently full, Luke didn't expect complete privacy, but he did hope to talk to her without any interruptions.

Once they were seated, and Sierra had fastened the seat belt across her tiny waist, Luke followed suit. The scent of her perfume tickled his nose and made his cock throb. No flowery fragrance for this woman. The scent was sharp, yet subtle, a hint of spice and something erotically stimulating. Her perfume suited her nicely.

"Mr. McCoy, I hope you know what you're doing," Sierra stated, her voice but a whisper, and for a moment, Luke thought he imagined it.

"Always," he assured her, turning his head to look at her. Those silver-blue eyes pierced him, and he noticed she was no longer smiling.

His attention was drawn to the last few people easing down the aisle, making their way to the few seats left in the back. His eyes locked with Cole Ackerley's and memories from that one night flooded through him. When Cole's eyes darted to the woman sitting next to Luke, something akin to fire developed hot and fierce inside of him. The other man's interest was evident, but Cole turned his gaze away and managed a smirk, not saying a word as he passed by.

"Do you know him?" Sierra asked, catching his attention.

"Why?"

Sierra looked at him in disbelief and then turned to face forward once again. "No reason. And remind me not to ask any more questions."

"Why's that?" Luke asked, but Sierra simply laughed – without mirth – and it donned on him that he was answering her questions with questions of his own.

For the next half hour, they both remained quiet as the plane departed from the terminal and then made its ascent into the clear blue skies over Dallas, on their way to Las Vegas, Nevada.

Luke hadn't seen Logan and Samantha, but he figured they had managed to secure seats at the front of the plane. Since he had been so engrossed in trying to locate Sierra, he likely just overlooked them. Although he wasn't sure exactly where Cole was located, Luke could feel the man somewhere behind him.

"So, are we going to spend the next four days with me asking questions and you answering with questions?" Sierra's husky voice broke the silence.

"Why would I do that?" Aiming to get a rise out of her, he hit his mark. "Damn you're pretty when you get irritated."

A sweet, rosy blush crept up Sierra's neck and stained her high cheekbones, and the sight struck something deep inside of him. He didn't know a damn thing about this woman, other than she was an interior designer who grew up in Tennessee, her mother worked for Xavier Thomas, and she was feisty as hell, but what he did know he liked. A lot.

"Ok, you win. I'll tell you about myself," Luke offered, wanting to put a smile on her pretty face. When she turned slightly in her chair to face him more directly, his body tensed, but he forged on.

"I was born and raised in Dallas, my parents died when Logan and I were about eight, leaving us to live with my ornery old grandfather, and truth be told, we couldn't have selected anyone better to put up with us."

"I'm so sorry," Sierra consoled him, and the feel of her silky fingers against the back of his hand had a different feeling flowing through him.

"We gave him a run for his money, but the old man kept up with us like a champ," Luke continued, not wanting to think about the soft feel of her hand or whether the rest of her was just as soft. "When we graduated from high school, Logan went off to college, and I stayed close to home, choosing to go to UTD for business.

"Up until about five years ago, I hadn't found what I was looking for, but I managed to get some experience under my belt working at various companies usually in management of some sort. Then the club came up for sale, and Logan and I used our inheritance to purchase it, turning it into what it is today," Luke said, glancing at Sierra.

"And that is?" Those glowing blue eyes were fixed on him as she asked.

He hoped she wouldn't ask that question, but given they were going to spend the next four days together, in one capacity or another, Luke felt it necessary to get it out in the open. "Club Destiny is a sex club."

"A swinger's club? Not a brothel, I assume?"

Her political correctness made him want to laugh. He was genuinely surprised by her reaction altogether. She didn't seem put off by the idea, and that was a first for him.

Granted, Club Destiny had nearly one hundred exclusive full time members and another fifty or so part time members, all of whom shared the same lifestyle and interests in some form or fashion as Luke and Logan, but he rarely met anyone off the street who didn't give him a questionable scowl when he mentioned his profession.

"That's correct. It's more of a lifestyle club that caters to the needs of our members."

"Is it limited to married couples?" Sierra asked, and Luke realized she knew more about his world than he expected.

"No. Single, married, it doesn't matter. However, membership to Club Destiny is steep, which is a requirement to keep the sort of clientele we're looking for." Steep was almost an understatement. For the price, an interested party knew what they were signing up for when they joined.

"What about nonmembers? Can they engage in any activities?"

"No. Our policies are finite and extremely strict as we aim to ensure the anonymity of our clients. As you saw the other day, we have a public facing club that we open to anyone, but the other is limited to members only."

"Are there rooms on site?" Sierra asked in all seriousness.

Luke didn't know what to think about Sierra's inquisitions. She knew all the right questions, the same ones that he frequently received from those applying to become members of his club.

"Yes." Realizing they were venturing into unchartered territory, Luke was reluctant to continue answering her questions without throwing out a couple of his own. "You sound familiar with this type of club. Have you ever been a member of one?"

When Sierra's cheeks brightened once again, and her eyes averted, Luke wondered if he had nailed it. Unsure of what he hoped her answer would be, he held his breath as he waited.

"No. I haven't," she admitted, but she didn't turn to look at him again.

"Is that because you didn't want to?" He had to ask.

"Yes," she said, her bright blue eyes flickering with some hidden emotion. "Yes and no, I mean. It isn't that I have anything against the lifestyle, it's just that I have never ventured down that path."

Luke exhaled deeply. He hadn't realized how much he hoped she would say that until the words were out. For some reason, the fact that she hadn't been a member of a club like his, spurred on his possessive nature. But something in the way she answered said there was more to the story than she was letting on.

"Have you ever been married, Sierra?"

Her head jerked in his direction, but then she covered her reaction smoothly. "Yes."

"Are you married now?" he asked, trying to hold back the fury starting a slow pulse deep inside. There were boundaries he would cross without hesitation, but he would never, without explicit permission, be with another man's wife.

"No. I'm divorced. Eleven years now."

Luke tried to do the math in his head, but since he didn't know how old she was, he wasn't able to pinpoint an exact timeframe. Based on her appearance, and what he did know about her, Luke assumed she had been remarkably young when she got married.

"How about you? Are you married?" Sierra asked, turning the tables on him.

"No. And before you ask, no, I've never been married. So, what happened?" Luke felt there was more to her story than just the normal irreconcilable differences, and when the question tumbled out, he didn't try to hide his interest.

"What happened with what?" He could see her attempt to deflect the question, but Luke wasn't going to let her off that easily.

"With your marriage," he clarified, hoping to back her into a corner.

"It's a long story," she said, turning to face the seat in front of her once more.

Luke took a chance and placed his hand on her arm, aching to touch her, and wanting her to know he was genuinely interested. He made a show of glancing down at his watch, then back at her. "We've got time."

~~*~~

Sierra remained as still as physically possible, the warmth of Luke's hand on her arm sent sparks straight through her.

His dark, tanned hand was a remarkable contrast to her much paler skin. As if that wasn't enough, the size of his hand compared to hers, the coarse feel of his skin, made her insides do flips. She wondered what those hands would feel like on the rest of her.

She didn't want to talk about this, but she had no one else to blame for the direction their conversation had taken. After all, she had been the one to start it, which meant she would have to be the one to finish it. Either she would sit back and share the next hour and a half with Luke, telling him her deepest, darkest secrets, or she could shrug him off, tell him that it was none of his business. The crazy thing was, she wanted him to ask these questions, she wanted him to be interested in her. Answering him was the only downside.

"I was eighteen years old when I got married to my high school boyfriend," Sierra began, feeling the loss when Luke pulled his hand from her arm. "We had just graduated from high school, and my mother had just moved to Dallas. I think I had some abandonment issues, which made for some downright lousy decisions. We were married for less than three months before I filed for divorce, realizing that he wasn't able to give me what I was looking for."

"Was it mutual?" Luke inquired, making Sierra relive those days that she had pushed to the far recesses of her memory.

"In a sense, yes, I think it was," Sierra stated, and then turned to look at Luke. "Be careful where you go with this conversation, Luke. I want to make sure you're ready for the answers you're going to get."

The look of pure lust on his face had her insides quivering. Sierra had always known there was something different about her, something that burned just a little too hot, but she had never found anyone who could extinguish the flames inside of her. With the way Luke looked at her, the things she knew about him, Sierra wondered if she had finally met the man who could at least sate the unfulfilled need that was a living, breathing thing.

She wished she had recognized her own idiosyncrasies long before she said 'I do', but, unfortunately, for both her and Brian, she hadn't. Granted, Sierra wasn't sure how she would have known since she had been a virgin when she married Brian, and not long after they were married, they both realized they were completely incompatible when it came to sex.

"I'm always careful." Luke's tone was more a warning than anything. "Tell me, Sierra."

"We weren't compatible. Sexually." Sierra tried to keep her voice low, not wanting the other passengers to hear their conversation.

"How so?"

The look she shot him was her attempt to get him to stop with the intimate questions, but he didn't look at all worried. In fact, he grinned, that slow, seductive tipping of his sensual lips that made her want to climb over the armrest and straddle him just so she could get a little closer.

Sierra leaned in, hoping to keep her words between them. When Luke leaned in as well, Sierra breathed in the spicy musk of his cologne, his intriguing scent rushing through her bloodstream like a drug.

"I might look sweet and innocent, Luke," Sierra whispered, then leaned just a little closer until her lips nearly brushed his ear. "I'm anything but."

His deep inhale told Sierra what she needed to know. He was affected by her, and since he owned a club that catered to the sort of lifestyle she had always been fascinated by, she didn't think he was turned off by her admission. When he gripped her wrist, hard enough to get her attention, but not hard enough to hurt her, Sierra moved back, her eyes locked with his.

"Honey, you might not be sweet and innocent, but I'm the one that needs to be handing out the warnings. Tread lightly when you try to tempt me."

Sierra's eyes went wide, and she tried to comprehend what he was telling her. Apparently he realized she needed further clarification because he leaned in so that his mouth was up against her ear, ensuring she was the only one who would hear him.

"I'm not some little boy you can toy with or one that you can tease with your so-called needs. In case my brother didn't tell you, I'm the real deal. I don't have any qualms about stripping you naked right here in this seat and burying my face between your legs until you scream my name. You might want to think this one through because until now, until me, you haven't met the man who will make you own up to those fantasies of yours."

Sierra's entire body went rigid; heat pooled between her legs and her clit began to throb just from the gruff sound of his voice and the words he said. And for the first time in her life, she wondered if she might have actually met her match.

"Do you understand what I'm telling you, Sierra?" Luke asked, his breath still warm on her ear.

She couldn't speak, but she managed to nod her head in understanding. Oh, she knew what he was saying all right, and though she couldn't tell him, those embers that had been glowing deep inside of her sparked to a full blown inferno.

"Answer me. That's the only rule I have. You must always answer me because it's imperative that I know exactly where you stand."

"Yes." Was that *her* voice? God, she was breathless. "I understand."

Luke pulled away just as the stewardess approached, offering them drinks and peanuts. She needed a drink all right. A strong one. But the only thing she was hungry for wasn't served on an airplane menu.

Chapter Six

From the moment Sierra walked off of the airplane in Las Vegas she'd been overwhelmed with a strange feeling. Maybe it was the fact that Luke had insisted on remaining close to her, or maybe it was because she wanted him to.

They had met up with Logan, Sam and Veronica when they entered the airport terminal only for Luke to let them know he would be escorting Sierra to the hotel, so they wouldn't need to wait.

There were two limos, Logan told them; so Luke and Sierra would be taking one while the other three would go in the second.

Luke had shown his disapproval of her immediate need to argue with him, but that hadn't stopped her in the least. Although Luke might, in fact, be the one man that Sierra didn't feel as though she could walk all over, she damn sure wasn't going to back down so easily.

After all, she might have a profound longing to be dominated in every way, but she certainly wasn't at all interested in being a submissive. There was a difference between finding a man who would stand up to her, not conform to her every whim, and changing everything about who she was and letting said man control her life.

Her initial reaction was to tell him that she would just ride with her mother, but Luke had simply glared at her, then turned his attention back to the others stating that he would handle getting her there safely.

Somehow she managed to rein in the need to stomp her feet and tell him to take a flying leap off of a very short building. Instead, she had conceded to him that time. Let the man think she'd be easy to tame. He would soon find out the hard way that she wasn't going to give in easily.

Even Brian, her ex-husband, hadn't known what to do with her need to be dominated, to be forced to let go of all control. No, sweet, oblivious Brian, fresh out of high school, had just been fortunate to be getting laid any way at all. Unfortunately, it was always the same. He wanted to *make love* while Sierra wanted to spice things up. When she even mentioned something different, Brian would tense up, and it didn't take her long to realize that they were polar opposites when it came to sex.

Though somewhat amicable, the two of them parted ways before they were fully invested in the marriage. Since then, Sierra hadn't held out hope that there was a man strong enough to handle her needs.

Until Luke.

Even in the short time she had known him, the two times she had actually talked to him, Sierra knew he was the dominant alpha male she was searching for. Only there was a problem that she hadn't yet figured out how to deal with. Luke McCoy owned a sex club, a swinger's club to be exact. And based on her understanding of the man, he had experience beyond her wildest imagination. Trying to figure out exactly how she would be able to satisfy the needs of a man like him had plagued her for the last two hours.

On top of that, Sierra had been privy to a rumor that alluded to Luke being bisexual, and though the thought didn't turn her off, she wondered just how that would work. How did a woman handle a man who needed more than she was even able to give him?

Her first hint of the truth behind the rumor was Cole, the man who had captured her attention with his physical beauty as he walked past them on the airplane. The look in his eye, the one that was pinpointed on Luke, said so much more.

The way Luke tensed hadn't been all in her mind either. He'd gripped the seat like the plane might fall out of the sky, although they were still grounded in the terminal. He visibly relaxed when Cole passed them, but when she had asked Luke about it, he'd blown her off. Still, Sierra couldn't help but wonder if Luke did know Cole, and if so, who he was to Luke.

As they descended the escalator into the luggage area of McCarran International Airport, Sierra was overwhelmed with the same exhilaration that she usually felt when she arrived in Vegas. There was just something about the place, something that relaxed her, made her want to let the weight of the world fall from her shoulders if only for a few days. Glancing over at Luke, she noticed that he looked more tense than usual – apparently Sin City didn't have the same effect on him.

"Is everything ok?" she asked as she tried to keep up with his long, steady strides as they made their way toward the baggage claim. There was a man wearing a suit holding a sign that said 'McCoy' and Sierra assumed that would be for either Luke or Logan. Luke ignored her question, walking toward the man and pulling something from his pocket.

A few minutes later, after the man had retrieved their bags, she was once again following Luke. This time he held her hand in his, and when he stopped abruptly, she damn near plowed right into him. They stopped just inside the doors, and there, in front of them, was Cole.

"Don't say a fucking word. We'll talk when I'm ready." Luke's voice was harsh and left no room for argument from the other man.

Well that answered her original burning question. Apparently the two did know each other.

When Cole nodded his head, almost submissively, Sierra had to keep her jaw clamped tight so that it wouldn't hit the floor. Here was this man, just as sturdy and compelling as Luke, not to mention devastatingly handsome, yet he was taking direction as though that was what he was born to do.

Sierra watched the entire thing play out, the tension arcing between the two men, the hint of defiance in Cole's eyes, and although Luke lowered his voice, she still heard the meaning behind the words clear as day. When Luke tipped his head toward the limo driver, mentioning that Cole was "with them", she noticed the mirrored look of surprise in the handsome blond man's navy blue eyes.

When Luke pulled on her hand, she realized he was once again on the move, so she followed obediently. He led her to a black stretch limo, opened the door for her and then waited patiently while she climbed inside. Cole climbed in on the other side and moved to the seat across from them.

Their eyes met, locked on one another, and Sierra couldn't control the sensual shiver that raced down her spine. So, she hadn't imagined her initial reaction to this man. Being embarrassed at the thought of finding both of them so incredibly attractive was a fleeting thought. Her reaction was foreign, but not unexpected.

When Luke got in behind them, the space suddenly felt too small, not enough oxygen for the three of them to share. Sierra didn't know who to look at, or whether she should look at either of them. The glass partition between the back and the front was closed, so they had complete privacy, yet Sierra suddenly wished they didn't.

Luke had warned her on the airplane; he'd told her that he wasn't a man who played games, and she was starting to believe him. Then the car was moving and Luke directed his attention on her, making her almost squirm in her seat. All of the courage she'd manage to scrape up since the day she had met Luke had vanished like a thief in the night.

"Let's see what you're made of." His voice was hoarse, rough with need, and for the first time, Sierra began to wonder if she should truly be scared of him.

Without a second's hesitation, he moved closer, lifting her onto his lap, one hand diving into her hair. She couldn't suppress the shudder that overcame her, her body reacting immediately to his rough touch, aching to be closer while her brain was sending up flags telling her to run.

"I've wanted to do this since the first day I saw you." The deep timbre of Luke's voice washed over her seconds before his lips touched hers.

She wouldn't deny she'd had a fantasy or two about this very thing, but Sierra was inexperienced when it came to this. She could want, she could ache, but she would never go after it with the intensity she felt from Luke.

His mouth was softer than she expected, yet firm. Demanding. She was sitting awkwardly in his lap, unable to get closer, yet her instincts were urging her forward. When he moved again, Sierra took the opportunity to get more comfortable, turning herself in his arms while their mouths ate at one another until she was straddling him, the hard ridge of his erection pressed between her thighs.

He kissed her deeper, tilting her head so their mouths aligned perfectly, his tongue melding with hers while one hand remained entwined in her hair, tipping her head back and successfully holding her in place. As if she would try to get away. Not a chance.

He didn't touch her anywhere else. His other hand rested on her thigh while she cupped his jaw, grinding intimately against him, trying to get their bodies closer, much closer than their clothes would allow.

When he broke the kiss, Sierra whimpered involuntarily, but she was so hot, her body burning, all good sense and logic completely vanishing, replaced by the need to kiss him. The grip on her hair tightened, and a sharp, thrilling pain shot through her scalp as he pulled her back, putting space between them.

"This isn't all or nothing, Sierra. I'm doing my damnedest to control myself, but I can't make any promises. If this gets too hot, or goes too far, just say the word and I'll stop. But, you have to tell me."

Sierra remembered his instruction from earlier, and she responded with a confident "yes" before his lips locked with hers once more.

She wasn't sure how much time passed while she devoured him, her hands roaming over the hard planes of his chest, the taut muscles bunching and flexing beneath her fingers. She used her hands to get familiar with his body, feeling the thick, corded muscles along his shoulders, the hard, rounded muscles of his biceps, the restrained, tense sinew on his forearms. The man was a complete work of art, all suppressed power and dark, swirling passion.

When the limo stopped, and Luke pulled back, she realized they had already made it to the hotel. Instead of leaping off of his lap, she pulled back and looked into his eyes, noting the churning hunger in the sensual, almost amber color, waiting for his next move. She wanted this – *needed this* – and Sierra was scared that if she took matters into her own hands, he would disappear, or she would end up running fast and hard. If her brain had a minute to catch up with her libido that might just happen, so she remained where she was.

"Let's check into the hotel, then we'll pick up where we left off later," Luke instructed, his eyes darting from hers to the man sitting behind her.

Holy shit. Sierra turned abruptly, realizing that Cole had been in the limo the entire time she and Luke had been making out for the last how many ever minutes. What the hell was she thinking? How did she forget that they had an audience?

Luke situated himself and then moved her from his lap before he opened the limo door and exited, waiting patiently while she climbed out behind him. Once she was out, she stepped just out of his reach, trying to put a little distance between them.

He might've made her lose all common sense for the fifteen minute trip from the airport, but Sierra wasn't going to give in that easily. She hadn't spent her entire life looking for a man who could tolerate her need for independence only to give in the second he kissed her.

She needed a moment to regain her equilibrium and being close to Luke wouldn't help matters.

~~*~~

Cole had to adjust himself because his jeans were now painfully tight. After having a front row seat to Luke and Sierra's prelude to what would likely be the most explosive sex any of them had ever known, no amount of counting backward from one million was going to disperse the blood pounding insistently in his cock.

The way Sierra had taken charge, straddling Luke, had Cole's breath hitching in his chest. The only thing that would have been hotter was if she had turned that intensity on him.

During the flight, Cole had managed not to think about Luke and Sierra sitting so close, their heads tilted toward one another as they spoke in hushed whispers. He hadn't heard what they were talking about, but the couple of times that he heard Luke laugh, he'd been fixated on the seats they occupied. Luke McCoy didn't laugh. At least not often. But, he had with Sierra which surprised the hell out of Cole.

When he had first ventured down the aisle in search of a seat, he had been initially surprised to see the two of them sitting together, but after his own reaction to Sierra, he understood Luke's attraction. But he couldn't help notice that she was not the type of woman that Luke was generally attracted to. First of all, she was too small. Luke stood damn near six and a half feet tall and a frame that large was heavy in its own right. Add to that the muscle that Luke carried around on his massive frame and Luke dwarfed Sierra.

Not that it had stopped Cole from thinking about how she would feel beneath him, or better yet, between him and Luke. That thought had sent the blood rushing to his groin, his cock throbbing incessantly. Thankfully, while on the airplane, sitting next to a couple who had to have been in their eighties, Cole had managed to rein in his thoughts. That hadn't been the case in the limo.

Luke's low growls mixed with Sierra's insistent whimpers had Cole wanting to release his cock and stroke it as he watched the couple make out like he was watching live porn. But then they'd arrived at the hotel, and when Luke's eyes had made contact with his, Cole felt the heat that simmered between them begin a rolling boil. They might have avoided one another for the last couple of months, and they might have had issues to work out, but this trip was going to be the *coup de grace* so to speak. What they had circumvented was quickly becoming something that neither of them could deny.

No matter how much Luke wanted it to just go away.

Temptation

Exiting the limo, Cole fell into step beside Sierra, not making small talk because it appeared she was trying to regain her composure. The way her eyes widened when she realized he was still there told Cole more than she knew. She might be open to new sexual experiences, but she clearly wasn't familiar with those preferences.

Hopefully by the end of the four days, they'd be able to change all that.

Chapter Seven

Luke conceded to Sierra's need for space when she successfully put a few feet between them. For now. She insisted on walking a step or two in front of him, and with a view like that, he wasn't about to complain. The way those jeans hugged her heart shaped ass and molded to her toned thighs had him wishing he could remove them just to see what she wore underneath.

Once inside the hotel, he headed straight for the concierge desk, doing his level best to get his mind out of the gutter. He wasn't surprised to see that Sierra had stayed back a considerable distance with Cole.

"Checking in," Luke told the friendly woman who eyed him with a questionable look. Giving the woman all three of their names, advising that they needed three rooms, Luke added a few instructions of his own.

If things went the way he hoped, one of those three rooms would go unused anyway, but he wasn't going to predict the future just yet. If he knew anything about the mysterious woman he'd just spent three hours with, he knew she would give him a run for his money.

The woman was a firecracker, and when he had pulled her onto his lap in the limo, the way she had lost all of her inhibitions had nearly been his undoing. He was secretly drawn to her unbridled fascination, yet apparent innocence, regarding his lifestyle. If he wasn't mistaken, she was intrigued by his dominant nature, though Sierra Sellers was anything but submissive.

The thought of a woman who wanted to be dominated, yet didn't want to hand him the reins was compelling, and still so far outside of his realm of experience Luke was almost at a loss. Submissives were a dime a dozen back at Club Destiny, some of the actual D/s variety, so finding a woman who went up in flames when he took control, but in the same sense didn't give in easily, was new for him. She was a challenge that Luke looked forward to.

He was inherently attracted to a woman who wasn't afraid to go after what she wanted, but in his world, they were few and far between. Most of the women he came into contact with wanted to be told what to do and bowed their heads, diverting their eyes because they thought that was how it worked. Maybe that was the case for some men, but not Luke.

That was a significant part of his attraction to Cole. The underlying hostility that was on constant simmer in Luke's bloodstream wasn't satisfied with a simple submissive. The temerity that both Cole and Sierra possessed struck a tense, sensual chord inside of him, and Luke looked forward to the challenge.

His initial apprehension had immediately been thwarted when Sierra easily molded to him in the limo, her hands reading him like a book while her soft, sweet tongue dueled with his, searching, pleading for more. She didn't make excuses for her desire, nor did she back down when she was just as overwhelmed by the sexual tension as he had been.

Luke's natural inclination to dominate, to control, was stronger than even him, and having her so pliant and willing in his arms had been a temptation he was barely able to resist. Although he sensed that Sierra forgot Cole was even there, she hadn't been intimidated when realization dawned.

The woman in front of him clicked away at the keyboard, and ran a few plastic key cards through some gadget before turning her attention back on him. A moment later, she handed him a small paper folder containing the room keys as a genuine smile tipped her lips when she sweetly said, "Enjoy your stay, Mr. McCoy."

He intended to.

"I'll send someone over for your luggage, sir."

Luke nodded his head, then dared a quick glance behind him. He found Cole and Sierra standing beside one another only a few inches between them. They were smiling, not an ounce of awkward tension as he had initially anticipated.

Yes, he fully intended to enjoy his stay.

A few minutes later, Luke was walking Sierra to her room and handing over her key card. The air sizzled between them as he waited momentarily before kissing her lightly on the lips, then urging her inside of her room. Alone.

He'd give her a few minutes. It's the least he could do… considering.

Once her door clicked shut, he turned his attention back toward the man whose mere presence filled Luke with a foreign sensation. Something he couldn't pinpoint. Animal magnetism maybe.

It was almost as though that constant, overwhelming aggression that filled his bloodstream had found an outlet, which explained the way his body reacted to Cole's heated stare.

"We'll talk, but not right now," Luke told Cole, turning to walk down the hall where the other two rooms were located.

Overheated or not, Luke wasn't ready to deal with this... this attraction in its simplest form. That didn't mean he could ignore the unwavering desire to include Cole. To include the one man who had detonated a pleasure of atomic proportions within Luke, the one man he trusted implicitly, and knew from experience would help him to fulfill every one of Sierra's sexual fantasies.

Cole nodded his head slightly, his eyes backlit with that hint of defiance Luke was drawn to, yet the underlying willingness was still there.

Cole wasn't the reason for the heated aggression that boiled just beneath the surface, but he was one of the reasons for the driving hunger that sought an outlet for release. Luke couldn't define it, nor could he ignore it.

"Meet us downstairs in twenty," Luke demanded, locking eyes with Cole. A quick nod was Cole's acknowledgment before he disappeared inside of his room.

A heavy sigh escaped Luke as he slipped into his own room, leaning against the door. Taking a look around the empty hotel room, partly dazed by the events of the last hour, Luke exhaled deeply. He had a brief reprieve from the overwhelming urges that Sierra seemed to inspire within him, urges that Luke hadn't realized until now.

For two months he'd managed to abstain from the pleasure he'd built his life around. Managed to ignore the lust that sizzled hot and wild through his veins, with the hope that he could come to terms with what he wanted.

He'd invested hours of thought trying to understand what that even meant. It wasn't even until that one night, the night he'd taken Cole with savage intensity, given himself over to the primal needs he'd always managed to keep a lid on, that Luke had realized he was searching for something. Something more than the frequent release that never seemed to go deep enough.

For the first time, Luke had felt a momentary reprieve from the yearning and here he was, smack in the middle of a temptation that defied imagination. There was Sierra, a mystery he wanted to unravel. The mere sight of her overwhelmed Luke with urges he hadn't expected. Add Cole into the mix and the possibilities were endless, all of the pieces seeming to fall into place.

The mystery that was Sierra Sellers was going to require some restraint, but Luke sensed she was the woman who could sate those needs. The needs that weren't just physical. Bold and open to the desires that most people tried to ignore, Sierra made him ache. On top of that, she was slowly breaching a barrier that he had erected unknowingly, a barrier that slowly crumbled each time he was near her.

She was the answer to the confusion Luke had been wrought with after that one night with Cole.

He was man enough to admit his sexual urges weren't the same as most men, but he wasn't naïve enough to believe that one woman couldn't satisfy those urges. He might revel in sharing, the combined pleasure that could be found when two men focused on the needs of one woman, but Luke was possessive by nature and Sierra had ignited that instinct.

Maybe it was too early to admit, but Luke wanted something from Sierra. Everything, actually. The thought had occurred to him that maybe Cole hadn't been the one to make Luke realize he was missing something in his life; maybe it was Samantha who had done that. Samantha and the way she looked at Logan, the way the two of them seemed to be more complete when they were together.

Either way, Luke felt something stronger than mere physical, sexual attraction when he looked at Sierra. And if he had anything to say about it, after the next four days, either the two of them would walk away from one another, the time they spent together just a pleasant memory, or they would move forward.

Luke walked to the windows and threw back the heavy curtains, taking in the concrete jungle that was the Las Vegas strip. The view was so different during the day when the tall resorts were bathed in sunlight; the stunning mountains a backdrop to the energy that flowed steadily even in the early morning hours.

Turning back to the room, Luke took in the king sized bed, complete with a thick beige comforter and rows of oversized pillows and a surge of lust thumped through his veins. Picturing Sierra sprawled out on that bed, her long, silky black hair fanning out around her, wearing nothing but a smile, had his dick throbbing.

The rest of the furniture, all nondescript and miniscule in the small space mirrored that of any other hotel room he'd ever stayed in. A small couch, two wooden nightstands, a desk, and a cabinet that housed the television completed the room. The smell of stale cigarettes was faint in the air, likely embedded into the walls and the dark maroon carpet.

Luke didn't care about the room, as long as he had a place to sleep; though sleep was the last thing on his mind at the moment. This was Vegas, and there were things to do, places to go, eccentricities to take in, and of course, Sierra Sellers.

He'd be lucky if he got any sleep at all.

Luke dropped a couple of dollars onto the bed for when the bellhop delivered his bags and opted to go down to the casino. Sitting in the room with Sierra so close was a distraction he didn't need.

~~*~~

Thirty minutes later, Luke was back on the twenty-seventh floor knocking on Sierra's door. He had somehow managed to pass the time by attempting to rein in his feelings, his needs, those dark desires that fueled his hunger.

Now he wanted to see Sierra, and to get on with what would come next, though he wasn't sure what that was. For the first time in his life, Luke didn't have a plan, he didn't know what to expect, but he knew what he wanted and he was never one to sit idly by without going after it.

The door cracked open, Sierra's beautiful face stared back at him, spurring his heartbeat to a full gallop once again. It was odd how one woman, still such a stranger to him, had him so riveted. He vowed to himself that he would take the next four days to explore her in ways she had never imagined, ignoring the trepidations that still lingered.

"Come in." Her voice was low, seductive, yet he could see the purity and confusion in her eyes.

Sierra didn't know what to expect from him, but that was ok because he wasn't quite sure either. She probably expected him to pounce on her the moment he walked in the room.

As attractive as that idea was, Luke wasn't built that way. He would go after what he wanted, but part of the lure was the anticipation. Oh, he would have her if he had anything to say about it, but it would be on his terms.

"Are you ready?" he asked as he stepped into the room that looked exactly like his own.

Sierra had pulled the curtains back, the view of the Las Vegas strip the same from where he had stood only minutes before. Not nearly as appealing as when the night bathed the streets with dark energy and the lights of the casino's flashed bright, but it was Vegas nonetheless and not another place in the world felt the same.

Sierra grabbed her purse from the desk and turned toward the door.

Never one to let an opportunity pass him by Luke crowded her against the wall, halting her midstride. The confusion he'd seen in her eyes was now replaced by pure ecstasy, causing the blood that pumped hard and fast through his veins to make a sudden detour to his cock.

"I want to taste you, Sierra," Luke growled, pushing her flush against the wall, his body pressing against her much smaller one. "Have you changed your mind?"

He had to know the answer to that question before he allowed this to go any further.

"No." The word was exhaled on a breath as she stared up at him; the silver striations in her blue eyes glowing, her lips parting slightly.

"Good."

Not wanting to push this further than a simple kiss – though the way Sierra kissed him was anything but simple – Luke had to tamp down the hunger.

Brushing his lips lightly against hers, Luke relished the soft, sweet taste of her; his body heated from the way she pleaded for more. Pushing things a little further, Luke cupped her ass, lifting her so she had to wrap her legs around his waist, aligning their bodies perfectly. Pressing her into the wall, her breasts crushed against his chest, Luke fused his mouth with hers in a passionate kiss to rival all others.

He barely registered her soft moans over the roaring in his ears. The sweet pain that ignited in his scalp when she plunged her hands in his hair had Luke needing more, but he forced himself to stop.

"Woman, you're going to be the death of me." He fought for breath as he rested his forehead against hers. "You don't know what you do to me."

"Tell me."

The eagerness he detected in her voice was overwhelming; she was just as willing to see where this would lead as he was.

"I want to strip you naked, run my tongue over your luscious curves and bury it deep inside your pussy." He felt her body tense as his blunt words lingered in the air between them. "I want to watch as you take my cock deep inside that sweet mouth of yours." Luke brushed a finger over her swollen bottom lip, enjoying the way she fought for breath, the way her legs tightened around him.

"And I will, I promise you that."

Chapter Eight

Sierra moaned as she crushed her breasts against Luke's hard muscled chest, pressing closer, wanting nothing more than for him to do the wicked things he said, but she felt his control, felt the way he held himself back.

She didn't have any doubts that he would show her things she'd only ever dreamed about, that he would make her body burn unlike any man before him and any man after. Sierra had never wanted a man as much as she wanted Luke, never knew the same hunger that ate at her insides when she thought about him.

The fact that Luke didn't touch her in any other way, besides the hot kisses, wasn't lost on her either. Not that she was quite ready for something to happen between them, but her body throbbed for something more.

"We have to go down and meet Cole." Luke broke the kiss and pulled away, lowering her feet back to the floor.

Her body felt cold without the warmth of him, but she situated her clothing and ran a hand over her hair, trying to gain some composure.

Luke held the door open, and she led the way down the hallway toward the bank of elevators that would take them to the casino level. Between trying to keep her feet steady when her adrenaline was coursing at an all-time high and praying she could get her breathing under control, Sierra attempted a glance at Luke. From the looks of it, he didn't appear to be paying any attention to her.

The man was an enigma. A force to be reckoned with. Tall, dark, handsome – all of the adjectives used to describe the hero in her fantasy novels rang true for him. But there was something stronger, more powerful, that coursed just beneath the surface and that's the part of him that she wanted to tap into.

Breaking the silence as the elevator descended, Sierra asked the question that had plagued her for the last half hour. "Is there something I should know about Cole?"

As soon as the words were out, Luke looked at her, and she saw the storm brewing in the multi colored hues of his eyes. At first she thought he would shrug her question off, but then he faced forward just as the elevator dinged the arrival at their destination.

"There's a lot you should know about him. And you will."

That wasn't much to go on, but it was more than he had given her earlier on the airplane.

Sierra suspected that she had been right about the two of them. She couldn't pinpoint what their relationship was, but she had an idea that it was more than friendship. How much more, she didn't know, and she took the hint not to push it any further just yet.

Moving forward when Luke placed his hand at the small of her back, she allowed him to usher her out of the elevator and into the chaos that was the casino.

The world came into sharp focus the second her feet landed on the lush, velvety carpet of the casino floor. Inundated with the sights and sounds synonymous to Vegas, she tried to take it all in.

Though it was still early morning by Vegas time, the casino floor was littered with people, some standing near the elevators talking, some sitting in the large food court sharing breakfast while many were seated at the wide variety of slot machines that stood proud and tall as far as the eye could see.

The smells of food drifting from the food court made Sierra's stomach rumble. The breakfast she had consumed a few hours ago had long since burned off, and she realized that, with the time difference, it was lunchtime back at home.

As though he could read her thoughts, Luke turned toward her. "They're serving lunch at the conference in just about an hour. Let's find Cole, and head over."

Sierra nodded, remembering that she was in Vegas for a reason, and not just to find a way into Luke McCoy's bed.

An incredulous laugh threatened, but Sierra choked it back. Finding her way into any man's bed was about as foreign as the way her body had lit up like the fourth of July when Luke had touched her that first time in his club. The only companion she'd invited into her bed was of the silicon, vibrating variety.

Confidence was something Sierra prided herself on, yet when it came to men, Luke McCoy in particular, she wondered how much she could pretend. Being led around by her overactive libido for the last few days, Sierra had conjured up some pretty steamy images, with Luke playing the lead role, but when it came down to it, she was going on sheer determination alone.

Instead of hiding out in her hotel room like she had contemplated, she walked alongside Luke, feeling her fortitude return in small measures.

He might be a mystery, but Sierra was pretty sure she understood what drove him. She recognized the hunger in his eyes because it consumed her. She knew the determination he felt when he touched her because she desired it.

She admired his confidence, the respect his mere presence demanded, and the graceful way he moved as though he owned the place. In fact, there wasn't a single thing about the man that she didn't want to know more about.

The silence that lingered between them wasn't as awkward as she anticipated as they ventured through the casino to the main doors that would lead them out on to the strip. She was grateful for the short walk that did wonders in driving down some of the hunger that had been lodged in her belly since the limo ride.

This roller coaster she was riding on was a series of dips and valleys based on sexual highs and lows and it required concentration just to take one step at a time when she wanted nothing more than to grab Luke's hand and run, not walk, back to the hotel room where she could explore him with more than her hands.

Just when her mind was wandering dangerously close to the gutter again, Sierra was distracted by Cole, who fell into step beside them.

For the second time that day, she damn near ran right into Luke, this time having to put her hands out to keep from plowing into him. Ok, so his abrupt stops were beginning to irritate her.

"Cole Ackerley, this is Sierra Sellers. She's Xavier Thomas' admin's daughter, here on business. Sierra meet Cole. He's a representative of CISS, Corporate Investigative Security Services. Here to attend the conference as well."

Sierra hadn't expected such an in-depth introduction, especially coming from the one word responder, so she tried to hide her astonishment. When Cole held out his hand, acting as though they hadn't already been introduced days before by Samantha, she reached for his in turn and watched the way her fingers disappeared into his large palm.

Just like the first time they touched, Sierra felt the heat spiral low, swirling insistently in her belly. Her eyes were riveted to his long, tan, muscular arm, the light dusting of golden hair covering the ridges of muscle that flexed with each movement.

A spark jolted from her fingertips to her nipples, and she hoped her blush wasn't evident. Turning her face up to meet his, their gazes collided, and Sierra felt her skin grow warmer.

The man was masculine beauty personified, attractive from a distance, but a true masterpiece up close.

She would've described Luke as being ruggedly handsome which was the polar opposite to Cole's perfection. He was a big man, nearly the same height as Luke, but his body was thicker; the muscles in his shoulders starkly defined beneath the soft, navy blue button down he wore. His chest was broader, all hard angles and planes that she suspected no amount of clothing would disguise.

"Nice to meet you, Sierra." The rich timbre of Cole's voice wrapped her in sexual awareness.

She was in so much trouble here.

"Nice to meet you," Sierra managed to get out when Luke cleared his throat.

She flipped her gaze over to Luke and was surprised by the devilish grin on his face. Here she was, visually ogling the man she had just been introduced to and he was smiling about it.

When Luke took her hand in his, – did he actually pull her closer? – Sierra tried to ignore the fact that she was now surrounded by two of the most sexually arousing males she'd ever come into contact with.

Damn this was going to be a long day.

Chapter Nine

Six miserably long hours later, Sierra found herself sitting in a corner of the large banquet room, cursing her shoes and wanting nothing more than to slide into a hot bath. For a man she had somehow been convinced didn't like to talk, Luke had taken to introducing her to anyone and everyone he came into contact with, and somehow she had managed to keep up with him all day, which is where the miserable came into play. Her feet ached, her calves were on fire, and her back had long since gone on strike.

Her mother had instructed her to network, and that's exactly what she had done. All day.

Despite the fact that Luke was not employed by XTX, or CISS for that matter, no one would have been the wiser based on the way he spoke of the two companies in such high regard as he easily greeted each and every person they came into contact with.

He introduced Sierra to people from all around, many of whom resided in the Dallas/Fort Worth metroplex. And all of the information he'd garnered about her had been during their walk over that morning, when he had asked for a brief rundown of the types of services her company provided.

She'd given him high-level details, and apparently Luke had memorized every word based on the way he offered her name and a brief description of her services to everyone she met.

Being an entrepreneur himself, Luke was well versed in the ways of public relations. He knew how to market without making people feel overwhelmed or as though they were speaking to a sales person. Sierra was also well versed, and she had easily picked up the conversation from Luke as though the two of them had been doing the same thing for years.

By the end of the first day, she had already scheduled two appointments to meet and show her portfolio to a couple of big wigs in the Dallas area.

Sitting up straight in her chair, Sierra watched as Cole and Luke closed in on her, making their way from across the room where they had been talking to Xavier Thomas, the man she had been introduced to earlier in the day by Veronica.

It dawned on her that she'd often referred to those she generally associated with as being big, but she realized as she watched the two men that she had been speaking in relative terms. At four feet, ten and three quarter inches – yes, she tacked on every fraction – she often felt inadequate.

However, seeing these two predatory males as they approached, both of them standing well over six feet tall, with broad shoulders and wide chests, carried by powerfully thick thighs, Sierra realized she hadn't known what big actually meant. These men took up some serious real estate with their massive forms.

The smile Cole threw her way sent a warm shiver straight down her spine, and she immediately felt some of the strain of the day wear off. Secretly, she had wished that Luke would smile at her similarly, but he looked distracted and intent.

"Are you two nearly finished?" she asked, rising from her chair.

With both men so close, sitting was not an option. Though she was a full foot and some change shorter than either of them, standing was the only way to bring herself to a more even playing field. Never having been intimidated by those who were larger than she was, there was something about them that made her feel much smaller and vastly more feminine than she ever had before.

"I need to take care of a few things, so why don't you and Cole have dinner and meet me back at the casino in two hours," Luke offered, moving in close to her.

Standing beside him, she had to look up to see his face, the warmth of his body and the spicy, sexy scent of his cologne an all too familiar feeling at this point. A surge of disappointment came over her at his inability to join them for dinner, but when Sierra looked up at Cole, the disappointment faded.

"I made reservations for two at the steakhouse in the hotel under Cole's name. I'll try and get away as soon as possible," Luke stated as he leaned down and planted a gentle kiss on her lips.

Unable to hide her surprise, Sierra was forced to hold herself upright. His kiss was tender and familiar. Like they had shared that same kiss every day for as long as she could remember. Keeping in mind where they were, and who was still hanging around, Sierra pulled back quickly, giving Luke a flashy smile.

Before she had a chance to say anything, Luke was walking away and Sierra was left staring after him. When Cole cleared his throat, she darted her eyes to him, seeing the sexy smile that eased some of the tension she had felt moments earlier.

"Shall we?" he asked, holding out his arm so she could hook her hand inside the crook of his elbow.

"Absolutely." Without hesitation, Sierra took hold of his arm, feeling the play of his well-toned muscles beneath her fingers as he led her through the banquet hall, back through the casino and out onto the strip.

The wonders of Vegas were upon her when she stepped outside to find it was already dark, and the lights of the strip filled every crook and crevice of the buildings around them. Snaking through the throngs of people, she stayed close to Cole as they made their way across the pedestrian bridge.

"How did you meet Luke?" Sierra asked when they had to stop to let a large group of people go by.

"At the club," he offered, glancing down at her when he spoke.

His uniquely masculine scent was equally as arousing as Luke's but in an entirely different way. Sierra found that she liked being close to Cole, and she was strangely attracted to him despite the fact that she found herself overwhelmingly attracted to another man at the same time. Maybe it was the vibe she got from both Luke and Cole.

If the rumors were true, then there might be something more going on between the two men than met the eye, but deep down, Sierra got the feeling that they weren't looking to be exclusive. The club was all about threesomes, and though she had never experienced one of her own, she definitely wasn't opposed to the idea. Especially not one that involved men like Luke and Cole.

"Are you a member?" she asked as they descended the outdoor escalator that would take them to the sidewalk on Las Vegas Blvd.

"I am."

"Does that mean you're active in the lifestyle?" Sierra knew the answer to the question before he answered, but she was trying to make small talk.

Cole glanced over at her, one golden eyebrow lifted as though trying to read her. "Yes," he said solemnly, followed immediately by, "Does that bother you?"

Sierra hadn't had a chance to talk to Cole much throughout the day, having seen him only briefly, but she already felt comfortable with him. She could read his hesitancy; feel the way his arm tensed briefly as he anticipated her answer.

"Not at all," she stopped walking so that she could look up at him. "I'm not aware of the dynamic between you and Luke, but I want to get to know you better. If I overstep my boundaries, feel free to let me know."

When Cole stepped closer, placing his hands on her hips, Sierra struggled to maintain her composure, her hands instinctively going to his chest.

"I'd like that more than you know," he whispered.

When his eyes moved to her mouth, Sierra fought the urge to reach up and kiss him. And where the hell had that come from? How could she even consider kissing Cole after what she had done with Luke earlier that morning? There was just something... something familiar about him that made her want to get closer.

Cole was a stocky man, muscular and tall, intense, but he didn't emit the illusion of danger that she felt from Luke. Cole made her feel safe somehow, and standing so intimately close to him now, wanting to feel his lips on hers, was a little disconcerting... All things considered.

"I'm not sure what's happening here," Sierra whispered softly.

"I'm not either, but whatever it is, I like where this is going." Cole slid one finger down the side of her cheek in a gesture so tender, Sierra felt tears prick behind her eyelids.

Had a man ever touched her so sweetly, while still making her feel desired?

When he lowered his hand, he took hers and twined their fingers together before turning toward their hotel.

"Hungry?" he asked as they stepped inside their hotel's casino, the bright lights, the sounds of slot machines, and the overpowering smell of cigarette smoke assaulting her senses all at once.

"Starving. Have you ever been to this restaurant before?" Sierra asked as they walked down the aisles that intersected the casino floor, a bright red carpet and gold accents giving it an elegant, upscale feel.

"No. Vegas isn't my thing. I've come out a couple of times, but I don't frequent it enough to have tried many of the restaurants. How about you?"

"Once. I wasn't disappointed, I know that much. My friends and I made it a goal to try a different restaurant each time we came. Needless to say, we've had both good and bad."

Cole approached the hostess desk and offered his name. The girl glanced down at the book in front of her and then beamed a smile back at them. "Right this way."

With Cole's hand on her back, Sierra followed the woman through the dimly lit restaurant to a table in the back. Before she could do it herself, Cole pulled out her chair and waited for her to take her seat. Once he was seated, and their drink orders were taken, Sierra gave him her full attention.

"Tell me what you do for a living." Sierra started the conversation, hoping she could get him to share some information about himself.

He didn't seem to be any more forthcoming with information than Luke was, but Sierra figured there was a time and place for everything. With nothing else to do, hopefully Cole would find talking easier than staring blankly at one another.

"It's complicated," Cole said.

Sierra got the sense that Cole had some hidden insecurities, though based on what she had heard throughout the day, he was exceptionally sharp and communicated easily with the type of people they had been in contact with.

"I'm intelligent. I think I can handle an explanation." Sierra grinned, then sat back in her chair as a waiter placed two wine glasses on their table, then filled them.

"Technically, I'm self-employed." Cole took a sip of the wine, then nodded at the waiter with his approval. "Give us a few minutes," he instructed the man hovering over them.

"What is it that you do?" Sierra asked when they were alone again.

"I contract out my services."

Sierra's eyes went wide. *Was he saying...?*

Cole laughed, a deep, thunderous rumble that went straight to her core, lighting up all of her nerve endings along the way. Unlike Luke, this man had a laugh that came out easily.

"Not those services, naughty girl," he clarified. "Let's order and I'll tell you anything you want to know."

Glancing down at the menu in front of her, Sierra tried to focus on the words. She smiled despite herself. The way he called her naughty, thrilled her.

"You like steak?" he asked, interrupting her thoughts.

"I do."

"My kind of woman." And with that, they were silent for a few minutes while they both scanned the menu, placing their orders when the waiter returned.

"Back to what you do, you know, the services you contract out."

"Aside from living off of my trust fund," Cole began, watching her for her reaction, "I do various odd jobs. Sort of like a handyman might contract his services, I do the same, although not manual labor. For example, this conference, I'm filling in for Alex McDermott, the owner of CISS. I've got a head for business, and I enjoy the political aspect."

"A public relation's front man?" she asked.

"Exactly. I go in, learn what I need to know about the company, and then attend various events in their place."

Sierra didn't question Cole about his trust fund, though the way he had gauged her reaction told her that he expected her to. She wasn't interested in the man's money. She was interested in the man and Cole's profession stimulated the intellectual side of her brain.

Sierra got the impression that Cole wasn't much on offering personal information, appearing to be just as private as Luke. How the two of them managed to engage in the types of relationships they did, namely threesomes, was beyond her. Those seemed a bit personal in her opinion, but what did she know.

"Are you from Dallas originally?" she asked, resting her arms on the table, her fingers twined around the stem of her wine glass as she gave Cole her attention.

"No, I was born and raised in Oklahoma," he responded to her question, and she saw the glint of shyness shining in his beautiful eyes.

"What made you move to Dallas?" Sierra detected the hesitance in Cole's eyes, and she wondered if she was asking too many personal questions.

"I needed a change. I earned a degree from OU and then moved south, not sure what I was looking for. Somehow I ended up in Dallas, and I've built my business from there. It wasn't until about seven years ago that I became involved with the club. Although seven years ago, it was named Destined Hearts, and it wasn't nearly what it is today."

"Destined Hearts?" Sierra laughed. "That sounds more like a singles website."

"That's what Luke thought, so he changed the name to Club Destiny when he and Logan bought it five years ago, figuring he wasn't changing it entirely, just giving it a facelift per se."

"Well, I'm not sure I would have named it Club Destiny, but it's a definite improvement. And you said you met Luke at the club?"

"I did." The hesitation in Cole's answer was evident.

"I'd like to know more about the lifestyle. Luke mentioned the club isn't exclusive to married couples, so I'm assuming you aren't married."

"Not married. Never have been," Cole stated, watching her carefully. "And no, Club Destiny isn't limited to married couples. I've been a member of Luke's club since inception. And as for my lifestyle… What is it that you want to know?"

Sierra grinned, realizing she was definitely treading on personal territory and based on Cole's reaction, he wasn't all that happy about it.

Thankfully the waiter chose that moment to interrupt them, bringing their food and refilling their wine. Allowing Cole a temporary reprieve, Sierra focused on eating, doing her best to leave Cole be for a few minutes. As much as she wanted to believe that Cole was just shy, and a little startled by her questions, Sierra got the impression that he didn't want to talk about himself. *To her.*

"Cole," she said, placing her fork and her knife down on the table beside her plate. When he looked up, holding his fork in front of him, halting midway to his mouth, Sierra continued. "I want to know everything there is to know about you."

Watching the internal struggle Cole waged with himself had her wanting desperately to reach out and touch him. For such a strong, masculine man, Sierra felt there was something much deeper, which explained whatever was going on between him and Luke.

"Tell me," she encouraged him, then picked up her fork and tried to continue eating. Truthfully, she wasn't all that hungry, but she didn't want their time together to end.

Right now, right here, with Cole, she felt at ease. He knew who she was, at least superficially, and he knew about her interest in Luke. He also knew of her interest in him, based on the way he looked at her. Apparently he didn't have a problem with her wanting another man. She wished she could be just as comfortable with the situation. This was the part of her that she had never been able to explain, the part of her she always felt was abnormal. Daydreaming about being that woman in her romance novels, the one who was showered with love and attention from two men, was a frequent fantasy.

When it came to sex, Sierra was open, wanting to express her deepest, most intimate desires, and if she wanted to be with two men, then the rest of the world be damned. She'd just never thought of it as more than just a dream. As long as everyone was on the same page, what did she have to worry about?

The only question was whether Luke and Cole were thinking the same thing she was.

"Let's just say I'm very open."

Of course he wouldn't go into detail. Sierra smiled, wanting to laugh at his inability to tell her more. "Ok, we'll leave it at that. But, you have to tell me one thing."

He shot her a skeptical look but didn't turn away.

"Are you bisexual?"

Cole hesitated, but then he nodded his head. "Yes."

Well, that answered most of her questions all in itself. It explained his relationship with Luke and being that he was a member of the club it told her that he wasn't discriminatory when it came to gender. Club Destiny was a swinger's club after all.

"You think that answers all of your questions?" There was a hint of suspicion in Cole's tone.

Had she actually spoken out loud?

She hoped she hadn't, but the way he looked at her as if she'd grown two heads said maybe she had.

"It tells me enough." She paused momentarily. "I don't judge, Cole. I'm not interested in picking apart your life or determining whether it's right or wrong. I just want to get to know you."

Seemingly satisfied with her response, Cole clarified. "I engage mostly in ménages with married couples. Which makes me the third."

He was letting her know who he was so she could make up her own mind.

"Now, tell me more about *you*," Cole stated, turning the conversation to something much safer for him, but not so much for her.

With a deep, fortifying breath and a long swallow of wine, Sierra proceeded to tell him the details of her life. If he trusted her enough to share, she might as well divulge everything.

Chapter Ten

Cole charged dinner to his room, although they insisted that Luke had already instructed them to do no such thing. Taking the waiter aside momentarily, when Sierra had slipped away to go to the ladies room, Cole told him in no uncertain terms that he didn't give a shit what Luke had instructed. That had changed the waiter's perspective and resolved their issue entirely.

When Sierra returned, Cole was waiting, and the two of them wandered through the casino until they came upon an empty blackjack table. Insisting that he play, he found himself unable to tell her no. There was something so compelling about the woman that Cole wondered if he would *ever* be able to tell her no.

He didn't bother to tell her that he had no idea how to play the game, so when he started losing she turned to him in wide eyed wonder.

"Have you played before?"

"Nope," he admitted, grinning. "Can you tell?"

When Sierra laughed, Cole's insides tumbled repeatedly. Her laugh was the sexiest sound he had ever heard. Her carefree attitude and always-there smile was refreshing, and Cole found that he would do whatever it was she wanted, lose as much money as necessary if he could only keep her smiling.

His admission apparently didn't sit well with her, so she ordered two beers from a passing waitress and insisted on teaching him how to play. He was doing relatively decent until a couple joined the table, but at that point, he didn't give a damn how much money he won or lost, he just wanted to sit beside Sierra and watch the beautiful way her face lit up when she would win the hand.

The dealer turned her attention on Cole, and he glanced down at his cards. Two aces. *What the hell was he supposed to do with that?* "Hit me?"

"Wait," Sierra pleaded. "Split them," she urged, and Cole had no idea what she was talking about. "He wants to split them," she told the dealer who then looked at him for confirmation.

"Whatever she says."

Sierra told him what to do with his money, adding more to the table that he was likely going to lose, but what the hell did he care. Then the dealer proceeded to deal out more cards, and Sierra squealed in delight.

"Blackjack! Twice!"

Cole wasn't sure what that meant to him, other than he had won, but when Sierra threw her arms around his neck, wrapping him in her sweet, spicy scent, Cole no longer cared. When she buried her nose into the crook of his neck and her warm breath whispered across his skin, he damn near came up off the chair. His dick swelled and throbbed, making his jeans increasingly uncomfortable – a sensation he was becoming all too familiar with.

"You won," She told him when she pulled back, and Cole could only stare back at her.

Did she feel the same thing when they touched as he did? That sharp tingle that started somewhere deep inside and radiated outward. When their eyes met, and held, he knew instantly that there was definitely something going on between the two of them.

Throughout dinner, Cole had continued to answer Sierra's questions, although he admittedly was trying to determine her motive. Yes, his insecurities had led him to believe Sierra was grilling him only to find out more about Luke. He'd been there before. On more than one occasion and he had to say, it wasn't his favorite pastime. So when she seemed to be genuinely interested in him, Cole had let down his guard a little.

He'd tested her with his admission about his trust fund, and her reaction, or lack thereof, surprised him. Yes, Cole had money. Boatloads of it. More than he could spend in a lifetime thanks to his grandparents and his parents.

Did the money define him? No. But, he was the first to admit that the money was part of who he was. It allowed him to do what he loved without the worry of whether or not he would be able to eat. That was a blessing that he didn't take for granted.

The one thing he had learned about his money... it changed people. Other people. They measured him based on the sum of his bank accounts. Which was partially why Sierra's personal interest in him had been so shocking.

The questions that she asked weren't related to Luke or to Cole's money, and for the first time, Cole had been taken aback. Almost to the point that he hadn't known how to answer her questions.

But he did and here they were, enjoying what was left of the evening without awkwardness and without the need to run off to bed in order to make the night tolerable. Not that he didn't want to get Sierra in bed because he definitely did.

He fought to keep the blood flowing through his veins, rather than pooling in his groin. That was difficult when just the sound of her voice, the easy way she laughed, and the way the soft skin on her arm rubbed easily against his made him hotter than hell.

Sierra cleared her throat and smiled before turning her attention back to the dealer who was waiting for her to make her play. Cole shifted his gaze down to her hands, noticing the slight tremor in her fingers. He couldn't suppress the smile that broke free. This night only continued to get better and better.

He just wondered how it would turn out after Luke showed up.

~~*~~

Luke returned to the hotel nearly an hour later than he anticipated, and instead of calling Cole to find out where they were, he opted to take a walk through the casino to see for himself.

He spotted them quickly at a blackjack table, another couple sitting beside them while they ribbed the dealer, laughing and joking and obviously enjoying each other's company.

He paused to take in the scene, noticing how Sierra sat close to Cole, their arms brushing one another, the heated way that she looked over at him.

He couldn't pinpoint what he was feeling, but the sight triggered that possessive instinct he harbored. When it came to the couple sitting at the table, their gazes locked on one another, Luke was overwhelmed with the need to keep them close, but there wasn't an ounce of jealousy when it came to the relationship they were building.

Forcing his feet to move forward, he closed the gap and came up behind Cole, lightly brushing his arm against the man, then placing one hand on the back of Sierra's slender neck.

"Hey." Sierra smiled brightly, and something caught inside Luke's chest. The way she reacted to him settled something deep; something that he hadn't realized was insecure.

"Are you winning?" he asked, glancing down at the mountain of chips growing up from the green felt.

"I'm on a good streak, let's put it that way. Though Cole hasn't fared nearly as well. I think I've won the same amount that he's lost."

Cole didn't seem to mind, if the grin on his face was anything to go by. As much as Luke hated to put an end to their good luck at the tables, he had other activities in mind. Naked activities. After nearly nine hours of business, his mind having been on Sierra most of the day, Luke was ready to get her to his room. He gave Cole a knowing look and the other man caught on quickly.

Offering up his chips to the dealer, Cole stood from his chair. "I say we call it a night. Cash me in?"

"Me too," Sierra said, obviously unwilling to be left behind.

Luke's body hardened, his dick twitched, and a slow burning heat started deep in his gut as he watched her. She seemed to anticipate what was coming next, and unless he missed his mark, she was eager.

Sierra tipped the dealer before they walked away, and Cole took her chips to cash them in with his. Luke continued toward the elevators with painstakingly slow movements giving Cole time to catch up. The man had better get a move on, or Luke would be getting on without him.

While they waited, Sierra slipped a twenty dollar bill into one of the dollar slots and stood beside it and played. After two tries, the machine lit up and started making noises.

"Oh my goodness! Did I..." Sierra stared at the machine like she wasn't sure what happened.

Luke watched her expressions, the beautiful way her face lit up with happiness. For the first time in his life, Luke wanted to be the reason her face lit up like that, not the flashing numbers across the screen that announced she had won.

"Lucky today, are you?" Luke asked, lowering his voice so only she could hear when Sierra threw her arms around him, right there in the middle of everyone. Instinctively he wrapped his arm around her, holding her close and kissing her forehead, breathing in that sweet, sexy scent of her perfume.

"I'm hoping to get luckier," she whispered in his ear, her fingers lacing in the hair at the nape of his neck, softly brushing against his skin.

Luke was afraid he just might lose his control when it came to Sierra. He could feel the need to take her building from the inside, the need to dominate her, to show her exactly the man he was.

Sierra pulled away when the casino attendant came up to pay her winnings.

"Shit, she's on fire," Cole added as he walked over.

"She is that," Luke agreed, but he wasn't referring to her lucky streak.

~~*~~

Ten minutes later, they were walking into Luke's suite, choosing his over hers since he had an adjoining room with Cole. Once inside, Cole went directly to the minibar, making drinks for the three of them while Sierra took a seat on the small couch. The curtains were pulled back, the lights of the strip glowing and flashing brightly down below.

Luke removed his suit jacket and tie, tossing them onto the side chair, then unbuttoned the top two buttons on his shirt, and rolled up his sleeves. All the while, he kept his eyes on Sierra, watching her as she fidgeted.

She was nervous, but he couldn't necessarily blame her. She'd been all spark and flames early that morning on the airplane, thinking she knew what she was getting herself into until he'd called her on it.

Truth be told, Sierra hadn't even dreamed about the type of man Luke was. Those books that she likely read wouldn't touch on the darkness that swirled inside of him. In order to control some of his own hungers, he'd opted to engage in his brothers' sexual exploits, allowing Logan to control the situation. They were safer that way.

Right now, he just wanted to strip Sierra down, to feel her writhe beneath him, to fill her completely while she came around his cock. He wanted her to watch while Cole dropped to his knees, and Luke buried his cock in Cole's mouth hard and fast. He wanted to crush her between the two of them while Cole filled her pussy and Luke took her sweet ass.

She might have some fantasies about what she truly wanted, but tonight would be the first test. Tonight he would see what she was made of. Despite the fact that they were still getting to know one another, Luke didn't give a damn. He wanted her. And he wanted her now.

"Sierra." Luke controlled his words, the hunger rising, the ache throbbing harder. "Come here."

Cole subtly jerked to attention, turning to look at Luke, waiting for what would come next. He carried the drinks forward, handing Luke his before passing Sierra one.

Still sitting on the couch, Sierra looked confused, but she slowly moved to the edge.

"Now," Luke growled, staring at her, not moving from the wall he was propped against.

She jumped, standing from her seat and glancing over at Cole as though he might be able to help her. Luke wasn't going to tell her again. She'd learn soon enough that when he said something, he expected compliance. She took tentative steps toward him, her hands faintly trembling as she held the glass in one hand.

"Do you know what you're getting yourself into?" Luke asked, figuring now was the time to get this out in the open. He might be dominant, he might expect complete surrender, not submission, from his partners, but he didn't take them against their will. He'd never been with anyone who wasn't completely willing, and he wasn't about to start now.

"I could ask you the same thing," Sierra retorted, and Luke caught the twinkle in her eye when she smiled so sweetly.

"Baby, I always know," he assured her.

"Then I think we have something in common. I wouldn't be here if I didn't know what I was doing." The confidence in her brilliant blue eyes glowed brightly.

"When I tell you to do something, I expect full compliance. Understand?"

"Yes."

"I need you to be absolutely sure about this, Sierra. I need your complete trust. I won't hurt you, but that doesn't mean I won't push you to the point you feel like you might break. If you get scared, I need to know."

"Like I said, I wouldn't be here if I didn't trust you." Sierra then turned to address Cole. "Or you."

So she did understand the dynamic of what was happening between the three of them. She didn't seem scared, but Luke could tell she was uncertain, more so than she was admitting.

"Have you ever done this before?"

"Done what?" she asked innocently.

So she wanted to play it that way.

"Have you ever been with two men at one time?"

"No."

Luke pushed away from the wall, watching as Sierra took one step back, her reaction belying her cool confidence.

"And you plan to now?"

"Yes."

Cole had taken a relaxed position standing near the window, one shoulder propped against the wall, his ankles crossed as he watched the scene playing out before him. Figuring now was as good a time as any to give Sierra a glimpse of his true nature, Luke addressed the man.

"Cole." Luke only had to say his name before Cole was standing tall again, all strength and masculine grace. "Take your shirt off."

The defiance in Cole's gaze spurred Luke on, and he had a feeling the other man knew it. The way Cole battled his internal need to defy him turned Luke on more. "See baby, even Cole doesn't understand me all that well." Luke turned Sierra in his arms so her back was to his front, focusing her eyes on Cole. "He still seems to think that when I say something, I'm making a request. Take the damn shirt off, Cole."

Sitting his drink on the side table, Cole unhooked one more button on his shirt, keeping a leisurely pace. With one hand, he reached behind his head, gripping the collar and pulling the shirt over his head, slowly revealing his impressive abs, followed by his smooth, well defined chest and then his massive shoulders.

Once the material was out of the way, Cole locked his gaze with Luke's once more.

"He's a fast learner," Sierra commented, her sharp intake of breath letting them both know how much she appreciated the view.

Admittedly, Cole was a sight to behold – smooth, tan skin; hairless except for the small trail of blond hair that disappeared into the waistband of his jeans.

"Now it's your turn, baby." Luke placed his empty glass on the top of the television cabinet, then putting his arms around Sierra, over her shoulders.

He began teasing her by trailing his fingers over the sweet curves of her breasts, lower until he reached the hem of her t-shirt.

Never taking his eyes from Cole, he watched the man's reaction, seeing the hard outline of his erection coming to life in his jeans as more of Sierra's body was unveiled.

"You want to see her naked? You've thought about it all day, the same as I have," Luke spoke softly, his voice hoarse with need.

"I've hardly thought of anything else," Cole admitted, watching as Luke slid the soft, black fabric up her torso, revealing smooth, pale skin.

When Sierra leaned into him, Luke took her response as her approval, and then took her glass from her hand, setting it beside his. Pulling the shirt up and off, he held her wrists in one of his hands, above her head.

"Put your hands around my neck," he instructed, letting go of her wrist when she did, the movement thrusting out those perfect breasts, encased in sexy black lace.

None too gently, Luke palmed the luscious curves, squeezing, listening to the way her breaths became erratic; barely hanging on to his sanity when she ground her ass against his rock hard cock.

His next move rid her of the lace, baring her breasts, tipped with small, dusty pink nipples that he longed to put his lips on. Holding back the urge Luke kept her facing Cole, watching the other man's eyes lock on those two hardened points, his hand instinctively going to his crotch, rubbing the hard shaft behind the zipper of his jeans.

Sierra fit nicely against him, her head settled perfectly beneath his chin, which allowed Luke to lean forward and view the sweet skin he was uncovering. Sliding his hands down over her flat stomach, he found the button on her jeans and deftly unhooked it before lowering the zipper, more soft skin coming into view.

"You see what you do to him? What you do to every man who looks at you? I guarantee he's hard as granite."

"Show me," Sierra whispered.

"You heard her. Take the jeans off," Luke demanded, liking that Sierra was an active participant.

Cole didn't hesitate before he easily removed his jeans and boxers, letting them sit on the floor where they fell. Luke made sure Cole felt the heat of his gaze as he raked his eyes over the hardened perfection of his toned body. "What do you think, baby?" Luke asked.

"Beautiful." Some of the confidence and surety had returned in her voice, but Luke felt the faint tremble as she anticipated his next move. "Absolutely stunning."

"I want to watch as he slides his cock into your mouth, watch while he holds you in place while your tongue bathes him," Luke whispered, and he witnessed Cole's body harden with anticipation. "But first I want you as naked as him. Take them off," Luke said, moving his hands to the side, but not taking a step away from her.

When she bent forward, lowering the denim down her legs, Luke bit back a groan as she ground her shapely ass over his throbbing hard on. Once her clothes were disregarded on the floor, she returned to her place against him, now a few inches shorter since she removed the shoes. Leaning forward once more, he let his hand trail down to the smooth, hairless skin between her thighs, using his index and middle finger to separate the soft, plump lips of her pussy, baring her for Cole's eyes. Her sharp intake of breath and the way she swayed in his arms assured Luke that she was just as turned on as they were.

"I'm eager to put my mouth on your pussy, Sierra. To fuck you deep and hard with my tongue while you scream my name, begging me to let you come." Luke let his middle finger rake over the sensitive bundle of nerves that he'd uncovered, slowly teasing her with gentle strokes.

"Please," Sierra begged.

Glancing up at Cole, Luke caught his breath at the sight of the other man slowly stroking his thick cock, the tip glistening with moisture. Making good on his promise, Luke pulled his hand back and then placed one firm hand on the top of Sierra's head, letting her know what he expected as he directed her to her knees.

"I want to watch while you put those pretty lips on his dick."

Cole took a step closer, then another until they were less than a foot apart. Sierra lowered herself to the floor, her eyes focused on Cole.

"That's it, baby, wrap those lips around him." Taking a step back, Luke moved to the edge of the bed where he could get a better view.

Sierra looked momentarily at him, then back at Cole who took another step closer, bringing his cock close to the promise of heaven.

When Sierra raised a tentative hand, wrapping her small fingers around Cole, Luke noticed that she couldn't circle him completely. He also noticed Cole's sharp intake of breath as her delicate hand closed around him while she placed teasing, open mouthed kisses on the engorged head.

Temptation

God she was sweet. So fucking hot as she slowly bathed Cole's cock with gentle, teasing flicks of her tongue before she slid down and over him, taking him completely inside the hot cavern of her mouth. The only thing that could've been better was to have her mouth on his cock.

Instead Luke just watched the strain on Cole's face as he tried to stand still while Sierra's hot mouth slid around him, Cole's cock disappearing inside while her velvety soft fingers slowly jacked him when she began to move.

When Sierra started to look up, obviously realizing she wouldn't be able to see him unless she released him, Cole quickly gripped her hair, holding her in place. Luke's cock jumped at the sight. Seeing Cole take control, unleashing some of his own need to dominate, was truly a sight to behold.

"Suck him, Sierra. Take him deep in your throat while he fucks your mouth." Luke spurred her on while the gruff sound of Cole's groan filled the room.

"That's it baby. God that feels so fucking good." Cole's voice was raspy with need.

No matter how many times Luke had fantasized about this moment all day, he had never thought it would be like this.

She opened wider; taking Cole in as far as she could before she closed her teeth around him and let them scrape sensually down his shaft, making him groan louder. Luke could damn near feel the tingling in his own throbbing cock just from watching.

"Holy shit!"

Cole quickly pulled his cock from her mouth while Sierra angled her head and slid her lips and tongue down the sensitive underside of his shaft before she sucked his balls into her mouth completely.

Just the sight of it was nearly Luke's undoing, and she hadn't even put her mouth on him yet. Her tongue bathed Cole's balls with warm, wet heat, forcing Cole to lock his legs to keep himself upright.

Returning her attention to his shaft, Sierra continued to fondle his balls with one hand while slowly stroking him with the other, sucking on the engorged head before once again taking him inside her mouth.

"Fuck her mouth," Luke growled, no longer wanting to be the voyeur, he moved behind Cole, shedding his shirt in the process.

There was only an inch or two difference in their height, but Luke still managed to reach around Cole, pressing his chest against Cole's back so he could reach around him and grip his cock. Placing his hand over Sierra's much smaller one, Luke forced her to stroke Cole faster.

"So fucking hot. You like having her mouth on you." Luke pressed his lips close to Cole's ear, wanting him to hear the intensity of Luke's need.

Cole didn't respond to Luke's words, but he used Luke's body to help hold him up as Sierra began to increase her pace, the sweet suction forcing him closer to the edge.

"Faster, baby. I want to watch as he comes in your mouth," Luke growled, grinding his denim covered dick against Cole's bare ass, the hair on his chest scraping sensually against Cole's smooth back.

"Fuck," Cole groaned. "Baby, I'm going to come. Take me deeper. That's it." Gripping her head, Cole pulled her closer, thrusting into her mouth until his knees damn near buckled.

With an unrestrained roar, Cole let go, coming long and hard into the sweet, hot mouth wrapped around his dick.

"Your turn, baby." Luke quickly released Cole and then rid himself of his remaining clothes.

When Sierra was back on her feet, he pulled her against him, and then lowered them both to the bed, laying her on top of him, the soft swells of her breasts pressed against his chest, the hardened points of her nipples scraping sensually against him. He pulled her head down until his mouth was on hers, tasting the essence of Cole as he devoured her.

"I want to watch your face while Cole eats that sweet pussy," he told her. "Raise your ass, so he can lick you, baby." Luke widened her legs, then pressed a hand against the small of her back.

Sierra did as she was told and the bed shifted when Cole climbed between their splayed legs, the other man gripping Luke's thighs as he maneuvered into place. The way he and Sierra were aligned brought Cole's mouth right in line with his dick and Cole's hot, warm breath caressed him, sending a chill down his spine.

"Look at me," Luke told Sierra when Cole began his sensual assault, his tongue teasing Luke's hard cock every so often as he pleasured the woman above him.

"Oh God!" Sierra moaned.

"Tell me, baby. Tell me how it feels."

"So good."

"Is he sucking your clit?" Luke asked, cupping her head and forcing her to look at him. "Keep your eyes open."

"Yes. He's…" Sierra gasped. "Oh, God! It feels so good."

"Does it feel good to have his warm tongue sliding between your pussy lips? Teasing your clit?"

Sierra didn't utter a single word, but the moans that escaped were music to Luke's ears. Whatever Cole was doing, he was doing well.

"Are you going to come, Sierra?" Luke asked.

"Yes. Oh! Right there. Oh, God! I'm going to…" Sierra's body tensed in his arms as she came against Cole's mouth, her eyes closed, her head thrown back.

It was the hottest thing Luke had ever seen.

Holding her through her first orgasm, his hands stroked over the gentle curve of her spine. Before Luke could contemplate what to do next, Cole took Luke's cock deep into his mouth, making his muscles tense. Instinctively he gripped Sierra tightly while Cole's talented fucking mouth stroked him, causing a maelstrom of pleasure to take up residence in his groin

"I want to watch," Sierra stated, pulling out of Luke's arms.

The sensations were so intense Luke couldn't hold onto her and concentrate on the sensual assault at the same time. Lifting his head, he saw the top of Cole's head as the other man sucked him harder, his rough, callused hand gripping the base of his dick, doing his best to drive him to the edge, but clearly unwilling to let Luke come just yet.

"Oh, God," Sierra moaned from beside him, making both Cole and Luke look her way. "That's the hottest thing I've ever seen."

Luke followed her gaze back between his legs where Cole had doubled his assault, one hand fondling his balls, one finger brushing the sensitive skin just underneath, making Luke groan as he gripped the comforter beneath him. He tried to thrust up into Cole's mouth, but he was bracing his body on Luke's thighs, making it damn near impossible to move.

Throwing his head back onto the mattress, trying to hold himself together, but overcome with the magnitude of the way Cole expertly sucked him, Luke didn't think he could.

Then, in a move that damn near stole his breath, there was another mouth on him, another hand. Softer, gentler, yet just as thrilling and they were both licking and sucking, pushing him higher, faster.

"Fuck!" Luke growled with a fierceness that reverberated through the room as he came.

Chapter Eleven

Before Sierra could catch her breath, still reeling from the wildly erotic blow job she just witnessed, Luke pushed himself up off of the bed while Cole came down on top of her, pressing her into the mattress. His mouth found hers, fast and hard, his tongue delving deeper while she tried desperately to wrap herself around him.

The ferocity in which they had all three come, albeit individually, left her wondering how they could keep going. But she found her body was primed and ready, her pussy wet and aching to feel one of them inside of her.

She heard the crinkle of a foil wrapper, but she knew it wasn't Cole because he was still on top of her, both hands braced by her head, keeping him suspended above her so she didn't burden his full weight. Spreading her legs, she attempted to guide him where she wanted him, only to feel hands pass between them where she assumed Luke was sheathing Cole's cock with a condom. She couldn't wait any longer, and the feel of Cole's rock hard body pressed against hers suffused her with a warmth she wasn't ready to part with.

Another foil wrapper opened, followed by the distinct sound of a cap being flipped open. Sierra assumed Luke was taking care of the preparations. For what, she didn't know, but she had a fairly decent idea.

When Cole pulled up from her, breaking their kiss, Sierra attempted to look over his shoulder, but could barely make out Luke's form standing at the edge of the bed.

"Please. Fuck me!" Sierra pleaded, once again grinding herself against Cole, trying to align them so she could take him into her body where she needed him to be more than she needed her next breath.

"Off the bed." Luke's husky voice interrupted Sierra's intention, causing her to still. What were they going to do?

The warmth of Cole's body disappeared as she was suddenly jerked to the edge of the bed, her butt resting on the side while Cole slipped his arms beneath her knees, spreading her wide.

This was new for her. Hell, everything they were doing was new for Sierra.

"Bend over." Once again Luke was directing Cole, and he was rearranging himself without reservation, aligning Sierra's body so he still hovered just out of her reach.

"Just like that." The satisfaction in Luke's voice was unmistakable as it rumbled from behind Cole.

Sierra was awash with a heat that threatened to send her over before Cole slipped inside of her. She was torn between wanting to watch as Luke took Cole, the thought making her body tremble and wanting to watch the pleasure on Cole's face while Luke fucked him so desperately. In the position she was in, she could only focus on the man above her, so Sierra locked her gaze on Cole's handsome face.

Torn between not knowing what to do and not knowing what she was supposed to want, Sierra waited, anxiously anticipating what would come next. This was new for her, every part of it − from the desperate need that filled her to the ache to be with these two men.

Her nerves were rioting and she wished they wouldn't give her time to think it through because if her brain was allowed to take over, she knew she would retreat, go back to the comfort she knew from not being with a man, not being in a situation that robbed her of all reason and left her with nothing but desire.

In two seconds she was going to panic, to pull away if they didn't do something. Instead of waiting, she locked eyes with Cole and issued her own demand. "Inside me! Now!"

In an instant, Cole shifted, lifting her ass off the bed, her knees bent and hanging over the crook of his arms as he plunged inside of her to the hilt in one swift motion that left her breathless.

She screamed, the invasion so sudden, it was both painful and erotic, each sensation overwhelming the other until they merged as one. Instinct had her body fighting to resist, yet trying to adjust to his size at the same time.

When she attempted to move, Cole gripped her wrists in each of his hands, pinning them to the mattress beside her hips, rendering her immobile. His head lowered as he sucked a nipple into the hot furnace of his mouth sending tingles down her spine and making her internal muscles clamp around him. That earned her a desperate groan rumbling from deep in his chest.

"Hold still, baby." Cole's body went instantly rigid as he appeared to be bracing for Luke's impalement while he was still buried deep inside of her.

Temptation

Then there was more movement, and she felt Luke's fingers brush her calves as he gripped Cole's hips, the bed dipping slightly below her as more of Cole's weight came down on the mattress, though he was still mindful of his grip on her wrists. How the man managed to think at all with everything that was going on was beyond her.

And then there was blessed friction, movement, though slow and steady, still just what she needed. Cole's iron hard cock tunneled inside of her in a slow glide; retreating just as slowly at first. She watched his face tense, felt his body harden; only sheer pleasure written on each of his handsome features.

The man was a masterpiece, so hot, so damn sexy; Sierra was nearly blinded by it.

A few more grunts and thrusts and then, somehow, they managed to find a rhythm that rocked Sierra to her core. Cole's thick cock buried deeper, only to retreat and thrust harder, faster until Sierra lifted her hips to better the angle, her stomach muscles screaming with the motion as she tried to take him deeper inside of her.

"Fuck yes!" Cole groaned, slipping one hand free to palm her breast, squeezing gently at first, then harder, his thumb and forefinger pinching her nipple, a bright burst of sensual pain shooting directly to her clit, making her muscles tighten.

And then there was only feeling. An overwhelming pleasure that lit her entire body from the inside out, stars danced behind her closed eyelids as she pressed her head into the mattress, letting the sensations wash over her until she couldn't take any more.

Sierra screamed when her orgasm ripped through her, her body clamping down on Cole as he thrust harder, faster, being rocked by Luke from behind until both men's groans thundered through the room, sending another orgasm rocketing through her.

Then the darkness took her.

~~*~~

Luke awoke to sunlight flooding the room, the feel of a soft body pressed up against his side. Her fresh, clean, feminine scent mixed with the sultry smell of sex that still permeated the air. Rolling to his side, he slid his hand over the rounded curves of the woman in his bed and found himself smiling.

Sierra.

The memories of the night before, the way the three of them had come together, the way they had connected, still shocked him. Despite his need to take Sierra, to bury himself in her tight body, Luke hadn't been able to make it that far. After Cole and Sierra made him come with their mouths, he'd been overcome with a savage intensity that he feared would cause him to hurt her.

Instead of taking that chance, he'd buried his cock into Cole's tight ass and hung on while they'd both inadvertently fucked Sierra, Cole having the pleasure of being inside of her while Luke was rocked with the intensity of being inside of Cole again.

As many times as Luke had been part of a threesome, he'd never done that. In fact, Luke had never taken a man so intimately, until Cole. Until the night at Luke's house when the overwhelming need had been too strong to ignore, the lure of Cole and all of the things the man made him feel had pushed him past the boundaries he'd inadvertently set for himself. Just like the last time.

Until that night, Luke hadn't realized he had even been attracted to a man in that way. And maybe he just hadn't found the right man. Deep down inside, he'd felt that with Cole and despite his reluctance to accept it, Luke knew it for the truth that it was.

Despite the intense sexual need and the desire that plagued him, Luke didn't feel the overwhelming protective instinct for Cole the way he did with Sierra. Maybe that's because Cole was strong enough that he didn't need Luke to be protective of him. Sierra, on the other hand, he had a feeling that the woman was easily getting under his skin, though she hadn't even tried.

Last night, Luke realized that although he enjoyed the pleasure that he found with Cole, he still longed to be buried inside of Sierra's soft, slender body and to feel the depths of what the woman could give him.

He had refrained.

Afterward, when both he and Cole collapsed on the bed beside Sierra, he had managed to put up that barrier that would inadvertently push Cole away.

Luke might be able to accept the fact that he could find pleasure in Cole's body, get lost in the heat and urgency, but that didn't make it any easier to face the aftermath. And Cole must have seen the invisible walls fall into place because after he disappeared into the bathroom, returning moments later with a damp cloth that he gently and effectively used on Sierra, before he disappeared into his own room without another word.

Lying on the bed now, Sierra's luscious body pressed up against him, Luke knew he needed to get up, to wake Sierra so they could get ready and meet Logan and Sam at the conference. He couldn't bring himself to do it. Yet. Since the moment Cole slipped from the room, Sierra had been sleeping soundly, and Luke wasn't anxious to wake her. Instead, he settled on watching her sleep.

She looked so innocent, the dark fan of her eyelashes brushing the tops of her cheeks, the silky, black, tangled tresses spread out around her, a dark contrast against the white sheets.

She was an angel. And she scared the shit out of him.

Luke was startled from his thoughts when he heard the shower in Cole's room turn on. Doing his best not to wake her, he slipped from the bed and made his way into the adjoining room in time to see Cole's reflection in the bathroom mirror as his naked form stepped into the shower. Luke was torn between what he wanted and what he shouldn't want. And that was Cole. His body wanted the man. Fiercely.

Truthfully, Luke was scared shitless about the desires Cole brought out in him. He didn't feel the need to deny the physical attraction between them. Luke was open to his sexuality, always had been, going after what he wanted for the sheer pleasure of it. Luke wouldn't deny that he needed variety, and apparently he'd found what he needed in Cole.

Before he knew what he was doing, Luke was in the bathroom, pulling back the shower curtain and climbing in. Cole stood beneath the spray of hot water, his forearms resting against the tile while he leaned his forehead against them.

Need pierced him as he took in the sight of Cole's strong back, his trim waist and perfect ass.

Unable to say a word, Luke simply moved up against him, pressing his chest to the other man's smooth, well defined back, sliding his cock between Cole's legs. The sharp intake of breath was Cole's only acknowledgement, and when Luke leaned against him, reaching around with his right hand to stroke Cole's rock hard erection, he gave in to his desires.

"I need you," Luke stated firmly. Using his left hand, he guided his cock between Cole's firm ass cheeks, teasing the puckered hole. "Right here. Right now. But I won't be gentle," he warned.

Cole nodded his head and leaned farther into the wall, giving Luke better access as Cole used his own hand to stroke the steely length of his cock.

Luke made quick work of rolling on a condom, his cock hard as stone and pulsing with the need to be lodged deep inside of Cole again.

He caught sight of a tube of lubrication sitting on the edge of the tub and wondered whether Cole had anticipated this, or if the man had just intended to satisfy himself. Quickly flipping the cap open, Luke squeezed the cool gel over his cock and stroked gently. He was primed and ready, just from the remembered feel of Cole's welcoming body.

With little finesse, Luke guided his cock into Cole, thrusting hard, burying himself to the hilt, slipping through the tight ring of muscles, the tense grip of Cole's body milking him. Being inside of him was a pleasure Luke had never known before Cole and one he feared he would never know after.

Cole gasped, pressing back against him, his hand stroking harder and faster along his cock while Luke gripped his hips and pounded into him. Luke's insides tightened; the tension building, Cole's body gripping him, pulling him deeper. Grunts and groans erupted, echoing in the small space, barely heard over the sound of running water as Luke thrust deeper.

Until last night, he'd avoided this for two long months, the desperate need to own this man, to take him like this, to unleash all of his desire on one person. The one person who could handle Luke like no one else.

"You're so fucking tight. I'm gonna come deep in your ass, and you better fucking come with me," Luke growled, pressing Cole down with one hand on his back as he continued to pound into him. "Come for me, Cole!"

With that, both men growled out their release, the warm water pounding over them as they fought for breath, using all of their remaining energy to continue standing.

Luke slid from Cole's body, pressing against his back, laying his head against Cole's, taking a moment to relish the feel of the man. The differences between Cole and Sierra were like night and day, and for the life of him, Luke didn't understand what he was drawn to. What he did understand was that no matter how hard he pushed, Cole continued to come back. What that ultimately meant, Luke had no idea.

Luke didn't understand the conflicting feelings; the need to possess Cole – mind, body, and soul. Those feelings piggybacked on his need to have Sierra – the woman he had thought about constantly since the moment he first laid eyes on her. Both of them consumed every waking thought, every conscious desire, and for the life of him, he couldn't explain it.

As much as he wanted Cole, as much as he was coming to care for him, Luke was scared shitless that it would all be taken away in an instant…the underlying reason Luke kept himself from getting attached, the very real knowledge that the ones you loved could be ripped from your life so easily. Like his parents had been.

Even as a small child, unsure of what it meant to love and lose, Luke vowed never to let anyone get close, never to rely on someone to be there because in the end, what happened to them was out of his control. And he couldn't bear to lose anyone else.

Sierra brought on the exact same fears. Luke didn't know her well enough, and he hadn't pushed her far enough. Last night had been mild compared to what he wanted to do. Although she gave herself over to them both freely, trusting them with her pleasure, Luke still worried that he would scare her. Even though he wouldn't be able to hold back forever, at least for now he had Cole who didn't ask any questions.

When Cole turned in his arms, Luke took a step back, surprised when Cole latched on to the back of his neck, pulling him forward until they were just a hairsbreadth away, their foreheads touching. For a second, their roles were almost reversed, and Luke anticipated what Cole was going to say, holding his breath.

"This won't be over, Luke. I'll tell you that right now. What's going on between us, the three of us, this doesn't fucking happen every day." There was an intensity to Cole's words that Luke had never heard before.

"You own me," Cole continued, his voice lowering, "you own every fucking part of me, and I won't back off this time. From you or from Sierra. Don't make me."

The denial Luke had somehow come to terms with reared its ugly head, reminding him of what he didn't want – or more importantly what he didn't want to lose.

Before he had a moment to blast Cole with exactly what he thought about the whole thing, Cole pulled Luke to him, crushing his mouth down on his. Luke reluctantly gave in to the kiss, relishing in the hard, masculine feel of Cole's mouth as they both fought for dominance.

Luke knew who would win the battle, but for the first time in his life, he wasn't so certain he would also win the war.

~~*~~

Sierra woke up alone in Luke's bed; the sound of water running in the next room had her stirring until she couldn't fall back asleep. Instead of tossing and turning, aching for the loss of the warm body she had been curled up against all night, she ventured into the next room, just to see where Cole and Luke were. What she found rooted her in place and stole her breath.

Through the sheer shower curtain the outline of two masculine forms were visible, Luke behind Cole, thrusting deep and hard. Overwhelmed by the sheer eroticism of the act, the warmth of her juices trickled between her thighs as she looked on, fascinated. Although their words were muddled by the sound of running water, she heard their desperate male cries of release loud and clear.

She should have stepped out of the bathroom, should have given them the privacy they deserved, but she couldn't tear her eyes off of the sight before her. When Cole turned in Luke's arms, the words he said much clearer than only moments before, Sierra's heart practically stopped beating.

What's going on between us, the three of us, this doesn't fucking happen every day. You own me, you own every fucking part of me, and I won't back off this time. From you or from Sierra. Don't make me.

Though her body had succumbed to the pleasure the night before, shutting down completely, Sierra's mind hadn't been so easily deterred. During fits of sleep, waking to find that she wanted to get closer to Luke, her sleepy brain wondering where Cole had gone, Sierra had had dreams about the two men.

As much as she wanted this to be strictly casual, her heart fearful of what damage two powerful men like Luke and Cole could inflict on it, she wasn't able to grasp the concept. Having only been intimate with them for a few hours, Sierra found that she was starting to want more. Likely a huge mistake, but an emotion she couldn't quell.

The confirmation from Cole's mouth that what she had felt the night before was not something she was experiencing alone left her feeling elated, a flash fire of hope burning in her chest. Granted, Luke hadn't said a word, but he didn't have to. She had seen it in his eyes the night before, the way he had looked at her told her more than words ever would. All of this she had garnered from a man she knew so little about.

Sierra wasn't sure if she had made a sound, but the shower curtain suddenly pulled back, and Luke stuck his head out, his hand reaching for her until she was stumbling forward, being pulled into the steamy shower between both men, the sheet she had wrapped around herself dropping to the cool tile floor, forgotten. Her heart drummed double time, and she couldn't hold back the smile, even though she was worried that they would be upset that she had been standing there, invading their private moment.

"It's your turn, baby," Luke whispered as she was pulled back against Cole's rock solid chest while Luke went to his knees in front of her. "I've wanted to do this all damn night."

"Oh, God. What are…?" She swallowed the rest of the words on a moan as Cole swiftly lifted her against him, cupping her rear as she braced her feet on the sides of the tub.

When Luke buried his face between her legs her muscles went lax, and she was grateful that Cole held more of her weight. A quick rearrangement of bodies had Luke shifting her legs up over his shoulders, kneeling before her as he feasted on her sensitive pussy.

"Did you like what you saw?" Cole asked as he nipped the delicate skin of her neck while Luke did unspeakable things with his mouth, his tongue buried deep inside of her, thrusting slowly. "Does it turn you on to watch Luke fuck me? To take me with the same overwhelming desire that I've taken you with?

"Yes." She wouldn't lie, and she wouldn't avoid the questions. She had liked what she saw. The raw passion between these two men was a turn on like no other. Seeing the way they held themselves back, yet gave themselves freely made her long to belong, long for them to look at her the same way that they did each other.

"Luke!" Sierra screamed his name as he sucked her clit into his mouth and thrust two fingers inside of her, curving them at just the right angle, stroking the sensitive tissue that would guarantee her orgasm. He was moving quickly, forcing her to the precipice, but she didn't want it to end. She tried to press harder against his mouth, to increase the friction of his wicked tongue, but he held her in a position that allowed her little movement. He controlled her pleasure.

Cole pushed her hair aside and latched on to the skin at the base of her neck with his lips, sucking roughly, an apparent erogenous zone she was completely unaware of. Sierra saw stars. The world erupted in a whirlwind of color and sensation as she exploded; her orgasm was so powerful, she was grateful both men were holding her because she would have collapsed to the floor without them.

Moments later, once again standing on her own two feet, they were washing her, then themselves, and before Sierra had fully come back down to earth, Luke was carrying her from the shower, wrapped in a fluffy white towel. He laid her gently on the bed and then climbed over her.

"If we had more time this morning, I would bury my cock deep inside of you just to feel that sweet, warm pussy wrapped around me."

Sierra couldn't help it, she moaned, the mental image bringing her body quickly to life again.

"Later, baby. I promise," Luke whispered and then kissed her softly, tenderly before he climbed off of the bed and went in search of clothes.

Sierra rolled over onto her side and watched his beautiful, masculine form as he moved effortlessly around the room, completely comfortable with his nudity. He was perfection, and Sierra knew she was falling hard and fast for a man who liked to hold himself back in every way that counted, other than with sex.

She glanced over at the clock, realizing they needed to be at the conference in less than thirty minutes, and it took nearly half of that just to dry her hair. Bolting up off of the bed, she wrapped the towel tightly around her while she searched for her clothes. She needed to get back to her room so she could get ready.

As she pulled on her jeans, unable to locate her panties or bra, Luke came up behind her with his shirt and slipped it over her back. She stood upright, sliding her arms into the sleeves, the soft cotton smelling faintly of that sultry cologne he favored, but more of the unique man. Although the shirt dwarfed her completely, she managed to button three of the buttons before she went to the door, her shoes in hand.

"I'll be ready in thirty minutes. If you and Cole need to go over beforehand, I can find my way." She gripped the door handle but not before Luke had her bracketed between his arms and the door. Turning in the circle of his arms, she looked up at him and smiled.

"We'll wait. You've got time," he whispered, and then leaned down and kissed her again, another sweltering hot kiss that spoke of promises and hot orgasmic sex. God, she would never get enough of this man.

Nodding her head, she pulled open the door and peered out. Seeing that the hallway was empty, she ran to her door and let herself in.

Though she had just spent the night with Luke and Cole, she wanted nothing more than to get right back to them as fast as she could.

~~*~~

Friday passed quickly. Luke, Cole, and Sierra spent the day talking to vendors and potential clients, as well as managing to have lunch together, all three of them. Tonight they were all invited to dinner for XTX at a Brazilian steakhouse located on Las Vegas Blvd. Sierra had rushed back to the hotel, leaving both men to finish up at the conference, despite their arguments that at least one of them should accompany her back.

Well, that would have been nice, but she feared it would also be a distraction she could ill afford. During the thirty minutes she'd garnered that morning to get ready, she had managed to get presentable enough to spend the day walking and talking with vendors from all over, but tonight... Well, tonight she needed a little extra time.

Luke mentioned that, after dinner, they would likely go to one of the prestigious nightclubs Vegas was famous for, and Sierra wanted to dress up. She was a girly girl to her marrow, and since she had not one, but two men she was trying to impress, she figured she would go all out.

Once inside of her hotel room, she stripped and jumped into the shower. She wasn't in a rush since Cole had told her that they had at least two hours before dinner, but Sierra didn't want to waste any time. As she stood under the warm spray, she remembered what had happened that morning, specifically what she had watched happen. She felt a zing of pleasure course through her womb at the remembered way Luke had taken Cole in the shower, and then the words Cole had spoken afterwards. Was she crazy to think that something could actually come of this, other than mind blowing sex? Knowing Luke for only four days made her feel a little overzealous about the potential for this to turn into a lasting relationship.

Maybe it was hope, or maybe it was insanity. Either way, Sierra felt something for both of these men, and if the way they looked at her was anything to go by, she didn't think this was casual on their part either.

From what she gathered during her brief conversations with both men, Luke and Cole had known each other for approximately five years, but until recently hadn't gotten close. Even though Luke hadn't admitted anything to her specifically, Sierra was under the impression that Cole managed to satisfy Luke's sexual urges. She longed to be included in that.

Working conditioner through her hair, Sierra remembered the way Luke had looked last night, the vulnerability she was sure she recognized in his beautiful eyes. She might not know much about him, but she knew intuitively that he wasn't one to leave himself susceptible to emotion unless he wanted to be. Perhaps she was being naive, thinking that he would possibly feel something for her more than just an easy lay, or someone he could have fun with for a little while.

Sierra wasn't into casual sex, never had been, which was why she had chosen not to be with another man since her ex-husband. When she and Brian married, they had been young and incredibly stupid, but they had genuinely cared for one another, and he had been the first and only man she had ever given herself to, until last night.

Even if she and Brian weren't looking for the same things out of life, or even out of their relationship, when they said their vows, they had meant every word. Brian might have been intimidated by her aggressiveness in the bedroom, or more importantly, her need to be controlled, but he had never been cruel. Sure, he had told her in no uncertain terms that he couldn't give her what she wanted, but he did it gently, although she had felt like an abomination thanks to his rejection.

And then, they had gone their separate ways.

Sierra never shared her innermost thoughts with anyone after that. Not one person, aside from Luke and Cole, knew her desires. And until Luke had told her that he wasn't into playing games, Sierra had been misguided in how she had approached him. Just one look into his eyes told her everything she needed to know about the man. He was strong, masculine, and utterly alpha, but he was also tender, and just as exposed as the next person when it came to matters of the heart.

She got the impression that he was guarded, and he had reason to be. Luke needed something more than he showed the world. He was demanding, and she felt the underlying aggression that flowed steadily just beneath the surface; his need to protect himself from anyone who might expect too much from him. That would explain his desire to be a participant in other people's relationships, rather than to have one of his own.

The same went for Cole.

Except with Cole, Sierra knew he was more open to expressing his feelings. He didn't hide who he was or what he wanted. From the outside looking in, he appeared just as dangerous, just as closed off as Luke, but she saw it in the way he looked at Luke. He had come to the point in his life where he needed something more. She just wasn't sure if Luke had come to that point yet.

Rinsing the conditioner from her hair, then lathering up and scrubbing her body puff over herself, Sierra finished in the shower and resumed getting dressed in her room. Allowing the steam to dissipate from the bathroom, she pulled on her silk robe and sat on the couch for a few minutes, glancing out at the strip.

Her mind drifted to a conversation she had heard earlier in the day between Logan and Sam. They were talking about Luke, and from what she overheard, the two of them were talking about inviting him to their bed again. *Again.*

Something dark and possessive had taken root in her soul. Dark enough that she had asked Cole about it when they had taken a break to sate a much needed afternoon caffeine fix.

Cole reassured her that although Luke had been involved with Sam a time or two, nothing had happened between them for at least two months that he knew of. He didn't go into detail about the actual incidents, but she understood a little more about Logan and his own kinks. Being Luke's identical twin, she wasn't sure why she hadn't seen it before.

According to Cole, Logan enjoyed sharing his wife with other men, but he was very selective about who he would allow into their bedroom. His obvious first choice was his twin brother, but since the last night, which Cole hadn't gone into detail, Luke hadn't been back to their bed.

Sierra genuinely liked Samantha, and she completely understood Luke's physical appeal, but aside from the fact that Sierra had shared a bed with two men – something she was still surprised by – she wasn't into sharing either of them with anyone else. But she couldn't tell Luke that. He wasn't the type to take orders from anyone, nor would he take kindly to stipulations, and she would sound like the crazy, jealous girlfriend if she did. So that was out of the question.

Suddenly feeling a little depressed about the state of her newfound relationship, or whatever it was called, Sierra wondered if maybe she should just back off. Was she strong enough to handle a man like Luke? Or Cole? They were both successful, confident men who knew what they wanted and went after it with all that they had. She was living proof of that.

Neither of them had shied away from showing her who they really were, from introducing her to a part of themselves that she knew they didn't show the world. How many women had they shared between them? Not many, if she had to guess. From what she gathered from Cole, he was generally the third in his sexual exploits, being included with married couples. She could only assume Luke was the same, especially if he had been included in Sam and Logan's relationship.

God she was crazy. What the hell was she getting herself into? She had spent the last eleven years of her life walking around with a false sense of bravado that was based on her carnal needs and unfulfilled desires. So when it came to a relationship with men like Luke and Cole, she didn't have any previous relationships to compare this one to. Never had she had the confidence to even attempt to find out more about this lifestyle that she felt was so much a part of her.

She was a coward. And here she was, easily jumping into being with two men, and though she was thrilled with the idea of it, her heart was already searching for more. On top of that, she was just getting her business off the ground, utilizing the small nest egg she had established, but other than that, she didn't have anything to offer them.

She should just enjoy the sex while she had the opportunity. No strings, no complications. Why did she have to go in search of love? What made her think that Luke or Cole would even feel something for her the way that she already felt for them?

Cole had made reference to it just that morning, but maybe she had been mistaken. Maybe he was talking about the ménage, the fact that he was able to be with Luke, the way he apparently wanted, and she was just the extra that came along with it?

Shit.

She was doing it again. Thinking too damn much.

Forcing herself up and off of the couch, she went back to the bathroom and proceeded to get ready. Maybe, if she spent an hour or so fixing herself up, she could dredge up a little of that self-confidence she seemed to have left on the airplane when she arrived in Vegas.

Chapter Twelve

By the time Luke made it back to the hotel, he was ready for a shower. More importantly, he was ready to see Sierra, but there wasn't time for that. He needed to take a few minutes to clean up so that they could make it to dinner on time. Logan had been adamant that they not arrive late, and Luke didn't want to disappoint his brother. He wasn't sure why not exactly, but he wasn't going to fight it.

Once inside of his room, he noticed that the maid had changed the sheets and made the bed, neatly organizing the other items he'd left out that morning, including Sierra's panties and bra. The blood rushed south as he pictured her removing them. With that mental image playing on constant repeat he quickly disrobed and got in the shower, doing his best to hurry.

The temptation to take his semi-erect cock in his own hands and stroke himself to completion was more than he could resist. Throughout the day, he'd been tortured by the thoughts of what happened the night before, the pure eroticism and the intoxicating lust they had shared. The tryst in the shower that morning, with Cole, had sent him over the edge, but his body still ached for Sierra in a way he couldn't understand.

She had been on his mind throughout the day, so much so that when Logan briefly hinted at Sam's desire to have him join them again, Luke had blatantly turned him down. He'd seen the disappointment on Logan's face, but then, there was recognition. Thankfully, Logan didn't ask any questions, and Luke didn't offer any excuses. A simple no was all he could muster.

As far as he was concerned, at least for the time being, he didn't have the energy, or the desire, for anyone other than the two people who were filling every lustful thought, every carnal desire already.

Glancing down, Luke focused on stroking his cock with soap lathered fingers. He had no idea how he could even get it up after that morning, the way Cole had milked him dry, but he was hard as granite, and he was sure he wouldn't last five minutes once he was alone with either of them again, so he quickened his pace, closed his eyes and pictured burying himself deep inside of Sierra. He had yet to experience the exquisite sensation of her beautiful body.

Within minutes he groaned out his release, but the hand job didn't sate the hunger that still beat like a bass drum inside of him.

Tonight he had something in store for her. Something that would push Sierra past the boundaries she wasn't aware she had erected. Though she wanted to indulge in his lifestyle, which was nothing more than uninhibited sex, Luke was still confident that she didn't understand the full depth of that commitment.

~~*~~

Dinner went off without a hitch. Luke had ensured they made it to the restaurant on time, though that had been a difficult task. The second Sierra opened her hotel room door, he'd lost all common sense. She had stood before him and Cole, dressed in a barely there red dress that rode high on her toned, creamy thighs and accentuated the voluptuous curves of her breasts. The knee high, black, leather boots nearly had him coming in his jeans.

For the last three hours, he'd been tortured by the mere sight of her. Luke watched the confident way she spoke, the assurance in the way she moved, the sexy way she tossed those silky, long tresses over her shoulder when she laughed. He even watched the way other men looked at her and for the first time in his life, he felt a killing rage.

He got the impression that Cole felt the same, which was amusing considering the company they were in and the fact that he was sure Sierra wasn't quite ready for the world, or her mother, to know that she was currently playing the filling in a carnal delight sandwich.

However, Luke had barely contained the desire to punch a few men who glued their eyes to her sinfully hot body for longer than they should have. Based on the way Sierra had smiled at him, she was aware of the burning fury in his gut, and the damn temptress had laughed. She'd pay for that later, he promised himself and her as well.

"Thanks for dinner, Xavier." Luke graciously thanked their host as the entire XTX party began going their separate ways. "I appreciate the invite and please, let me know if there is anything else I can do."

During dinner, Luke briefly discussed with Xavier some of the vendors that he needed some help with for a few deals he had in the works. Both Cole and Luke listened with half an ear, their attention mostly on Sierra, but somehow through his lust hazed brain, Luke had understood and offered to contribute during the last day of the conference on Saturday.

"Thanks for all your help, Luke. You too, Cole. I know Alex greatly appreciates you being available on such short notice. You kids have a good night, and we'll see you bright and early in the morning." Xavier stated and then joined Veronica on their way out the door.

Sierra was saying her goodbyes to her mother as Xavier approached, and as soon as she was alone, both Cole and Luke descended.

"Let me tell Logan and Sam goodbye, and I'll meet the two of you in the parking lot. The limo should be waiting," Luke stated, and he noticed a slight frown shape Sierra's glossy red lips. "Is everything ok?"

Sierra immediately smiled, though the gesture didn't quite reach her eyes. Luke wanted to find out what was bothering her, but the restaurant wasn't the time or the place, so he shrugged it off for now and went in search of his brother.

By the time he made it to the parking lot, Cole and Sierra were already in the limo waiting for him. He quickly joined them after informing the driver of their destination. They'd be taking the scenic route.

Sierra was sitting beside Cole on the opposite side as Luke, and she looked nervous. Figuring she'd just spent the better part of the evening wining and dining her mother's employer, Sierra probably needed a little time off from having to work. Luke had just the plan to help her relax.

"Cole got the pleasure of having his dick in your mouth last night. Tonight it's my turn," Luke said crassly, not caring for a minute how he sounded. Based on the way Sierra shuddered, her eyes lighting up like a flame, he knew he'd hit his mark.

He slowly unbuttoned his jeans and slid the zipper down, pulling his cock free and stroking it slowly. "Come put your mouth on me."

With something that resembled determination, Sierra slid to her knees on the floor of the limo and leaned over him, her eyes watching as his hand stroked up and down. When she was close enough, he put his hand on her head and pulled her forward roughly, a spark of defiance shining in her brilliant blue irises. He liked that about her. He liked that she wanted to be dominated, but she needed to be forced. Sierra wasn't the type of woman to just do what she was told.

No, she was feisty.

"That's it, baby. Take me all the way in, wrap your lips around my cock," Luke groaned as he guided her head down on him, shoving his cock as far as he could without making her gag. Her slim fingers were wrapped around the base of his shaft, squeezing gently as she began to rhythmically move her hot, wet mouth over him.

"Have you ever sucked two cocks at the same time?" Luke knew the answer to that question, but he was going for the shock factor. When she managed to shake her head negatively, he once again pulled her closer, shoving his cock deeper. "God that's good."

Luke made eye contact with Cole and the other man knew exactly what he wanted. Without hesitation, he moved over to sit directly behind where Sierra was kneeling on the floor as he released his cock from the confines of his jeans. Gliding his hand into her glossy hair, Cole turned her head, forcing Luke's cock from her mouth before he eased past those ruby red lips.

"Damn that's hot. The way you want to take us both," Luke added, moving closer.

Sierra got the idea when she took him in her hand and slowly stroked while she bathed Cole's shaft with her tongue, then turned and gave Luke the same attention. Before long she had managed to get her mouth around the engorged heads of both of them, just barely, licking and sucking while they watched her intently. The sensation of her mouth, mixed with the feel of Cole's dick rubbing against his own was hotter than hell.

"Fuck." Cole grabbed her by the head once more, burying his dick in her mouth, and fucking with wild abandon. "Take me, Sierra. Take all of me. That's it, baby. Fuck! Just like that."

Cole's commentary was making Sierra bob faster, her cheeks hollowed until Cole could no longer hold back, coming deep in her mouth.

Sierra didn't hesitate before she swallowed and turned her attention back to Luke, performing the same ministrations until Luke was gripping her head roughly, shoving his steel hard shaft deep into the wet, hot cavern of her mouth.

"Fuck!" Luke growled and came, hot spurts filling her mouth. He didn't release his grip on her head until she'd milked him dry.

~~*~~

Sierra wasn't sure how much time had passed, but the next thing she knew, the limo had pulled into one of the prestigious resorts that catered to the young and trendy and housed one of the hottest, most exclusive clubs in Vegas. She was surprised to see that both men had tucked their spent cocks back inside of their jeans, which she was eternally grateful for because the limo door opened and the driver stood patiently by as Luke exited, followed by Cole. Both men waited for her to join them, each of them taking one of her hands in his and leading her to the main entrance to the club.

There was a long line that wrapped around the front, but apparently Luke didn't believe in waiting. If the limo ride was anything to go by, the man wasn't big on patience.

Once they reached the bouncer manning the door, Luke spoke quietly to the man, then slipped him what appeared to be money before the burly man took a step back, unhooked the rope and allowed them to enter. Luke wrapped a protective arm around her and pulled her up against his side as they walked inside.

Sierra was visually assaulted by bright flashing lights and a sea of bodies moving and dancing to the music that blared from various speakers throughout. She could barely hear herself think, much less be able to have a conversation with anyone.

Cole separated from them as Luke led her up a set of stairs to another level where there appeared to be private tables. Surprisingly the sound was somewhat muted, and Sierra's brain stopped pounding out the familiar beat.

"I take it you know someone," Sierra stated, taking a seat in the velvet covered, half-moon booth while Luke took a seat beside her, keeping her close.

"I know a lot of people," he said without arrogance. "What do you think?"

"It's nice. I've been here once before, but it was years ago and I was here for one of my best friends bachelorette party's so suffice it to say, I don't remember a lot about that night."

"Party girl, are you?"

"Not really." Sierra never had been one to go out to the clubs, or take part in the trendy night life, but when she came to Vegas, all bets were off. It was about having a good time and going with the flow.

Luke leaned in closer, putting his mouth up against her ear, and Sierra held her breath. The heat of his breath sent a shiver over her, and the way his big, rough hand traveled up her thigh set her blood to boiling. She wasn't sure how she was going to make it through the night if he continued to make her crazy with lust. Quite possibly that was his intention.

"You don't know how bad I want to feel you wrapped around my cock. Watching you ride me hard and fast."

Her womb spasmed. *Spasmed!* And she clenched her thighs together. Thankfully the noise was loud enough to drown out her sigh, or there would be people looking at her to see what was wrong. Sierra longed for the same thing, wanted to feel him inside her, though her fantasy was of his big body covering her... However, she was willing to compromise.

"I don't know how long I can wait."

His admission went straight to her heart, and Sierra found herself hoping against hope that she would never stop hearing those words. She looked deep into his eyes, trying to read him, trying to let him know just how much she wanted him. "I need you," she whispered, and if he didn't hear the words, he at least understood what she was saying.

Luke's hand trailed farther up her thigh, and Sierra glanced around to see if anyone was watching. They were tucked into a private table, with a miniscule amount of privacy, but not nearly enough for what Luke was doing. He slipped his hand between her thighs, parting her legs until he was able to use his finger to part her labia, another finger lightly caressing her clit. Sierra nearly lost it, the feeling was exquisite. Even if the atmosphere was all wrong the man was oh so right.

"Luke." She couldn't hold back a moan as she leaned against him, ducking her head into his shoulder where she felt his pulse beat in his neck and was able to breathe in the essence of the man. His scent was unique; something dark and forbidden, and tempting.

What was it about this man that made her lose touch with reality? Do things she only imagined doing, but never having the guts to?

"Do you ever touch yourself, Sierra?" Luke continued to torture her with one finger while his calm, smooth voice whispered in her ear. She could tell he was in no rush, but wondered how long they would go unnoticed in a crowded club.

"Yes," she admitted easily, her body burning hotter as he forced one finger, then two, deep inside of her.

"How many men have you ever been with?"

The way he carried on the semi casual conversation nearly had her groaning, but somehow she managed to answer. "Including last night?"

"No."

"Before last night, I've only ever been with one man. That man was my husband."

She swore she felt Luke's hand stop moving, but only for a second before he drove deeper, curling just right so he stroked the one spot he knew would send her into hyperspace.

"What else are you wearing under that dress?" Luke asked, his eyes focused on her.

She hesitated for only a second before she answered. "Nothing."

Sierra wasn't sure where Luke was going with all of the personal questions, but her body was on fire. Maybe it was the dress, or the way he was fingering her in public, or maybe it was the way he looked at her, as though she were completely naked sitting in the middle of an overly crowded nightclub.

"Show me."

Was he serious? There were people around and feeling naked and being naked were two very different things.

Despite all of that, Luke's deep, penetrating voice sent chills down her spine and made her shiver. He wanted her to show him that she wasn't wearing anything under the dress. Right here. Right now. She hadn't gone without her bra and panties intentionally, but the way the dress molded to her body wouldn't allow for anything to be worn underneath without showing lines, so she opted to go without. Now she questioned her judgment.

"Now," Luke insisted.

Sierra jerked at his tone, her pussy spasming around his finger as she nearly came from the gruff sound of his voice and the sensual intrusion. The smirk on his face told her that he knew exactly what he was doing to her. He knew what she wanted, and he was pushing her.

Fine. He probably thought she wouldn't do it.

Taking in a deep fortifying breath, and wondering why the hell she didn't have a drink, Sierra slowly slid the dress down over her breasts, the cool air making her nipples pucker.

"Beautiful," he said, and Sierra felt his appreciation all the way to her toes.

Sierra lifted her bottom off of the seat an inch so that she could pull the clingy fabric farther up her legs. A cool draft drifted between her thighs, the bare skin of her mound tingling from the sensation.

"Do you like putting on a show? Or just being told what to do?"

She wasn't sure which it was, or whether it was a little of both. Giving it some thought, she finally answered him truthfully. "Both."

Now sitting on display, her breasts bared completely while Luke's hand continued its sensual assault, Sierra fought for breath. When Cole walked up, his eyes glossy with what appeared to be lust, Sierra thought she might just come. When he moved into the booth on the other side of her, shielding her even more from any unexpected, prying eyes, Sierra was hanging by a thread.

"I want to watch Cole lick your sweet pussy."

"Right *now*?" She was struck with disbelief. It was one thing for him to finger her beneath the table, or even for her to bare her breasts in the darkened corner, but if Cole were to bury his face between her legs, they would surely attract some attention.

"Right now. Right here," Luke confirmed. "Think you can handle it?"

No. "Yes," she said, fierce determination replacing her sudden modesty.

Sierra glanced at Cole as he moved to situate her in the booth so that he could slide between her legs. He pushed her legs open wider, giving him full access to her dripping wet pussy right there in the booth. Luke maneuvered himself so that he was shielding them both from view. God, she was going to come just sitting here, the anticipation was driving her crazy. The remembered feel of Cole's tongue made her want to thrust forward, to force his mouth on her. Instead, she waited patiently as she met Luke's intense stare.

"Put your mouth on her, Cole," Luke instructed in that low, hedonistic tone of his, and then moved closer; still blocking them from anyone else's wandering eyes. He didn't touch her immediately, but she felt his gaze like a physical caress. "You are so damn beautiful."

His words lit the flames inside of her while Cole's mouth fanned them.

Sierra was suddenly awash in sensation, the cool air in the club caressing her exposed skin while the warmth of Cole's talented mouth played over her, his tongue flicking back and forth over her sensitive clit. She wasn't going to last, and whether it was due to the fact that Cole could play her body like a violin, or because she was practically naked in a public place with two of the sexiest men she had ever met, she didn't know. Either way, her orgasm was building to a crescendo, and when it took her, she feared she wouldn't survive it.

Luke bent his head, placing his lips on her puckered nipple, using the flat side of his tongue to tease, before sucking her fully into his mouth. At the same time, Cole drove his tongue deep inside of her while he used his thumb to press against her clit until her body exploded and she was unable to hold on.

When Sierra came, Luke covered her mouth with his, swallowing her cry of ecstasy, even though no one would have heard with all of the noise anyway. As her body loosened, her breathing returning to normal, Luke watched as Cole fixed her dress, covering her once again.

"Tell me, Sierra. Tell me what you want," Luke coerced as she returned to a sitting position between both men, her face hot from embarrassment.

"I want you," she admitted. "I want you, Luke. Any way I can have you."

Luke looked at her, and Sierra half expected him to lift her from the seat and carry her out of the club. Raw, passionate, hunger swirled in the brown and green hues, a promise of things to come.

She hadn't even noticed the three drinks now sitting on the table, apparently Cole's doing. A quick look at him and she saw the same passion in his eyes, but before he said anything, his mouth was on hers as Luke slid his hand up her thigh again. His hot, insistent tongue dueled with hers and Sierra tasted herself on his lips.

Temptation

My God, they were in a public place, sitting in a booth that didn't offer significant cover, and she'd already had one explosive orgasm while more than half naked, mind you. And was now being groped by one man and playing tonsil hockey with the other. Surprisingly, she didn't want to be anywhere else. Unless of course she was naked and they were taking her to places she'd never been before, preferably not in public.

Cole gripped the back of her head and held her close as he devoured her mouth, and Sierra couldn't get enough of him. Despite the need, the urgency, his kiss was incredibly gentle. When they came up for air, he pressed his forehead against hers.

"I've waited all night to do that," he said, running his finger down the long strands of her hair, brushing the outside curve of her breast and then teasing her nipple. So the man might be gentle, but he was in no way innocent.

Then Luke turned her head, palming the back of her neck as he locked his mouth to hers. Sierra knew she should worry what others would think about the woman in a red dress making out with two men at the same time, but she couldn't come up with the urge to care. With Luke's talented mouth kissing her like she had never been kissed before, both hungry and gentle, Sierra didn't give a damn about anyone or anything except him.

"I would ask you to dance, but I fear I'll strip you naked and fuck you right there on the dance floor, people be damned," he said as he kissed her chin, then her jaw. "As much as I wanted this to be a night out, I don't think I can take much more."

Those were the words she longed to hear. As nice as the club was, as much of the Vegas vibe that flowed through the place, Sierra wanted nothing more than to go back to their hotel, or shit, even the limo so she could get her hands on this man.

"I'm ready when you are," she said, and before she could take another breath, Luke was pulling her out from the booth, and she had to fight to fix her dress, not wanting to flash half the place as he led her and Cole down the stairs and back out through the main doors they'd come in only minutes ago.

Her only thought… She hadn't even had a chance to have a drink.

Chapter Thirteen

Luke felt like a teenager who was about to get laid for the first time. He had fully intended to merely tease Sierra, but when he had buried his finger deep inside her, finding her slick and warm, he hadn't thought of anything more than making her come. Thinking about how she would feel wrapped tightly around his cock hadn't fared well for him. Hell, if Cole hadn't shown up when he did, the other man might have been looking for a ride home. Instead, Luke insisted on making Sierra come, but he couldn't do it himself. Not yet. He wouldn't have been able to bury his head between her legs and be satisfied with just that.

So, Cole had obediently licked her pussy until she came right in the club, and now the three of them were climbing back into the limo, heading back to their hotel. For Vegas standards, it was still early, just a little after midnight, but Luke didn't give a shit. He'd gladly spend the remaining night hours buried deep inside of the woman who was sitting beside him now. He didn't even have the strength to tease her, for fear he would come in his jeans long before he ever got them off.

Thankfully the drive back to the hotel was a short one, and once they arrived, the three of them exited like the limo was on fire.

Luke had to make a conscious effort to tip the driver, then to walk through the casino rather than run. He was holding Sierra's hand while Cole held her other, and she was nearly running just to keep up with their long strides. He had to give her credit; she made walking in heels look like child's play.

Once inside the elevator, Luke pressed her up against the wall, cameras be damned. For her sake, he didn't use his hands, but he did crush his mouth to hers as she twined her fingers into his hair.

"Remember, there are cameras in here," he warned her as she attempted to climb his body.

"At this point, I don't mind an audience." Her soft laugh made him smile. He liked that she was so hot, so responsive to his touch.

The elevator dinged, announcing their arrival at their floor and Luke allowed her to walk out in front of him so he could enjoy the view. Cole fell into step beside him, but on the way to Luke's room, Cole stopped at his own.

"What are you doing?" Luke asked, clearly confused.

"Giving you some space."

"If I wanted space, I would have fucking asked for it," he told him, taking one step closer. "When I want to be with her alone, I'll let you know." Gripping the back of Cole's neck, he brought his face close to the other man, his eyes raking over his near perfect features.

Cole had the ability to turn him on like no one he'd ever met before, until Sierra. And yes, he was more than a little confused about what it was he wanted, but tonight, his intentions were clear. He didn't trust himself alone with Sierra. Not yet. His emotions were all over the place and being alone with her would likely result in him thinking something stupid.

Partly because she had him scared shitless of all that he might want from her.

Cole nodded his understanding, and they moved down to Luke's door, where he ran the key card through the reader and pushed the door open hard enough to slam into the wall.

"I want you naked," he ordered Sierra, crowding her against the wall as the door slammed shut behind them. "Fuck. Leave the boots on."

Without finesse, Luke helped her to remove the dress, pulling it up and over her head – thank God for spandex. When she stood gloriously naked in nothing but those fuck me boots and a smile, Luke took a second to look his fill. Her skin was a creamy white, her long, glossy black hair a stark contrast against her pale skin. Her eyes sparkled like the clear blue waters of the ocean and were focused on him.

Luke pressed her into the wall as she tried to hurriedly unbutton his shirt. Apparently she was frustrated with the pace because she pulled and buttons went flying, and then her hands were on him. He started on his jeans, but she shoved his hands away, deftly undoing the button and then quickly and, bless her, gently eased the zipper down. Luke knew he couldn't wait. He managed to push his jeans down over his hips and then he lifted Sierra, pressing her back into the wall, her legs wrapped around him as he thrust inside of her. Damn she was so fucking tight.

He held still for a moment, allowing her body to adjust to his size, but then she was wrapped around him completely, her legs around his waist, her arms around his neck, and she was trying to impale herself on him.

"Slow baby," he warned, knowing he wouldn't last this first time.

"I don't want slowly," she argued and then crushed her mouth to his. Sweet, erotic whimpers told him how much she needed him.

"Put your hands on my shoulders," he told her, breaking the kiss and gripping her tighter.

When her hands were braced, he gripped her ass, holding her up as he rammed into her again and again.

"Luke!" she screamed his name, her body gripping him like a velvet vice and he had to grit his teeth to keep his head from exploding. Literally.

"Fuck, baby," Luke growled, continuing to pound inside of her, unable to stop himself. He leaned forward, nipped her shoulder as she came around his cock. When her body stilled, he carried her over to the bed. He needed more room, better traction. Still buried deep inside of her delectable body, he followed her onto the bed, never unsheathing himself from her body, lifting her legs over his arms so he could get a better angle.

Angling as deep as he could, Luke slowed his thrusts, wanting to hang on a little bit longer. When he noticed Cole in his peripheral vision, standing beside the bed, his jeans unbuttoned, stroking his cock in rhythm to match Luke's thrusts, another thread loosened inside of him and he barely restrained himself. Sierra began moving; lifting her ass to meet his thrusts, and Luke couldn't hang on. He pressed her into the mattress, bending her nearly in half as he pounded into her over and over, harder and faster.

"Fuck!" he growled, and he came with a fury, nearly falling on top of her as his body spasmed out of control.

Managing to roll off of her, he fell onto the bed, pulling her against him.

"Luke." Cole's voice broke the silence, and he managed to move his arm from over his eyes long enough to glare at the other man. The look on Cole's face was not what he expected, and he glanced down, his eyes moving in the direction of Cole's to see what the other man was referring to.

"Son of a fucking bitch!" Luke sprang up from the bed, unsure of what to do or where to go. "Mother fucker!"

"What's wrong?" Sierra asked as she pulled a sheet over her nude body, concern and what resembled terror on her pretty face.

How the hell did he let that happen? Not one fucking time in all of his thirty-nine years had he ever had sex *without a fucking condom. Never.*

He'd lost his control, lost all sense of what he was doing, who he was with. How could he not think about protecting her?

Cole stood firmly rooted in place in the middle of the room, staring at him with wide-eyed confusion. He shot a look at Sierra and then back at Luke, never saying a word. The silence in the room was unnerving, and Luke had the sudden need to get away from them both, but an even stronger urge to keep them close.

"It's ok, Luke," Sierra said quietly, apparently realizing what he had freaked out about, and Luke stopped pacing just to stare at her.

"How the hell is this *ok?*" Was she out of her fucking mind? He could have gotten her pregnant.

"I'm on birth control," she said, sitting up on the bed and moving toward the edge, pulling the sheet tighter around her naked body. "To regulate my periods."

Luke let out the breath lodged in his chest and felt marginally better. Only momentarily though. He still didn't understand how he could have been so thoughtless.

This woman screwed with his head. He'd been blinded by lust and burying himself inside the sweetest woman he had ever known. This wasn't like him. He couldn't afford these types of distractions in his life.

Fuck.

~~*~~

Sierra watched as Luke panicked despite her reassurance that they were protected. Admittedly, she was slightly unnerved that she had never even thought about protection. She'd only been with one man in her life, so she was clean, and based on the way Luke was reacting, he religiously used condoms. Until now.

Wondering what he was going to do next, she tracked his movements as he paced again, then went to the closet and pulled out another shirt. He disappeared into the bathroom and she heard the water running.

She glanced at Cole who now sat on the couch, his jeans once again buttoned, his head hanging low. She wanted to ask him what they were supposed to do next, but he didn't look like he had the answers any more than she did. A minute later, Luke answered the question when he walked right out the hotel room door without a backward glance.

What the hell?

"Where is he going?" she asked, pulling the sheet tighter around her, anger bubbling up in her chest. Aside from being hurt, she was pissed as hell.

"He's fucking running," Cole growled and stood.

Well, he could just run for all she cared. Sierra stood from the bed, the sheet still around her, and headed to the bathroom. She grabbed her discarded dress on the way. Within minutes, she was cleaned up and dressed. When she returned to the room, Cole was no longer there, but the adjoining door was open. She contemplated sticking her head inside, but as far as she was concerned if he had wanted company, he wouldn't have disappeared.

Salvaging what little pride she had left, Sierra walked out of Luke's hotel room and down the hall to her own room. If she were going to fall apart, she'd be damned if she would do it in front of anyone else.

Cole took a deep breath, trying his best to contain the fury and rage that had ignited within him the second Luke stepped out of the hotel door, effectively running away from yet another situation in which he couldn't control. Not that he hadn't expected this sort of behavior from Luke. He'd lived it once, so Luke's reaction was true to form.

What pissed him off the most was Luke's ability to turn his back on Sierra. It was one thing for Luke to walk out on Cole, or to ignore him entirely, but it was not ok for him to do the same to Sierra. At least not as far as Cole was concerned.

The selfish bastard thought of no one but himself, and when he got like this, there was no reasoning with the man. So instead of following him out the door, chasing him down and beating some sense into him, Cole leashed in some of the rage that had threatened to break free. One look at Sierra's stunned face allowed Cole to hang on to that frayed thread of sanity, and he'd slipped into his room, hoping for a minute to breathe.

Apparently he had more than a minute, based on the fact that the door to Luke's room clicked shut, and Cole knew Sierra had likely disappeared into her own room. Gripping his hands into fists, his short nails digging into his palms, Cole stood in the center of his room and fought to breathe. It was something he'd grown used to over the years.

Ask anyone and they would tell you that Cole Ackerley was a calm, even gentle, man. What they didn't see was the fury that bubbled like acid deep in his gut. Those same people would tell you that Luke was the aggressive one, the one with the temper, the loose cannon that could go off in the blink of an eye. That's where the two men were similar; however, Cole had spent years reining in that temper, burying the aggression and single-handedly convincing everyone he was a gentle giant without a mean bone in his body.

Sometimes he wondered why he even bothered. Especially when it came to Luke. The man was dominant, he was aggressive. And Cole loved that about him. Yes… loved. Luke McCoy was the one man that Cole had given himself to whole heartedly. Without thought.

After that one night in October, Cole had accepted what Luke still made a conscious effort to deny. There was something between them, something that they could fulfill in one another that no other person, man or woman could satisfy.

He'd learned early on that he was bisexual, although he wasn't all that fond of the term. In his opinion, there wasn't a single term that would define the satisfaction to be found in another human being, when it came to intimate contact in any form.

As far as sex was concerned, Cole had never thought to set boundaries on himself or question his preferences. There were numerous women he'd enjoyed over the years, and a handful of men. Either way, Cole found satisfaction in the person, not their gender.

Which led him to Sierra and the way his body responded to her. From the moment he'd laid eyes on her at Club Destiny, Cole had accepted that she was the one woman who would likely change him forever. Did he believe in love at first sight? Not specifically. Does that mean it doesn't exist? No. And Sierra Sellers was living proof because Cole had found himself fantasizing about the woman in more ways than one since that fateful day.

And now, Luke had gone and dismissed them both as though they weren't worth the effort because he couldn't maintain his control when he was around them. That's how Cole knew there was something more between the three of them. Something more between Luke and Sierra and something more between Cole and Sierra. When another person has the ability to make you lose your mind in sheer, unadulterated bliss, they will be worth pursuing.

Grabbing his cell phone and pacing toward the window that overlooked the strip, Cole dialed the familiar number.

"What the fuck is wrong with you?" Those were the first words out of Cole's mouth.

"Look, I'm catching a plane back to Dallas tonight. What happened…?" Luke sounded calmer than he had earlier, but Cole knew he wasn't thinking rationally.

"That's fucked up, man." Cole let out a frustrated breath, jamming his fingers through his hair. "How can you walk out on her like that?"

"It's for the best," Luke stated, followed by a few seconds of silence. "This isn't what I want."

Right. Cole had been down this road before. Luke could say the words all day long, but the only person who might believe them was him. Cole knew better. This was everything Luke wanted, but since the man didn't have the power to control what was happening, he was going to run fast and hard.

"Keep telling yourself that, Luke. Maybe one day you'll believe it." Cole clicked the end button, tossing the phone on the bed to keep from heaving the damn thing at the wall. He felt the blood begin to pound in his head, every muscle going rigid, and he knew he had to calm down.

He wanted to go to Sierra, to check on her and make sure she was all right, but he needed some air first.

~~*~~

An hour after she had come back to her room, Sierra had showered and put on her pajamas. At three o'clock in the morning, she knew she should be asleep, but she just couldn't do it. Hell, she'd even tried to lie down, but thoughts of Luke and what happened were scrambling her brain. Part of her wanted to know if he had come back or not. Her pride told her that it didn't matter. What he had done was unforgivable.

One last ditch effort to get some rest had her filling a glass with water, downing it quickly, then heading back to the bed. Just as she pulled the blankets back, there was a knock on the door. Her traitorous heart started pounding harder, anxiety filling her chest like a helium balloon.

She stopped at the door, her hand resting on the knob, but she didn't turn it. What would she say to Luke if he showed up now? She dared a glance through the privacy hole and saw Cole standing there, and she immediately opened the door.

"What's the matter?" she asked, taking in his weary appearance.

"Did I wake you?" he asked, looking her directly in the eye.

"No." Sierra took a step back so he could come inside. "I couldn't sleep."

"Me either," he admitted, thrusting his hands into his pockets and strolling toward the window.

Despite everything that happened over the course of the last few hours, the pain that Sierra now felt deep down from Luke's abandonment, one look at Cole and all negative thoughts vanished. The man had a body to die for, his broad back rippled with strength, and she could see the flex and give of his muscles beneath the thin fabric of his t-shirt. Tanned arms flexed with restrained energy as he turned to face her.

Sierra took a step forward, realizing exactly what Cole had come to her for. The same thing she realized she now wanted from him. Comfort.

"I want you, Sierra," Cole said, a flash of insecurity fluttering on his handsome face before it was masked with a deep, dark hunger.

Sierra understood the vulnerability, and she suspected that he wouldn't want her to know exactly how much Luke's abandonment had affected him, as well. Standing before her, Cole's emotions were masked entirely, but she figured they weighed heavily on his mind. Neither of them could control Luke. Neither of them had the ability to help Luke understand that he couldn't blame himself for so many things that were out of his control.

The feelings.

The need.

Just from the amount of time she had been around him, Sierra knew that Luke thought he could control everything, every situation, but then when he realized he was just as human as the rest of them, he panicked. Based on the concern reflected in Cole's beautiful deep blue eyes, Sierra accepted what Cole already had. Luke wouldn't be back tonight.

Unlike Luke, Sierra wasn't going to walk away. Not from him and not from Cole. She needed to reassure Cole. He'd taken a chance coming to her room, and if the words Cole had said that morning rang true, he wasn't going to back down either.

Taking a step closer, she gauged his reaction, but he didn't move. His eyes locked with hers and Sierra held her breath, waiting for that moment when he might push her away. Instead, he took a step closer and her heart pounded harder.

"Make love to me, Cole," she whispered.

In an instant, Cole was on her, his hard body pressed firmly against hers, the feel of his erection pressed between her legs. Sierra latched onto him, melding her lips with his, relishing the comfort that she found in his arms. Without hesitation, he managed to rid her of her clothes, along with his own, claiming a condom from his back pocket before he had her flat on her back.

"I can't be easy, Sierra. I need to be inside of you right now."

"Please," she whispered, pulling his head down, and when their lips touched once again, she realized just how much he had been holding back.

"I need to feel you," Cole stated, pushing up from her as he opened the foil packet and sheathed himself before aligning his body with hers once again, driving into her in one hard thrust.

"Oh God!" Cole was buried to the hilt, filling the empty, lonely spaces that Luke had left when he had walked out on them earlier. And suddenly Luke no longer mattered because Cole was here.

Sierra pulled him closer, the weight of him on top of her felt like heaven. When he tried to pull back, she held him closer, wanting to feel all of him against her. Then he was kissing her again, gripping her hands and lifting them above her head as he drove into her over and over again. As her body tightened around him, he slowed his pace and then pushed back, allowing her to gaze deep into those all seeing, all knowing eyes.

"I need you to love me, Cole." The words were out before she could stop them, and the look on his face nearly broke her heart.

"Always, Sierra."

Chapter Fourteen

Sierra was happy to be home. Four days in Vegas were more than she could handle and considering the circumstances, she thought she had managed to hold herself together pretty well. When she and Cole had woke up Saturday morning, he'd excused himself to his room to shower before returning to walk with her to the conference. It wasn't until then that he told her Luke had flown back to Texas, although she was pretty sure he had known it when he had come to her during the night. She had been glad he waited to tell her because the news broke her heart all over again.

Granted, the edges of her heart were still cased in anger and fury at the man, but the net of it was that he'd hurt her. Badly. The things Luke made her feel, both with the way he buried himself deep inside of her body, and eased his way into her heart weren't normal for her. And because the man was just as out of control as she was when they were together, made it nearly impossible to think that he could have walked away so easily. Although that was awfully pretentious – or maybe just naïve – considering they hadn't been in any sort of a committed relationship before they had finally done the deed.

But now…

Now they definitely weren't, and it hurt to even think about it. Despite her failed efforts to convince herself that casual sex with Luke and Cole was better than no sex, Sierra knew she wasn't programmed that way.

Somehow, probably thanks more to Cole than anyone, Sierra managed to hold herself together for the rest of the weekend. He made going through the motions bearable. And when he stayed the last night with her, Cole managed to take her mind off of Luke completely. After hanging out at the Blackjack table for a couple of hours, then catching a late dinner, the two of them had retired to her room where they ended up ravishing one another numerous times on Saturday night, both of them realizing it could very well be the last time.

Her biggest fear? That her heart was already as attached to Cole as it was to Luke. On the other hand, no matter how amazing sex with Cole was, Sierra suspected they were both trying to find comfort in one another, a desperate attempt to compensate for the devastation that was Luke McCoy.

Temptation

Her mother had realized something was wrong right away, but Sierra brushed her off when they came face to face at the convention center. She couldn't talk about it, mainly because she didn't know what had happened herself. The facts were clear, but Luke's reason for running wasn't. Unless it was because he was scared of what was happening between them.

Although she wasn't the type to use sex as consolation, Sierra wasn't so sure Cole didn't see *her* as a stand in for Luke. He hadn't given her any impressions that he was using her, but neither of them had spoken about Luke or of what had happened. Instead, they had consumed one another. Yet afterward, hidden by the dark shadows of night, Sierra's mind had drifted to Luke numerous times.

The situation was unfamiliar. She had never been with another man other than her husband, yet she had been with two different ones in the span of just a few days. Initially, being with both of them seemed almost normal. But when Luke walked away, leaving her and Cole alone, she couldn't help but feel as though a part of her was missing. Though she doubted he had even cared.

The one thing she refused to do was to settle. Not that she considered Cole a consolation prize by any means. He was so much more than that. She had begun to care about him, but she knew in her heart of hearts, things weren't going to get any easier between them. The best thing for her to do would be to back off of both of them, no matter how much it hurt. In the end, the pain would be less than the total agony she would feel if she allowed something to develop that wasn't based on true feelings.

Now the only thing left to do was to get back in the swing of things.

Her first networking gig was behind her, and she had a business to get up and running. In addition, her little rental house needed a little TLC. She hadn't been able to part with her house in Nashville, the one she inherited from her grandmother, partly because she wasn't particularly versed in dealing with ambiguity. Moving to Dallas was probably the biggest decision of her life, so not selling allowed her to keep the comfort of home within arm's reach.

So instead of selling, she rented her Nashville house out, knowing that if it came down to it, she had a place to go back to. At this point, she wasn't quite ready to put down permanent roots in Texas, which left her with a rental that she needed to make as comfortable as possible for as long as necessary.

Until she was ready to commit to staying in Dallas, she would give it her all. There were so many things that needed to fall into place before she would concede to staying – getting her business up and running, getting a feel for the lay of the land, and above all else, convincing herself that Dallas was home.

The ringing of her cell phone jarred her from her thoughts as she walked from room to room wondering how she could make the place feel just a little homier. Furniture would likely help.

"Hi Mom," Sierra cheerfully greeted her mother. They hadn't shared the same flight out because Veronica opted to go back on Saturday morning with Xavier while Sierra stayed until the end of the conference.

"You make it back all right?" Veronica asked, sounding a little worried.

"I did. I just got home a few minutes ago."

"What happened to Luke? Xavier said he had an emergency and had to get back home before the conference was over."

Emergency? She doubted that being a coward would constitute an emergency, but if it made Luke feel better, who was she to say anything different.

Nonetheless, Sierra felt the all too familiar ache at the mention of Luke's name, but she did her best to hide it. "I'm not sure. Cole said he had something to take care of." That wasn't exactly a lie, but Sierra definitely wasn't going into further detail. Not with her mother anyway.

"Is there something going on between you and Cole?" Veronica asked, always right to the point.

"Why do you ask that?" Although Sierra and her mother were close, she'd always found it difficult to talk to Veronica about matters of the heart. When it came to the fact that Sierra found herself in the middle of some sort of convoluted love triangle, she didn't have the slightest idea what she would even say.

"I don't know. The two of you seemed rather close on Saturday. I got the impression he was worried about you."

"Cole's a good man, Mom. And I'm sure he was just worried about making sure I was taken care of since my date had to leave so suddenly." There, that was the truth. Cole had been worried about her, the same as she had been worried about him.

There was a moment of silence on the phone line before Veronica picked right back up, side stepping the personal issues as she always did. "Did you strum up any contacts at the conference?"

That question was so much easier to answer, so Sierra proceeded to tell her mother about the appointments she'd made with a few business owners in the Dallas area, including one personal consultation with a prominent Dallas lawyer looking to make some significant changes to her house. In the end, when it came down to how her business faired over the weekend, Sierra was satisfied.

If only she could say the same for her personal life.

After a few more minutes of mundane conversation, Sierra let her mother go.

With nothing else to focus on, Sierra's attention was once again on the sparsely furnished rental she inhabited. Part of her wanted to run out and drop a chunk of change on making the house a home, maybe some furniture, some art work, whatever it took to focus on something other than Luke and Cole.

Instead, she gave in to her exhaustion, both mental and physical. Thanks to the time difference between Vegas and Dallas, it was already closing in on dinnertime, and Sierra hadn't eaten since early that morning. A quick perusal of the refrigerator told her she would have to go to the grocery store if she wanted to eat. Since she was too tired to even do that, she opted for a slice of bread before heading to her room for a quick shower and then off to bed she would go.

~~*~~

Two weeks later, Sierra found herself riding on a high thanks to having landed a promising job with one of the two appointments she had gone on. She had also been hired by the Dallas lawyer, Susan, for a job that she anticipated would take at least three months.

The Monday after she came back from Vegas, she had immediately gotten on the phone with those potential clients and confirmed the meeting times. Her persistence had paid off, and she landed her first clients.

Immersing herself into work was the only thing that remotely kept her mind off of Luke and Cole. Not that she had heard from either of them since she got back from Vegas. Not hearing from Luke wasn't surprising, but not hearing from Cole... She was almost speechless. Not that she would know what to say to them anyway. Especially Luke. And now, the distance she and Cole put between them would only make a reunion awkward.

Initially hope bloomed, but that was doused rather quickly after the first day when she never heard from him. She'd secretly willed her phone to ring, only to be disappointed time after time until finally she gave up completely. Sierra never was the type to pine after a man. Or two.

Once again her cell phone rang, interrupting her from her thoughts. She lurched for the phone, half hoping that fate, or karma, had heard her silent pleas and her random thoughts hadn't been for nothing. Glancing at the phone, she didn't recognize the number, and doubt settled in. Figuring it wasn't Luke or Cole, she realized it could be one of her potential clients.

"Sierra Sellers," she answered, trying her best to sound cheerful and professional.

"We're having a little get together at the house and wanted you to come." The female voice on the other end of the line stated. "Sorry, this is Sam, in case you didn't recognize my voice."

Sierra was a little taken aback by the sudden request, but she laughed despite herself at Sam's quick talking. "Wow, that's one way to say hello."

Sam laughed. "Sorry, I've been so busy today and then I realized I hadn't actually invited anyone yet. Work has been a little hectic, with Dylan officially onboard and Alex being all wrapped up in Dylan's sister."

"Oh, that's right." Sierra remembered their last conversation when Sam had given some rather interesting bits of gossip. "Didn't you say Ashleigh, I think that's her name, was moving back to Dallas?"

"Yes. She came back for the XTX Christmas party, and from what Logan told me, she is officially supposed to move back in the next week."

"I'm guessing Alex is a nervous wreck." Sierra hadn't actually met the man, but based on her conversations with Sam, she felt as though she knew him.

"Like you wouldn't believe. He's grumpy. Well, I should say grumpi*er*." Sam laughed.

"Well, that should be interesting." The details had been all based on pure gossip rather than any fact, but Sam was convinced Ashleigh and Alex were going to go up in flames in the very near future.

"It is. I've invited them all to the house tomorrow night, so you have to be here. There'll definitely be fireworks."

"Fireworks in February. Count me in."

"Oh, thank goodness." Sierra heard the relief in Sam's voice. "So, tomorrow night, eight o'clock. Our house. I'll text you the directions."

"Is there anything I need to bring?"

"Just your bright smiling face."

Sierra smiled at her friend's excitement. "All right then. I'll see you tomorrow at eight."

Disconnecting the call, Sierra stared down at the phone.

She and Sam were quickly developing a close friendship, spending quite a bit of time together. They'd ventured out on a couple of shopping excursions, along with several lunch dates, and they had recently taken to talking on the phone. Being that Sierra was still new in town, she hadn't made many friends, so developing friendships like those she left behind in Nashville was making the transition a little easier.

At first she was surprised by all of the attention she received from Sam, and Sierra had an idea that part of it was because Sam felt guilty. Sierra advised the other woman that she wasn't responsible for what happened between her and Luke. Of course, she hadn't gone into detail, not wanting to share that belittling piece of information, but Sam was worried all the same.

No matter what brought the two women together, they found they had enough in common to keep them talking for hours. Sam openly admitted she wasn't the type to make many friends but that she felt comfortable with Sierra. The heartfelt comment struck something deep inside and Sierra found herself looking forward to spending time with Sam.

Surprisingly, they didn't spend much time talking about Logan and thankfully, Sam didn't bring up Luke or Cole at all. In the back of her mind, Sierra wondered if Sam was once again engaging in threesomes with Luke, but she couldn't bring herself to ask. She honestly didn't want to know.

The pain of knowing would have been detrimental to her fragile peace of mind.

~~*~~

"Kane, where's the invoice from this morning's delivery?" Luke asked as he neared the bar where Kane was stocking inventory. Thursday nights were busy for Club Destiny, an apparent time to celebrate the coming of the weekend, so Luke knew his bar manager was frantically trying to get everything ready for when the doors would open in just three hours.

"I asked Jacob to bring it to you." Kane said, making reference to one of their nightly bartenders.

Club Destiny was open to the public on weekday evenings starting at six and Friday and Saturday starting at three, closed on Sunday. Due to the large volumes of people they saw coming through their doors, they employed three full-time weekend bartenders, and two more alternated shifts during the week, plus a handful of waitresses and kitchen staff. Kane was the only bar manager and he worked roughly six days a week, by his choice. Since their deliveries had been coming up short, Kane was coming in early and staying until well after closing to ensure he kept tabs on everyone and everything that was going on.

"When? I haven't seen it yet." Luke was a little irritated by the fact that since he had come back from Vegas, they had once again come up short on one of their deliveries, and all fingers were pointing to one of his employees. He just hadn't figured out who it was yet.

"I gave it to him a little while ago and asked him to drop it on your desk on his way out."

Luke hadn't checked his desk thoroughly, but he had given it a quick glance and didn't see it. Giving Kane and Jacob the benefit of the doubt, he opted to look once more before he lost his temper.

Something he'd been doing more and more in the last week.

Since coming back from Vegas, Luke hadn't been himself. He'd been distracted and frustrated, and, unfortunately, he wasn't one who could rein in his temper easily. When it came to his customers, Luke did his best to be pleasant, but those who worked for him knew he could be a world class asshole. Much more so since the incident with Sierra in Vegas.

Just the thought of the black haired vixen with her smooth, creamy skin and sexy legs made Luke's heart pound. He hadn't heard from her, or seen her at all since he'd come back and based on the way he had lost his head, he didn't expect to. Sierra had way too much class for a man like Luke. He'd hurt her, Cole had driven that point home the one and only time he had seen him in the last two weeks. After that clusterfuck of a conversation, Cole hadn't come back to Club Destiny, and Luke wasn't sure he'd be back.

Not that he didn't take full responsibility for his own actions. He did. He'd been so far out of his mind with lust that night that he had taken Sierra without a condom, putting her at risk. Luke had never had sex without a condom, and due to his promiscuous lifestyle, he was checked routinely for disease, so he knew he hadn't risked her in that sense. But, he could have gotten her pregnant, and where the hell would that leave them? Luke wasn't ready for a family.

At least he didn't think he was.

Until that night, he had never given much thought to having a family of his own. A wife. Maybe a couple of kids. Those things were so far out of his reach, he had never considered them. But with Sierra, the dream could have easily become a reality, which would have altered the course of their lives. That wasn't something Luke could come to terms with.

Did he even want kids?

That was a question that plagued him often since that night. The answer wasn't an easy one, yet he found himself daydreaming about Sierra carrying his baby and surprisingly the thought didn't make him cringe the way he expected. He knew that his brother didn't have any intentions of having kids, making it clear that he and Sam weren't interested. For Luke, the answer wasn't that simple. Until Sierra, he had never considered the idea, but something had changed with her.

Hell, *everything* had changed with her.

He wanted things he never wanted before. He wanted her. He wanted every damn thing she would give him, but his loss of control had proven that he wasn't capable of handling a woman like her. A woman like Sierra required a man who could take care of her. One who could provide for her and protect her. Apparently Luke wasn't that man.

Oh, he could give her any material thing she dreamed of. He had money. Lots of it. But she didn't seem to be one who cared about that. If that were the only thing he had to give her to make her happy, he'd do it freely and without question. Instead, Luke knew Sierra needed love and security. Something he obviously wasn't capable of giving.

No, when it came to taking care of her, Cole was better suited for that role. Luke's only option was to back off, thinking if he did, Cole and Sierra might have a chance to find what they were looking for in each other. He'd seen the way Cole looked at her, touched her, made love to her.

Luke was even privy to the fact that Cole hadn't engaged in any of his normal sexcapades since the Vegas trip. He figured one of these days he'd hear that the two of them were getting married.

Fuck.

Shaking off that derailing train of thought, Luke opened his office door and went in search of the missing invoice. He didn't have time to think about Sierra or Cole. He was a damn possessive man by nature, and though his heart hurt for them both, Luke knew it was in everyone's best interest if he moved on to something that would require less of a commitment from him.

Luke was just about to call Jacob to find out where the man put the invoice when his cell phone rang. He glanced at the caller id and bit back a groan.

Logan.

"Hey, bro. What's up?" Luke answered reluctantly, half tempted to let the call go straight to voicemail.

"Not a damn thing. What about you?"

"Same ol' shit, different day," Luke admitted, rummaging through a stack of papers on his desk. "You're not ass deep in some sort of HR violation or something?" Luke provoked his brother.

"Oh, fuck off." Logan laughed. "I'm calling to invite you to a party tomorrow night at my house." Amusement laced Logan's words. Apparently Luke's irritation was something Logan had gotten used to.

"A *party*?" He couldn't hide the skepticism in his tone.

"Not that kind of party, man. Just a get together. We've invited several people over, and I expect you to be there."

"You know I can't do anything on Friday nights. I've got a club to run."

"And you know as well as I do that Kane can handle anything, and he's got you on speed dial. I don't want to hear your excuses. I haven't seen you but for five minutes in the last two and a half months."

Luke knew Logan was right. They hadn't seen much of each other in months, and that was solely Luke's doing. He'd been hiding out from anyone and everyone, including his twin brother. "Fine. What time?" He was giving in too easily, but Luke had let Logan down enough times lately, he couldn't bring himself to do it now.

"Eight."

"I'll be there. But, I'm warning you. If the club needs me, I'll have to bail."

"I hear ya." Logan sounded content with at least a commitment from Luke. "Did you find anything out about the missing liquor?"

"No. I'm looking for an invoice from this morning's delivery to verify that, but it seems to have been misplaced."

Logan was the only person Luke had shared his concerns with, not wanting the person that was responsible to know Luke was on to them. Since his twin was a silent partner in the club, he figured Logan deserved to know they were losing money.

"The invoice or the delivery?"

"Both."

"Did you check the cameras Alex installed last week?" Logan asked, referring to the security cameras they hired CISS to install the week before.

After the last delivery had come up short, Luke had been at the end of his rope.

"Not yet. I'm doing that now," Luke confirmed.

"Let me know if you need my help with anything. I've got to run to a meeting, but I expect you at the house tomorrow at eight."

"I'll be there."

With that, they ended the call and Luke pulled up the security cameras on his computer, running through the footage from that morning's delivery. This would've been the first delivery since the cameras were installed. Since Luke kept the installation on the down low, not even Kane knew they were being put in.

Five minutes later, Luke was watching with disbelief as Lucie Werner, Club Destiny's weekday bartender was handing the delivery guy what appeared to be cash as he set aside two cases behind the dumpster near the delivery dock. *Sonuvabitch.*

Lucie? Seriously?

Luke couldn't deny the fact she was the one on the screen, but in all of his life, he would have never expected Lucie to steal from him. She'd been employed by Club Destiny for three years and aside from being one of his most loyal employees, she was also a single mother of a four year old. Why in the hell would she be stealing from him?

A knock on his office door had Luke closing the window on his monitor. "Come in."

Jacob Hayman walked in, holding the missing invoice in his hand. "Sorry, boss. Kane said you were looking for this." Handing over a slip of paper, Jacob turned to leave.

"Hey, Jacob. Have you seen Lucie today?"

Luke watched the other man intently, noticing the slight wince as he shrugged his shoulders. "Not today."

Was Jacob helping Lucie?

"If you see her, let her know I'd like to speak with her," Luke said, and then turned back to his screen as nonchalantly as he could manage. There was no sense letting on that he suspected anything just yet. He'd known Lucie for a long time, and she was the last person Luke would expect to do something like this. If she was stealing from him, she had a damn good reason.

Luke wanted to know what that was.

When Jacob left his office, Luke called downstairs. "Hey, Kane. You see Lucie this morning?"

"I did. She stopped in rambling about leaving something in her locker. She wasn't here long though. Why?"

"If you see her again, let her know I'm looking for her." Luke wasn't going to go into details.

"Will do, boss."

Chapter Fifteen

So this was how the incredibly wealthy lived, Sierra thought to herself as she navigated the streets of Sam and Logan's gated community. The houses that lined the well-manicured streets were nothing short of mansions with giant oak trees lurching toward the evening sky while branching out in all directions.

When she pulled into the circular drive of Sam and Logan's massive estate, Sierra took note of the numerous cars lining both sides of the driveway and the handful pulled into the extra spaces in front of the three car garage. She pulled into an open area and sat motionless, her car idling while she tried to convince herself this was where she should be.

Finally, after putting off the inevitable for far too long, Sierra climbed out of her car and headed up the walkway toward the house. Just as she reached the front door, a male voice called her name, and she turned in time to see Cole strolling in her direction, looking so damn sexy her heart hurt.

He looked just the same as she remembered, confident and gorgeous, even in his casual, faded jeans and a black polo shirt that encased all of those sexy as hell muscles.

"Hey." She was at a loss for words, her heart beating fast and hard against her ribs. She hadn't seen him since that last day in Vegas, nor had she heard from him. Momentarily she was struck by his sheer masculine beauty until she realized *she hadn't heard from him*. And here he was, acting as though they were long lost friends and he just happened to run across her while they were both out at the same place. What happened to him not backing down?

"How've you been?" he asked tentatively as he stepped closer, keeping a safe distance, but Sierra felt the warmth of his presence all the same. Apparently he was acknowledging the fact that he hadn't bothered to call her either.

"Busy." Well, it was the truth. She'd been busy doing a lot of things. Thinking about him. Thinking about Luke. Wondering what the hell happened and how she had experienced ecstasy for only a brief moment before it was ripped away from her all too quickly.

"I heard you landed a couple of clients from the conference. Congratulations."

"Thanks." Sierra figured her mother was the reason for the gossip, or possibly Sam, which didn't surprise her.

She must have been staring blankly at him because Cole placed his arm around her, as though they hadn't spent the last few weeks not talking, and led her to the front door. Rather than knocking, he walked right in like he owned the place.

The second they were inside the brightly lit foyer, they were greeted by a big black dog, his tail wagging, and his tongue lolling out of the side of his mouth. Sierra stopped momentarily, instinct telling her to tread carefully. The animal was a beast, and she didn't want to become dinner.

"He won't hurt you. Bear's just a big teddy bear. Aren't you boy?" Cole leaned down and gave the dog a firm pat on his back.

"Is he Logan and Sam's?" Sierra asked, offering a tentative hand toward the dog. When Bear merely pressed his giant head into her palm, Sierra smiled and offered him a gentle rub.

"No." The one word answer was said with a little irritation, but Cole didn't offer any further explanation and Sierra didn't ask.

"There you are!" A cheerful voice called from the living room, and Sierra looked up to see Sam coming her way.

The woman was dressed casually in a pair of faded Levi's and a red t-shirt that accentuated her shoulder length blond hair, and a pair of Dr. Marten's on her feet. Sierra hadn't bothered to ask what the dress code was, so she felt a little overdressed with her jean skirt, black t-shirt and her favorite suede black boots, but she wasn't uncomfortable. She was somewhat grateful she had taken the time to dress up since she had run into Cole.

When Sam reached in for a hug, Sierra returned the gesture, but when she stepped back, Cole was no longer beside her. She didn't want to look obvious, so she kept her eyes on Sam, not wandering around the immaculately decorated house looking for him like she wanted. What did she care? He hadn't bothered to call her at any point in the last few weeks, so her pride shouldn't let her be curious about where he went.

Even if her body was begging to find out. *Damn hormones.*

"Did you have any trouble finding the house?"

"Not at all. Your directions were spot on," Sierra stated, taking a step back. "I love your house, by the way."

"Thanks. Technically it was Logan's first, but I can't complain." Sam smiled sweetly. "You look like you could use a drink."

She did? Well, the fluster was likely thanks to Cole's unexpected presence. "That sounds great."

"What can I get you? Wine? Vodka? Soda?"

"That's a tough one." Sierra grinned. A few minutes ago, before she saw Cole, Sierra would have been satisfied with a glass of wine. Being that her body had ignited despite her insistence that it sit down and shut up, she figured she'd probably fare better with the hard stuff. "I'll take a vodka and 7Up if you have it," Sierra said as she followed Sam through the living area into the wide open kitchen complete with stainless steel appliances and all the bell's and whistle's.

Sam smiled. "My kinda girl."

~~*~~

From the moment Cole caught sight of Sierra from the corner of his eye, he'd been mesmerized yet again. For the last two weeks, he'd done everything in his power to stay away from her. He hadn't called. He hadn't shown up at her house. Nothing. All in hopes that somehow Luke would come to his senses. Apparently the man was more stubborn than Cole had given him credit for.

Seeing Sierra was a complete surprise, especially knowing that Luke was in attendance at this little shindig put on by Logan and Sam. The instant he saw her, Cole knew Luke's twin had an ulterior motive. And Luke's new sister-in-law was a matchmaker with a heart of gold, but Cole feared she was getting in over her head this time. Not only had they invited Luke and Sierra, they'd also invited Ashleigh Thomas and Alex McDermott. If they were expecting fireworks of epic proportions tonight, Cole suspected they were in for a show.

Granted, when Logan extended Cole the invitation, he'd attempted to say thanks, but no thanks. Logan hadn't let him off the hook that easily, which explained why he was standing in the shadows watching Sierra as she disappeared into the kitchen with Sam. His preference would have been to hang around, continue to breathe in the uniquely fascinating scent of the woman and to see the smile that shone on her sweet face. Instead, the second he'd had a chance, he'd walked away from her.

Why? Well, that he couldn't explain. And maybe he wasn't the martyr that he tried to make himself out to be. Staying away from Sierra for the greater good wasn't his only motive. No, he'd found himself getting too attached to her. Too quickly at that. After that last night they spent together in Vegas, wrapped in each other's arms, his cock sheathed deep inside her luscious body, Cole damn near lost his mind. And his heart.

The only conclusion he had come to was that he had already fallen hard and fast for the woman, and after everything that Luke had put her through, he didn't want to be the rebound guy. Part of him hoped that by giving her space, she'd come to him. When that didn't happen within the first couple of days of being home, Cole figured he was right. Sierra had needed comfort after Luke had so recklessly smashed her heart.

Oh, he wouldn't be the one to tell Sierra that he had held her that first night when she cried. Considering she had been asleep, deep, soul wracking sobs torn from her chest, Cole hadn't been able to wake her, so he settled for doing the only thing he knew to do. He held her until she finally settled back into a restless sleep. After that, Cole had been filled with hurt and anger and... confusion.

He loved Sierra. He'd be the first to admit it. At least to himself. But he wouldn't share that little bit of knowledge with her because apparently she hadn't felt the same way about him.

So in a matter of weeks, Cole had found love, only to let it slip so easily from his grasp. And what was worse than that, it was the second time it had happened in the last few months. As far as he was concerned, he had met his quota for a lifetime. No sense in torturing himself any longer, so he had let her go, right along with Luke.

Tonight he would settle for watching Sierra, knowing she was doing well and hoping like hell that once Luke realized she was here, all hell didn't break loose.

~~*~~

For two hours, Sierra managed to mingle with the other guests, even being introduced to two more prospective clients. Cole was still nowhere to be found, but Sierra did her best not to care. That was much easier said than done. Thankfully Ashleigh seemed to be looking for an escape as well, so the two women stood on the back patio overlooking the beautiful pool and talked briefly. Neither woman admitted why they were trying to put distance between themselves and the party, but Sierra found solace in the fact that she wasn't alone.

By the time she figured she had finally put in enough face time to call it a night, Sierra managed to find the guest bathroom where she was able to take care of business and wash her hands. As she exited the bathroom, determined to seek out Sam so she could say her goodbyes, Sierra heard a familiar voice coming from farther down the hall.

"Don't you get it? I'm not interested in that right now. You might have chosen to ignore everything that happened, but damn it, I can't," a male voice said, anger and frustration lighting up his words.

"I've moved on. You should, too."

The second voice brought her up short. She dreamed of that voice.

"You're a heartless bastard, you know that?" the first voice said, sounding as though he were moving closer to where Sierra stood motionless in the hallway. "You might be able to give her up, but I can't. It's killing me, Luke."

Was Cole talking about her? Sierra's heart pounded erratically in her chest, her hands beginning to shake.

"That's the fucking problem. I can't give her up, but I don't have a choice. She needs someone better than me, someone who can put her first."

At that point, Sierra was certain they were talking about her, but she couldn't move from where she stood. She couldn't go back toward the party, and she couldn't go forward. She was rooted to the ground, hanging on every word.

"You do what you need to do. You're a selfish bastard as far as I'm concerned, and one day you'll realize just what the hell you missed out on. I only hope I'm around for that day."

The voice came closer and just when Sierra realized Cole was stepping around the corner, she also recognized she didn't have time to run.

"Sierra." Cole's seductive voice washed over her, sounding hurt, yet hopeful.

Her eyes darted from Cole to the man standing just a few steps behind him, then back again. She was overwhelmed with a sense of déjà vu, feeling as though she had been here before, alone with these two men. The way they stared at her, she felt as though she was completely naked, and more than a little vulnerable. Unable to move, at least she managed not to fidget.

"Sorry, I was –" Sierra let her voice trail off, not knowing what she was going to say. The only thing she did know was that she was going to make her feet move, no matter what the hell they wanted. She had to get away from them because this was too awkward, and she felt as though the bottom of her stomach had dropped out. Shooting one last glance back at Luke, Sierra made sure he saw all of the emotion that welled up inside of her before she turned to go.

"Sierra, wait," Luke called after her, but she didn't stop.

Fuck him.

She heard what he had to say. She knew he didn't have any intentions of apologizing, so why the hell did she need to hang around? It would only make things worse. Instead, she pretended not to hear him and kept moving toward the front door. She only hoped Sam wouldn't come out because she didn't think her voice would work long enough to say goodbye. As she reached the front door, she heard Cole call out her name, but again, she didn't stop.

She was fumbling for her keys in her purse as she reached her car. She clicked the remote to unlock the doors, but before she had her hand on the door handle, Luke's voice bellowed from behind her.

"Sierra. Stop."

She froze in place, trying to hold back the sob that threatened to tear from her chest. There was no way she was going to get all emotional. Not after what he had done. When she moved her arm to reach for the door handle, his big, strong hand clamped onto her wrist.

She twirled around, jerking away from him and taking a step back until she was trapped between his massive body and her car. "Don't touch me," she ordered, keeping her voice low and controlled.

"Luke." Cole's deep voice thundered from behind Luke, but Sierra couldn't see him. "Let her go."

Temptation

She was surprised when Luke turned abruptly, an angry glare directed right at Cole. Seeing an opportunity, she reached behind her and gripped her door handle, pulling up until the car door opened. Thinking she might actually have a chance to sneak away from them unscathed, Sierra took a step to the side, trying to get the door open farther.

Then that angry glare was turned back at her, and Sierra saw something else in Luke's gaze.

"I need to go," she stated, but it came out almost like a question. As though she was asking his permission. But that couldn't be because Sierra didn't give a shit what Luke wanted.

"You weren't supposed to be here," he stated.

That took her by surprise. "*What?*"

"You heard me."

"Fuck you. I was invited." Anger surged hot and fierce inside of her as she tried to figure out where Luke was going with this.

"I wouldn't have come if I had known you would be here." He looked thoroughly pissed, and Sierra would have taken another step back if she wasn't already pressed up against her car door. When Cole stepped around to Luke's side, she did her best not to tear her eyes away from Luke.

"Well, that makes two of us. Next time Sam invites me, I'll make sure I ask so I don't intrude. Now, if you'll excuse me, I need to –" She was about to say *go*, but before she could get the word out, Luke was on her, his mouth crushing down on hers and damn her body, she couldn't resist him as she threw her arms around his neck and pressed closer. The emotions were a whirlwind, sparking the flames, and Sierra was lost, taken back to that night in a hotel room in Vegas.

Luke gripped her hair, twining it around his big fist, pulling her head back and breaking their kiss. Sierra could only stare up at him, her lips still tingling from his kiss.

"You don't deserve this, Sierra." Luke sounded tortured as he stared down at her. "But, I'm not strong enough to resist you."

The strangled whimper that escaped betrayed her. She didn't want to let him know just how much she still wanted him, despite what he had done. Despite everything. Sierra wanted him with an intensity she couldn't control.

"Go home with me," he said, and Sierra heard an underlying plea in his tone, even though the words were more a command than a request.

"I can't." She couldn't. Damn it.

He brought his head closer, his lips hovering just above hers, his hands gripping her hips and pulling her flush against him until she felt his erection pressing against her belly.

"Go home with me, Sierra," he demanded again.

Sierra wanted to stay strong.

She wanted to give in.

The pleasure she knew she would find in his arms, in his bed, was almost more than she could bear, but this was Luke. The same man who ran like a frightened child when things got too damn hot to handle.

"No." She was startled by the conviction in her tone.

Luke took a step away from her, still staring down into her eyes, and though it was dark, Sierra could see the energy swirling in the green-brown hues. He wasn't a man who was used to hearing that word, but as far as Sierra was concerned, he'd burned that bridge.

"I'm not as easy as you seem to think I am, Luke. I'm not one of those girls you can throw down on your bed, have your wicked way with, and then walk away from. I deserve better than that."

"I agree." He didn't elaborate.

"Well," Sierra choked back the emotion bubbling up, wanting this man to fight for her before she added, "have a nice life then." When she turned this time, he didn't stop her. She managed to get her door open completely and was just about to step inside when Luke got her attention once more.

"Don't." He sounded tormented, and Sierra knew exactly how he felt.

Instead of giving in to her traitorous body, Sierra forced herself into her car, turned the key in the ignition with shaking hands and managed to drive away without giving him another glance.

Too bad she only made it two streets over before she had to pull over while she broke down and cried.

~~*~~

Luke didn't move from the driveway as he watched the tail lights of Sierra's car disappear into the darkness. What the hell had just happened? How did he end up standing there, begging her to go home with him when the only thing he wanted to do was to watch her walk away. Actually, that was a bold faced lie. The *last* thing he wanted was for her to walk away. But, he had been honest when he said she deserved better.

Sierra deserved a man who could satisfy her in every way, one who would put her first, not his own needs. Luke wasn't that man. He couldn't understand, much less explain, what it was he needed from her. There was something there though. Something so strong Luke couldn't just walk away again. He was starting to wonder how he managed the first time.

The memories flooded his mind, the night he finally let himself get lost in her exquisite body, buried to the hilt while she clamped down on his cock. He'd been delirious with pleasure, more so than he had ever known.

His thoughts were interrupted by the sound of footsteps coming his way. He turned, fully expecting to come face to face with Cole, but he wasn't standing there. Instead, he found Sam standing only a few feet behind him, her arms crossed beneath her breasts, staring at him like he had grown a third eyeball.

"What did you do?" she asked, no longer the sweet, submissive woman he had been with in the past.

"It's best this way," he told her and started to walk off.

Sam put her hand on his arm, gripping firmly, and he halted, staring down at her small fingers where they latched onto his bicep.

"I may not be the best person to give advice, especially when it comes to running away, but Luke, damn it, you can't keep doing this to yourself."

"Doing what?" He tried to play ignorant.

"You can't stand here and tell me you didn't find something in Sierra that makes you feel more complete than you ever have before. It doesn't matter how scared you are, you have to own up to what is happening between the two of you."

"I don't know what you're talking about, Sam," Luke stated firmly, noticing his brother now walking their way. *Shit.* This was the last thing he needed. An intervention.

"You know exactly what I'm talking about," she insisted, glancing behind her, then back at him. "I won't pretend to know what happened between the two of you, or how Cole plays into all of this, but I know for a fact that something has changed in you."

"This is none of your business," Luke bit out, the hostility lurking just beneath the surface.

"I'm making it my business. You're family, and I care about you, Luke. I also care about Sierra. She's a good friend, and although she might not know you like I do, I can assure you, she doesn't deserve for you to run from her."

"Who's running, Sam?" Luke's irritation was growing. "I'm the one standing here. She's the one who left."

"This time. But that isn't what happened in Vegas."

Luke wondered how much Sierra shared with Sam. He didn't blame her if she needed someone to talk this through with, but he didn't want his sister-in-law involved in his love life. "Look, Sam —"

"No, *you* look," Sam said defiantly. "I don't know what happened, and I'm not asking for details. I just know that for the last few months, ever since that night at your house, you've been an ass. To everyone. You haven't had time for your brother, and you've now blown off everyone else in your life while you run and hide from whatever demons are haunting you."

Luke stared incredulously at Sam, listening to her rant.

"It's your life, and I won't interfere, but I will tell you that whatever happened that night between you and Cole should have been an eye opener for you. Now that something seems to have happened between you and Sierra, you're an idiot if you continue to push these people out of your life. You can't control it all, Luke. It's just that..." Sam stopped talking, clearly frustrated with the entire situation, but Luke didn't know what to say.

Those were the same things he'd thought for quite some time now, but it didn't make the situation any easier. And right now, he didn't have the patience to talk about it with her or anyone else. Instead of responding, he nodded his understanding and walked off. It was time that he went home. Time for him to get away from this debacle and move on.

Temptation

A minute later he was pulling out of his brother's driveway, and a minute after that, he was pulling in behind a familiar car parked on the side of the street. Barely able to get the truck in Park, Luke bolted out, heading for the driver's side door, fear and worry beating away at his insides.

Had something happened? Was she ok? When he tried the handle, the door didn't open, so he tapped lightly on the window. When he saw the tears on Sierra's face, his heart stopped beating. Grabbing his cell phone from his pocket, he dialed Logan's number.

"Bring someone down the street to get Sierra's car. She's going home with me." He didn't wait for an answer before hanging up and sliding the phone back in his pocket.

With deft movements, he reached into the car, lifted her and carried her to his truck. She was so upset, Luke figured she didn't know what was going on, but for now, he just needed to get her back to his house. They'd talk about it there.

Chapter Sixteen

Sierra wasn't able to argue with Luke when he pulled her from her car, carrying her easily to the passenger side of his truck. She didn't bother as he drove either. Not because she didn't want to, but because she was too emotionally drained.

After leaving Logan's, she planned to go straight home to bed; hoping sleep would allow her to escape the emotional overload to her system known as Luke McCoy. Instead, she found she was too distracted to drive and a moment after she pulled alongside the curb, the tears began to fall.

Sierra knew she was a strong woman. She was independent and self-sufficient, but she couldn't deny that she had feelings too. Seeing Luke again brought every one of those feelings to the surface, making her want something she knew she couldn't have. Apparently that thought had been too overwhelming, and the emotional breakdown she had successfully dodged for weeks descended upon her.

Thankfully, she managed to fight back the tears once she was in Luke's arms, or maybe he was the reason they stopped altogether. He wasn't saying anything, thank goodness, and she wasn't going to try and explain either. Not that she could if she wanted to.

That damn hope bloomed in her chest once again, and she was afraid to say anything for fear she would wake up, and it would all be a dream. Walking away from him was the hardest thing she had ever done, but it had been the right thing to do.

Ten minutes later, Luke pulled into a house that rivaled Logan's vast estate easily. The lawn was lit up with strategically placed accent lights, but those all disappeared when he pulled into the four car garage, closing the door behind them and shutting off the truck.

"Don't move," he said as he opened his door, causing her to jump at his tone.

She watched him warily as he made his way around the front of the truck, his gaze intent and his posture ramrod straight. Sierra fought the urge to move back when he opened the door, leaned over and unbuckled her seatbelt before lifting her into his arms and carrying her to the door that would lead to the house.

"I can walk you know." She could pretend his caveman behavior was beginning to wear on her nerves, but secretly, deep down, Sierra enjoyed the feel of his arms around her.

"Hmmphh."

Luke moved with purpose, going quickly through the house, barely giving Sierra time to take in her surroundings. What she did see was immaculately decorated with absolutely no clutter anywhere. The decor was wholly masculine with stone accents and heavy wood beams, along with large pieces of furniture scattered about.

Before she could say another word, Luke was pushing open a door, and before them was a monster of a bed, four large wooden posts and a heavy wooden headboard and footboard encasing the mattress which was covered with a brown suede comforter and several decorative pillows.

She dared a glance up at him as he made his way to the bed, sitting her on the edge and then standing before her. The look in his eye was so hot, so fierce, Sierra expected to feel her skin singe from the heat. And before her eyes, Luke's features softened, the hard lines around his mouthed eased, and his massive shoulders seemed to loosen.

"What do we do now?" he asked, clearly bewildered.

"I don't know." Honestly she didn't. What she wanted from this man was so powerful, so all-consuming, she didn't know how to tell him everything she wanted from him.

His body.

His heart.

His soul.

Though the last two weren't up for grabs, Sierra wanted them all.

Luke bent at the waist, placing one large hand on her thigh as he eased the zipper down on one boot, sliding the suede boot off and to the floor, followed by the other.

"Luke." His name came out as a whisper in the silent room and his gaze traveled up her body until those mesmerizing eyes locked with hers.

This was the first time they had been alone together, and Sierra found she wanted him selfishly to herself. When it came to Luke, Sierra knew the man owned her, heart and soul, and though she was still so utterly confused when it came to her feelings, especially for the two men who had so easily invaded her life recently, she wanted to have Luke all to herself. At least for a little while.

"I need to touch you, Sierra." Luke's words were low, a rough baritone that stroked every one of her sensitive nerve endings.

He was edgy, Sierra could see the restrained power in his flexed biceps and the strain in his neck muscles, but there was tenderness in his tone. Her emotional breakdown had left her weak, or maybe Luke was the one who was making her weak, but either way, Sierra wanted him to take away the pain if only for the night. Even if dawn broke, and Luke was out of her life for good this time, Sierra wanted nothing more than to spend the night in his arms, getting to know every part of him by touch and taste.

Sliding her feet to the floor she stood before him, feeling more vulnerable than she ever had, but needing him. Wanting him. She reached for the buttons on his shirt, and he inhaled sharply, his eyes locked with hers. Slowly she released each small circle from its mooring while they maintained eye contact, neither of them saying a word. Once she could access the glorious naturally tan skin of his chest, Sierra ran her fingers through the soft black hair, making a point to lightly scrape her nails over his nipples.

When she reached his neck, she cupped his face until he leaned closer, his palms cupping her head in turn as he pulled her closer, their lips meeting in a gentle, seductive mating of mouths. His tongue slid over her bottom lip, and Sierra opened for him, letting her tongue duel with his until she reached a fever pitch.

~~*~~

Luke managed to hold back the hunger, wanting to savor the taste of Sierra for as long as she would allow him. Unsure how he'd been given this second chance, though he never would believe he deserved it, he found himself kissing her, her hands cool on his face as they held on to one another while the rest of the world fell away. Never in his life had he felt this overwhelming tenderness, a need to mate with a woman so completely. He wanted to worship her body until she was ruined for any other man until she knew with every breath she took just how much he wanted her.

When he had come upon her car, finding her in tears in the front seat, Luke had known then exactly what he'd been fighting since he bailed on her in Vegas. This one small woman had weaved her way around his heart so quickly he was left nearly breathless by the sheer intensity of it. And here she was, back in his arms, the soft, subtle scent and the sweet taste of her overwhelming his senses to the point he wasn't sure he'd make it through the next few minutes.

Breaking the kiss, needing to take a moment just to look at her, Luke slid his hands down over her shoulders, then her arms until he reached the hem of her sweater. Gripping it gently, he lifted, forcing her to raise her arms, allowing him to sweep the material up and over her head. Standing before him like some exotic goddess clad in only a short jean skirt and a turquoise blue demi bra, her small, puckered nipples peeking through the lace, beckoning him to taste her. Oh how he wanted to taste her.

Backing her against the mattress, forcing her to sit, Luke hovered over her, forcing back the urge to climb on top of her just to feel her writhe beneath him. Apparently she was reading his mind because before a single word was spoken, Sierra maneuvered into position on the bed, lying flat. With hardly any grace whatsoever, Luke rid himself of his shirt, seconds before he climbed over her, pressing a knee between her soft thighs, feeling the warmth of her sex through his jeans.

Lord have mercy, the woman sparked a fire in his blood, and he had to focus on his original intentions. When a soft moan escaped her lips, his dick jumped and his skin tingled, the memory of what it felt like to be inside of her so fresh, so vivid, he wasn't sure how he'd survived the last few weeks without her. But tonight was all about taking his time, making this moment last and building her need until she was blind with it.

Her nimble fingers quickly got rid of the bra, leaving her breasts on full display while his eyes roamed the gentle curves, lingering on those dusky rose colored nipples that beckoned him to taste her. He started with her lips, lightly kissing, teasing, before descending down her jaw. Taking his time, licking the sexy column of her neck, feeling her heartbeat rapidly against his tongue, and noticing how her body shuddered when he sucked her fragrant skin inside his mouth. Trailing farther down, he planted open mouthed kisses on every inch of skin he could reach until he reached the upper swell of her breast.

"Luke," Sierra breathed his name, and he pressed against her, holding his weight up with his arms as she wrapped around him, her arms circling his neck, her knees bracing his hips.

Bending his head, he took one puckered nipple into his mouth, her sweet taste hitting him like a drug, making his body harden, his blood heat. She was such a sensual woman, her entire body receptive to his touch.

Her long hair fanned out around her as she gripped the back of his head, pulling him closer as he suckled one nipple, then the other. He cupped one soft, firm mound, squeezing lightly while laving her nipple with his tongue, using his teeth to scrape gently before flicking the hardened nub.

He would never get enough of her, the way she moaned her pleasure, the way her thighs squeezed him as he covered her body. And as much as he wanted to prolong this sensual torture forever, Luke needed to feel her wet heat. With quick movements, he pushed off of her, pulling her ankles until she was at the edge of the bed, quickly removing her skirt and the little scrap of turquoise lace that covered the heart of her before shedding his own clothes.

"I need to feel you, baby."

"Yes," Sierra agreed, trying to pull him closer as he held her ankles against his shoulders, guiding himself into her easily, this time not bothering with the condom because after having already felt heaven inside of her body there was no other way he wanted to go.

She was so wet and so damn tight Luke had to grit his teeth as he eased inside of her, letting her body accommodate his size. In her position she wasn't able to move easily, but that didn't stop her from trying. A smile tipped his lips as he lifted her ankles, raising her hips from the bed slightly, offering him a better angle as he held her thighs against his stomach and pushed into her slowly, then retreated. Over and over, he repeated the gentle glide, going deeper, pulling out.

"So tight." Her internal muscles clamped down around him, holding him to her, pulling him deeper and Luke groaned. She was milking him for all he was worth and Luke was barely holding on to the last remnants of his control.

"Faster," Sierra pleaded, gripping the comforter beneath her, unable to reach him due to their positions, attempting to thrust her hips upward. "Harder. Luke, please."

Luke leaned over her, bending her body until her thighs were pressed between them, her calves over his shoulders as he began to increase the rhythm, slamming into her and pulling out, over and over until she was moaning his name, the sweet sound echoing around him until Luke was lost to the sensation.

He groaned, shattering the silence, coming harder than he expected, and praying he'd be in one piece when this was all over.

~~*~~

Sierra fought to catch her breath, her body spasmed out of control as her orgasm detonated, his name on her lips once more. While they lay in the dim light, neither of them moving an inch, she steeled herself for what would come next. Luke had just made love to her. They'd come together, both body and soul in one instant that Sierra knew would change her forever.

Although he had been unable to go slow – hell, she hadn't wanted slowly – she knew Luke would look back on this with a critical eye and realize this hadn't been only about sex. When he eased from her body, Sierra couldn't tamp down the rising panic until moments later when he returned from the bathroom, a soft, warm cloth in his hand. When she reached for the cloth, he batted her hand away, insisting on cleaning her himself. Moments later, he disappeared once again.

A quick glance at the clock beside the bed explained her sudden bone deep tiredness. It was already two in the morning, and if she didn't do something soon, she'd fall asleep in his bed, and that was the last thing she wanted.

"Can you take me home?" she asked when he returned as she sat on the edge of the bed.

"No." The one word came out firmly, and Luke surprised her as he climbed onto the other side of the bed after pulling the blankets back. "Come here."

Sierra was dumbfounded momentarily as she watched. Sure, she had spent a night in his bed, but that had been different. That night she had practically passed out from the orgasms. But tonight, no, tonight there was plenty of time to think things through. Unfortunately she didn't want to think. She wanted to feel Luke's warmth infuse her. At least for a little while longer.

She stood and pulled the blankets back before joining him on the bed. Her heart was still racing, a constant *thump thump* in her chest as she braced herself mentally. Before she could prepare her next thought, Luke caught her arm and pulled her closer, then lifted her into his arms before launching from the bed.

Sierra was startled, and now that she was flung over Luke's shoulder, naked as the day she was born, she felt her face grow hot. "What the hell are you doing?"

"After that mind blowing orgasm, I figured you might relax, but apparently that's not so," Luke said as he strode through the house just as naked as she was.

She was tempted to wiggle in his arms, to make him put her down, but her breath was caught in her chest, still stunned by his sudden movements. She felt the jarring impact with each step, and unable to see where they were going Sierra wasn't sure what to do next.

"Where are we going?"

"To relax." He sounded calm, but Sierra was beginning to wonder.

A second later, she heard the sound of a door being unlocked before he stepped out into the brisk night air. She tried to look around to see what he was doing, but he kept her close with one arm across the backs of her legs while she hung upside down over his shoulder.

Before she could panic or even scream Sierra caught sight of the water as Luke descended the steps into a swimming pool. She had a second to pray that it wouldn't be cold before he easily slid her down his chest until her feet touched the bottom of the pool. Thankfully the water was blessedly warm considering the chill in the air. Luke pulled her against him as he walked farther into the water. Taking the opportunity to get closer, she wrapped her legs around him, aligning their bodies almost perfectly until he groaned.

"I know a better way to make me relax," Sierra whispered into his ear, licking the lobe with her tongue.

"I like where your mind is going," he told her as he lifted her slightly before sliding home.

"Oh God!" Sierra latched onto him as he filled her completely, the water washing up over them.

"That's what I was thinking." His words were a rumble against her ear as he gripped her hips, lifting and lowering her, the water lapping around them as it dispersed from his movements.

"More," she begged, and heaven help her, she wanted to beg even more. With the buoyancy of the water, Luke was able to thrust up into her while she held onto him, her arms around his neck, her mouth fused with his, their bodies in sync and hers tingling from the inside out.

"That's it baby, ride me," Luke urged her on, holding her close as she continued to raise and lower on his steel hard shaft, taking him deeper, her mind whirling with the pleasure, her body overcome with the sheer ferocity of it.

"Luke." She was so close.

"Fuck me, Sierra. That's it baby." Luke's words were enough to send her spiraling into the ether. When he growled in her ear, holding her close, Sierra let go, her orgasm taking her while he followed her right over.

~~*~~

The next morning, Luke found himself alone in his bed trying to figure out just what had happened. Throughout the night, he had taken Sierra as many times as he could, never seeming to get enough of her until finally she was too exhausted and he let her sleep. Not exactly sure, but somehow they managed to damn near christen every single room in his house.

Now he was alone, and he wasn't sure if he was pissed or relieved, or maybe a little of both. Sierra was getting to him in ways he never expected, and honestly, he would have been damn happy to wake up beside her. Instead, his bed was empty, and his instincts told him she wasn't in the shower or even in the kitchen making something for breakfast.

Grabbing his phone off of his nightstand, Luke did the unthinkable. Dialing quickly before he thought better of it, he called Cole.

"I'm assuming you picked Sierra up from my house this morning?" He didn't even bother to greet the man, just needed to get down to business.

"Yes." There was a hint of volatility in the single word, but Luke didn't ask anything more.

"Thanks."

"Yep." And the line went dead.

Fuck.

Luke knew he had to do something about Cole. They needed to talk. Luke was still confused though. After spending the night with Sierra, the first woman he'd actually brought home to his bed, Luke knew his life and his outlook had changed forever. And although he might be distracted to the point of insanity by the woman, he knew it wasn't ok for him to put Cole on the back burner without telling him how he felt. But how did he feel?

He desired Cole, that was a given. He found himself wanting to be lost in the masculine serenity that was the man, but he was still confused. Was he leading Cole on? Was he leading *himself* on? For the life of him, Luke didn't understand what it was that he wanted from Cole and after the night with Sierra, he was even more baffled by the way he was drawn to both of them the same.

And the hardest question of all still eluded him. Did he want more from both of them?

Sure, he'd been a world class jackass when he panicked in Vegas, storming out after he realized he'd done the unthinkable. But after the night he'd just spent with Sierra, he wondered where he had mustered up the strength to even walk away.

For the first time in his life, Luke wanted more. He wanted a commitment, a solid, monogamous commitment from a woman. Or possibly both of them. He might have burned that bridge already, but that didn't stop him from wondering what that would even be like.

Everything had changed when that woman walked into his life. And for the first time, Luke wanted her all to himself, but at the same time, he was willing to share her with Cole if it would keep the man close. Did that make him selfish? Undoubtedly. It didn't stop his thoughts from drifting to the *what if's* when it came to the two of them.

What if he loved Sierra? What if he loved Cole? What if the three of them tried to make a go of this? What if they failed?

That last question fogged his brain and made his usual doubts surface. Luke accepted the fact that what he wanted from his sexual relationships were against the norm. And he didn't know of anyone who had openly tried to explore a threesome relationship on a more permanent basis. Was it even possible?

Hell, Luke didn't know, and he didn't have enough energy to spend contemplating the idea. Forcing himself from the bed he ventured to the shower. Time to get on with his day because no matter what he did or said, he wouldn't be able to change what was happening and at the moment, he wasn't sure he wanted to.

Temptation

Chapter Seventeen

Two hours later, Luke was strolling in the front doors of Club Destiny. After a quick glance around, he headed directly toward his second floor office. A morning delivery was scheduled, and he wanted to have a front row seat to the action. It was time he had a little talk with his day bartender and figure out just what was going on with Lucie Werner.

He took the steps two at a time and made his way to his office before anyone else saw him, hoping to have the element of surprise. Lucie wasn't scheduled to work on a Saturday so the woman would have to come up with a damn good excuse for being on the premises if she was because Luke wasn't going to believe in coincidence. Not this time.

Unfortunately, not five minutes later, Lucie was filling his computer screen handing something that appeared to be cash to the delivery guy standing on the back dock. *What the fuck?* Luke waited until the man dropped off the cases, and just before he went back to the truck, Luke headed out of the office at a dead run.

Down the stairs, through the main room, and down the hall that would lead to the store room. He came to a halt just inside the door, watching as the delivery guy unloaded two additional cases behind the dumpster before getting in his truck and driving away.

Luke hated what he had to do next, hated that Lucie would deceive him this way rather than come to him if she needed help. He slipped out the door as quiet as possible and took his position on the other side of the dumpster. The alley reeked of garbage and booze, but Luke ignored everything except for the task at hand. He wasn't disappointed because not two minutes later, Lucie's ten year old Honda was pulling down the narrow alley, coming to pick up her loot.

Luke felt like an asshole, but he actually gave her time to load the liquor into her car before making his presence known. When she got behind the wheel and started the engine, Luke opened the passenger door and climbed in.

"Is this a lucrative side business?" he asked calmly, staring down one of his best bartenders.

"Oh my God! Luke, you scared me!"

"Well, that's payback. You took me by surprise too. Pull the car around to the garage and let's go inside and talk while I decide whether or not I'm going to call the cops."

Lucie stared at him in disbelief, tears filling her eyes. She did as he told her, pulling around the building and into the underground parking garage. After she parked the car, they both exited, and she followed obediently into the club's back entrance. As they walked through the main bar room, they caught the attention of a few employees and Cole, who was sitting at one of the tables. Upon seeing Luke with Lucie, Cole stood abruptly and headed in their direction.

Luke did not have time for this right now, but he wasn't about to call Cole out in front of an audience, so he just kept walking, leading Lucie to his upstairs office.

"What's going on?" Cole asked as he followed the two of them into the office.

"That's what I'm about to find out," Luke responded, still remaining calm while Lucie appeared to become even more nervous than before. Not that he blamed her, the woman should be terrified. She had a small child at home and she had just been busted stealing from her employer.

"Mind if I hang out?" Cole asked, his eyes darting over to Lucie who had taken a seat in one of the guest chairs across from Luke's desk.

Luke got the hint. After all, he wasn't dense. He wouldn't put himself in a position where Lucie could make any accusations against him. Not that she would, but when backed into a corner people sometimes did strange things.

Stepping into the office with Cole directly behind him, Luke made his way to the desk chair before turning his attention on the pretty bartender.

"What's going on, Lucie?" Holding up his hand before she started to speak, he continued. "And before you start off with a lie, I want you to consider this your only warning. You were captured on camera, so your reason is the only thing that might keep me from calling the police."

Lucie seemed to give his statement more consideration before she opened her mouth.

"I needed money." That was her only explanation.

Luke understood that, but he needed a reason. Instead of asking the question straight out, he stared back at her waiting for her to elaborate.

"My daughter is sick." This time her eyes filled with tears and Luke leaned forward in his chair, giving her his full attention. He might be a hard ass, but when it came to kids, Luke could almost forgive a parent a lot of things.

"What's wrong with her?"

"She has chronic ear infections. Constantly getting strep throat. Her doctor said she needs to have her tonsils removed and tubes put in her ears. I can't afford any of that. Not on my salary." Lucie sobbed. "I know what I did was wrong, but you have to understand –"

Luke waited for her to calm down a moment. "What should I understand, Lucie? Talk to me."

He was a little offended that Lucie would rather steal from him than come to him in the first place about her financial problems. She'd been working for him for years, and Luke knew her hardships. Hell, he knew the hardships of several of his employees.

He had always tried to be fair, and for a couple of years, he had even given large Christmas bonus' hoping to help as much as he could without them thinking he was offering charity. His employees had pride, and he respected that. But that didn't stop him from wanting to help.

"Her father doesn't pay child support, and I don't want to get government assistance. So, I started working a second job, but I couldn't handle spending that much time away from her, so I had to quit. I didn't know what else to do."

Luke was dumbfounded. Here was a woman who had a four year old daughter, single handedly taking care of them both, but instead of coming to him for help she decided to break the law.

"Why didn't you come to Luke for help?" This time Cole was dishing out the questions, moving closer, resting a hip on the edge of Luke's desk.

Luke sat back allowing Cole to take over. He watched as Lucie stared back at the man, her eyes going soft while her chin darted out in defiance.

"How is he going to help me?" she asked, the intensity of her chocolate brown eyes focused on Cole.

Luke suddenly felt like a bystander as he watched something transpire between Cole and Lucie right before his very eyes. He was tempted to get up and walk out of the room, leave the two of them to hash out the issue, but this was his business. He couldn't let Lucie off the hook without at least some sort of punishment.

"He damn sure couldn't help you while you were stealing from him," Cole stated, his tone heated with restrained anger. If Luke wasn't mistaken, these two had a history.

"I didn't know what to do." Lucie admitted, her eyes darting to the floor while her hands fidgeted in her lap.

Luke felt sorry for the woman, but he was thoroughly pissed at the same time. She'd cost him a lot of money. He couldn't imagine she had made a lot of money from selling the liquor on her own, but obviously that little extra had inspired her to keep going.

"How much money do you need?" Cole asked, surprising both Lucie and Luke. Luke stared at the man as he waited to hear where he was going with this.

"I don't know yet. I've been saving the money I made so I can at least pay something to the doctors. She's so sick." The tears returned to Lucie's eyes and Luke's heart broke for the woman. Apparently he was going soft.

He'd met Lucie's little girl a time or two when she brought her by to pick up her paycheck, and once at a company function. Now that he thought about it, the little girl was frail and unusually quiet, but Luke never considered the girl might be sick.

"When is her next appointment?" Cole asked, concern in his voice.

"What?" Lucie asked, her eyes darting back up.

Luke watched as an unknown emotion singed the air, arcing between Cole and Lucie and he wondered for a moment what the hell was going on.

"You heard me. When's her next doctor's appointment?"

"I haven't made one." Lucie admitted, sounding defeated.

"Make one. I want to go with you," Cole said firmly, leaving her no room to argue.

Luke expected her to do just that, but he watched in stunned fascination as Lucie locked her gaze with Cole and nodded her head.

Then Cole turned his attention on Luke, and he saw the concern written on the other man's face. He also recognized Cole's understanding of the situation. Lucie had to be punished for her actions, but Luke couldn't bring himself to call the police.

Turning his attention back on Lucie, Luke forced the words out. "How do you propose we handle this situation? I don't want to call the police, Lucie, but I don't know what else to do. You've cost me a lot of money, and, unfortunately, I'm not the only one who knows about this."

Tears began to fall from Lucie's eyes and Luke felt like a total shithead, though he had no reason to feel guilty. He sensed Cole's body tense, and he felt the other man's sudden need to protect this woman. He again wondered if something had happened between these two or if he was just imagining things.

"Please don't call the police. I'll pay you back. I promise," she sobbed, her eyes pleading with him.

Luke sat silent for a few minutes, letting her fidget as she waited for him to respond. He wasn't going to call the police. He never intended to call them, but he did intend for her to pay the money back. That was the least he should do in this situation. Based on the way Cole was reacting, Luke got the impression that Lucie Werner wasn't going to have to worry about any doctor's bills.

"We'll work out a payment plan," Luke stated, glancing up at Cole and then back to Lucie. "I need to talk to Logan, and then I'll get back to you."

Lucie nodded her understanding and then her eyes darted back to Cole who stood up from his perch on the desk.

Luke watched, still fascinated by the way Lucie reacted to Cole and the way she stood from her seat as Cole nodded his head in the direction of the door.

What he wasn't happy with was the inexplicable jealousy that he felt watching the two of them.

Cole shut the door to Luke's office as he followed Lucie from the room. Admittedly he was astonished at what just happened. Both by the fact that Lucie had been stealing from Luke and by Luke's reaction to the entire situation. Had he really just let her walk out without any sort of finite punishment? The changes he noticed in Luke were astonishing, and he wondered if Sierra had to do with it or if Luke was just getting soft in his old age.

"Lucie, wait," Cole called out to her as she began descending the steps that would take her to the main bar area. "We need to talk."

Lucie stared back at him in disbelief, and he wanted to smile. This woman was a total enigma. So totally devoted to her daughter, the single mother had worked for years to provide the support the little girl needed. Cole was pretty sure that no one other than him knew the full story, or the fact that Lucie opted to be a single mother all on her own. Her daughter, Haley, had a father. And Cole knew who that man was, but he also knew Lucie didn't want anyone else to know. Especially the father.

So, for years Cole sat back and kept his mouth shut. He'd also sat back and thought he and Lucie had become friends. Apparently she didn't think so.

"What is it that you think we need to talk about?" Lucie asked, both fear and wariness etched into her features.

She knew Cole had the ability to blow the whistle on her. To share with the world, and Haley's father, the entire situation. What she didn't know was that Cole would never do that. Although he tried to encourage her to. It killed him to sit back and watch the man, a very good friend of Cole's, unknowingly go about each day oblivious to the fact that he had fathered a child.

And yes, Cole was absolutely convinced that Haley's biological father had no idea he'd given in to urges that resulted in the birth of that beautiful little girl.

"I'll stop by your place tonight so we can discuss this. Make Haley's appointment and let me know when it is. I'll be there, and we'll take care of the money issue."

Lucie peered back at him, and he could see her need to argue, to turn down his generosity. Surprisingly she didn't, and Cole understood how desperate she must be because Lucie Werner had never accepted anything from him or anyone else.

Watching her intently, Cole saw the way her brain churned overtime as she tried to come up with a feasible excuse. When she opened her mouth, closed it again, before nodding her head in defeat, Cole rested a hand on her shoulder.

"It'll work out, Lucie. I promise."

With that she turned and walked away, not glancing back. Cole had never made a declaration like that one before, but based on the changes he was seeing, he had never been more certain that things would actually work out.

~~*~~

Sierra sat in the plush home office of Susan Toulmin, Attorney at Law, waiting for the woman to hang up from the call she had been on when she answered the door. Susan called Sierra the night before and told her she had time the next day to meet with her to go over Sierra's initial design changes for Susan's eight thousand square foot home. Mansion would be a better name for it, but Susan tried to pretend that the monstrosity of a house was nothing more than the average person had. Yeah, right.

After spending several hours with Susan, getting a feel for the woman's personality as well as her likes and dislikes, Sierra came up with a design she hoped the lawyer would be happy with. The woman was multifaceted and after their first meeting, Sierra had left feeling a little out of sorts. Eccentric was another adjective Sierra would use to describe Susan, but not out loud. Based on what she knew of the hard working attorney, Susan wouldn't appreciate it.

As she waited patiently, trying not to eavesdrop on the call, she wondered how Susan would react. This wasn't a new experience for Sierra, but she couldn't deny the fact that she was nervous. She was just grateful she hadn't had much time to dwell on this meeting after what had happened the night before with Luke. Sierra hadn't been able to think of much other than what had transpired between the two of them during the early morning hours.

Knowing she had gotten in over her head, Sierra had reluctantly called Cole before Luke had woken, asking if he could come and pick her up. That was a decision she had contemplated long and hard before actually dialing, but with no one else to turn to, she had ended up making the call.

Thankfully he hadn't asked any questions when he came to get her, nor when he dropped her at Logan's so she could pick up her car. She'd quickly thanked him and hurried out of his truck, feeling out of sorts. After everything that happened between her and Cole in Vegas and the way he had so easily written her off when they returned, the few minutes they had been in his truck had been awkward.

She'd felt incredibly guilty asking Cole to come get her, knowing she couldn't look him in the eye ever again. Though their time in Vegas had been special to her, and an experience she would never forget, Sierra couldn't deny the overwhelming satisfaction when she had had Luke all to herself. The way he devoted every touch, every kiss to only her, Sierra found herself wanting him all to herself.

As much as she hoped he felt the same way about her, needing only her, Sierra wasn't naïve enough to believe that to be the case. Hence her reason for sneaking out of his house at the break of dawn. If she could walk away with the memories of last night, without having to endure Luke's rejection again, Sierra might be able to remain in one piece. Doubtful, but she was holding on to that thread of hope.

"Thanks for waiting." Susan said anxiously, placing the cell phone down on her desk and interrupting Sierra's wayward thoughts.

"No problem." Sierra smiled, hoping to mask the emotion she knew had been written all over her face.

"What have you got for me?" Susan asked, getting right to the point, her tone a little more harsh than Sierra expected. During their initial conversations, Susan had been almost sweet. Apparently that was her *I just met you, and I want you to like me* persona because Sierra definitely wasn't getting that vibe from the woman now.

Grateful for the distraction, Sierra spent the next two hours with the successful Dallas lawyer, going over plans and designs and making changes. Lots and lots of changes. So much so, by the end of the meeting, the design no longer resembled anything Sierra would have come up with. Susan hadn't even agreed to one single compromise. When she finally conceded to what Susan wanted, Sierra was exhausted and wanted nothing more than to go home and slide into a hot bath.

As she drove the short distance back to her house, Sierra couldn't help but wonder what Luke was doing at that very moment. Part of her hoped he would call and give her hell for walking out on him. Instead, she figured he'd probably been thankful that he didn't have to let her down easy.

She had to fight the tears that threatened to fall, realizing she was much too emotional to play these little games and reinforcing the fact that she couldn't handle casual sex. Which was frustrating as hell because here she was, independent, successful, and she'd even give herself credit for being intelligent, but let her emotions get the best of her and she was just a mess.

When she turned down her street, trying to rein in her emotions, Sierra noticed a familiar truck parked in her driveway. By the time she managed to pull her car alongside it, her heart was pounding in her chest. Hope had her chest expanding, her palms sweating as she shut off the engine and slowly climbed out of the car.

Luke was making his way around the big Chevy when she reached the small walkway that would lead to her front door. She was tongue tied, unable to say a word as she took him in. Wearing a white button down shirt, untucked and unbuttoned at the throat, with the sleeves rolled up past his thick, ropey forearms, Sierra had never seen the man look more mouthwateringly sexy than he did right then.

"Invite me in, Sierra," Luke growled, and Sierra knew he wasn't making a request. She could feel the fury radiating from him, and for the life of her, she didn't know why it turned her on so damn much.

Rather than say anything, her mouth was too dry to speak anyway, she made her way up the short walkway, unlocked the door and then managed to take two steps inside before she found herself pressed up against the wall, and Luke's imposing body pressed against her.

She inhaled sharply as their eyes met, the hunger she detected in the light hazel depths sending a sharp bolt of heat between her thighs.

"You walked out on me this morning."

Sierra knew better than to say anything. What could she say? She *had* walked out on him, and by the looks of it Luke was none too happy with her. Part of her wanted to be defiant and taunt him, but the hard lines on his face said he wasn't in the mood to argue.

She wouldn't win anyway. Her resolve was nothing when it came to Luke McCoy.

Chapter Eighteen

When Luke pressed a hard thigh between her legs, Sierra restrained her immediate need to grind down on him. When he gripped her wrists in one of his big hands and lifted her hands above her head, she somehow managed to hold back a moan.

God he felt good against her; the solid thud of his heart beating in his chest was evident even through the soft white cotton. He was just as affected by their nearness as she was, but Sierra was hanging on by a thread and he knew it.

His mouth hovered just above hers and Sierra was tempted to run her tongue over his lips just to taste him. Instead she squeezed her lips together to keep from giving in.

"I think you need to be punished." Luke's voice was a dark, provocative grumble that, along with his warm breath fanning her face, had goose bumps forming on her flesh.

Oh yes, she couldn't argue with that. She only wondered what he had in mind.

Before she could say anything, Luke lifted her up and tossed her over his shoulder, similar to the way he had the night before when he had taken her outside to the pool. The only difference was this time they were both fully clothed. Hopefully not for long.

Since he had never been to her house before, Sierra was surprised when he headed toward her bedroom. He couldn't have known where it was, although her house wasn't very big, so it wasn't that hard to navigate.

Once inside the room, Sierra half expected him to toss her on the bed. Instead he slowly slid her back down until her feet touched the floor. Knowing better than to try to back away from him, Sierra anticipated his next move; only what he did next took her completely by surprise.

He pulled over the hard back chair she kept against the wall, and he sat down easily, his eyes still locked on her. She followed his every move, her body throbbing with need while the shrill sound of warning bells started going off in her brain. He didn't look all too happy. Strangely, she wasn't scared of what he *would* do; she was more worried about what he *wouldn't* do.

"Take off your panties," he ordered, and Sierra fought to process his words. The long flowing skirt she wore nearly touched the floor, and for the first time that day, she wished she had worn pants. She loved the black and white gauzy material and the way it brushed against her legs when she moved, but she never thought about how vulnerable she was no matter what she was wearing when she was around Luke. He wouldn't get any argument from her. At least not yet anyway. She lifted the soft, lightweight fabric until she could slip her hands underneath and remove the now damp fabric that covered her sex. She eased her panties down her legs and stepped out of them, leaving them on the floor behind her. Her belly fluttered with arousal while her hands began to tremble.

"Lift the skirt and come here," he instructed.

Luke's husky, thunderous voice reverberated through her, a shiver starting at the base of her spine and creeping up slowly until the hair on the nape of her neck tingled. Once again she lifted the material that hung to the floor until she exposed her legs up to mid-thigh.

"Higher." He sounded impatient now, and Sierra saw the intensity in those sexy, bedroom eyes.

She did as he said, lifting the material to her waist, baring herself to him completely.

"Now come here."

Sierra took a hesitant step forward, then another until she was standing directly in front of him.

"Let me see how wet you are. Show me." Luke's eyes darted upward, meeting her gaze and then back down as he waited for her to do as she was told.

Sierra had yet to say a single word to the man, and she found she could hardly focus on her next breath, much less any coherent thought. Using her index and middle finger on her right hand while still holding her skirt with her left, Sierra separated the bare, wet folds of her pussy, watching Luke as he focused intently on her fingers. The heat that spiraled low and fierce matched what she saw in his eyes, and Sierra felt empowered, if only briefly.

When he lifted a hand, one finger coming forward to slide over her clit, Sierra thought she might just crumble to the ground. He quickly flicked her clit, and then pulled his hand back before pulling her down across his lap. Startled, she yelped as she found herself lying across his lap, humiliation coursing through her.

"Damn that's beautiful," Luke's voice boomed through the room as one callused hand caressed her bare bottom.

Oh, God. What was he going to do? Sierra tried to move, tried to get out of his grip, but his other hand came down to rest on her back, effectively holding her in place. His hard thighs pressed against her stomach while she gripped the side of his leg to hold herself up.

"Luke!" Sierra screamed his name as his hand came down on her bare ass, a burning sensation shooting down her legs.

"Spread your legs."

Sierra could barely focus on his words, but then his hand came down again, harder this time, stinging her ass.

"Now."

Now *what*? Sierra didn't know what he wanted her to do. She tried to think, tried to comprehend what he had said, but the pain and humiliation consumed her. Another hard smack landed and Sierra sobbed.

"Open them."

Sierra instinctively spread her legs, hoping that was what he wanted her to do. Another slap landed on her ass, but before the pain could register, Luke buried one long, thick finger inside of her and an orgasm unlike anything she had ever known ripped through her, her entire body held together by the magnitude of that single pulse radiating outward from between her legs.

As she came back down from the sensual high, Luke slipped his finger from the depths of her pussy and Sierra fought to hold her upper body up, all of her strength zapped from the intensity of that one orgasm.

Somehow, Luke managed to lift her without Sierra needing to use her legs and then she was placed face down across the bed. Her body was still in shock from the intense pain and the mind numbing orgasm, so she barely registered her skirt slowly sliding down her legs. Her energy was so depleted she couldn't move a muscle, but Sierra felt the throb between her legs intensify. That one orgasm was only a prelude to what was to come, she knew, and despite the fact that Luke had just spanked her – yes, the man had *spanked* her – Sierra longed for more.

Without any help from her, Luke managed to remove the rest of her clothes and Sierra remained lying face down on the mattress, her head turned to one side as her body tried to recover from the intensity of her climax. She thought about trying to turn over, but then Luke took one foot in his big, strong hand, kneading the arch and eliciting another groan from her.

~~*~~

"Do you think you've learned your lesson?" Luke asked, not expecting Sierra to answer him.

He was impressed when she sighed a "yes", though still not moving a muscle. At least she remembered his demand for her to answer him whenever he questioned her.

Since the moment he stepped foot into her house, Luke had been overcome with the need to teach her a lesson for walking out on him that morning. The desire to spank her sweet ass had made his dick throb hard and insistent for the last two hours until he couldn't take it anymore. He'd driven straight from the club to her house, not knowing whether she would be home or not.

When he arrived, she hadn't been there, so he had decided to wait her out. Unsure how long he would have to wait, he was pleasantly surprised when she pulled down the road only a few minutes later.

The mere sight of her caused his heart to beat double time, his cock throbbing just as insistently. With the hunger barely restrained, Luke managed to appear as civilized as possible while standing on her front lawn. Once inside the house, he hadn't been able to contain that need any longer.

Looking at her now, lying naked and sated on her bed, Luke had so much more in store for her. Her beautiful ass was bright pink from his hand, and although he wanted to spank her again, just to make sure she learned her lesson, he wanted to explore her entire body with his tongue more.

"That didn't sound very convincing, Sierra."

Luke moved his hands up over her calf, then up the soft skin of her thigh, continuing to massage her. He managed to avoid the temptation between her legs and moved back down her other leg until he was once again massaging her foot.

He continued the sensual assault, teasing her when he reached the top of her thighs but never delving into the depths of where he knew she wanted him.

Lifting her left leg, Luke placed a soft kiss to the bottom of her foot, then to her heel, then allowed his tongue to trail up over the back of her calf until he reached the sensitive spot behind her knee. Just as he expected, Sierra began to writhe against the bed.

"Be patient, baby," Luke said as he trailed more kisses up the back of her smooth thigh until he reached the sexy, rounded globe of her ass.

He spread her legs farther apart, allowing his tongue to tease the heated flesh he had reddened only moments before. He nipped her with his teeth and then soothed the sting with his tongue. Shifting slightly, Luke spread her legs a little wider, then parted her cheeks with his hands until he could easily slide his tongue down the crack of her ass, teasing her relentlessly until she nearly came up off of the bed. He darted his tongue inside of her, reaming her ass while she moaned and screamed his name, her body once again tensing beneath him. He wanted to bury his dick inside of her tight ass, but he hadn't come prepared to take her there, so he had to settle with tongue fucking her for now.

When her body loosened up, she began to thrust backward against his tongue, and Luke knew what she wanted. Without lubrication he would hurt her, but he could still fuck her sweet, hot pussy. Pushing up off of the bed, Luke went to remove his clothes, and when Sierra began to turn over, he ordered her to remain still.

"Don't move from that position."

Sierra dropped back down, once again grinding against the mattress and Luke knew what she needed. The same thing he did. He needed to feel her velvety, hot pussy sheath him. Within seconds he'd shed his shoes, jeans, boxers, and shirt and was back on top of her, spreading her thighs so he could ease between them.

"Up on your knees." Lifting her hips, Luke placed a hand between her shoulder blades, situating her just the way he wanted her. At this angle he could thrust deep and hard.

"Luke! Please!"

Luke's cock jerked in his hand, her demand making him harder than he thought possible. Positioning his cock at her entrance, he slid the head through her slick folds before sliding in easily only to pull back. When she tried to thrust backward, Luke gripped her hips and growled.

"Don't move."

This was part of her punishment. He wanted her to burn with the need, to remember the desperation she felt until he fucked her the way she wanted. Sliding in slowly once more, he retreated, pulling out until only the head of his cock penetrated her. Sierra once again tried to force him inside of her and he brought a hand down on her ass, the sound reverberating through the room.

"I said don't move." This time she listened, and Luke gripped her hips, shifting her a little so he could slide in once more.

When he was satisfied that she wouldn't move, he increased his pace, her soft, sensual moans floating in the air, the smell of her arousal permeating his senses and making him hungry for more of her. Pulling out again, Luke slid one finger into her pussy, using her juices as lubrication before he slid his cock back inside her warm, wet heat. He then plunged his finger into her ass, as he began to thrust fast and hard, recognizing his own need to come was barreling in on him.

How he managed to maintain a rhythm was beyond him, but Luke thrust his finger in her ass while driving his cock deep inside of her until she screamed his name and her internal muscles clamped onto his cock, his balls drawing up tighter as a rocket of sensation started at the base of his spine and shot through him.

"Fuck!" Luke growled out his release as he shot his seed deep inside of Sierra before crumbling to the bed, shifting his weight so he didn't crush her.

He had no idea how much time had passed, nor did he care, as he laid beside Sierra, holding her against his chest, her deep, even breaths signifying she had fallen asleep. Luke fought the overwhelming urge to close his eyes. He didn't want to fall asleep, didn't want this moment to end. After waking up that morning, alone in his bed, Luke didn't want to ever go to sleep if it meant he would wake up without this woman by his side.

Somewhere in the last twelve hours, Luke had come to terms with the intensity of his feelings. He'd also come to terms with the fact that he wanted more from her. His only concern was how she felt about Cole. The fact that Luke hungered for something darker, more potent, and more aggressive than any woman could offer him meant that his need for Cole would never be sated, yet it didn't mean he couldn't live without it. If that was what Sierra wanted.

Since Sierra seemed to demand more than Luke ever thought a woman would demand when it came to sex, Luke held out hope that those dark desires of his wouldn't go unsated. She completed him in ways that Cole, or any other person, man or woman, ever had. Based on the satisfaction that consumed him at the moment, Luke didn't doubt he would get what he needed from Sierra.

Or maybe he was worrying for nothing. It was possible Sierra hungered for more than he alone could provide her. Did she prefer another man in their bed? After all, she had been so eager, so willing to participate in the threesomes they'd shared in Vegas. Which meant what? That they wouldn't be happy just the two of them?

Shit. This was the very reason that Luke didn't do relationships. There was too much emotional drama that needed to be settled and quite frankly, it was giving him a headache.

Luke rolled over, easing his arm out from under Sierra until he could sit at the edge of the bed, his feet firmly on the floor. He didn't want to walk out, didn't want to leave Sierra, but he didn't know that he could stay. He had run before, and though he had his doubts, this didn't feel like running. Yet he didn't feel like talking, and if she woke up, talking would likely be on the agenda.

Resigning himself to at least taking a little time to himself, Luke kissed Sierra and grabbed his clothes, sneaking out of the bedroom before she had time to wake up. Dressing hurriedly, he snuck out the door, locking the bottom lock on his way.

He'd be back.

If she let him after this.

~~*~~

Sierra woke to an empty bed, but she didn't have to wake up to know Luke had left. Though he thought she was asleep, Sierra had been lying in his arms, listening to him breathe and relishing the feel of his strong heartbeat beneath her ear. She didn't need to open her eyes to know he had been thinking too much. Instead of asking him to share with her, she'd pretended to be asleep until she had actually fallen asleep.

Now as she lay in her bed, staring at the slow turning blades on her ceiling fan, Sierra wondered what he had been thinking about. The last two times they had been together, they'd been completely alone. Was Luke thinking about Cole? Or the fact that they didn't have another person to share their bed? She certainly hadn't been.

Oh, Sierra remembered vividly what it felt like to be pleasured by two men, but she had never even thought about anything other than the way Luke felt inside of her when it was just the two of them alone. And the same had been the case when she and Cole indulged in one another in Vegas. Guilt flooded her at the realization. Yet her heart still yearned for both men. Equally.

Since Cole hadn't tried to get in touch with her, the only assumption she could make was that Cole had been using her for comfort during their time in Vegas. Or maybe he just didn't feel the same about her, and he had waited until their return to Dallas before sneaking away, hoping to avoid confrontation. After all, she had seen the way he looked at Luke, heard his declaration that morning in the shower.

If those words he'd spoken with so much conviction were actually true, how had it been so easy for him to give up on her? As much as it hurt, Sierra didn't fault him for it. Deep down, she acknowledged the dark fantasies that consumed her, knew that others had the same urges, but quite possibly Cole was only interested in being close to Luke.

The sound of her cell phone beeping caught her attention. After Luke's unexpected arrival, her brain had been fuzzy with lust, and she dropped her purse, forgetting all about it when Luke pressed her into the wall. As she went in search of it now, she wondered who it could possibly be. It was Saturday after all, and it wasn't like she had many friends. Being that Luke had just walked out on her, she didn't figure it was him.

When she reached the living room, her phone went off again, making her dig through the endless contents of her purse just to find it. Glancing at the screen, Sierra's breath caught in her throat.

"I'll be damned," she whispered, staring at the text that lit up the screen.

Dinner. My house. Tonight. 8pm.

So he might have snuck out, but Luke hadn't forgotten about her. As much as she wanted to punish him for walking out on her, Sierra couldn't bring herself to do it.

The clock on her cell phone told her she didn't have long to get ready if she expected to be at his house by eight. Her body flushed at the remembered punishment she'd received earlier. Heading directly to the shower, Sierra couldn't help but wonder what he would do if she were late.

Chapter Nineteen

A couple of hours later, Sierra was pulling into the circular drive at Luke's. She had purposely planned to be a few minutes late, and her body heated at the thought of how he would react. A hint of humiliation fluttered through her at the thought of what he had done earlier. Worse than that, she was a little embarrassed that she had enjoyed it so thoroughly. Of course she wouldn't share that tidbit of information with Luke.

As she walked to the front door, she admired the massive two story stone house. When he brought her to the house the night before, she hadn't seen much of the outside, but taking it in now, she saw his personality all over it. The house was strong and masculine, just like the man. White stone slightly discolored from age and weather, gave it a uniquely distressed appearance, accented by the thick, heavy wood posts that made it appear wholly masculine and suitable to the man.

Just as she was about to knock, the door flew open, and Sierra came face to face with the sexiest man she had ever laid eyes on. You would think by now she would have gotten used to looking at him, and his striking appearance wouldn't still give her the chills.

"Bear. Sit," Luke barked, and Sierra's eyes were immediately drawn to the large black dog now heeling at Luke's side. The same dog that had been at Sam's.

"I take it he belongs to you." Sierra smiled down at Bear, pushing her hand forward hesitantly. Though the animal had taken kindly to her the last time she had been around him, she didn't know how he would react around his owner.

"That he does," Luke stated and took her other hand, pulling her inside the house to close the door behind her. "Hope you're hungry."

Sierra looked up into Luke's eyes, and for the first time, she didn't see the hunger that she was used to seeing. Instead she saw... confusion. "I'm starving," she conceded, suddenly worried about his reasons for inviting her over.

Allowing Luke to lead her farther into the house, Bear's nails clicked on the hardwood floors as he followed. Two steps into the immaculate, top of the line kitchen, she was assaulted by delicious smells.

"You cook?" She didn't mean to sound skeptical, but Luke didn't seem like the type of guy who dabbled in gourmet cooking.

"It's not one of my favorite things, but yes, I can get by," Luke told her, and for a brief second, she caught the familiar gleam in his eye.

"Can I do anything to help?" A sudden need to keep busy overcame her.

"You can set the table," Luke stated as he turned his back on her, returning to the stove to stir something.

Sierra couldn't tear her eyes from the man. Although she sensed something was off, he was still a sight to see. Wearing only a pair of those sexy ass jeans that hugged his hips and ass nicely, she was offered a stunning view of Luke's naked back. The corded muscles moved gracefully as he worked, which she admired immensely, especially the intricate tattoo that wound from his upper arm and then over his back.

She was suddenly starving, and it had nothing to do with the glorious smell of food emanating from the pan Luke was stirring.

"You keep looking at me like that, and we might not even make it through dinner," Luke growled as he turned and faced her.

Sierra could handle that. Based on the fact that her mouth watered at the mere sight of him and a consistent ache had taken up residence between her thighs, she wondered if she would even be able to make it through the meal.

A low growl broke the sudden silence, and when Sierra instinctively looked down to see where Bear was, she was confused to see him lying in a corner of the room, eyes closed, snoozing as if he didn't have a care in the world. If the growl hadn't come from Bear, then that meant…

Before she could think better of it, Luke lifted her in his arms and planted her butt on the granite countertop, easing himself between her legs. When he cupped her jaw, turning her head so she was staring directly into those sexy brown green eyes, she managed a sharp intake of breath. Then his mouth was on hers, and her hands were all over his gloriously exposed skin. When he broke the kiss, Sierra let her mouth linger, trailing kisses down his neck, over his shoulder until she could outline the hot as hell tattoo on his left arm.

She had seen the tattoo before, but she had never paid much attention to it, always having been too distracted by other things. Sierra traced the outline with her tongue, following the muscular curve of his shoulder, then slowly trailed down his chest until her tongue found his nipple. Using her teeth, she nibbled and licked until it hardened, spurred on by his groans and the way he held her head against his chest. At this rate, they definitely were going to miss dinner.

~~*~~

Luke reached behind him and flipped off the stove burner, his body burning as hot as the flame he had just extinguished. When he'd asked Sierra to dinner, he fully intended to spend some time talking, but the sight of her when she walked in the door had him thinking a quick change in course was critical. The loose fitting sweater she wore did nothing to hide the luscious curves of her breasts and that damn mini skirt had made his dick stand up and take notice.

The way she looked at him like he was the meal made his body harden, and his brain malfunction. The way her hot mouth latched onto his nipple had his cock threatening to burst out of his zipper. And the way those soft, deft fingers of hers were trailing lightly across his skin sent a shiver up his spine.

Screw dinner. He wanted to feast on Sierra.

"How hungry are you?" Sierra whispered as she trailed those mind numbing kisses over his tattoo once more.

"Starving," Luke growled, spreading Sierra's legs farther apart, his fingers trailed up the inside of her thigh only to find she didn't have on any panties. He didn't hesitate before he speared two fingers inside of her.

He was hungry all right.

When she screamed his name and dug her fingernails into his back, Luke had to grit his teeth. The woman was so fucking responsive, so damn hot, he could barely control himself. He slowly retreated, shoving his fingers back inside of her. "That's it baby." Luke leaned over her, allowing her to press her forehead into his shoulder as he continued to finger fuck her right there in the middle of his kitchen. "You like when I fuck you with my fingers?"

"Yes."

"Come for me, Sierra."

"Harder," Sierra begged, and Luke gave her exactly what she asked for until her pussy clenched his fingers and she moaned. A second later, her body went lax right there in his arms.

But he was far from done with her.

Lifting her from her perch on the counter, he carried her over to the granite topped kitchen table and leaned her back, pushing her skirt up and over her hips so he could see her. Damn the woman was beautiful. Her long black hair fanned out around her as she lay open and waiting for him. Using his thumbs, he separated her lusciously swollen pussy lips, his eyes glued to the soft, wet folds. When she pushed up onto her elbows, her eyes tracking his every movement, Luke's dick jumped right onboard with her wanting to watch.

"Beautiful," he groaned as he leaned closer, teasing her clit with his thumb. "Take your sweater off," he ordered, watching as she awkwardly managed to pull the soft, black sweater over her head, tossing it to the chair beside the table.

Clad in a red lace bra – the woman was going to kill him with her various colored underwear – her breasts beckoned him, the pebbled tips teasing him.

"Now the bra," he told her as he leaned forward, licking his way from her navel up over her rib cage as she managed to unhook the clasp.

Once she was bared to him, Luke sucked one hardened tip into his mouth, caressing her with his tongue while she moaned and writhed beneath him. He gave her other breast the attention it was due before standing back to his full height and pulling her skirt down over her legs until it fell to the floor.

Laid out before him, naked except another pair of those fuck me boots, though this time they were of the cowboy variety, Luke looked his fill. The way Sierra stared back at him, propped up on her elbows as she watched intently, made Luke's body hum. Making sure she could see his every movement he parted her with his fingers again and then leaned in and raked his tongue over her clit. Her body jerked beneath the onslaught of his tongue as he began to torture her clit, flicking back and forth over the sensitive bundle of nerves.

In order to give him better access, he scooted her backward on the table a little, propped those sexy as hell boots on the edge and then went at her like the starving man he was. Within seconds Sierra was thrusting her hips, trying to force him closer, whispering his name until her body tightened, her clit throbbing insistently and she came right there on his kitchen table. Damn that was sexy as hell.

Before he could decide what to do next, Sierra was off the table, standing before him in all of her naked glory pulling at the button on his jeans. He looked down at her, his eyes locked on the way her tiny fingers deftly eased the button from its mooring and then slid the zipper down slowly. She eased his cock from his jeans and the feel of her velvety soft hands gripping his dick had him jerking in her hand. When she looked up, those crystal, blue fire eyes full of heat and determination, Luke sucked in a breath.

"My turn," Sierra told him and then pushed him up against the wall, as forceful as her small body versus his much larger frame could manage.

Luke willingly backed against the wall and watched as she slid to her knees, pulling the confining denim down his legs as she went. The one and only time she'd had his cock in her mouth was in the limo in Vegas and Luke admittedly thought about that night so many times as he'd used his hand to get himself off.

Now, he watched in utter fascination as the woman before him eagerly brought his steel hard shaft to her lips. Their eyes met, and her little pink tongue darted out to lick the glistening tip. Her hands were planted on his thighs, and she proceeded to tease him relentlessly with only her tongue, lapping at the engorged head, then sliding slowly, ever so slowly, down the sensitive underside.

He knew this was payback for the times he had tortured her, but he longed to spear his hands in her hair and pull her closer, shoving his dick inside her warm, wet mouth until he came deep in her throat. Instead he managed to latch on to his fragile control while she continued to taste and torment him with her tongue.

"So fucking good," he groaned the words out past clenched teeth as he kept his eyes riveted to her mouth. When she smiled up at him, Luke knew he was a goner. This one tiny woman had, in the span of such a short time, managed to own him mind, body and soul.

Her fingernails raked up his thigh until she cupped his balls with her satiny smooth hand, squeezing gently. He wanted to tell her to increase the pressure, to suck him deep and hard, but he didn't. She was right, it was her turn. Sierra wasn't experienced at this, but the determination he saw in her eyes was the only thing he needed. Her willingness to please him nearly brought him to his knees, and no matter the dark desires that swirled inside of him, or his need for a rougher touch, none of it compared to what he needed from this woman.

He watched as her mouth closed over the head, managed to keep his eyes open as her tongue bathed the underside of his cock. He was so lost in her sensual ministrations that he hadn't even noticed when she slid one finger into the crack of his ass, teasing him like no one had ever done before. Then her eyes closed and she gripped the base of his cock with one hand, thrust her finger inside of his ass as she sucked him deep into the hot confines of her mouth and Luke had to bite his lip to keep from exploding.

A minute or two was too much before he was unable to hold back any longer. He gripped her hair with both hands and guided her head as he thrust forward, deeper into her mouth, over and over as she sucked him.

"Fuck." The word slipped out through gritted teeth as he continued to fuck her mouth while she so skillfully fingered his ass. "I'm gonna come, baby. Fuck." He wasn't ready, but she was pushing him past the point of no return.

Her hand squeezed, stroking harder, faster, as she matched the rhythm with her mouth and Luke couldn't hold back any longer. He stilled her head with his hands, thrust deep and came with a rush.

Never in his life had Luke experienced anything like the erotic high that he received when he was with Sierra. He only hoped that when he told her the true depth of what she made him feel, what she made him want, that she didn't walk away from him.

~~*~~

Two hours later, Sierra was sitting at the edge of Luke's hot tub clad in one of his shirts with her feet dangling in the warm, bubbling water, sipping a glass of wine. She laughed when he first attempted to join her with a glass of his own wine, but after two sips, he hadn't been able to keep up the facade. He downed the rest of his glass in one quick swallow, put it aside and reached for a beer instead. Admittedly, that small, fragile glass had looked so out of place in his big, masculine hand, but she hadn't said anything.

Thankfully dinner hadn't been ruined, so they sat at the bar in the kitchen, neither of them able to look at the kitchen table without thinking about what they had just done. They managed some small talk, but other than talking about work they hadn't broached any personal subjects. Sierra got the impression Luke was nervous about something, but she hadn't had the guts to ask him. Now that they were outside, she wanted nothing more than to ask him the questions that she had longed to ask. However, he had somewhat closed himself off, so she once again thought better of it.

For early February, it was unseasonably warm, but the chill in the air sent a shiver down her spine, and the next thing she knew, Luke was sitting behind her, his bare chest brushing against her back.

"You should get in the water. It's warmer in there," he told her as his arms came around her, holding her close.

"Only if you'll join me." She placed one hand over his. The way he held her made Sierra feel safe and secure, a feeling she hadn't felt in so long, and one she didn't want to let go of.

When he didn't move immediately, Sierra thought he was ignoring her request, but then his hands moved slowly, easily unbuttoning the shirt she was wrapped in before sliding the soft cotton over her shoulders. Sierra had never been much for modesty, and for some reason, being naked around Luke, even outside, didn't bother her in the least. Thankfully his backyard was private, with tall trees that shielded them from prying eyes.

With his oversized shirt now resting at her elbows, her nipples puckered from the cool air that caressed her overheated skin. Moments later, his hands cupped her breasts, his fingers fondling the sensitive tips, pinching lightly, but not enough to bring pain. He continued to fondle her for long minutes as she pressed farther into his hands, a low, insistent throb starting between her legs. She wanted to feel him inside of her, to ride him until they both came, but when she tried to turn in his arms, he gripped her breasts and stilled his hands.

"Not yet. I'm going to enjoy teasing you for a while," he whispered against her ear, squeezing each breast a little harder than he had before. "You had your fun. Now it's my turn to torture you."

The gruff words he murmured in her ear made her nerve endings buzz with longing. The feel of his callused hands as they abraded her hypersensitive skin had her moaning his name, her body bursting into flame once again. How this man managed to set her blood to rapid boil with just a simple touch was foreign to her. Sierra wondered if she would ever stop longing for his touch.

Then, as though he couldn't wait any longer, he managed to strip them both of what little clothes they had on before submerging them into the gloriously warm water. Just when she thought he would turn her in his arms, and thrust inside of her, he surprised her by pulling her onto his lap, but her back was against his chest once more. She could feel his erection as it pressed against her lower back, but he didn't press into her. No, the frustrating man only continued to tease her.

He gripped her breasts, pinching her nipples as she watched his movements, the sight so erotic, so sensually stimulating, Sierra thought she might come before he ever got inside of her. Her breasts had always been sensitive, but never had she dreamed she could have an orgasm just from a touch.

The water lapped against her chest as he pinched and squeezed, but then he lifted her with his thighs until her nipples were exposed to the brisk night air. A shot of pure ecstasy raced through her at the sudden shocking sensation, the erotic mixture of cold and pleasure/pain, before lowering her into the water once more. He continued to do this over and over until Sierra was grinding her ass against his thighs, trying desperately to ease the throb between her legs.

"I keep thinking about the way you looked with your mouth wrapped around my cock."

His lewd words sent a jolt to her system, making her moan out her pleasure as he continued to fondle her repeatedly, never once moving his hands from her breasts.

"Then I think about the way you came with my tongue buried in your sweet pussy."

Oh, God. He was going to make her come just from the rough sound of his voice.

"Or how about when I spanked that pretty little ass of yours while you came around my fingers. Did you like that, Sierra?"

She nodded her head, unable to find the words to tell him just how much she liked it, although she knew she should feel shamed at the very prospect of being spanked.

"Tell me," Luke demanded, the growl in his tone telling her he wasn't requesting her obedience. He was demanding it.

"Yes," she whispered as she pressed into his hands.

"Yes, what?"

"I liked it." Sierra forced the words past her lips though she was on sensory overload, her body burning for that little bit that would push her over the edge.

"Tell me," Luke bit out, nipping the sensitive area where her shoulder and neck came together.

"I liked it when you spanked me." She felt her face redden from embarrassment, but she couldn't bring herself to care because she was so close to detonating.

"You like to be punished, don't you?"

Sierra had never thought she would find pleasure in that little bite of pain, but she had. She had loved every second of it. "Yes."

"Is that why you were late? You hoped I would bend you over my knee and paddle your ass again?"

Oh, God.

"Yes." She hated to admit the truth, but she knew there was no holding back with Luke. It was as though he could read her body.

"Stand up."

What? Sierra stopped moving, trying to figure out what he was going to do before she did as she was told.

"Now."

Reluctantly, Sierra put her feet on the concrete floor of the hot tub and pushed herself to a standing position. Her body was flush from embarrassment, her nerve endings humming with arousal as she waited for what he would do next.

"Bend over the side so I can see that sweet, little ass."

He moved over, giving her room to do as she was told. With a quick glance at him, she noted the lust sparkling in his eyes, and she immediately did as she was told. The air was brisk against her wet skin, the concrete cold as it scraped against her nipples, but Sierra didn't dare turn back now.

When she felt Luke move against her side, she knew he was moving into position so he could easily do what he threatened to do and she felt her pussy grow wetter, her clit throb with eager anticipation.

The first slap to her ass startled her, a strangled cry escaping, but she didn't move. The sensation was different than earlier in the day, sharper, biting into her wet skin. Then another, harder than the first, landed, and she bit her lip to keep from crying out. The humiliation nearly overwhelmed her, but the excitement was almost more than her overstimulated body could take.

The next two slaps were in rapid succession, but then he moved, the water sloshing up over her exposed thighs before he separated her ass cheeks and buried his tongue in her pussy while she fought to hold on. Fought the urge to come hard and fast because she didn't want it to end.

But then he was gone, another slap landing on her ass, then two more before he once again buried his tongue deep inside of her and she moaned out her pleasure. The concrete was rough against her skin, but she couldn't do anything to stop it as the sensation washed over her. He repeatedly alternated between spanking her and thrusting his tongue deep inside until she was overloaded with need. Just when she thought she would explode, he stopped.

"Luke," she pleaded, but he only placed his hands on her ass, separating her now burning cheeks as he slid his tongue downward until he breached her puckered hole with his tongue, slowly, sensually bringing her to the brink again.

Sierra never imagined someone touching her like that, never thought she would ache for more as his tongue thrust inside of her ass. She knew she shouldn't like it, shouldn't want more, but she did. God help her, she did. She wondered what it would feel like to have him inside of her there.

Long minutes passed as Luke continued to use his tongue to drive her wild, alternating between her ass and her pussy until she knew she couldn't take anymore. Her orgasm built slowly, sharp and sudden tingles rushing out from her core until she felt nothing but sensation through every extremity and then…

She exploded.

Bright, blinding light flashed behind her closed eyelids, and her body spasmed out of control.

Chapter Twenty

When Sierra's body relaxed, Luke wasted no time lifting her and carrying her back into the house. As much as he enjoyed teasing her he couldn't take much more. Once inside, he placed her firmly on her feet before grabbing a towel from the closet and drying them both. When she stirred to life, thanks to his wandering hands, he led her to his bed, directing her until she was on her hands and knees.

"God that's pretty," Luke stated as he reached for a bottle of lubrication in the bedside drawer. "I think spanking you is my new favorite hobby."

He had to admit that Sierra amazed him. Her innocent appearance belied her openness to sexual foreplay. She didn't shy away from him, though he could feel her hesitation, her concern that she enjoyed what he did to her. Truth be told, he hadn't expected her to embrace this type of foreplay, much less enjoy it.

Climbing onto the bed with her, Luke placed a hand between her shoulder blades and pressed her into the bed. "Don't move from that position," he ordered, watching as she relaxed into the blankets.

After lubricating one of his fingers, Luke paused only briefly before sliding his finger into her anal passage, going slowly, not wanting to hurt her. When she whimpered, he paused, but didn't retreat. She had admitted she had only ever been with one man in her life before she had been with him or Cole, and Luke had to assume she had never been taken this way. The thought of being the one and only man who would bury himself inside of her ass had his dick twitching and an overwhelming sense of possessiveness making his chest expand.

"Easy, baby," Luke coaxed when she began to move. "Relax."

Sierra was tensing up, and he knew if she started thinking too much she might panic. Leaning over her, he slowly pushed his index finger deeper as he placed open mouthed kisses over her bare back.

"I can't tell you how many times I've thought about burying my cock deep inside of your ass. The thought makes me so fucking hard, Sierra," he told her, realizing she liked the way he talked to her. No matter how vulgar his comments, Sierra reacted to each and every word.

Just as he expected, she slowly began to thrust back against his probing finger. He reached for her hand and pulled it around, guiding her until he could press her fingers against her clit. "Play with yourself, baby."

With little help from him, Sierra began to stroke her clit, her breaths growing more ragged. While she was distracted, Luke squeezed more lube onto his fingers and then slid two inside of her, easing them gently and encouraging her with more verbal instructions. After what seemed like forever, but had only been a few minutes, Luke managed to press three fingers inside of her as she moaned, the initial pain she felt slowly melding into pleasure.

"That's it baby," Luke urged as he pulled his fingers from her and lubed his cock, stroking forcefully as he lined himself up behind her. "I need to be inside of you. Are you ready for me?"

He hadn't expected her response, so when she moaned her affirmation, Luke didn't hesitate, guiding his cock into her, the sensitive tissue accepting him. He had to restrain the urge to slam into her, knowing he had to go slow, be easy with her. As his cock slowly disappeared inside of her ass, Sierra lay completely motionless until he reached around her, guiding her fingers over her clit once again.

"So fucking tight, baby," Luke groaned, his control quickly slipping out of his grasp. The way her body gripped him, her muscles flexing around his cock had him gritting his teeth.

"Luke," Sierra whispered his name, and he stilled inside of her. He was only in halfway, but he feared he was hurting her too much to keep going.

"What, baby? Tell me."

"Please Luke." Sierra's voice became stronger as her body began to rock, her fingers quickening their pace on her clit.

"Tell me what you want, Sierra," he said, holding his breath, expecting her to tell him to stop.

"Fuck my ass," she demanded as she tried to thrust her hips backward. "Now!"

The last threads of his control shattered, and he plunged deeper, holding her hips as he began to move forward, then back. When Sierra pushed up onto her hands, pushing against him forcefully, Luke lost it. He thrust hard and fast, deep inside of her ass as her sensual cries spurred him on. Somehow he managed to reach around her, finding her clit with his fingers as he thrust forward, her backward momentum pushing him deeper until his balls drew up tight and his spine tingled.

"I'm going to come, baby. Come for me, Sierra," Luke barked out the words, unable to slow down, unable to think of anything but coming inside of her.

"I'm coming!" Sierra screamed, and Luke lost all train of thought as his orgasm ripped through him, his cock exploding inside of her.

After carrying Sierra to the shower, managing to wash them both before returning to the bed, Luke half expected them both to pass out from exhaustion. As he lay in the dark room, Sierra's small frame curled up against him, her head resting on his chest, he knew he would be able to sleep soundly for the first time in forever.

For whatever reason, he couldn't close his eyes as his brain was overloaded with so many thoughts. He had originally invited Sierra to dinner so that they could talk. Not that he was a man who talked much or often, but there were questions he wanted to ask her. As he lay there, trying to form the words, Sierra threw out a question of her own.

"Are you in love with Cole?"

He was pretty sure she couldn't have asked him a more unexpected question. Although, based on their time in Vegas and Luke's own confusion for the last few months, he could understand where she was coming from. He answered truthfully. "I don't know."

That very question had plagued his mind for so long, ever since that one night when Cole, Logan and Samantha had joined him at his house. That night, because so many months had passed, was almost a blur. Everything except that moment when he had taken Cole with wild abandon.

Luke pressed against the base of Cole's spine, pushing him deeper into the mattress, using three fingers to fuck him, gripping his own cock painfully tight. Cole didn't make a sound, but the way he thrust against Luke's fingers told him everything he needed to know.

Unable to contain the animalistic growl that tore from his chest, Luke drove his cock forcefully into Cole's ass, his fingers gripping painfully hard into Coles hips as his entire body hardened, coated in a sheen of sweat..

"Fuck." Luke began moving inside of Cole, going deep, then pulling back, not being gentle, finally unleashing all of the pent up tension that coursed through him. "So fucking tight." His words were clipped as he fought to hold on, needing to lose himself in the hard, tight grip of Cole's body. He slowed his thrust, going deeper, over and over.

"Deeper." Cole made his own demands, beginning to thrust backward. "Fuck me, damn it! Fuck me!"

And with that, Luke let himself go, their bodies a blur of motion as Luke pounded himself into Cole, grunting and thrusting, leaning over him, holding him tighter, Cole using the strength in his arms to push back against the sensual invasion.

"Damn you!" Luke groaned, unable to restrain the pent up fury, unable to hold back what the man made him feel.

The room erupted in powerful groans and sensual moans as the two men maintained their defiance, seeking what they longed for from the other, but still holding something back.

"Come for me, damn it!" Luke ground out the command as he impaled Cole repeatedly, harder, faster, then reached around grabbing hold of Cole's cock and stroking in time with his furious thrusts.

Cole howled out his release, a deep, sensual cry interrupting the otherwise heated silence while Luke thrust deeper, once, twice, then he followed Cole over, leaning forward and clamping his mouth on the other man's shoulder as he groaned out his release.

Even though he thought himself to be in denial for quite some time, Luke knew he had claimed Cole that night. And based on the feelings he had for Sierra that he could very well be in love with Cole.

"You don't know?"

Luke understood her confusion because he was riddled with it himself. He gave the question more thought. He considered Cole a friend, a very good friend, but he knew there was more to it than that. He cared about him; that much he could admit. But he cared about a lot of people and what he felt for Cole was decidedly different. He cared about Samantha, but he didn't love her the way that Logan did. And he didn't yearn for her the way that he did for Cole and Sierra.

"Cole is the only man I have ever been with, so I think there might be something to that, but I still don't understand it."

"He's more than just a friend," Sierra stated matter-of-factly.

"Yes. However, Cole and I have never been together by ourselves, with the exception of that morning in the shower. It has never been like that between us."

"Do you want it to be?"

Luke was beginning to get uncomfortable with the questioning, but he understood Sierra's need to know. Hell, he wanted to know.

"Maybe. Shit, I don't know."

"I think he has feelings for you," Sierra said, her fingers trailing circles over his chest.

And Luke thought that maybe she was right. He had gotten the impression Cole felt something which surprisingly hadn't disgusted him. No, disgust would have been the last term he would use to describe anything about Cole. But he couldn't help but think about the way Cole had reacted to Lucie Werner. It was possible Luke had misinterpreted Cole's interest, which bothered him more than he was willing to admit.

"What about you? How do *you* feel about Cole?" Luke asked, needing to know.

Sierra tensed in his arms, and Luke knew the answer, no matter what her next words would be.

"I care about him. I wouldn't have slept with him if I didn't."

Luke changed positions, easing out from under her until he could look down into her eyes. "Do you love him, Sierra?"

"I don't know," she admitted, staring back at him with something akin to fear in her eyes.

"Tell me, Sierra."

"I feel something, yes. The same way that I feel for you."

The way Sierra inhaled deeply told Luke she hadn't expected to reveal that much of herself. He wasn't about to let the opportunity pass him by though. "And how do you feel?"

Sierra didn't answer his question and Luke needed to hear her answer. He moved quickly, flipping her onto her back until he hovered above her. He could see the brilliant blue flame of her eyes in the dim light shining from the bathroom, but he couldn't read her expression. Pushing her legs open, Luke slid between her thighs, aligning himself intimately with her.

"Tell me, Sierra," Luke whispered, leaning closer, propping his upper body with his arms so they were touching from knee to chest while brushing his lips against hers.

"I –" Luke kissed her before she could finish the statement, but he knew she was only going to make an excuse anyway. Slipping his tongue inside of her mouth, Luke was overcome with tenderness where this woman was concerned. Her fingers slid into his hair, her fingernails gently scraping his scalp, and a shudder rumbled through him.

When he pulled back and stared into her eyes, Luke saw everything he needed to see. The way she looked at him, the way she kissed him, hell, the very way she gave herself to him, told Luke exactly how she felt. His heart swelled at the thought.

As he watched her, Sierra slid her hand down his face, cupping his jaw but never taking her eyes off of him.

"Tell me, Sierra," Luke whispered, almost begging. "I need to hear you say it."

Sliding home, Luke thrust inside of her slowly, letting her wrap her legs around his waist. She was wet and warm, and he lost himself to the feel of her just as he allowed himself to get lost in those crystal blue eyes.

Sierra clung to him, and her body spoke the words he knew she wouldn't say. He wanted to hear them, but he couldn't blame her for not being able to assign the words to the feelings because he was having the same difficulty. When tears formed in her eyes, Luke was overcome with emotion. He poured himself into his movements, burying himself inside of her slow and deep, angling his hips when he was seated fully, only to retreat and return.

Admittedly, Luke wanted to hear those three words from Sierra, and he knew they would change his life forever. But, he couldn't force her. He wanted her to tell him because she was overcome with the emotion, the same way that he was. Instead, he settled on making love to her, their feelings transferring between their bodies, emotions stronger than any words could ever define.

When she gripped his jaw tighter, forcing him to look at her, he saw every emotion written on her face. He continued his torturous pace, thrusting deeper. When she leaned her head up, his mouth met hers, and he kissed her with everything he had.

When he pulled back, he met her eyes again as Sierra's internal muscles clamped around his cock. He wasn't ready for the moment to end, but he couldn't hang on. The tight warm clasp of her body milked him. For some reason, he couldn't get the words out, but Luke prayed Sierra could feel everything he felt.

Sierra pulled his face down to hers, thrusting her tongue deep in his mouth and Luke's orgasm pummeled through him just as Sierra came.

Heaven help him. He might not be able to speak the words, but he was in love with Sierra Sellers and the mere thought of what that meant scared the shit out of him.

~~*~~

Cole pulled into Lucie's apartment, and he wondered if she would even be home. He hadn't seen her car in the parking lot, but it was dark and he hadn't looked that hard. It was very possible the woman had taken her daughter and disappeared for the night, hoping Cole wouldn't confront her. Resolutely, he parked the truck, turned off the engine, grabbed the bag he'd set in the passenger seat and headed to her door on the second floor.

After two solid knocks, he was about to give up, but before he turned to walk away, he heard the chain rattle and the deadbolt click, telling him that Lucie was in fact home. And she was letting him in.

Progress.

"Hey," he greeted when her beautiful face appeared beside the edge of the door.

"Hey," she replied, taking a step back and letting him in.

"I thought you wouldn't be here," Cole said the words out loud, wondering when he'd become so honest.

"You said you were coming by." Lucie stated though he could tell from the look on her face that the thought of disappearing had definitely been on her mind. "What's in the bag?"

Lucie's curiosity had her expression briefly turning from distrust to wonder as she stared down at the plastic sack he was holding.

"Where's Haley?" he asked, ignoring her interest but smiling just the same.

"She's in her room. I told her she had to take a shower before you got here, and she just got out."

"Have you had dinner?" Cole asked, glancing around the apartment, taking in the small table in the kitchen that was set with plates and forks.

"We were just about to." Lucie responded, glancing back at the table he was eyeing before turning her attention on him once again. "I made enough for three if you'd like to join us."

Cole hadn't eaten since lunch, and he was starving, so her offer was easy to accept. He nodded his agreement and they stood staring at one another.

He let his eyes roam her face, scrubbed clean of makeup and looking so incredibly young and beautiful, Cole felt something deep inside of him give. Lucie couldn't have been but in her late twenties, but with her dark, chestnut brown hair pulled back in a haphazard ponytail, those deep chocolate brown eyes lacking the normal makeup, she didn't look much older than twenty.

During the week, when she was working at the club, she was generally all dolled up, looking much older than she was, and Cole decided he liked the clean, fresh look on her better. Not that he would say a word because either way, Lucie was a beautiful woman.

"Let me get Haley." She broke the strained silence before heading down the short hallway, calling out to her daughter in the process.

Cole turned to the small kitchen, noting the array of pictures decorating the small refrigerator, all created at the hand of a small child. He smiled to himself as he looked over each one, noting the creativity that only a child could possess. One picture reflected a small square box, topped with a triangle and housing two smaller boxes and a slanted rectangle. Obviously a picture of a house. Along with that, there were others containing stick figures of a small person with long brown hair and a taller one that looked almost the same. Apparently a family portrait.

His eyes travelled to another that was hidden behind the edges of the family portrait. This was almost the same, but included a taller person with short hair along with what looked to be a small animal. A dog maybe. So, apparently little Haley had included a man and a dog in her family portrait and Cole wondered what conversations that one had sparked between mother and daughter.

"Mr. Cole!" Haley's exuberant, if not fragile, voice called out from behind him. When he turned, the little girl launched into his arms, wrapping her arms around his neck while Cole returned the gesture.

"Hey pretty girl," he said, patting her back and holding her close. "I'm so glad to see you."

"You are?"

The wariness in her little voice shocked him, and he glanced over at Lucie. She didn't make eye contact with him, which he expected.

"Of course I am," he said, pushing her back so he could look into her eyes. The same chocolate brown eyes as her mother, yet her hair was much lighter, almost blond. "Look. I even brought you something."

"For me?"

"For you," he confirmed as he brought the plastic bag up so she could reach it.

"What is it?" she asked as she squirmed in his arms, trying to get down and grab the bag all at the same time.

Cole set the little girl on her feet and handed her the bag, smiling to himself at the look of joy on her face.

"A Barbie!" she squealed and then turned to look at her mother. "Look, Mommy, it's a Barbie!"

"A very pretty Barbie." Lucie confirmed, standing a few feet away, still not looking at Cole. "Let's sit down and eat before we open her though."

Cole followed Haley to the table where he sat in the spot she designated just for him. For the next thirty minutes, the little girl dazzled him with her stories of preschool and her apparent trip to the zoo the week before. Or maybe the month before. Haley didn't seem to have a good concept of time, but her recollection of the event was vivid.

For the first time in as long as he could remember, Cole was able to forget about all that was going on in his own life and focus on the wonder and excitement of one four year old little girl.

"Did you make an appointment?" Cole asked Lucie a little while later as he helped her to clear the table while she washed dishes in the small sink before sliding them into the dishwasher.

The three of them had shared dinner, laughing and talking. Once they were finished, Cole had helped Haley to open her new Barbie and then Lucie whisked the little girl away because it was well past her bedtime. Waiting patiently in the living room, Cole distracted himself with his own thoughts while Lucie read Haley a bedtime story, returning when the little girl had finally fallen asleep.

"Yes, I made the appointment. Next Thursday." Lucie stated, scrubbing one of the pans she had used to cook dinner unusually hard.

Cole watched while she continued to attack the pan, clearly some of her emotions were coming to the surface. A moment later he removed the pan from her hand, turning off the water before pulling her into his arms.

"It's going to be ok," he promised her; unsure exactly what he was promising. He could guarantee that financially Lucie and Haley would be fine. He could make sure Haley received the medical attention she needed, and that mother and daughter wouldn't go without food because of the cost. He, however, could not promise that what was bothering Lucie would get easier.

"It'll never be ok." Lucie sobbed against his chest. "How does he not even know that it happened?"

The question was redundant, and one Cole couldn't answer. He knew who she was referring to and he knew it was about the night Haley had been conceived, but he didn't know how to answer. He couldn't imagine being inebriated to the point that he didn't know what he was doing.

Lucie pulled back, wiping her tears with the back of her hands before turning back to resume washing dishes. Cole had other ideas. They needed to sit down.

"Let's talk. The dishes can wait."

Surprisingly less reluctant than earlier, Lucie wiped her hands on a nearby dishtowel before heading back to the kitchen table. "Would you like some coffee?" she asked, obviously trying to play the part of a good hostess.

"I'm good. Sit," he directed her before taking the seat to her left.

After a moment of silence, when it was apparent he was going to have to initiate the conversation, Cole asked the question that had been burning on his mind. "Why did you do it?"

"I didn't know what else to do." Lucie started, staring at her hands resting on the table. "I needed the money in order to pay the doctor bills —"

"Not that. I know why you stole the booze." He wasn't asking about her recent crime spree of stealing liquor from her employer and apparently selling it for extra money. That was a given. "Why did you keep Haley a secret from her father?"

Apparently the question startled Lucie because her eyes darted quickly to Cole's before she turned and glanced down the hall. She must have been satisfied because she turned her attention back to Cole.

"He doesn't remember what happened. At all." Lucie stressed the last two words.

"That doesn't mean he wouldn't want to know he has a daughter." Cole lowered his voice, cognizant of the fact Haley was still within ear shot, even if she was asleep.

"How would he even have time for her? He spends all of his time at the club."

"You know he would help." Cole could argue until he was blue in the face, and likely Lucie still wouldn't change her mind, but he had to try.

"Financially, maybe. But that's not what she needs."

He begged to differ, especially if her mother was out stealing just to pay her medical bills. Instead of stating the obvious, he waited patiently until she continued.

"Haley needs a father. I get it. That still doesn't mean I am going to tell him. He wouldn't have time for her and quite frankly, I think that would be harder on her than not knowing."

Reaching out and placing his hand over hers, Cole looked Lucie directly in the eyes. "Listen to me. You need to seriously consider this, Lucie. He deserves to know he has a daughter. It's only fair to let him make that decision on his own. I know the last four years have been hard on you, but that doesn't mean it has to continue to be that way."

"What am I going to say to him? I mean seriously." Lucie said, clearly exasperated. "Oh, and guess what? Almost five years ago you slept with me, and although I know you don't remember, you have a daughter? Right. Like that's going to happen."

"He cares about you, Lucie."

"That's only because I work for him," she argued.

Cole knew it was time for him to make his exit. He was only making the situation worse, and he couldn't very well make Lucie's decision for her. "Think about it, Lucie. That's all I'm asking." Standing from his seat, he noticed the relief on Lucie's face. She didn't want to continue this conversation, and he would grant her that reprieve.

When he reached the door, he turned back to her one more time, not knowing quite what he was going to say.

"You know him better than I do, Cole. What do you think he would say?"

He wasn't sure either, but at least she was starting to consider the implications. "I don't know, honey. I really don't, but I think you'll be surprised. The three of you deserve to have a chance to figure it out together."

Temptation

Lucie looked at the floor for a moment before she nodded her head. "Thanks for coming by."

"I'll see you on Thursday. I meant it when I said I wanted to go to her doctor's appointment." Cole tilted her chin so she had to look up at him. "And I mean it, give it some thought. He might be angry at first because you kept this from him, but he'll come around. And she deserves it, Lucie."

With a look of clear defiance, Lucie straightened her spine, those chocolate brown eyes fixed on him. "I still don't know how telling him he's a father is going to make a damn bit of difference, but I'll think about it, Cole. Goodnight."

With that, Cole left. On his way to his truck, he thought about Lucie's parting words, and he could only hope he was right.

Yes, Cole was sure Kane was going to be livid that Lucie had kept such a life changing secret from him, but in the end, it would work out. At least he prayed that it would.

Chapter Twenty One

"Feel like having dinner with me?" Luke asked Sierra when she answered the phone.

That was Luke, no other greetings, just right to the point.

"Tonight?"

"Can't think of any better night."

"Are you taking me somewhere? Or are you cooking for me?" Sierra asked, remembering vividly what happened two weeks before when Luke attempted to make dinner. If she thought about it too much, she might just break out in a sweat.

"Will your answer change depending on what I say?"

"Probably not," she stated truthfully, infusing a smile into her voice.

"Then my place it is," he told her, a wicked promise in his tone. "Be here at six."

"Make it six thirty and you've got a deal," she told him, remembering she had an errand to run that would likely make her late for a six o'clock dinner date, and despite the way her body hummed at the thought, she wasn't used to making promises she couldn't keep.

"See you at six thirty," Luke said, and the phone clicked off.

Unfortunately Sierra wasn't able to make it by six thirty, but she called Luke and told him she would be a few minutes late so he didn't worry.

At fifteen minutes after seven, Sierra was pulling into Luke's driveway only to see a familiar truck parked close to the house. Leary of what was going on, she took her time exiting her car, grabbing her purse and her cell phone. On her way to the door she listened closely to see if she could hear the sound of their voices. The silence that greeted her was either a blessing or an omen, and she wasn't sure which it would be.

When it came to Luke and Cole, especially with the way things had been between them lately, she couldn't begin to assume the outcome of any interactions between the two men. When she reached the door, she rang the doorbell and stood patiently as she waited for Luke to appear.

To her surprise Cole answered, looking just as devastatingly handsome as he had the last time she saw him at Sam's party. Or rather the morning after when he came to pick her up at Luke's.

"Hey," Cole greeted, a small smile on his lips.

"Hey." Sierra was stunned silent by his appearance at Luke's house. As far as she knew, the two men hadn't spoken much in recent weeks.

"Come in," he urged her when she didn't move forward. "I don't bite."

The blush that suffused her face was unavoidable, but she tried to cover it with a smile. "Thanks."

Once inside, she expected to smell dinner cooking, but to her dismay the house was eerily quiet and the only smells she could make out were those of wood and some sort of lemon cleaner. Her stomach rumbled in protest.

"He's out back." Cole shut the door behind her and led the way back through the living room.

Sierra wanted to ask Cole what he was doing there, but then that would sound rude. Obviously Luke invited him. Although the thought hadn't occurred to her, it wasn't a completely foreign idea.

When they walked out onto the back patio, she was taken aback. One of the patio tables was set, three plates and utensils to go along with them while overhead, soft lights hidden in the beams of the overhang illuminated the area with a romantic glow. What in the world was going on?

"Don't tell me you didn't realize today was Valentine's Day," Luke stated firmly when he walked up to her, gently pulling her into his arms before planting a scorching hot kiss directly on her mouth.

Valentine's Day? No, she had no idea. How had she missed that?

"And tonight is all about you," Luke whispered seductively in her ear, using his teeth to nip the sensitive lobe before he took a step back. "But before I ravage you, I'm going to feed you."

Sierra felt as though she had stepped into an episode of the Twilight Zone. She had apparently been so wrapped up in work that she had forgotten it was Valentine's Day and to top it all off, Cole was standing there like this was just any normal day. Despite her confusion, or maybe because of it, heat suffused her. Just what did Luke have planned?

"Dinner will be ready in two minutes," Luke stated before turning back to the grill. "Cole, can you get the wine and a couple of beers?"

Cole didn't say a word, he just turned and walked back into the house, leaving Sierra standing there, trying to figure out if this was all just a dream. The evening air was brisk, but the heater that sat on the patio chased away the chill, adding an orange glow to the area around it.

"Can I help?" Sierra asked, trying to pretend she wasn't flummoxed by the strange things going on.

"Not tonight. You can take a seat and we'll have dinner on the table in under a minute," Luke told her as he pulled what appeared to be steaks from the grill, laying them on an extra plate.

She wandered to the table, sitting her purse down on one of the others and took a seat. She felt out of place, and wondered if she should pinch herself just to make sure she was awake. Before she had the chance, Cole returned with a single wine glass, a bottle of wine and two beers.

Apparently the men wouldn't be sharing the wine, and she was more than fine with that. At this rate, she wasn't sure one bottle was going to be enough for her.

Along with her confusion, a serious case of nerves had settled over her and her stomach no longer rumbled from hunger. Instead it was churning with anticipation. Yes, anticipation of what was going to come after dinner.

Thankfully dinner didn't take all that long to consume because yes, she was starving, and apparently Luke and Cole were as well. Either that or they just wanted to get on to the next course. Which she assumed would be dessert. She hoped.

After consuming two glasses of wine, she was feeling a little less anxious and more relaxed. The men didn't allow her to help clear the dishes, so she sat at the table glancing out over the sparkling dark waters of the pool and listening to the water in the hot tub gurgle gently. And then the moment of truth arrived when both men returned, Luke following behind Cole and closing the French doors gently behind him. They took the seats they had vacated moments before, and Sierra did her best not to look at either one of them. At least not until Luke chuckled.

"What?" she asked, trying to sound normal.

"Are you a little nervous, baby?" Luke asked, leaning back in his chair like he didn't have a care in the world.

Yes. "Maybe."

"And why are you nervous?" he asked in complete Luke fashion, fully expecting her to answer truthfully.

"I – I don't know." Ok, so maybe that wasn't the truth, but she hoped it would suffice.

"You don't know," Luke said, glancing over at Cole and then back at Sierra. "Well, why don't I help you to remember?"

Oh hell.

"Come here, baby," Luke said, his tone gentle, yet commanding, and Sierra found herself doing exactly as he said.

~~*~~

Luke watched Sierra as she stood from her chair. From the moment she stepped out onto his back porch the woman had been strung so tight, he thought she might break. Even through dinner, when the conversation was light, she had a hard time focusing. It was evident what his intentions were, but he had opted to have dinner first to give her a chance to gracefully back out if that was her choice. Not that he really thought she would.

When Sierra took a step forward, Luke sat up in his chair, placing his hands on her hips and gently turning her until she was facing away from him. He then settled her onto his lap, pulling her back against his chest and twining his fingers with hers. She was shaking, and he didn't think it had anything to do with the cold.

He had given some thought to how this night would play out long before he called Cole and asked for his help. That had been a huge step for Luke and surprisingly after he laid out his plans, Cole had easily accepted. Tonight would be only about Sierra. Her pleasure was their ultimate goal, and they were both up for the challenge.

"Relax," Luke whispered in her ear as he pulled her closer against him. "We won't bite. At least not unless you want us to."

That elicited a laugh from her which was his intention. When she finally settled, her body relaxing into him, Luke released her hands and placed his palms flat against her stomach. Tonight she wore another skirt, but this one was long, hanging nearly to the floor on her petite frame and he couldn't help but wonder what she was wearing beneath it. Hopefully nothing.

Her sweater was soft, and he brushed his palms over her stomach, then up to her rib cage before going back down and easing them under the hem so he could feel her smooth, warm skin. When her stomach muscles tightened beneath his hands he smiled. Apparently she was enjoying it so far.

He glanced at Cole, nodding slightly, giving the other man the go ahead. They agreed that tonight would be about her and Luke would not be in charge. Ultimately Sierra would by way of her reaction. Cole agreed to Luke's request to do as he wished, focusing solely on Sierra.

When Cole eased from his chair, moving down to his knees on the concrete in front of her, Luke felt her body tense once more, but she didn't try to move away. He continued to use his fingertips to tease the velvety soft skin of her belly, moving up to the underside of her breast before resuming his innocent ministrations. He wouldn't rush this. Not tonight. No matter how much she begged. And Luke knew she would because they planned to overwhelm her with pleasure.

Luke watched as Cole took one of Sierra's legs in his big hands, gently kneading her calf while removing her shoes one at a time and discarding them behind him. He continued his mini massage, using his fingertips along the well-defined muscles of her legs and easing upward slowly, lifting the gauzy skirt as he went until the fabric pooled on her thighs while Cole maneuvered in between her legs.

Damn. From where he sat, looking down to see Cole in front of them, he had a front row view. His dick liked the idea as it swelled and throbbed behind his zipper. Luke kept his eyes focused on Cole still kneeling between Sierra's legs, his lips trailing along the inside line of her calf. When he reached the inside bend of her knee, Sierra sucked in a breath, her stomach muscles tightening more. Sliding his hands down, Luke lifted the edge of her skirt higher, bringing the sexy purple silk of her panties into view.

"You're going to kill me with all of those silky colors," Luke whispered in her ear, licking the edge of her ear lobe in the process.

She smelled good, a subtle hint of lavender and vanilla. He wasn't sure if it was from her shampoo or possibly her perfume. Either way, the scent made him want to lick her more.

Luke focused on kissing her neck, holding her in place on his lap while Cole eased aside those sexy as hell panties so he could expose the bare lips of her pussy. He loved how she kept herself bare down there, and he could tell by how smooth she was that it wasn't from shaving.

"My dick's hard just from watching Cole between your legs. I bet your pussy's soaked, anticipating what it will feel like to have his tongue buried deep inside of you."

Luke wasn't anticipating an answer, Sierra seemed to be riveted by what was going on between her thighs, so when she spoke up, he stilled his lips on her neck.

"Lick me, Cole," she urged, but she wasn't pleading. She was demanding. "Now."

Cole did as he was instructed, using his index finger and middle finger to separate her labia, sliding his tongue slowly from her clit, down her slit and then back up. He didn't thrust his tongue inside of her, but Sierra didn't seem to mind.

"Just like that," Sierra encouraged.

Luke was riveted by the site of Cole licking and sucking Sierra like a starving man. His eyes were closed, and he was intently focused on using his tongue to taste and torment every inch of her.

"I think it's time you were naked," Luke stated as he left the edge of her skirt pooled in her lap while he gripped the hem of her sweater and lifted up until she maneuvered so he could remove it entirely.

Clad only in another sexy as sin demi bra, this one purple to match her panties, Sierra surprised Luke when she immediately unsnapped the front closure, freeing her breasts. Damn that was hot. The way she slid her hands over the full, luscious mounds, palming herself as she groaned. Luke kept her from moving, not allowing her to press against Cole's inquisitive tongue, so it appeared she was going to take matters into her own hands so to speak.

"I love to watch you touch yourself," he told her as he moved her hair to the side, ensuring he had a good view. "Do you touch yourself when I'm not around?" He had asked her the question before, but he wanted more detail.

"Yes."

"Tell me what you do. Do you have a vibrator?" he asked, imagining Sierra lying on her bed, her hands between her legs as she fucked herself with a silicone toy. The image was so erotic his dick hardened even more than before.

"Yes," Sierra stated, her hands slowly sliding into Cole's hair, but she didn't try to pull him against her. "It's blue," she continued. "Oh! Yes! Right there," she groaned when Cole began flicking her clit with his tongue, ensuring both she and Luke had a perfect view of his movements.

"Fuck," Luke groaned. "Spread your legs, baby."

Luke helped Sierra to open her thighs farther, using his own thighs to hold her open so Cole could continue.

"What do you do with that vibrator?"

"I press it against my clit." Sierra was breathless, her fingers still twined in Cole's hair. "Cole!"

Luke held onto Sierra, using his fingers to tweak her nipples as Cole increased the pressure. They needed to send her over, at least once before they moved on to the next part. Gripping the inside of her thighs, Luke spread her open and Cole buried his face fully between her legs, using his tongue to delve deeper until Sierra screamed his name once more, her orgasm blasting through her.

"That's it, baby. Come in his mouth," Luke urged.

~~*~~

Cole eased from between Sierra's legs, keeping his hands on her legs, unwilling to stop touching her. The way she had come apart, he'd been hell bent not to do so himself. She was so fucking hot and so responsive Cole had barely managed to restrain himself. And wouldn't that have made him look like some randy teenager getting laid for the first damn time? Instead, he focused on her, using his tongue how she instructed until she came in a rush.

"Let's go inside," Luke stated, but he couldn't move with Sierra slumped back against him, so Cole took the opportunity and lifted her into his arms, easily carrying her inside the house.

He waited for Luke's instruction because he didn't quite know where they were taking this. When Luke nodded his head upstairs, Cole turned and carried her.

This was going to be interesting. The last time they were upstairs was when Logan and Sam had been there. And they all knew how that turned out.

Once inside the room, Cole carried Sierra to the bed and laid her down gently. When Luke made his way over, Cole realized he'd picked up a couple of things on his way. Either that or he had brought them to the room earlier.

Luke didn't say anything as he moved around the bed, and Cole wasn't about to ask. He would follow Luke's lead, and by the end of the night, Cole only hoped Sierra was still willing to look either one of them in the eye.

Luke crawled up on the bed, holding a thin strip of black fabric in his hand. "I'm going to blindfold you now," he told Sierra, his voice low and gentle. "You up for it?"

"Yes," she said, her eyes still shut.

"Good." Luke lifted her head, putting the fabric over her eyes and tying it until it was firmly in place. "Can you see?"

"No," she whispered, obviously realizing what was really happening.

"This will only heighten your senses," Cole stated as he moved closer to the bed. Watching Luke, he waited for the man to tell him what the plan was. When he didn't, Cole took it upon himself to get rid of his shirt. When Luke nodded toward the bed post, Cole wondered what he was doing, but the answer was clear when Luke pulled out two more scarfs, tying one around the bed post closest to him and tossing the other to Cole.

Shit. They were going to tie her to the bed.

Luke eased the scarf around Sierra's left wrist, and Cole waited for her to protest.

"You trust us, Sierra?" Luke asked.

"Implicitly," she responded, and based on the assurance in her tone, Cole realized he was worrying for nothing. With her apparent permission, Cole followed Luke's lead, using the scarf to tie her hand so she had limited movement against the bed. He watched in utter fascination as she writhed, a sensual moan escaping from those sexy lips.

"Damn. You're beautiful, baby." Cole hadn't meant to say the words, but they escaped him anyway, coming out husky, raw with need.

"Touch me," Sierra moaned, turning her head in his direction, though Cole knew she couldn't see him.

"Soon," Luke promised her, moving to the end of the bed.

Without another word, Luke climbed on the bed, still fully clothed, taking one of the two toys he'd placed on the mattress in hand. Cole watched, feeling like a bystander, before realizing he was standing there like an idiot.

Without further hesitation Cole climbed onto the massive bed, moving easily up beside Sierra and lying on his side. Using the tips of his fingers on his right hand, he traced circles from her collar bone, then eased down to the gentle swell of her breast.

The woman was sex personified. So stunningly beautiful with all of that thick, dark hair, and smooth, pale skin. His lips had a mind of their own when he leaned down and softly kissed the area he had just caressed with his finger. He licked gently around the outside curve of her breast, using his tongue to taste the sensitive underside. Without the use of her hands, Cole realized he was free to go as slowly as he wanted because her movements were limited.

While he continued to explore every inch of delectable skin, Luke was using additional scarves to tie her ankles to the bed posts, apparently not content with the fact that she had use of her legs. Sierra didn't ask questions, and Cole couldn't help but wonder how long she had fantasized about this.

Chapter Twenty Two

Sierra's senses were heightened, just like Cole said; at least all of those other than her sight. She was hanging on the precipice of an orgasm that would skyrocket her into the next century, and neither man had done more than touch her. And barely at that.

The idea of being blindfolded and tied to the bed was unfathomable, and honestly the most erotic thing she'd ever experienced. She didn't know who was who and couldn't anticipate their next move. The sound of the sheets rustling beneath her, along with the occasional creak of the bed springs had her ears perking up.

What were they planning to do to her? That was the question of the hour, but she wasn't about to voice it. She didn't want this to end. And as taboo as this felt, she couldn't bring herself to be embarrassed. This was heaven.

Having these two gorgeous men spending every ounce of their energy on her pleasure alone was more than she could imagine. It was sensual and carnal all at the same time. She wanted more, but she knew better than to say a word.

The tongue caressing her breast was gentle and lascivious and made her so hot she feared she would break out in a sweat. Not knowing which man it was only heightened the experience. Her instincts told her it was Cole because likely, unbeknownst to him, the man couldn't help but be gentle, despite the hunger she knew thrived inside of him.

When she felt her legs being spread wide, she fully expected one of them to seat themselves deep inside of her, but her breath hitched in her chest when she felt strong, masculine hands encircling her ankles, followed by a silky fabric. He was tying her completely to the bed, and she'd be damned if she didn't almost come from the idea.

Here she was, on full display, completely naked, exposed, and highly turned on. Her skin was hypersensitive, the cool air caressing her, followed by that hot tongue doing wicked things to her breast. She hoped he would suck her nipple into his mouth, apply more pressure, but he didn't. Instead, the tongue laved her nipple then the valley between her breasts before moving on to the other. The bed shifted slightly as he moved over her.

Oh hell. He wasn't moving on. There were now two mouths on her breasts, both doing different things and Sierra's mind was nearly overwhelmed by the sensations. She couldn't focus on just one. Listening intently, she tried to make out the breathing, see if she could determine who was who. Oh, she had an idea because the man who was now feasting on her right breast was much more aggressive, and she figured it was Luke.

Not that it mattered because she was lit up from the inside out, relishing in the intensity of two hot mouths on her while their fingers began trailing paths of fire down over her belly, stopping just short of her mound. God they were going to torture her to death.

And then, much to her dismay, they both stopped and the bed dipped once more, this time closer to her head. Sierra felt as though she were being turned upside down, the weight at the head of the bed forcing her backward.

"Open." Luke's gruff voice broke the silence and Sierra instinctively opened her mouth, waiting patiently to see what came next.

The object that touched her lips was satiny smooth, yet she could feel the underlying firmness, realizing one of them was about to thrust deep into her mouth, and she welcomed the intrusion. Turning slightly, Sierra used her tongue to flick the mushroomed head, reveling in the salty taste that exploded on her taste buds. Before she had a chance to fully engulf him, there was a hand in her hair, holding her still, and angling her head upward, not tilted to the side like she expected. And then there was another warm, salty male pressing against her lips. They were both above her, both of their iron hard erections pressing against her lips.

Sierra wanted to take them both inside her mouth, but since her jaw didn't unhinge, she had no choice but to use her tongue to explore them both. The satisfied male groans that filled her ears spurred her on, telling her without words they enjoyed what she was doing. Instinctively she tried to move her hands, wanting to grip them both in her fists while she lavished them with the same attention they had given her. Instead, her silky bonds pulled her arms up short, and she could only use her mouth.

"That's it, baby." This time Cole's raspy words tickled her insides, making her body flush with heat while her mouth was filled with one rock hard erection. "Suck harder," Cole encouraged her and Sierra did as instructed, part of her wondering whether he was actually filling her mouth or just encouraging her with words.

She could no longer think because she was overwhelmed with sensations, so she decided to stop trying to decipher who was who and simply gave herself over to the feelings. The hand in her hair tightened, a sharp bolt of pain tingling through her scalp.

"Damn, baby. Your mouth is so hot." And this time it was Luke. Oh, God. She was going to come from the libidinous act, not knowing who was who, yet still overcome with pleasure.

And then they were both pressing the firm tips of their cocks into her mouth, and she was forced to open wider, to wrap her lips around the engorged heads as they thrust slowly, yet firmly into her mouth. She focused on breathing, not wanting to gag, but their sizes overwhelmed her. Seconds before she thought she would choke, they both pulled away, leaving her feeling empty.

"Don't worry, baby. We'll both be inside of you before long."

The excitement of that promise had her moaning as she lay there, anticipating yet again what was about to happen. The bed shifted, and she once again felt righted when there was more weight on the end of the bed, though she could tell one of them was still beside her head.

A soft, almost purring sound interrupted the silence and Sierra couldn't place the noise, although it was relatively familiar.

"I want those pretty lips wrapped around my cock, baby," Cole said, his lewd words so unexpected, and yet so fiercely hot, Sierra turned her head in the direction of his voice, opening eagerly before he thrust inside. This time she gave herself over to the act, sucking him in deep. He was in full control as he slid between her lips, over her teeth, forcing himself deeper as she allowed him to use her mouth.

He began to thrust forcefully, faster, harder, filling her with his salty, musky taste and groaning out his pleasure, spurring her on as she used her tongue to the best of her ability to stroke him.

"Suck harder." His gruff tone ignited those slowly simmering embers that they had lit on the back porch when Cole had buried his tongue in her pussy so expertly.

Just when she was getting used to the rhythm, something touched her clit, both hard and smooth and... Oh! Luke was using a vibrator on her clit and her body lit up like the fourth of July.

She turned her head, releasing Cole's cock as she groaned, trying to move closer to the stimulation that was igniting sparks deep in her core, her orgasm building... Suddenly Cole gripped her hair once more, turning her head and thrusting into her mouth while Luke plied her clit with vibration causing her to moan around Cole's cock.

"Damn!" Cole grunted, holding more firmly. "Baby, I'm going to come in your mouth if you keep doing that."

She wanted that more than anything. Wanted to know that she could bring them pleasure, even without the use of her hands, so she groaned again, waiting, anticipating what was to come.

And just like that, Cole erupted, his unique taste washing over her tongue as he jerked repeatedly in her mouth, holding her head firmly yet gently. When he slowly pulled out, Sierra realized she could so easily get used to this.

~~*~~

Luke watched as Cole's body tightened, those rock hard muscles in his chest and his arms standing out as though he were bench pressing four hundred pounds, his groan signifying his release. Just watching the man come inside Sierra's willing mouth had his dick demanding attention.

Not yet.

He wasn't finished with her yet, and he fully intended to be filling her ass when he came.

Using the small, handheld vibrator, he continued to massage her clit, enjoying the way her hips began to thrust eagerly. When Cole's eyes landed on him, he tilted his head, pointing out the other toy lying beside him. It didn't take Cole long to realize what he wanted and the other man joined him at the foot of the bed, lying just outside of Sierra's splayed legs.

He flipped the switch, the much larger vibrator coming to life and Cole maneuvered so he could thrust the large pink toy inside of Sierra.

"Oh God!" Those were the first words she had spoken since reassuring them that she trusted them with her pleasure, and they were music to Luke's ears. She had been silent almost the entire time, aside from the random moan and groan that signified they were doing something right.

From Luke's position, he watched the head of the fake pink cock disappear inside of Sierra's tight, wet pussy, before retreating back out, over and over. She rocked her hips more forcefully, and Luke increased the pressure against her clit, using her own personal lubrication to smooth over her so he could begin slow circles over the hardened bundle of nerves.

"Don't stop! Please don't stop!" Sierra screamed as her body flexed, pulling against the scarves that confined her to the bed, her stomach muscles rippling with tension as she held on.

Cole moved once more, angling his body so he could thrust the silicon toy inside of her, deeper, faster, harder.

"Come for us, Sierra," Cole urged. "Come now, baby."

And as though only his words were needed, Sierra's body tightened, her sensual scream pierced the air as her orgasm broke loose.

Unlike before, Luke wasn't about to let her rest.

Removing the vibrator from her clit, he used her own juices to coat it before easing it beneath the pink toy still impaling her until he found the small, puckered hole that he intended to fill with his cock.

He increased the vibration level before thrusting it inside of her ass while Cole once again began a series of slow, sensual thrusts. Both of them leaned over, using their tongues against Sierra's clit and Luke reveled in the way Sierra began to thrash against the mattress. When Cole's tongue touched Luke's he took the opportunity to duel with him, taking his own pleasure from the moment.

Cole's eyes locked with his for a brief second before he plunged deep into Luke's mouth, igniting a bonfire of lust that ricocheted off of his insides. He wasn't going to survive this, and he had to remind himself that this was for Sierra. Moments later, they both managed to return their attention to Sierra's clit as she screamed their names repeatedly, coming hard and fast around both of the toys buried deep inside of her.

Luke eased up from the bed, careful with his movements because he feared one brush against his cock would send him into hyperspace. He'd never been so turned on in his life, and he longed to be buried deep inside of Sierra.

Tossing the vibrator to the side, he reached for the bottle of lubricant sitting on the table beside the bed. He waited for Cole to move from the bed, his hands lingering ever so lovingly along the soft skin of Sierra's thighs.

"Untie her," he told Cole as he flipped open the cap. With deft movements, Cole untied Sierra's arm and leg on one side while Luke did the honors on the other. They both massaged her hands and feet, helping the blood flow to return in the event the restraints had been too tight. He'd done his best not to tie them too tight, but with Sierra's fragile frame, he wanted to make sure.

"Sit up, baby," Luke instructed her as he quickly pushed his jeans down over his hips and left them to puddle on the floor. He'd been in such a hurry earlier that he hadn't bothered to remove them even after Sierra had rattled his thin control with her sweet, sweet mouth. Grabbing the bottle once more, he climbed up onto the bed, situating himself behind Sierra and then pulling her down against him, her back lying flush against his chest.

When she ground her ass against his erection, he thought he would lose it, wondering if the next few minutes even mattered. "Want to see how it feels to have two cocks inside of you?" Luke asked gritting his teeth and trying to create a diversion to keep him from coming too quickly.

Luke situated Sierra so she was in his lap, aligning their bodies so he could slip inside of her when necessary. He handed the lubrication to Cole, who would have better access from his position between Sierra's legs. With his eyes, he directed a warning to the man, hoping he understood how close to the edge he was riding.

Luke leaned back, holding Sierra atop him, his mouth lined up with her ear. "I've been waiting patiently to bury my cock in your ass again, baby. To feel the way you clamp down on me, riding me. It makes me crazy to think about it."

Luke felt Cole's firm grip on his cock, and he grit his teeth once more, doing his best to keep from crying out from the sheer pleasure of it. He hadn't admitted to anyone how much he ached for the man's rough touch, but it was there nonetheless. When Cole stroked him once, twice, he almost bucked Sierra off of him.

She was still blindfolded so she couldn't see what Cole was doing, and with her body over top his, Luke couldn't either. Apparently Cole was out for a bit of revenge of his own making and Luke wasn't sure he could take it. When he felt Cole's hot breath against his balls, he knew he was in for it. Thankfully, the man planted his mouth on Sierra instead of him, making her moan and grind against him.

While Cole feasted on her pussy, he used his hands to apply the lubricant to Luke's dick, using gentle strokes that were making him cross eyed.

"I want to hear you scream my name when I'm buried deep in your ass, Sierra," Luke groaned, trying his best to divert his attention from the firm grip expertly stroking his cock. "Then I want to feel Cole's cock glide against mine when he buries himself in your pussy. Do you want to feel us both inside of you?"

"Yes," Sierra answered, the single word sounding strangled as Cole continued to devour her pussy for the third time tonight. The man was insatiable, but Luke couldn't blame him. The sweet taste of Sierra's pussy was addicting.

"Cole's going to guide my cock into your ass." Because if the man didn't, Luke was going to explode. "Then you're going to have to angle upward so he can fuck that sweet pussy."

"Please," Sierra groaned. "Please fuck me."

Luke was seconds away from screaming the same thing. Finally, Luke felt Cole angling him so he could push up inside of Sierra. With more willpower than he thought he possessed, Luke managed to hang on for the torturously long seconds that it took to seat himself deep inside of Sierra. She was willing, but her body was so tight. "Relax for me, honey," he coaxed her. "Let me in."

Seconds later, he was buried to the hilt in her ass while she held perfectly still above him. Then Cole was maneuvering between her legs, his balls shifting against Luke's as he ever so slowly slid inside of Sierra until they were both inside of her.

She groaned, and Luke wasn't so sure she was groaning because it felt good or not. He began to move, knowing she would feel incredibly full with them both inside of her.

"Fuck me! Now!" Sierra screamed.

Then Cole was moving, rapidly and without finesse. He lifted Sierra's knees so they were astride his hips, changing the angle until Luke had to hold Sierra up slightly so they could move. And then, thanks to Cole's forceful thrusts, Sierra was riding Luke's cock and the room was filled with the sound of their harsh breaths, the wet sound of their bodies slapping against one another and Luke couldn't take it anymore.

"Baby, you're so fucking tight." He wanted to hang on, but he was at the end of his rope. "I'm not going to last." The feel of Cole's cock gliding against his, inside of Sierra was more than he could bear. Sierra began rocking, her ass riding his hips as he impaled her over and over again, Cole managing to fuck her furiously until a deep, thunderous roar shook Luke to his core. As he came hard and fast inside of Sierra, he wasn't sure whether it was him or Cole who had released the animalistic sound, and at that point, he no longer cared.

Chapter Twenty Three

Two days had passed since Valentine's, and Sierra was still sore in places she would have never imagined. After the most intense sexual experience of her entire life, Cole and Luke had cared for her by joining her in the massive bathtub that took up at least half of Luke's exquisite bathroom. Even though her body was fully sated at the time, they'd still managed another round. Apparently she would never get enough of those two.

And now Sierra was on her way to meet Sam and Ashleigh for lunch at one of Dallas' renowned steakhouses. This would be the first time she would be talking to Ashleigh for more than a brief introduction, and admittedly, Sierra was a little nervous.

After having met the woman at Sam's party, she had to admit she was a little star struck. Perhaps Ashleigh wasn't aware Sierra knew she was none other than Ashton Leigh, the well-known erotic romance author whose books had been dubbed some of the hottest ever written.

Not that she would blow Ashleigh's cover, but since the woman's books were on her own bookshelves at home, she longed to get insight into how she came up with the scandalous and highly erotic scenes that had kept Sierra up many a night. When Sam invited her to have lunch with them, Sierra assured her friend she wouldn't say a word unless Ashleigh brought up the subject.

Pulling into the parking lot of the restaurant, Sierra opted for valet parking, choosing to forego the torturous walk from the far recesses of the parking lot. She'd gotten in enough exercise for one week as far as she was concerned. The heated reminder sent a blush across her cheeks, and Sierra only hoped the valet didn't notice. Handing him her keys after he opened her door, she looked the other way, trying to avoid the man's inquisitive eyes, just in case.

Once inside, she gave her name to the pretty young woman standing at the hostess stand. Moments later, she was being seated alongside Sam at a table in the back.

"Ashleigh's on her way. She said she got sidetracked this morning, and the time had gotten away from her."

Sierra smiled knowingly. "Is Alex still pursuing her relentlessly?"

"That would be my guess, but I don't know for sure," she said quietly. "Logan mentioned that the two of them had been seen at the club over the weekend. Together."

"Well, that's progress at least." The waitress returned and asked for Sierra's drink order, in which she gave. Once the two women were alone again Sierra turned to her friend. "I know I'm not supposed to ask, and you are definitely not supposed to tell, but is Alex a member of the club?"

Sam glanced in both directions, as though trying to ensure there wasn't a Club Destiny spy hanging out in the near vicinity before lowering her voice even more. "Yes."

"Does he –" Before Sierra could finish the question – *engage in threesomes* – Ashleigh approached the table, a glowing smile gracing her beautiful features.

"Hey, ladies." Ashleigh greeted, as though they were all long lost friends. Since Sierra didn't have any close friends in the Dallas area, she and Sam had discussed on occasion reaching out to Ashleigh to see if the woman would be interested in joining their weekly girls' lunch get-togethers. Apparently Ashleigh had been onboard with the idea.

"Hey, Ash," Sam greeted, and then turned to Sierra with a conspiratorial twinkle in her eye. "Is it me or is she glowing?"

"Oh hush." Ashleigh said sweetly, taking the vacant seat between the two women. "I am definitely not glowing. Alex couldn't get that lucky."

Sierra grinned, relieved that Ashleigh could at least joke about the not so subtle man who was doing everything in his power to make his interest known.

"Well, that's a shame," Sam stated, perusing the menu. "I was hoping at least one of us could share some juicy details about their love life."

Was it her or did Sam sound disappointed? She heard the woman's attempt at light hearted banter, but Sierra got the impression there was some truth to the statement. Instead of responding, the three women reviewed their menus until the waitress returned to take their order. Once the girl was off to put in their lunch order, they all turned back to one another.

"So, since I'm fresh out of sexy stories, I'm all ears if either of you would like to share." Ashleigh stated with a grin.

Right. As if the woman didn't have lewd and lustful thoughts filling that brain of hers. How she managed to come up with some of the creative scenes in those books of hers was beyond Sierra. When both women's gazes landed on her, Sierra blushed. Profusely.

"*What*?" she asked, realizing the guilt was front and center in the single word.

"Spill it," Sam stated firmly.

"There's nothing to *spill*." Sierra knew how transparent she sounded, but good grief, she couldn't imagine sharing the intimate details of what happened between her and Luke and Cole with anyone. Even Sam.

"If the grapevine is accurate, and, unfortunately, it usually is, I heard Cole was invited to Luke's house on Valentine's night. Would there be any truth to that rumor?" Sam asked ever so bluntly.

Sierra stared back at both women, and for the first time she actually longed to share her thoughts with them. She longed to have the kind of relationships she had left behind in Nashville, ones where she could share her life with her friends and feel safe and secure in doing so. She hadn't had that since she moved to Dallas. After a second of thought, she shrugged her shoulders and decided to go for it.

"Maybe," she told Sam, glancing over at Ashleigh and noticing how the woman turned her full attention on her.

"Do tell." Ashleigh encouraged and Sierra found herself sharing some of the details – definitely not all – with the two women over lunch. By the time she was through with her story, her face was on fire, and both women were hanging on her every word.

"Who knew that I'd walk away from this lunch with so much material for my books?" Then, as though she just realized she'd spoken out loud, Ashleigh's hand flew to her mouth, and she looked stricken.

Sierra laughed out loud, and Sam joined in. "Don't worry, your secret's safe with us."

"Oh my God! Do others know?" Ashleigh asked, truly startled that her secret was out.

"Just a few," Sam told her, pushing her plate away. "I only have one question."

Ashleigh stared back at Sam in disbelief and Sierra hung on for the one question that was burning a hole in Sam's mind.

"Do you ever worry that you'll put something inappropriate in one of those children's books you write?"

Ashleigh's eyes went wide and then the woman laughed out loud, a sound so sexy, Sierra couldn't help but stare at her. Damn. It was quite possible that Ashleigh Thomas was close to perfect. Down to earth, friendly, beautiful, and apparently pretty damn horny. Every man's dream.

"I do actually. I know, funny, right? But seriously, could you imagine? Even if my editor were to read it, I'd be so mortified."

"If you don't mind me asking, how did you get your start in writing erotic romance?" Sierra asked the question, but Sam appeared to be just as interested in Ashleigh's answer.

"Since I was young I've been writing, whether in my journal or just some form of creative writing. I loved it. Then, as I got older, I started writing stories that I would just dream up in my head. And then I started writing children's books, figuring that was the safe, respectable way to go and no one would look at me cross eyed for talking about magical horses, or princesses. But, deep down, there's always been a part of me that I kept under wraps, and I would allow myself to write those stories, but never dreamed of publishing them.

"One day, on a whim, I decided I would publish anonymously, going the independent route because heaven forbid anyone ever find out that I write those types of stories. And then out of left field, they started selling. Like crazy." Ashleigh told them, completely serious, keeping both Sam and Sierra riveted on the story. "I'm not sure how anyone ever tied me back to Ashton Leigh, and I will be mortified if my grandfather ever finds out."

"Well, like we said earlier, your secret is safe with us. It isn't our place to tell. And honestly, I only know of two other people who know the truth," Sam stated, glancing from Ashleigh to Sierra and back again.

"Who?" Ashleigh asked, clearly concerned.

"Logan and... Alex." Sam didn't smile when she mentioned Alex's name.

"Oh God! Are you serious?" Ashleigh asked, her face turning bright pink. "Well, no wonder the man chases me around so much. He must think..."

"Wait. No," Sam interjected, placing her hand on top of Ashleigh's. "That's not it at all. I can assure you Alex has no preconceived notions about your sexuality."

Ashleigh looked down at her hand, the woman was apparently lost in thought and Sierra wondered about the situation between her and Alex. Did she really think that was the only thing Alex would be interested in? Was the woman really that clueless? Not that Sierra even knew Alex, nor had she even met the man, but one look at Ashleigh Thomas and Sierra knew, regardless of her moonlighting as an erotic romance author, men would flock to her like a moth to a flame. She was *that* beautiful. And fun.

"So, I think turnabout is fair play," Sierra suddenly said, hoping to divert Ashleigh's attention. "Since you and I have both shared our intimate secrets, I think it's time Sam gives up something as well." She smiled sweetly back at Sam who now looked like a deer caught in the headlights.

"Me? Why me?" Sam asked, clearly stalling.

"I agree." Ashleigh said, turning those piercing gray eyes on Sam as well. "I think it's your turn to talk."

The waitress returned to refill their drinks, take their discarded plates and offer them dessert. Each woman kindly declined the offer of dessert and waited for the waitress to get out of earshot before they focused on Sam once more.

"Ok. Fine." Sam tried to sound exasperated, but Sierra noticed the smile in her eyes. "It's no secret that Logan and I have had our share of threesomes, however, since the man we had originally chosen to come to our bed has so graciously declined because apparently the man is in love…" Sam paused for effect, grinning mischievously at Sierra. "Well, do either of you know anything about Tag Murphy?"

And with that, Sierra listened intently as Sam discussed her desire to incorporate the newest member of Club Destiny into her extracurricular bedroom activities. Although from what Sam said, they very seldom restricted those activities to the bedroom.

She only hoped Sam didn't see the sudden and intense relief that washed over her from the admission. Knowing that Sam and Logan had shared a bed with Luke and accepting that fact were two entirely different things. Since Sierra had developed strong feelings for Luke, she wasn't interested in sharing him with anyone else. Well, unless you counted Cole.

Chapter Twenty Four

Sierra spent the rest of the week trying to appease one very demanding, very selfish lawyer. Yes. Selfish. It was no wonder the woman wasn't in a relationship, or not that Sierra could tell anyway. She thought of only herself and Sierra found the trait rather annoying. However, that didn't change the fact that Sierra worked for her. So she continued to put her best foot forward, doing what Susan asked and gritting her teeth in the process.

The week droned on and thankfully Sierra had an appointment with one of the other clients she met at the conference and that meeting turned out to be the polar opposite of any she had had with Susan. The man, Mr. Brendon Cason, a well to do architect whose eye for design was right along the lines of Sierra's, was happy with her ideas. She had spent the better part of two days placing orders and tying up a couple of loose ends. Lucky for her, the weekend was in full force because she was more than ready for a break.

So when Sam invited her to Club Destiny for drinks, she hadn't been able to refuse. And here she was, sipping one of those drinks as she watched intently while various groups of people laughed and had a good time around her. She was all for the good time, but, unfortunately, Luke apparently had other plans for her. Upon her arrival, he immediately exiled himself to his office to do whatever it was that he did.

"How are you and Luke doing?" Sam asked, and although the question sounded innocent enough, Sierra knew Sam picked up on the apparent tension between the two of them.

Sierra just wished she knew where it was coming from. Since Valentine's Day, she hadn't seen much of Luke, both of them so busy that their schedules never seemed to sync up. Now Sierra wondered if that hadn't been planned on Luke's part.

Sierra glanced behind her, as though Luke might be lurking somewhere in the vicinity. As if.

"I don't know. Until tonight, I thought things were fairly normal. We've both been busy, so I haven't seen much of him."

Sam appeared to be lost in thought, as though trying to figure out what could have happened. "Logan said there was a problem at the club, so maybe that's keeping him busy."

Possible, but not likely.

How much time could it possibly take to determine the consequences for one of your employees that had been caught stealing? Yes, Sierra knew all about the problem Luke was dealing with. Luke had shared the details with her one night over dinner, the only night she had managed to coax him over to her place so she could spend just a little time with him. Luke had played down the actual theft, but strangely tried to play up his thoughts on Cole's relationship with the woman. Sierra had been stunned to learn Cole could possibly be seeing someone, and she hadn't believed it for a minute, but Luke had been rather convincing.

After what happened on Valentine's, Sierra found it hard to believe Cole would have volunteered to come over if his affections were diverted elsewhere. He wasn't that type of man, Sierra knew that much. But, instead of arguing with Luke, she'd let him tell the story and even asked the right amount of questions, all of which Luke continued to answer the same. Apparently Cole found someone and Luke wouldn't be surprised if he lost interest in the two of them. Sure, the comment stung, but Sierra hadn't argued.

That was the first sign that Luke was trying to withdraw from her. And likely Cole as well. If she had to guess, he was overwhelmed by what happened between them, to the point that he was running. Even if it was figuratively.

Not wanting to dwell on the depressing thoughts, Sierra changed the subject. "Luke told me CISS is taking on another big client. What does that mean for you?"

"I'm not quite sure yet. Dylan, Alex and I have talked a little about what I might be doing for them, but we haven't carved out the plan. The only thing I do know is Logan isn't too happy with the idea of me leaving XTX."

"Do you have to leave?" Sierra asked pointedly.

"Not necessarily, but if you want to know the truth, I'm kind of intrigued by the idea. My contract with XTX isn't up for another year and a half, so I've got some time to convince Logan."

Sierra's eyes were drawn to a group of people walking in the front door. Eight o'clock on Friday night seemed to be the time to go out based on the way Club Destiny was filling up. The noise level was increasing thanks to the hordes of people filing in, and the music had been turned up a few notches.

"Have you ever been here on a Friday night?" Sam asked, obviously noticing Sierra's interest in what was going on around them.

"No." Admittedly Sierra had never been big into the club scene, though she seemed to have developed a voyeuristic fascination with what was going on around her.

"If you watch long enough, you'll see all sorts of interesting things," Sam told her, turning her attention to the group of people Sierra was watching. "See, those would be the regulars, just coming in to have a good time. But see that woman over there in the corner?" Sam said, not out and out pointing, but damn near close.

"The one in the midriff red halter and the tight jeans?" The woman looked old enough to be Sierra's mother, though her own mother didn't look near that old.

"Yes. And believe it or not that outfit is one of the more discreet."

The woman obviously worked out. She also probably spent one too many hours a week in a tanning bed based on the way her skin looked like leather. She wasn't unattractive by any means, but Sierra got the impression the woman thought she was much younger than she was.

"She's also one of the regulars. Her name is Barbara, but she goes by Barbie – no shit, I'm not kidding." Sam grinned wildly as she took a sip of her drink. "She's in here every Friday and Saturday night, and the woman sees more action than most college girls."

"Is she a member of the club?"

"Not hardly," Sam said, glancing over at the woman.

"Is that her son with her?" Sierra asked, noticing the more than attractive young man who was standing close by.

The question must have been funny because Sam laughed out loud. "No, that would likely be her date for the night."

"Date?" Sierra couldn't hide her disbelief. "But he looks half her age."

"And that's why she's classified as a cougar."

"Cougar? What the hell is a cougar?" Sierra dared to ask, wondering if she even wanted to know the answer.

"You know, an older woman on the prowl for a younger man. A *much* younger man."

Holy crap. Sierra watched as the woman and the younger man cuddled up to one another, blatantly groping each other right in the middle of the club.

Thankfully Logan walked up behind Sam, wrapping his thick arms around her, deflecting Sierra's attention from the way the older woman was sucking the young man's tongue down her throat. Gross.

Sierra watched Logan, riveted by the way he looked exactly like Luke, yet the two men seemed so very different. A hint of jealousy coursed through her as she watched the way the two of them openly shared their affection for one another. The sight was so sweet, it made Sierra's teeth hurt.

If Luke harbored even an ounce of the affection Logan did, Sierra wouldn't be sitting alone at the table, feeling like a third wheel. Before she allowed her emotions to get the best of her, she downed the rest of her drink and made eye contact with Kane. He knew exactly what she wanted and nodded his understanding.

"Where's Luke?" Sam asked the question Sierra was dying to ask, but couldn't.

"He said he'd be down in a minute. He was talking to Cole in his office a few minutes ago."

Cole? The mention of the man's name made that jealous spark from a minute ago seem inconsequential compared to the rush that flooded through her. The way Luke had portrayed Cole as having been basically one foot into another relationship, she was under the impression the two men weren't talking much. No matter how hard she tried, every time she thought about the two of them together, her thoughts drifted to that erotic shower scene she'd witnessed in Vegas.

Even though Luke was doing his best to convince her that Cole was actually seeing the daytime bartender, Lucie, she had yet to see evidence of it. And, no matter what, that didn't mean Cole and Luke weren't willing to cross that line.

The thought depressed her.

When Kane walked up and placed her drink on the table, Sierra was tempted to tell him that she was leaving. Subjecting herself to these types of things wasn't in her best interest. Especially when Luke was managing to avoid her altogether.

"I hear that lawyer is giving you hell," Logan said as he pulled up a chair at the table. "Sam tells me she's one of those you just can't make happy."

"That's what I'm beginning to think. Susan is definitely an interesting character," Sierra answered, trying to turn her attention back on the two people at the table.

The lawyer Logan referred to, Susan Toulmin, had successfully made Sierra want to pull her hair out. Strand by individual strand. She had spent Tuesday with the woman, listening as she proceeded to tell Sierra that every idea she had was basically garbage.

It was hard to believe she had been so eager to take the job in the beginning, thrilled with the possibilities. She should have known better when Susan had so easily agreed to all of Sierra's ideas. At least until she was presented with them officially. Now she knew why. There was no pleasing that woman, no matter how hard she tried.

The problem was, Sierra needed the job. She needed the reference, so she had worked her ass off for two days trying to find exactly the things, no matter how ridiculous, that Susan wanted to use in the design.

"What did you say her last name was?" Logan asked, glancing from Sam back to Sierra.

"Toulmin," Sierra answered, her attention riveted on what he might say next. Did Logan know her? Sierra met the woman at the conference in Vegas, so odds were Logan either knew her from there or had at least heard of her. Based on the way his jaw tightened, Sierra believed it was the former.

"Fuck. Seriously?"

Sierra's attention was definitely captured. "Yes. She's the Dallas lawyer that I met while I was in Vegas. Do you know her?"

"Not personally, but Luke does. Toulmin is her maiden name which she uses for her law practice. Although she's not married anymore, she never dropped her married name… Mackendrick," Logan informed her.

Sam's head jerked toward Logan and Sierra caught the look of distaste written on her beautiful face.

"What? What aren't you telling me?" Sierra wondered out loud, looking back and forth between Sam and Logan.

"Susan used to…" Sam started to reply, but Luke walked up just in time for her to close her mouth abruptly.

"Hey," Luke stated as he took the vacant chair beside Sierra. Shockingly, he leaned over and kissed her softly on the mouth before turning his focus on Logan.

"Where's Cole?" Logan asked and for the second time that night, someone else had voiced the burning question.

"He had something to do. Said he might be back in a couple of hours," Luke replied, raising his hand to get Kane's attention.

"You didn't tell me Sierra had been hired by Susie Mackendrick," Logan stated bluntly, looking none too happy.

Susie?

Luke's head jerked like someone had slapped him. "*What?*"

Apparently Luke hadn't put two and two together or maybe Sierra hadn't mentioned the woman's last name. Either way, Sierra knew there was a story there, and she was pretty sure it was one she wasn't going to like.

"She's the client I've been telling you about," Sierra managed to say when Luke glared at her.

"Where'd you meet her?"

What did it matter, she wondered to herself. Apparently there was something personal between Luke and the woman Sierra was now working for, and just like Logan, Luke seemed a bit stunned by the news. "I met her at the conference in Vegas. I told you about her."

"I'm pretty sure I would remember if you had," Luke argued, his eyes darting around the room as though he expected the woman to pop up at any second.

"Why? How do you know her?" Sierra asked, leaning forward in her chair and placing her elbows on the table. She wanted the story, and she wanted it now. Unease settled like a rock in her belly and though she hadn't thought it possible, she knew her week was just about to go from bad to worse.

"It's nothing." Luke brushed her off, masking any emotion he had previously shown as he avoided looking at her directly.

"What do you mean *it's nothing?*" Her ability to brush things off had just reached critically low levels. Between Logan's reactions, Sam's apparent distaste of the subject, and now Luke's wandering eyes, she knew there was something personal between Luke and Susan. Luke blowing her off was just the icing on the cake.

"Just what I said," Luke stated, and Sierra could see from his expression that the subject was closed as far as he was concerned.

Well, that was all fine and good. She could play this game too. "Well, that'll be my cue to call it a night," Sierra stated, standing abruptly. All heads turned to her, but she didn't bother making eye contact. Offering a quick glance at Sam, she spoke. "Call me tomorrow? We'll do lunch if you're not busy."

Sam didn't say a word, but she nodded her head, her eyes darting back and forth between Sierra and Luke. Without further hesitation, Sierra grabbed her purse and walked away. Maybe she was being petulant, or maybe she just wasn't willing to play these juvenile games. Either way, she'd reached her limit tonight.

Sierra would have thought that the pounding bass and the consistent chatter would have drowned out the sound that had her stopping her tracks. The husky, sexy voice that called out to Luke was familiar. The same voice that had spent two days telling Sierra she was none too happy with her designs.

Susan Toulmin, better known as Susie Mackendrick apparently, seemed to know her way around the club, which told Sierra everything she needed to know. Despite the warning bells sounding off in her brain, she turned toward the voice, just in time to see the beautiful Dallas lawyer wrap her arms around Luke's expansive chest. That wasn't a platonic hug... nor was the kiss that followed.

Oh, God. Sierra forced her feet to move as her stomach lurched, the nausea making her dizzy. She was going to throw up, and it had nothing to do with the alcohol she had consumed. Thankfully her brain functioned enough to convince her feet to move toward the door, but the second she stepped out into the cool night air, the dam broke, and the tears burst free. Choking on a sob, Sierra lowered her head, hoping no one would see the woman who was having an emotional breakdown. She'd only gone two steps out the door before she came face to chest with a hard, unmoving form.

"I am *so* sorry," she sobbed, glancing up into familiar ocean blue eyes.

Why her? Why today?

"Sierra?"

Oh, great. The pity she saw in those exquisite eyes was nearly her undoing. When Cole gripped her arm, pulling her out of the path of the crowd, she wanted to just slink into a corner and die.

"Honey, what's wrong?" The tender tone of his voice didn't help the steady flow of tears, but somehow Sierra managed to pull away from him.

Everything. "Nothing. I – I need to – to go." With that Sierra skirted past Cole and down the narrow corridor that would lead her to the underground parking garage. Her feet didn't seem to move fast enough, but the farther she made it away from Luke, the stronger she began to feel.

Chapter Twenty Five

Luke was caught off guard when Susie walked up to the table, her sultry, southern twang a complete distraction to the fact that Sierra had just up and walked away. He stood, fully intending to go after Sierra, only to find Susie walking right into his arms. He abruptly wrapped his arms around her to keep from losing his balance, but before he could pull away, Susie planted a scorching hot kiss firmly on his lips.

Based on the death glare his brother shot him, and the look of horror on Sam's face, Luke knew Sierra had been witness to everything that just happened. And being the dumbass that he was, Luke didn't chase after her. Instead, time slowed to a crawl as the four of them stared at one another in fascinated shock. Well, everyone except Susie who appeared to be oblivious if her constant rambling was anything to go by.

Minutes later, Luke found himself sitting at the table with the three of them while Susie continued her incessant talking. "And you wouldn't believe this interior designer I hired," Susie stated, capturing the full attention of everyone at the table.

"Since I met her at the conference in Vegas, I figured for sure I would be getting top notch when I hired her. She's new to the interior design world and green as hell. Unfortunately, she's much more inexperienced than I originally gave her credit for. The woman just doesn't seem to get it. I'm not sure how she intends to make it in that business if she is too stupid to take any sort of direction. I mean seriously, how hard is it to understand when I'm telling her exactly what I want?"

Sam abruptly stood from the table, pushing her chair back so hard it nearly tumbled over. "It's time to go," she told Logan pointedly, not making eye contact with Luke.

If she expected Luke to say something she had another thing coming. Oh, he knew he should defend Sierra, he knew he should say anything that would make Susie put a lid on it, but he couldn't seem to come up with the words.

For the last few days, Luke's emotions had been all fucked up, and he didn't know how to even talk to Sierra. As it would appear, the night the three of them spent together had had a shocking effect on Luke. Unable to get his shit together, he'd successfully managed to keep her at arm's length all week. It appeared the arm had just turned into a football field.

Luke could only watch as Logan and Sam walked away, his brother's death stare boring a hole into him and promising retribution later. That was par for the course these days or so it seemed. If his conversation with Cole earlier was anything to go by, Luke had successfully morphed back into the world class asshole.

"So, it looks like it's just you and me now, cowboy." Susie's seductive whisper slid over him while her slender fingers snaked up his arm.

He'd always wondered what it meant to have an out of body experience. Now he knew. He glanced down at Susie, feeling like a bystander watching a train crash into another one head on at two hundred miles per hour.

The woman looked the same as always with her beautiful, golden blond hair, those piercing brown eyes, and those sinfully red lips, but for the life of him, Luke couldn't understand what he had been drawn to about her. Before he could give it another second's thought the other object of Susie's sexual infatuation chose that moment to walk up to the table and based on the look on his face, Cole was none too happy to see Luke.

"What the fuck are you doing?" Cole barked, glaring down at Luke, never even acknowledging Susie.

"What are you talking about?" Luke pushed to his feet, needing to get some height on Cole in order to deal with the man's anger. In all the time that he had known him, he had never seen Cole mad enough that his hands were balled into fists at his side. If Luke looked close enough, he'd probably see steam coming out of his ears.

"Cole, honey, what's wrong?" Susie interrupted.

As though seeing her for the first time, Cole glanced over at the woman at the table, but his attention didn't stray for long before he locked that penetrating stare back on Luke. "Sierra just stormed out of here. *In tears.* Although she didn't bother to tell me why, my money's on you."

The thought of Sierra crying tore at Luke's heart. If he was a smart man, which he was, he would high tail it out of the club and find her. Apparently his intellect had taken a back seat to the rage boiling just beneath the surface. "If I remember right, you lost your right to stick your nose into my business."

Cole laughed. The man actually laughed, but his eyes showed no reflection of humor. "I don't give a fuck about *you*." Cole's tone was deceptively calm, standing toe to toe with Luke. "It's her I care about."

"Her? You're going to stand here and tell me you care about her? You abandoned her, remember? You abandoned both of us." *Wow, where the hell had that come from?*

"Abandoned?" Cole's body went stone still. "I stayed away from her. Because of you. And then the second you invite me over, I'm there. And you want to tell me I'm the one who abandoned *you*?"

Cole jabbed a finger in Luke's chest, and the sudden, intense reaction to the other man's anger was shocking. Luke instinctively reared back, his fist clenched, every muscle geared up for a fight. His brain registered what he was doing, but a fraction of a second before impact, someone's steel hard grip latched onto Luke's arm and pulled him back, causing him to stumble.

"Not here, damn it." Logan's tense words broke through the red haze that consumed him. Pulling out of Logan's grip, Luke stepped forward, getting right in Cole's face again.

"We've got some things to talk about, you and me," Cole stated matter-of-factly, not giving an inch. "It's time we took care of that."

Luke processed the words, he even understood what Cole was telling him, but all of a sudden nothing seemed to matter except for one thing. Getting to Sierra.

"Luke? What's going on?" Susie's husky voice broke the strained silence that settled between the two men despite the loud music pounding through the sound system.

Tunnel vision consumed him, and he could only focus on the man standing inches away.

"Tell her," Cole stated through clenched teeth.

"Tell her *what*?" Luke's irritation level was reaching the critical point.

"Start with how you sent Sierra out of here crying."

"Sierra?" Susie asked, looking bemused. "Not Sierra Sellers, I hope. Please don't tell me that you've lowered your standards…"

Luke cut her off before the words could come out. He gripped Susie's slim arm, jerking her to face him.

"Don't." The word came out more as a snarl, but Luke couldn't contain his temper. "Don't say another fucking word about her. You're damn lucky she's even given you the time of day. And if I hear one more fucking word out of your mouth, you'll be out of my club so fast your head will spin."

Susie's eyes widened, locked with his and he swore he saw... Oh, hell, the woman was turned on by all of this? Good Lord. His suspicions were confirmed a second later when her eyes lowered. Her admission of surrender.

On a normal day that look would have Luke backing her against a wall and taking her hard and fast until she screamed his name.

Not today.

Not ever again.

He was right on one thing... Sierra deserved so much better than him. She deserved everything. And if Luke had a chance in hell of making her understand he was the man who would give her everything, he had to take that opportunity.

"Luke, I didn't mean..." Susie began when she realized Luke wasn't at all interested in her submissive act.

"That's enough," Luke scolded her like a recalcitrant child.

The woman had the audacity to lean into him, pressing her breasts against his chest, and the look in her eyes was smoldering. She was definitely getting off on this. Taking a step back, Luke took inventory of those around him.

Great. Just fucking great.

He'd gotten the attention of damn near everyone in the club, including Lucie and Kane. The two of them were staring at him like another head had just sprouted from his shoulders. They shouldn't be all that surprised that he would lose his shit like this. It'd been a long time coming.

"Fuck," Luke groaned, running his hand through his hair before turning away from both Cole and Susie.

He needed to get out of there, and he needed to do it now. A glance and a nod in Kane's direction and the other man knew exactly what Luke expected. Kane was likely getting used to being in charge. Maybe he should consider giving him a raise. At least the club would be handled.

Before he could get five feet away, Cole was breathing down his neck, gripping his arm and jerking him around to look at him.

"You and I... we're going to talk. Tonight. I'll be at your place in a half hour. Don't you dare fucking run away," Cole told him before walking away.

Luke didn't have a chance to argue. That was fine with him. There would obviously be time to do that later. He only hoped the fire that ignited his blood had extinguished by then. If not, he couldn't be responsible for his own actions.

"Sam is taking Sierra back to your place," Logan stated when he fell into step with Luke. "She was in no shape to drive, so Sam convinced her to let her take her home. Only Sam had a few ideas of her own, and you can thank her for it later."

Luke glared at his brother through the fading red haze. "Logan —"

Before Luke could get another word out, Logan took a step in his direction. "Save the explanations for Sierra. She doesn't deserve this shit, man. You're a ticking time bomb, Luke, and if you don't get your shit together, you're not the only one who's going to get hurt in all of this," Logan stated, his jaw clenched tight. "If you want to self-implode, you go right ahead, the rest of us can't seem to get through to you. It's your fucking life, so do what you will. But, don't... don't you *dare* take Sierra down with you."

That was a threat if Luke had ever heard one. The words were loud and crystal clear as they ricocheted through Luke's confusion riddled brain. His brother was right about one thing... Luke was a ticking time bomb and heaven help anyone who got in his way tonight.

~~*~~

Twenty minutes later, breaking at least a handful of traffic laws and possibly the sound barrier on one occasion, Luke was pulling up to his house. Rather than pull into the garage, he haphazardly parked the big truck in the driveway and stormed into the house. Thankfully he'd managed to cool off at least a degree or two during the drive home, but now he wanted nothing more than to see Sierra. To explain.

Explain what, he didn't know. He only knew she deserved more than what he showed her tonight. For the last week, ever since that night with Sierra, Luke's chemical make-up had been altered. She made him feel something… want something… and it scared the living shit out of him. So, instead of manning up, he'd been doing his level best to avoid her. And yes, Cole had nailed it accurately. Luke had run away. Maybe not physically this time, but he'd definitely managed to exile himself from Sierra, and the woman had tried to give him the space he needed. Instead of explaining himself, he'd been the selfish bastard he'd always been, and he'd pushed her away.

"Sierra," Luke called out when he walked in the door, but there was no sign that anyone was in the house. His sister-in-law had a key because she and Logan had taken care of Bear while he'd been away, so he'd fully expected to see them both inside.

Fuck.

She wasn't there.

Bear came ambling out from the bedroom, obviously picking up on Luke's mood and staying on the sidelines. "Hey, Bear," Luke greeted the dog, who still didn't head toward him.

Maybe Cole could take a pointer from the dog and give Luke some space instead of showing up because one thing Luke knew for sure… he damn sure wasn't in the mood to argue with Cole. Right, wrong, or indifferent, Luke made his own choices, and now he had to face up to them. But the only person he cared to discuss it with was Sierra.

Luke stopped in the middle of his living room, staring around like he could conjure Sierra up with just his thoughts. If that was the case, she would have been in his bed every night for the last week, no matter what he had told her.

A loud knock on the door jerked Luke's attention and sent Bear into a barking frenzy. That wasn't Sierra. He knew by the sound of a large fist pounding on the door. "Sit," Luke scolded Bear before heading into the foyer.

Yanking the door open, Luke fully expected to come face to face with Cole, but instead, his brother stood on his front steps looking none too happy to be there. Glancing around, Luke figured he'd find Sam standing behind him, but no, Logan was apparently alone.

"What?" Luke asked, not feeling up to having company.

"Why don't you invite me in, bro," Logan said as he sidestepped him, not waiting for an invitation.

What the fuck? Shouldn't Logan be at home with his wife?

"What's the matter? Where's Sam?" Suddenly worried that something was wrong, Luke shut the door behind him and waited for the bad news.

"She's at home. Where I should be," Logan stated, sounding irritated. Without further explanation, Logan veered toward the kitchen, and Luke fell into step behind him.

"Then why are you here?"

"Because my meddling wife said I needed to come talk to you. When I tried to talk her out of it… with my tongue… she cut me off." Logan glared at him, then turned his attention to the refrigerator. Pulling out two beers, he handed one to Luke before taking a seat at the bar. "Fucking cut me off."

Luke wanted to laugh. Remembering the way Sam heated up the room with just her presence made Luke take a seat beside his brother. Adjusting himself, he got comfortable, opening his beer and tossing back half of it before looking at his brother again.

"What did we need to talk about?"

"Shit if I know." Logan smirked. "You got anything stronger than this?" he asked, tossing back the rest of his beer in one gulp.

Luke knew where this night was going. He'd spent a couple like this recently. Although he'd been alone at the time with a single shot glass and his buddy Jack. Getting up once more, he moved to the cabinet above the refrigerator where he kept the hard liquor and pulled out the bottle of Jack Daniel's he'd gotten so acquainted with. It was almost half empty – or was that half full? Shit. What did he care?

Two shot glasses in hand, Luke made his way back to the bar, this time choosing to stand on the opposite side as Logan. He poured a healthy amount in each glass and then scooted one in Logan's direction. "What are we toasting to?"

"Threesomes," Logan stated flatly.

Luke damn near choked and he hadn't even taken a drink. "Threesomes?"

"Yes. Let's toast to threesomes. May every man be lucky enough to watch the pleasure another man can bring his woman."

"Frequently and in every possible position," Luke added before clinking his glass with Logan's and tossing back the amber liquid.

"Damn that's good. Another," Logan said, pushing his empty glass forward.

Luke wasn't in the mood to argue, so he filled their glasses once again and pushed the second in front of Logan.

"Your turn." Logan looked up, clearly waiting for Luke to say something.

"To sex." Luke lifted his glass, waiting for Logan to click his glass against it.

"Sex? Seriously?" Logan laughed. "Surely you can be more creative than that."

"Nope, I was thinking the same thing about sex that I was about threesomes – frequently and in –"

"Every possible position," Logan chimed in, clinking his glass against Luke's.

"Another." Logan slammed his glass down. "So now that we know the truth... my life is clearly lacking threesomes, and yours is lacking sex in general, why don't we solve both our problems and go back to my house."

And there it was. Luke knew his brother was disappointed in the fact that Luke hadn't been an active participant in their midnight rendezvous, but he just couldn't bring himself to do it. Not that he didn't want to feel Sam's mouth wrapped around his cock, or the silky, warmth of her pussy as he fucked her from every possible angle. Those would always be fond memories, but Luke had apparently evolved.

Or maybe he'd just lost his fucking mind.

"Don't be stingy with the liquor," Logan said as he pulled the bottle out of Luke's grasp and filled both glasses once again. "And don't worry; I'm only giving you shit about the threesomes," Logan clarified before tossing back the next shot, a toast apparently not needed.

Not wanting to be left behind, Luke took the shot and felt the heat wash through him, his vision becoming just a little fuzzy while his ears were starting to ring.

"I've actually thought about talking to Tag," Logan admitted, glancing up at Luke as though he expected a reaction.

"Tag Murphy?" As if Luke needed to clarify. How many Tag's did they actually know?

"One and the same," Logan slurred, reaching for the bottle again.

So apparently Logan had come over to comfort Luke, for whatever reason, and was seeking his own comfort in the bottle of whiskey that was now… three quarters of the way empty. At this rate, he'd have to pull out another bottle.

"So, why Tag?" Luke inquired, getting that backup bottle. Just in case.

"I've seen the way Sam looks at him. I mean, how could she not? The man's built like a brick shithouse."

That was the damn truth. Tag Murphy was one of the newest members of Club Destiny, and one mean looking son of a bitch. Apparently the women thought he was hot, or so he'd heard. Cole had actually introduced Luke and Logan to Tag and not long after, the man had asked about joining the club. Luke was a little surprised that Logan would even consider the man. "I figured you'd talk to Dylan."

Logan didn't seem surprised by the idea, but he turned his attention back on the bottle. "I thought about it. I just don't know if he's in the right place in his head right now."

Another round was poured and Luke tossed his back as fast as his brother, his legs suddenly feeling incredibly heavy. "No, you're probably right." Pulling out the barstool beside Logan, Luke slid into it, wanting to remain vertical as long as possible.

"What the fuck is going on with you and Sierra?" Logan asked after a few minutes of silence. Although he managed to butcher Sierra's name, thanks to the whiskey.

"Hell if I know."

Logan's face contorted, and he suddenly looked… sad. Shit, just what Luke needed, a sappy drunk that wanted to talk.

"From the moment I met that woman, I thought she would be your perfect match. Physically she isn't what you normally go for, I get that."

Logan was accurate in that respect. Luke didn't go for tiny, petite women. At six feet five, two hundred and forty pounds, women like Sierra scared him. He was damn near twice her size, and he feared he would hurt her. But she had proven just how fragile she wasn't, and the thought made his dick stir.

"But the woman's a firecracker," Logan continued, apparently not needing Luke to contribute to the conversation. When he picked up the bottle and began to slosh the liquid into the glasses, Luke knew they were damn near at their limit. How many had they had anyway?

"That she is," Luke agreed, taking the bottle from his brother and filling the shot glasses once more. This had to be the last one or they would both be flat on their faces in the next few minutes. "And she's hot as hell. Granted, she's not Sam, but the woman is a beauty."

Logan's words began to get closer and closer together and Luke had a hard time understanding him. Or maybe that was Luke's brain running the words together.

"I love her." *Holy fuck!* Where the *hell* had that come from?

Logan turned to Luke like his hair had just gone up in flames, and Luke knew he'd actually said the words out loud.

"I knew it!" Logan slammed the glass on the bar. "I fucking knew it."

As though Logan had just figured out the cure for cancer, his eyes lit up, and a smile split his face. Luke couldn't help but laugh. Yes, damn it, he loved her.

"Let's drink to that," Logan slurred, *drink* coming out more like *shrink.*

They tossed down another shot and this time Luke damn near fell off of the barstool. His eyes crossed, and his vision went gray on the edges. Time to call it a night.

No sense in staying up any longer… Logan had apparently been successful in getting Luke to talk.

~~*~~

Good God.

Someone must have hit Luke square in the face with an anvil. That was the first thought that sprung to Luke's mind the next morning when he awoke to the sun bathing the edges of the bed through the blind's wooden slats.

"Sonuvabitch." Apparently that was fast becoming one of his favorite words these days.

Throwing his arm over his eyes, he attempted to shut out the blinding light and to hold his brains inside of his head. Whiskey was not his friend in the morning that was for damn sure.

Temptation

Despite the throb behind his eyes, Luke's mind immediately drifted to the night before. And it didn't have anything to do with the fifth of whiskey he and his brother had downed. He couldn't get his mind off of Sierra. Or Cole. And the way he'd successfully managed to push the two of them away. Likely for good this time.

Fucking idiot.

What the hell was Luke supposed to do now?

When the answers didn't just spring forth, not that he really expected them to, Luke pushed himself to the edge of the bed. He knew of one thing. He had to get his ass out of bed and attempt to salvage the two things that actually meant something to him.

He just didn't know exactly how he was supposed to do that.

Chapter Twenty Six

"Yes, ma'am." Sierra rolled her eyes as she managed to remember her manners. The woman deserved to be called a few choice other things, but at the moment, Sierra knew her reputation was on the line. Not that she should care. She was going back to Nashville, right? At least that was the plan she had drafted in her mind the night before. It had sounded so finite when she had shared the news with Sam.

"No, ma'am." Once again Sierra let the woman drone on and on while she tossed in the expected answer where necessary. "Yes, of course I can be there this afternoon. I'll see you then."

Gritting her teeth as she pressed the end button on her cell phone, Sierra resigned herself to the fact that her shitty day had just gotten shittier. At least she had a few hours to build up the nerve required to spend another afternoon sitting in a room with Susan Toulmin while the woman proceeded to tell her in no uncertain terms what a terrible designer she was. The thought that this was the last time she had to see the woman was the only thing that would get her through the afternoon.

She needed caffeine in a bad way. And maybe some aspirin. A *bottle* of aspirin. After the night she had, most of it spent pathetically sobbing her eyes out as she curled into a ball on her bed, Sierra wasn't surprised by the furious pounding behind her eyes. Pushing her weary body up from the couch, she ventured into the kitchen. Coffee would go a long way toward ridding her brain of the fuzz left over from the night before. Maybe.

After she had rushed out of Club Destiny, almost plowing right over Cole, Sierra had managed to make it to her car just in time to realize she was in no shape to drive. Thankfully Sam must have known because the woman came to her rescue and offered to drive her home.

Well, not home exactly.

Her original intention was to take Sierra to Luke's, but she managed to tell her friend that under no circumstance would she be caught dead at Luke's house. She was done with the man.

Finished. Through. Kaput.
Damn him.

Through a haze of tears, Sierra made her way to the coffee pot. She'd be damned if she would shed one more tear for that rat bastard. Let him have Susan Toulmin… *the bitch*. They deserved each other.

At least that's what she tried to tell herself as she filled the carafe with water and tossed coffee grounds into the flimsy paper filter. Her brain was fully onboard with her plan to banish Luke McCoy from all conscious thought. Her heart not so much.

Standing barefoot in the kitchen, waiting for the coffee to brew, Sierra choked down two aspirin and then took the time to look around. Her little rental hadn't become much of a home in the last few months. Which meant she had very little to pack up and take with her. Mostly her clothes and a couple of pieces of furniture.

The thought of going back to Nashville was bittersweet. She hadn't yet gotten comfortable with Dallas. *Big fat liar*. Truth be told, when Sierra had been with Luke and Cole, she'd felt more at home than any one place she had ever lived. Her heart sank right into her stomach at the thought. None of it mattered. He'd made his choice, and clearly it hadn't been her.

To top it all off, Sierra received a call from Cole just before dawn. She'd answered the phone, still groggy from sleep, secretly hoping it was Luke on the other end of the line, calling to grovel at her feet and profess his undying love.

So not the case.

However, the sound of Cole's deep, familiar voice had her nerves settling and a spark of hope igniting in her chest. Whatever for, she had no idea. After she assured him that yes, she was all right, and yes, she did get home in one piece, they said their goodbyes. Little did Cole know that Sierra's goodbye had been more final than he might have thought. She was going back to Nashville and Dallas would be just a little blip on the roadmap of her life.

The coffee gurgled to completion and Sierra grabbed one of the boring, white coffee cups she had picked up at the dollar store when she had moved in. No need to go out and find something that would cheer her up. At least not yet. She'd have plenty of time to do that when she got back home to Tennessee where she belonged. She would likely have to buy another house since hers was currently rented. That would ensure she couldn't have a momentary relapse and wind up back in the Big D.

A pounding on the front door had her sloshing coffee in her cup, the hot, black liquid spilling over and onto her shirt. "Damn it."

Setting the cup on the counter and grabbing a hand towel, Sierra attempted to wipe off the now cooling liquid as she headed for the door.

The door. *Oh, shit.*

Who the hell would be at her door that early in the morning? Whoever it was, she shouldn't answer it. The knock thundered again, eliminating the hope that it might have been Sam coming to check on her. Definitely not a dainty, feminine knock. Her traitorous legs moved closer to the door and Sierra found herself glancing through the peephole, praying that it wouldn't be...

Whew! It wasn't.

Gripping the handle, Sierra pulled back the door, still trying to dry her now damp t-shirt.

"Hey." Cole's beautiful face peered down at her, those indigo blue eyes caressing every inch of her skin as he took her in.

"What's up?" she asked, doing her best to sound nonchalant but feeling a little unsteady from the intensity of his gaze.

"Can I come in?" He was halfway through the door as he asked the question, apparently sure of her answer. Good thing because she hadn't been... sure that is.

"Ok." Stepping back so he could come inside, Sierra felt incredibly small once again. She'd gotten used to being around Luke, but Cole still had the ability to make her feel utterly feminine and incredibly fragile.

Realizing she was still trying to dry her shirt, she tossed the hand towel onto the back of the chair and turned away from Cole. "I need to, um, change. I'll be right back." See, that wasn't so hard. She could talk to this man. There was no reason to get all flustered when he was around.

Sierra double timed it to her bedroom, ripped the stained t-shirt up and over her head, tossing it in the direction of the clothes hamper in the corner and missing it entirely. What was wrong with her? When she reached for the dresser drawer, she noticed her hands were shaking. And not some little vibration either. No, this was a full blown earthquake in her limbs.

Temptation

She wasn't aware how long she stood there, staring down at her hands, but the next thing she knew, Cole was coming up behind her, turning her in his arms and pressing her against his chest. She pressed her damp – *shit, she was crying* – cheek against his broad torso, her hands snaking around his waist. His masculine scent filled her nostrils and soothed her frazzled nerves.

"Baby, it's going to be all right," Cole muttered, running his hand through her hair as he cupped her head, holding her against him.

How did he know it would be all right? How did he even know what the problem was? She sure as hell didn't.

And when had he taken to calling her such an endearment? Baby?

A sudden flash of memory had Sierra gripping Cole tighter. The remembered way that this man made love to her while they were alone in Vegas had heat coursing through every limb, chasing away the icy chill that had been in residence since the night before. On top of that, she had the scorching hot reminder of Valentine's and the way he had settled between her legs…

What was she doing?

To her relief, Cole took a step back, but when he tilted her head back to meet his gaze, Sierra's stomach nearly plummeted to the floor. The heat in his eyes was hot enough to scorch the sun.

"God, I've missed you," he whispered.

Missed her?

"I've missed you too." *She had?* What the hell was going on?

Sierra was mesmerized by the midnight blue depths of his eyes, the way he looked at her, the way his fingers felt on her chin, the heat emanating off of his massive body… she was in trouble here.

"I'm going to kiss you, Sierra," Cole stated, his voice low and intense.

Heaven help her, the only thing she could do was nod and anticipate the sweet, seductive feel of his mouth on hers.

The room disappeared when his lips came down to meet hers, and she was lost to the tender, gentle way he plied her mouth open with his tongue. This wasn't hot and fierce, though her blood was boiling and she wanted nothing more than to climb his body. No, Cole was making love to her mouth, using his tongue to delve gently, taking up residence, filling her with longing and need.

The next few minutes passed in a blur, their bodies melding together, their clothes quickly falling to the floor to be forgotten as Cole eased Sierra down onto her rumpled bed, sliding between her thighs as she held on for dear life. If only he would take her like a starving man, she might stand a chance of surviving the sensual onslaught. Instead, Cole eased between her legs, his mouth devouring every inch of her skin, taking long minutes to tease her nipple – one and then the other – until Sierra was nearly blinded with lust. She needed to *feel* him.

"Look at me."

Sierra had been lost to the sensations, her eyes closed, her head thrown back, but his voice lured her to the present.

Opening her eyes, she was struck with tenderness. The way Cole looked at her said so much more than words ever could. This was so much like the last time they had been together in Vegas, yet so very different. His emotions were written clearly on his face, and Sierra choked back a sob as she pulled him closer.

"You don't know how bad I've wanted to bury myself inside of you again," Cole whispered, his lips a hairsbreadth away from hers. "It's nearly killed me having to stay away from you."

Sierra inched downward, trying to align their bodies, wanting to feel him inside of her. With his weight hovering above her, she couldn't move, so she did the next best thing. "Make love to me, Cole." The whispered words tore from her chest, the emotions coming out with them as she wrapped her arms around his neck, pulling him down until their lips met once more.

Her body opened to him, taking him in until she wasn't sure where she ended and he began; an all too familiar cliché she hadn't fully understood until that moment when their bodies joined in the most elemental of ways.

"You feel so good," Sierra moaned, unable to hold herself back.

He lifted her knee, holding it close to his side, changing the angle as he slid slowly in, before retreating. Over and over he filled her. Sierra wanted the moment to last forever, wanted to remember the way it felt in Cole's arms, making love to him, giving him her very soul. Because when it was over, she knew she would have to walk away.

She couldn't possibly love two men. And how could she ever believe she and Cole weren't settling?

"So tight, baby," Cole groaned.

Sierra lost herself to the sensations, Cole's impressive body above her, his seductive mouth doing wicked things to hers. When he slid his rough, strong hands down her arms until their palms touched, fingers intertwining together, then lifting them above her head, Sierra knew she was a goner. There was too much emotion involved. She wasn't going to survive with her heart intact if he kept doing what he was doing.

"Faster," she pleaded, trying to pull him closer, trying to buck beneath him, needing to ratchet the heat up a notch so he wouldn't look at her like that. Like she was all he ever wanted. Pressing her mouth to his, she closed her eyes, needing to put some distance between them, even if only in her mind.

"Look at me, Sierra," Cole stated once more, breaking the kiss. "Look at me."

The demand was unexpected, but she stared back into his eyes, hoping he'd see everything he wanted to find.

"I love you, Sierra," he whispered the words, but Sierra's heart heard them like they had been shouted through a canyon, the meaning ricocheting through her until… she shattered.

Cole groaned, his body tensing as he held still above her, his release filling her body while his words filled all of the dark spaces inside of her. For the life of her, Sierra couldn't say the words out loud, but she knew…

She definitely knew she would never be the same.

~~*~~

Cole couldn't have moved if he wanted to. Lying in the darkened room, Sierra's soft body pressed up against his side, he accepted that he'd died and gone to heaven. That was the only explanation for what had just happened. He had made love to Sierra. And what they had just done couldn't be categorized any other way.

He'd taken his chances coming to her house that morning. After spending the last two months sitting on the sidelines, waiting for Luke to make up his mind, to figure out what the hell it was he wanted other than mind blowing sex, Cole had somehow managed to fall in love with this one small woman. But that's where normal ended, and unusual picked up, because what Cole was feeling couldn't be described any other way.

Being pulled in two different directions was not uncommon for Cole, but when it came to his emotions, this situation couldn't have been more outrageous if he'd dreamed it up himself. The night before, he'd wanted nothing more than to pull up to Luke's house, barge in and demand the man wake the fuck up and take notice. Instead, he'd talked some sense into himself and gone home to an empty house. Too much had been at stake, and thankfully, Cole had come to his senses before he made the biggest mistake of his life.

Second biggest, actually. The first had been coming to Sierra's that morning and giving in to the temptation that had eaten away at him for weeks.

Lying beside her, Cole recognized the mistake, knowing he'd never be able to just walk away from her again. It didn't matter how he felt about Luke, there was a part of himself that was reserved solely for this woman.

Maybe he should have remained on the sidelines, played the third like he'd been doing for years. That would have been the easy way out. Unfortunately, he couldn't sit back any longer. He did what was expected of him, he walked away from Sierra although it tore him apart to do so. He sat back and waited for Luke to figure out what he wanted and where did that leave him? It left him wondering just what the fuck he was doing.

Coming to see Sierra hadn't been a calculated move. According to Sam, Sierra was leaving, and Cole couldn't bring himself to sit back and let her just walk away without showing her – no, telling her – exactly what he felt for her.

Sierra stirred in his arms and he pulled her closer. Her slim thigh slid over his while her hand drifted over his chest, and Cole wished like hell that they never had to leave the bed.

~~*~~

Luke felt the tension in his shoulders the second he pulled into Sierra's driveway, taking note of the all too familiar truck parked on the street in front of the house. There was no mistaking the huge black Silverado and that could only mean one thing. Cole had found another place to go the night before.

Temptation

After last night, Luke wasn't prepared to face Sierra or Cole, let alone both of them together. And he wasn't sure he could explain the emotions churning through him. His brilliant idea to show up at Sierra's house, pray that she would let him through the door, now seemed like a rash decision. What had he been thinking?

And wasn't that the fucking question of the hour. Luke had done nothing but think for the last two hours. Ever since he woke up in his bed alone, he'd contemplated the result of his actions. The way he'd purposely pushed Sierra away, the way he'd denied whatever it was he had begun to feel for Cole, although, for the life of him, he didn't understand it.

Explaining it away didn't make things any easier. The fact of it was, Luke was so totally screwed. He'd gone and fallen in love with Sierra. That wasn't all that surprising. The woman was incredible. In every single possible way. So sweet, so sensual, and so damn beautiful his eyes hurt to look at her. Those glowing blue eyes penetrated his very soul, and she saw so much more than anyone else had ever bothered to.

On top of that, he'd somehow let himself feel something for Cole. Sure, he'd been shocked by the way he had reacted to the man that night at his house so many months ago. When Cole had gone to his knees... *fuck*.

The top of Luke's head had damn near come right off when Cole had gone to his knees and sucked him into the deep, hot recesses of his mouth. Until that moment, Luke had never known anything like it. He had only known his own need to possess the man, to own him. He needed Cole's total surrender and he had received it. Cole's rough touch had assuaged an ache Luke had thought would never be soothed. An ache that had taken up residence inside of him and longed to be sated.

Shutting off the truck, Luke opened his door and stepped down. His heart was beating like he'd just run a mile. What was he about to walk into?

No, he wasn't naïve enough to believe Cole and Sierra hadn't found solace in one another. Hell, he'd pushed them away. Both of them. And neither of them had done anything except try to be what Luke needed.

He hadn't thought about Cole's declaration from last night until he stepped out of his front door that morning. Cole had said, or more accurately, threatened, that he was coming by. Unless Luke had been too damn drunk, which was quite possible, but highly doubtful, Cole had never made it to his house. And seeing his black Chevy in front of Sierra's house told him why.

With resigned steps, Luke managed to make it to the front door. He hesitated briefly before he pounded his fist on the wood, his heart suddenly lodged in his throat. What was he going to say to her? Would she even listen to him?

When no one answered, Luke tried the knob. Finding it unlocked, he pushed the door open and invited himself in. Gently closing the door behind him, trying to make as little noise as possible, Luke wondered what he was about to walk into. Before he could turn around, Luke found himself slammed chest first into the door, Cole's impressive size pressed up against him from behind.

"What the fuck is wrong with you?" Luke bellowed, pushing Cole off of him, making him stagger back a couple of steps before Luke turned and Cole was up in his face.

"*Me*? What the fuck is wrong with *me*? That's the same question I have for you." Cole's deep baritone reverberated through the room, bouncing off of the walls and back at them.

Luke felt the burning rage ignite inside of him once again, and he pushed Cole with everything he had, sending the man flying back into the opposite wall before Luke descended on him.

"Oh my God!" Sierra's shriek startled them both, and Luke staggered back when Cole launched himself at him once again, this time losing his footing as both men went to the floor. *Sonuvabitch.* They landed with a thud on the carpet, rolling until Luke was on top of Cole.

"What are you two doing? Stop it!" Sierra screamed, scolding them both like they were children.

Luke ignored Sierra, staring down into Cole's face, expecting to see rage, or anger, or anything except what he did see. The dark, midnight blue eyes staring back at him reflected none of those things, only… affliction.

"What the fuck are you doing here?" Luke growled, trying to keep his voice low, but knowing Sierra would hear everything regardless of how quiet he tried to be.

"I want him here," Sierra stated, answering the question for Cole.

Luke ignored her, waiting for Cole to answer for himself.

"She's leaving," Cole choked out, not trying to move.

What?

"What are you talking about?" With a huff, Luke pushed off of him and stood.

"Sierra's going back to Nashville," Cole stated, all of the anger seemingly draining from his body as he pushed himself up off of the floor, his eyes darting between Luke and Sierra, finally landing on Sierra. "She's leaving."

Luke stared at the beautiful woman standing in the middle of her living room, draped in a black sheet, her hair in disarray, looking like she'd just… crawled out of bed. *Shit*. He was too late.

"What does he mean you're leaving?" Luke asked Sierra pointedly, trying to ignore the fact that Cole and Sierra must have just come out of the bedroom. Sierra didn't answer; she simply glanced at Cole as though trying to figure him out.

"Sam called me last night," Cole admitted, taking a step closer to Sierra. "She told me you were going back to Nashville."

Fully expecting Sierra to set the story straight, to reassure both of them that she wasn't going anywhere, Luke held his breath as he waited for her response.

"I am," Sierra whispered, a single tear rolling down her cheek.

"What?" Luke's stomach knotted, and he clenched his fists at his side. The sudden need to hit something overwhelmed him and he had to remember where he was. "Why?"

"There's nothing for me here," Sierra said, wiping that lone tear away. "I tried. I really did."

Was she trying to convince him or herself? Luke knew she'd tried. She'd done everything that could be expected of a woman and he still succeeded in pushing her away. And now, as he stood in Sierra's house, only feet from the two people he needed more than he needed oxygen, Luke felt his body come to life. Apparently heartbreak wasn't even enough to dispel the sensual need these two aroused in him.

"Shit," Cole stated, turning his back on Sierra.

"I'm sorry," she said, taking a step closer to him, not looking at Luke.

Cole surprised Luke when he turned around quickly. "You don't have anything to be sorry about."

When his penetrating glare landed on him, Luke knew what Cole was getting at. "What do you want from me?" Luke growled back at Cole, fury lighting him up from within.

Cole turned to face him, and Luke noticed Sierra was stepping backward, leaving them alone in the living room. He wanted to call out to her, but the intent look on Cole's face captivated him.

"I don't know what's wrong with you, man, but this shit has to stop," Cole said, his voice low. "You've been running for too long."

"Fuck you," Luke barked, his hands clenching at his sides. He was sick and fucking tired of being told that. He hadn't run last night, had he? No, he'd gone home where he was supposed to go, looking for Sierra and waiting for Cole. Neither of them had shown up. But he didn't fucking run. "What the fuck does it matter to you, anyway?" Luke asked, suddenly feeling like the outsider.

"Are you serious? Are you that fucking dense, Luke?"

"Why are you even here?" Luke choked out. "Why aren't you with Lucie?"

"Lucie? Why the hell would I be with Lucie?" Cole asked, sincere confusion contorting his features.

"I saw the way you two looked at each other. I know you're paying the doctor bills. I know you care about that little girl." Luke found himself rambling, but couldn't seem to stop.

"Yes, I care about her, and I care about Lucie. She's a friend of mine, and that's what friends do."

"Friends? I saw the way you looked at her. That looked like more than friends to me."

"No, Luke. You saw what you wanted to see. Lucie and I are friends. That's it. That's all it ever will be." Cole's tone had cooled considerably.

Was that true? Had Luke projected his own thoughts on Cole? Had he tried to find something to explain the wedge he'd inserted between them all on his own? Yes, damn it. That's exactly what he had done. The same thing he had done with Sierra...

Sierra.

She was leaving.

For good.

"You're full of shit," Luke said, his voice coming out as a choked whisper. He wasn't sure if he was talking to himself or to Cole. All of the adrenaline drained from his body as he leaned against the wall thankful there was something to hold him up.

"The only woman I care about, the only one I have ever cared about is Sierra. Cole stated solemnly. "But she's not the only person I care about."

Luke stared into the depths of Cole's eyes, seeing something he'd always known was there, but something he hoped he'd been wrong about. Something he'd refused to acknowledge.

"It's always been about *you*." Defeat tinged Cole's words and Luke felt a hard tug on his heart.

What had he done?

Sierra's sharp intake of breath told Luke she was still there. He didn't look away from Cole. He couldn't. The man's admission had stunned him. Ok, so maybe he'd had an idea of how Cole felt about him, but the denial he'd shrouded himself in didn't allow him to dwell on it. And now… now he didn't know what the hell he was supposed to do.

"Obviously not nearly as much as you say. I know you were with her in Vegas. When I left," Luke said, not sure what the accusation meant at this point. Up until today, Luke had wondered if Cole and Sierra had gotten together. Hell, he had actually hoped they had at one point. But now he was certain of it. And by the looks of it, there was more between these two than just sex.

"I was. I've never denied it. She needed me and damn it, I needed her," Cole admitted, and the red haze began to cloud Luke's vision once more. The feeling was anomalous, considering the types of relationships, or lack thereof, that Cole and Luke had once engaged in. Luke wasn't used to this possessiveness that overcame him; the desire to have Sierra all to himself defied logic.

"Christ, Luke! What the hell did you expect me to do?" Cole asked, pacing the open area, not looking at Sierra. "You walked out on us – um… *her*. She needed someone to comfort her."

Luke looked at Cole. Really looked at him. The little slip of the tongue wasn't lost on him, but for the life of him, he didn't know what to say. Yes, Luke overreacted in Vegas. Yes, he walked out on Sierra. And yes, God help him, he walked out on Cole… numerous times. What did that mean for them? Did he want it to mean more? *Did* it mean more?

"But you fell for her, didn't you?" Luke asked, not wanting to hear the answer, but needing to just the same. Cole's penetrating gaze rooted Luke in place. He had. Cole had fallen for Sierra, the same way Luke had. Only Cole managed to stay away from her, at least for a little while. "You love her."

Cole didn't answer, and the silence told Luke everything he needed to know.

"Do you love him?" Luke asked, turning to Sierra. He was on the verge of having a breakdown and her response could very well send him over the edge.

Chapter Twenty Seven

Sierra didn't know how to answer the question.

If she told the truth, she would hurt Luke. Although the truth was much more complicated than just how much she cared for Cole. She was in love with Luke, was pretty sure she had been all along. But how did she explain that?

"I love you both." *Well, that was easy.* Sierra's gaze didn't waver from Luke's as she waited for his response. The words had tumbled out of her mouth before she had thought better of them. "But that doesn't change anything."

"What do you mean it doesn't change anything?" This time Cole was the one to speak up. "It changes *everything*."

"No. It doesn't," Sierra argued, turning back to her bedroom. She'd attempted to sneak away a few minutes ago so she could get dressed, but the turn in conversation had kept her rooted in place.

"Sierra. Stop."

Why was it that Luke's grumbling voice had the power to stop her in her tracks? She needed to get away from here. And not just to her bedroom. No, she needed to put some miles between them or she wasn't going to stand a chance of getting over Luke McCoy. But no… her perfidious body chose to stop before she made it out of the room.

"We have to finish this," Luke demanded, and Sierra jerked back toward him, ready to give him hell for all he had put her through.

"*Finish* this?" A giant bubble of anger and hurt swelled up inside of her and Sierra marched the few feet in his direction until she could smell that sexy, intoxicating scent of man. "*Finish* this?" she repeated. "As far as I'm concerned, Luke McCoy, you *finished* this last night."

Tears threatened behind her eyelids, and Sierra fought down the knot that formed in her throat.

"What do you want from me, Sierra?" Luke's voice lowered, a whispered rumble that shook Sierra to her core.

"Are you so dense that you really don't get it?" she asked, staring up into those green-brown eyes searching for something that would help her get through this. "I don't want anything *from* you." The terse words were loud in the silence of her house. "I only want *you.*" Turning to face Cole, Sierra caught the tortured expression moments before he masked it. "And I want you too. Heaven help me, I love both of you and this is killing me."

Sierra sobbed, the strangled sound forcing the tears from her eyes. This time there was no stopping when she turned and all but ran from the room. She couldn't take it anymore. Her heart was splitting in two, and through all of the pain, through all of the misery, she felt as though she had been torn in half.

When it happened, or how it happened, Sierra didn't know, but she had come to terms with the fact that she loved them both. With the backs of her hands, Sierra brushed away the tears. They were useless. They would get her nowhere. The fact of the matter was she was in love with two men. Two very different men and for the life of her, she didn't know how to deal with it.

She saw the way Cole looked at Luke. She knew he harbored some deep feelings for Luke, but she didn't know if he would ever divulge that information. Or maybe he had. And where did that leave Luke? To make a choice?

A quick glance at the clock told Sierra she didn't have time to sit around and figure out what Luke was going to do. She couldn't predict him any more than she could predict the weather. She had an appointment with Susan Toulmin in a few of hours, and though she didn't have any desire to be raked over hot coals twice in one day, Sierra knew she had to go.

Dropping the sheet to the floor, she walked to the bathroom and turned on the water. Hopefully Cole and Luke could let themselves out because she'd had enough for one day. The water hadn't yet heated up by the time she stepped in, so she let the icy rivers flow over her skin, through her hair. The blessed numbness that came along with it was a welcome relief from the emotion churning inside of her.

Closing her eyes, she tilted her head back, letting the water flow over her, trying her best to forget what had happened just that morning. The way Cole made love to her, the way he held her afterward, the thoughts heated her from the inside out.

The sound of the glass door opening had Sierra blinking her eyes open, expecting to see Cole standing in front of her, but surprised when he wasn't the only one. There before her were the two most impressive male specimen she had ever seen. Neither of them wore shirts, but they both still had on their jeans, so their next move startled her.

Before she had a chance to blink, both men were inside the glass shower stall with her, filling the space and crushing her between their two massive bodies.

"We don't all fit in here," she stated unnecessarily as the two men maneuvered around her.

"We'll fit." Luke's dark, hungry voice washed over her and the water temperature was no longer an issue because her blood heated despite her need to put space between them – both physical and emotional apparently.

Cole pressed up against her back, pulling her until she leaned into him, his arms wrapping around her.

"What are you doing?" she groaned as Luke went to his knees in front of her.

"What we should have been doing all along," Cole whispered in her ear, his rough callused hands roamed down her chest, cupping her breasts, making her skin sing with heated relief.

"Open your legs." Luke's voice sounded more rough than usual, making Sierra spread her legs without conscious thought. Standing between the two men reminded her of Vegas, when Luke had used his tongue to torture her in the most sensual of ways. She longed for him to do the same now, but the rational side of her brain was warning her that this was wrong. This wasn't doing anything to increase the distance between them that she so desperately needed.

But it felt oh so right.

The raspy feel of Luke's tongue as he snaked between the folds of her pussy, lapping at her, caressing her ever so slowly was enough to make her mind go blank. When Cole used his thumb and index fingers to pinch each one of her nipples, alternating between soft pulls and harder tweaks, Sierra leaned her head back and let the rapture take over.

"Open your eyes." Cole's warm breath teased her ear as he plucked at the lobe with his teeth. "Watch him."

Sierra couldn't watch him because the erotic scene playing out in her shower was hot enough to have her knees turning to rubber. She wanted to grind against Luke's mouth, to force him to that one spot guaranteed to make her body hum with pleasure.

"Open." Cole punctuated the word by pinching her nipples simultaneously and biting the sensitive skin on the back of her neck.

Sierra's eyes flew open, making direct contact with Luke's as he stared up at her, his tongue thrusting while he gripped her hips, pulling her forward, increasing the pressure. God the man could do wicked things with that tongue.

Then the warmth of the man behind her disappeared as Cole lowered himself to the tiled floor, his callused hands caressing every inch of her skin as he went down. Hot kisses trailed down her spine and Sierra's skin prickled, goose bumps igniting over every inch, her nipples puckering painfully. She needed more. She needed something...

Suddenly her legs were spread awkwardly, and she had to reach for the small shelf to maintain her balance as Luke's lips latched onto her clit, sucking and pulling while Cole's hands spread her butt cheeks wide, his wicked mouth doing the most erotic, forbidden things.

He wasn't shy about his intent, his tongue working easily to turn her into a quivering mass, doing those erotic things that she had only read about. Sierra had never known how good it could feel to have that hidden, forbidden part of her stroked the way both of these men tended to do. God it was agonizing and extreme all at the same time, pushing her higher, making her tingle. And although she had been the filling in their sandwich before, this was a different kind of torture, an entirely foreign experience that had her gripping the shelf, almost biting her tongue to keep from crying out until...

Sierra screamed as her orgasm rushed over her, starbursts shot behind her eyelids while warmth trickled through every limb, every extremity, her mind all but shutting down from the intensity.

Thankfully they were both there to catch her, to hold her as they stood to their full heights once again, keeping her crushed between them. And then it dawned on her that they were still at least partially clothed.

"Take your jeans off," she stated firmly, much more firmly than she anticipated. Both men glowered at her as though she had lost her mind and she followed up the direct order with, "Now."

Luke was more hesitant than Cole, but he did as she instructed, flipping the button out of the mooring and lowering the zipper, revealing that sexy patch of toned skin that disappeared farther into his jeans. After moments of turning her head back and forth, trying to watch both men at the same time, Sierra realized she could make this so much easier on herself.

The shower was too confining anyway, and the hot water heater was apparently running low, so she flipped the knob to off, and turned her attention back to both men.

"Out," she ordered, reaching for one of the oversized towels she kept on the shelf beside the shower stall.

"Bossy woman," Luke muttered beneath his breath and Sierra smiled in return.

She handed an extra towel to Cole and instructed him to dry Luke while she used the other to dry herself and then Cole. The look both men shot her was full of skepticism, but she easily ignored them. When Cole hesitated, she swatted him on the butt, catching his attention and making Luke smile.

He'd quickly replace that smirk with a groan if she had anything to say about it. After drying quickly and rubbing the cotton over Cole's magnificent form, Sierra tossed the wet towel to the floor, moving to stand just to the side of both men. "He's still wet."

Sierra wasn't sure where the overwhelming flood of feminine power had come from, but she was using it to her advantage for now. This might very well be the last time the three of them were together, which she wouldn't think about right now, and she intended to at least right a few wrongs in the process.

Cole rubbed the towel slowly over Luke's chest, their gazes locked on one another. Sierra watched as their chests began to rise and fall more quickly than before. They were turned on. She was turned on. Just watching the way Cole touched Luke, knowing he wanted to do so much more than just touch him, emboldened her.

"On your knees," she instructed Cole, and that caused the man's head to snap back in her direction like his neck was a rubber band. She kept her expression serious, hoping she could maintain her composure.

Suddenly Luke helped her out because he got Cole's attention with his gruffly muttered instruction. "On your knees."

The heat in his eyes radiated outward, making Sierra realize Luke had been waiting for this moment longer than she had. Apparently his denial kept him away from Cole, but if the hot, fierce way he consumed the man with his eyes was anything to go by, he wasn't holding back any longer.

When Luke added, "Both of you," Sierra raised a questioning brow. Since when had he taken control of the situation?

Oh hell, who was she kidding? Luke had always had control. He owned her, as Cole so eloquently put it that long ago day in Vegas. He owned every part of her.

She kicked the unused towel with her foot, moving it closer to Luke's feet, and she slowly went to her knees, waiting for Cole as he was much more defiant than she was.

Luke solved that problem by placing a hand on Cole's muscled shoulder, easing him down until they were both kneeling before him, his cock standing proudly out from his body. Luke slid his hand into Cole's shaggy, blond hair, holding his head firmly as he brushed the head of his cock against the man's lips. Sierra watched with utter fascination as Cole continued to defy Luke, keeping his mouth closed. The muscle ticked in his jaw, and Sierra could see the lust in Cole's eyes. He wanted this. He wanted this more than she did, but he didn't give in the way she had. Which was what Luke needed.

The sudden realization was enlightening. She understood what made Luke tick, what made him hold himself back. He might need to dominate, he might need to control, but he didn't want it to be easy. Knowing how easily he played her, how much she would give him, Sierra understood what he craved from Cole. Had he ever accepted that fact?

"Open," Luke groaned the word, apparently losing his grip on the control he so desperately sought to maintain.

Sierra watched, noticing the way Luke gripped Cole's hair tighter, seeing the pain etched on Cole's face from how hard Luke was pulling, but the man didn't seem to mind. Instead, his lips parted, and his tongue darted out in the most sensually erotic moment Sierra had ever witnessed. Sure, she had watched the two men in Vegas, but honestly she had been so overwhelmed by the sheer pleasure, the memories were faded. To see the scene before her so up close and personal, Sierra wanted nothing more than to be a bystander so she could take in every aspect, note every ounce of pleasure these two men brought to one another.

Luke thrust forcefully past Cole's lips, past his teeth and then held himself still as Cole enveloped his steel hard shaft. Sierra felt the moisture pool between her legs, felt her clit begin to throb as Cole began to consume Luke's cock, doing everything that Luke had taught her he liked. Effortlessly.

Luke's grip on Cole's hair didn't lessen, nor did Cole's apparent desire. Within seconds Cole was gripping Luke's hard muscled thighs, pulling Luke closer, giving himself over to the man while Sierra watched. She got the impression that Cole enjoyed her watching. Using her fingernails, she couldn't keep from touching him any longer; Sierra gently scored his back, raking her nails lightly up and down the taut, tanned skin.

"So fucking good," Luke groaned, shattering the silence in the small enclosed space and capturing Sierra's attention.

Looking up at him, she saw the sheer ecstasy etched on every one of his rugged features. Every muscle from his jaw down to his heavily muscled thighs stood out in stark relief as he held himself upright while Cole sucked him.

"Damn, I've missed that mouth," Luke whispered, and Sierra suspected Luke didn't mean to say the words out loud. Never did he share that much of himself, but he seemed to have let himself go. At least for the moment.

~~*~~

Luke didn't mean for his thoughts to project out of his mouth, but the pleasure Cole bestowed upon him was just too much. The way he used his tongue, coursing over the sensitive underside of his cock, bathing him in heat, was unlike anything Luke had known before. Except for the last time Cole had gotten on his knees before him.

Realizing he wasn't going to last, Luke pulled out of Cole's mouth, releasing his hair only to turn to Sierra who proceeded to blow his dick and his mind all at the same time. He couldn't take much more, and God help him, he hadn't wanted this to be about him. He needed to show both Cole and Sierra that he wasn't the selfish bastard he'd made everyone believe.

But he needed this. He had always needed this. The desire to own Cole, to have his complete and total surrender was stronger than he was. And the man's defiance still shook him to the core. Luke had realized he had to earn Cole's surrender, earn the right to pleasure him the way he saw fit. And it wasn't until that moment, with Cole on his knees before him, that he realized he did own the man.

Just as Cole owned him.

"I won't last…" Luke said the words as he backed away from Sierra, his back making contact with the wall as he fought for breath, fought for just a measure of control. For the first time in as long as he could remember, Luke felt as though he were in the right place. He felt safe with these two people, the ones who knew him better than even he knew himself. He closed his eyes for a brief moment as he tried to choke back the emotions threatening to take him down.

When Cole gripped the back of his neck, surprising him, pulling him roughly against him, the man's mouth crushing down on his, Luke let the trapped emotions loosen. All of the anger, elation, and confusion came roaring to the surface, released in the way Luke gripped him back, pulling Cole closer, rather than pushing him away like he had told himself he wanted to do. He flipped them so Cole was flush against the wall, Luke's body aligning until their dicks rubbed against one another, the truth of Luke's reaction to the man evident. He needed Cole.

And fuck, maybe that was the reason for all of the internal turmoil. Maybe he'd needed Cole all along, and his inability to accept what that meant… how that would change his life forever, had left Luke up in arms.

Their tongues dueled; their hands gripped one another roughly as they battled for dominance. Luke wouldn't back down. Not this time. He was in control. He was always in control, and if Cole expected anything from Luke, it was that he would be the one to decide their fate. Fighting to breathe, Luke broke the kiss, opening his eyes so he could let Cole see everything he was feeling. The two of them knew in that moment, as time seemed to stand still, exactly what they were doing.

And why.

Lord have mercy… Cole was in love with him. The acceptance was overwhelming.

"Turn around," Luke growled out the command and gripped Cole's arm, turning him until the man damn near face planted into the wall. "You want this?" Luke asked, trying to hold onto that tiny sliver of control he had managed to hold onto thus far.

"Yes." The word was laced with gravel, rough need making Cole's muscular body tighten as Luke pressed his bare chest against the massive expanse of Cole's naked back.

"No barriers this time," Luke said, and the words were meant as they sounded. A double entendre.

"None," Cole agreed.

Despite the rough handling, Luke couldn't suppress the aggression no matter how hard he tried, he wasn't about to hurt Cole. Never would he hurt Cole. But he wasn't sure he could hold himself back.

Once more, Luke turned Cole until they were chest to chest, mouth to mouth as he easily maneuvered them out of Sierra's bathroom, toward the bedroom. Time stood still as Luke pushed Cole down on her bed, laying atop him, biting Cole's shoulder in a pure act of dominance, showing him exactly who was in control.

When Sierra climbed up onto the bed, Luke watched as she crawled closer to Cole, her hands moving over his chest, massaging as they went. The woman had the sexiest, tightest body he'd ever seen and watching her move was erotic as hell. Especially when she was naked. She leaned down, her mouth taking Cole's in a kiss explosive enough to shake the walls.

Remembering what he was doing, Luke grabbed a bottle of lubrication from the bedside table, the thought of why Sierra even had it when she hadn't just a couple of days before flitting through his mind briefly before he flipped off the cap and coated his steel hard shaft. He was going to lose it.

Luke joined them on the bed, maneuvering between Cole's thighs, pushing them wider before trailing his hands up and over Cole's legs, his cock.

He needed to be inside of Cole, to join their bodies until neither of them felt as though they were one. He let one hand slide over the taut skin of Cole's stomach, easing back down slowly, caressing his rigid cock again briefly, before inserting two fingers in his ass. Cole groaned as Luke gently entered him. He wouldn't last long. He needed to be inside of this man more than he'd ever needed to connect with another person.

Removing his fingers, Luke stroked his own cock firmly, aligned their bodies and slowly gliding in while their eyes locked on one another. *Holy fuck!* He stilled momentarily as Cole's body took him in, his muscles contracting around him, squeezing him until Luke saw stars.

When Sierra pulled back, her eyes fixated on the place where Luke was joined so intimately with Cole, a spark of sheer lust ran through him, and Luke began to move. Slowly.

For the first time, Luke conceded to the fact that this wasn't just about sex, just about pleasure. It was all about need. His need. The need to have Cole beneath him, willing, wanting, just as Luke did. He tried desperately to maintain the slow pace, sliding deep inside of Cole, grinding his hips against his ass and watching the way his exquisite body tensed beneath him.

"Fuck me, damn you!" Cole grit out; pulling him, bringing Luke closer until their chests nearly touched.

And then the friction was almost too much. Luke began to thrust inside of Cole's warm body, gripping his hips, grinding deeper, only to pull back and plunge forward once again. Luke slid his hands up Cole's stomach, over his tense chest and slipped one hand behind his neck, pulling him closer until their mouths nearly touched. "Tell me," Luke growled.

"No." Cole leaned back, allowing Luke to bury his cock deep into his ass, but he held himself tighter, his powerful thighs unmoving.

"Fucking tell me," Luke demanded, thrusting deeper, harder, faster. Oh hell, he was going to come. The sight of Cole's powerful body, the muscles standing out in stark relief as the man held himself together, one hand snaking down to grip Cole's cock, Luke knew he couldn't hold back. "Tell me, goddammit!"

Sierra's breathing was becoming erratic as she sat just inches away, her hand between her legs as she rubbed herself, fixated on the two of them and making Luke's blood pressure soar. Having her there, watching, was more than he could have imagined, but in the same sense, Luke felt as though he and Cole were the only two people in the room and he needed, desperately needed to hear Cole admit what he was feeling. And yes, that was the selfish bastard coming out in full force because Luke had yet to tell either of them exactly how he felt, but he would.

"Fuck you," Cole ground out; lifting his hips, forcing Luke deeper; using his own hand over Luke's to stroke his cock. "I'm going to come," Cole whispered the last words and Luke slowed his movements.

"Tell me." Luke used the last remnants of his control to get the words out. "I need to hear you say it." Luke hadn't expected the words to come out, but once they were out there, he didn't want to take them back. He needed to know exactly how Cole felt.

"Fuck!" Cole gripped his hips, pulling him closer. "I. Love. You!"

Luke slammed his mouth down on Cole's as his world shifted on its axis and then exploded. His release was powerful, all consuming, as he thrust one last time inside of Cole, every ounce of his control shattered and he came with a roar.

Chapter Twenty Eight

A couple of weeks passed since the morning that Luke showed up at Sierra's, and in that time frame, he could count the number of hours he'd slept on both hands. Or at least it felt like it. He and Cole managed to talk Sierra into staying in Dallas, at least for now, while the three of them tried to work on how this situation was supposed to work. Rightfully so, Luke had to do some in depth explaining about his previous relationship with Susie before Sierra would let him off the hook. By the time his mouth was tired of moving, Sierra was finally forgiving him.

Whether they were at Luke's, Cole's or Sierra's, the three of them had taken to losing every ounce of their inhibitions – not that Luke had ever had any in the first place – and tried some interesting things. To say the least... the sex was phenomenal.

However, Sierra was continually questioning them both about the club. As much as Luke wanted to initiate her into Club Destiny, he was still hesitant. Not that it had anything to do with Sierra. No, he trusted her implicitly and would bring her onboard – hell, he'd pay her membership fees himself – if he thought it would be the right thing.

His issue? Well, he didn't want to share her.

Somehow he'd managed to repeatedly put her off, but he knew the moment would come when he would have to break down and have the conversation. As he sat at the big mahogany monstrosity that the original designer called a desk, Luke contemplated how he would do that. The night before when he'd been lying in bed, Sierra cuddled up against him, he'd spent a solid hour trying to come up with a plan.

He wanted to show Sierra what she was getting into when she joined, but he wasn't willing to introduce her to any of the other members. Not just yet anyway. So his tired brain had decided to bring her to his office and give her a taste of exactly what it meant to be a member of the club. She was disillusioned when she thought she had crossed all of the boundaries that she was going to cross when it came to sex. And though the last two weeks had been beyond his wildest imagination, Luke knew she still had some fantasies that they had yet to play out.

Part of him worried he would push Sierra too far and she would end up fleeing back to Nashville without a second thought. The other part of him prayed she would be open to his suggestions. Or rather, his demands. So, when he had woken up that morning, Luke had put his plan in motion.

Twenty minutes ago, he'd called her cell phone and asked her to meet him at the club under the pretense that he wanted her to take a look at his office. Considering he wasn't happy with the design, it wasn't a farfetched idea, and, in fact, he fully intended to hire her to redo it in the near future. But that wasn't why he invited her today.

Of course, before he called her, he had called Cole. Theirs was a longer discussion, Cole wanting to understand what Luke's overall objective was. And rightfully so. And now Luke waited for Cole to show up so they could discuss at length the reason for Luke's sudden decision to include Sierra in the club. He wasn't sure whether Cole was for or against the idea, but nonetheless, Luke respected his input.

A sharp knock at the door had Luke turning in his chair.

Right on time.

"Hey," Cole said as he walked in, shutting the door behind him. "What the hell is going on?"

Way to get right to the point. Luke glanced at the man, then turned back to his computer screen while he waited for Cole to have a seat. He exited out of the program and turned his attention to Cole.

"I've invited Sierra to the club."

"I gathered that much, but what I don't get is why." Cole's expression remained guarded, but he sat back in the chair, crossing one ankle over the opposite knee and resting his arms on the armrest.

"She's adamant she be given the opportunity to experience the club for herself," Luke told him.

"And just what does she think is going to happen?"

"Hell, I don't know."

"Considering most of what happens here, happens behind closed doors, with a few exceptions, I don't know what she's expecting. It's not like we have viewing rooms or anything like that."

No, they didn't. And yes, Cole was right. Most of what happened at Club Destiny happened behind closed doors between consenting adults. He knew the activities varied from the typical ménage to some hard core BDSM that a couple of the members preferred, but no matter the variety, it was usually done in private. Luke got the impression Sierra thought the double doors that closed off the member's only portion was a gateway to debauchery and kink. And maybe they were, but you wouldn't find members fucking in the hallway.

"So, what's the plan?" Cole asked, obviously waiting for Luke to give him more details.

~~*~~

Cole waited patiently for Luke to fill him in on what his intentions were for the afternoon. He still wasn't happy about Luke inviting Sierra to the club, but the fact she was more than a little anxious to be there wasn't a secret either. She'd asked him about it a couple of times in the last week or so, but Cole generally found a way to distract her. Apparently Luke hadn't been able to do that.

"I've asked her to take a look at my office, told her I was planning to redecorate," Luke said, sounding not so sure of himself.

"That's not a bad idea, actually," Cole stated, glancing around at the less than attractive surroundings. Luke's office never had held much appeal.

"And," Luke said, giving Cole that determined eye, "I'm not willing to let another man touch her, so my options are limited."

"I agree. She's off limits as far as I'm concerned," Cole said, giving the idea some thought. "That doesn't mean we can't have some fun with her."

"And just exactly what do you have in mind?"

Cole liked the fact that Luke was protective of Sierra. He also liked that Sierra was so open to new sexual experiences; however, he didn't think she'd given much thought to what that might really mean. Sharing a bed with two men was a radical next step for a woman who had only ever been with one man in her life, but Cole knew she had some secret fantasies she hadn't shared with anyone. Including him or Luke.

"I'm thinking a little voyeurism might be just up her alley."

"Voyeurism?" Luke said, apparently contemplating the idea. "Would she be the watcher? Or the watchee?"

That was a good question. Cole hadn't given it much thought, but the more he did, the more he liked the idea. A lot.

"And if you're thinking the latter, who do we know that we trust enough?"

"I'm thinking Tag Murphy," Cole blurted out before he could think better of the idea. The guy was not only a new member of the club; he was also Cole's stepbrother, although that little detail hadn't been shared with anyone other than Luke and Logan. Not even Sierra knew that. Although his kinks seemed to border on the extreme, or the man was just all talk. Either way, Cole knew Tag could be trusted. Obviously Luke must have thought so too, or he wouldn't have allowed him to join the club.

"Why the hell does everyone keep looking to that guy to fill their fantasies?"

What? Cole didn't know if the question was rhetorical, and he hoped like hell it was because he didn't have an answer. "Who else is looking at Tag?"

"Logan."

Seriously? Interesting.

Cole contemplated the idea for a few minutes, while Luke apparently did the same until they looked at one another. Yep. That was their best option. Now they just needed to come up with the details. "Call him. See if he's around," Cole stated, anticipation sparking the air like an electrical current.

This would definitely be interesting.

~~*~~

Sierra opened the door to the club and tried to insert a little confidence into her step. Luke had called her that morning and asked her to stop by. Apparently he was looking to redecorate his office, and although the idea intrigued her, she'd been overcome with a bad case of nerves on her way over. She was actually going to go past the double doors that separated the mainstream club with the private, member's only portion and she was more than a little excited by the idea.

She'd spent the better part of the morning visualizing all sorts of things that she might see once she crossed that threshold. Granted, she hadn't a clue what actually went on behind those doors, but it was a sex club. Surely there was... sex.

"Hey." Kane called out to her as she approached the bar. Luke hadn't said where she should go when she got there, so she opted to hang out with Kane until Luke showed up.

"Hey back. How are things going?"

"Same old stuff, different day. Can I get you a drink?" he asked, leaning against the bar as though he had nothing better to do than talk to her.

She sure could use a drink that was for damn sure. Before she had the chance to tell him what she wanted, her attention was directed to a man and a woman heading in the direction of the stairs. Sierra hadn't seen the man before, but she likely hadn't seen many of the members before. This one she would have remembered though.

He was sexy as hell. And ok, she might be in a relationship, but she sure as hell wasn't dead. The man was smoking hot. His head was shaved bald, right down to the skin and apparently he did this frequently because the top of his head was as tan as his face. His jaw was lined with dark stubble, the sexy, unkempt look that some men went for.

By comparison, he was probably as big as Cole as far as muscle went, but not as tall. Not that she was a good judge of height because she was on the short side and everyone appeared bigger than they probably were from where she stood. Standing next to the beautiful blonde woman, he looked bigger than average.

Still caught up in what was going on around her, she noticed the man crush the woman against him, his big hands planted firmly on her ass, squeezing as he... oh, my. He was grinding against her, right there in the club.

Not that there was anyone else around because they weren't open, and it was a Tuesday afternoon. In fact, they were the only other people in the room besides Sierra and Kane.

"Take me upstairs." The woman said in a sexy, raspy voice and Sierra found herself transfixed on the twosome.

"You know what that means don't you?" The man asked, still holding the woman. "It means you get naked, and I get to have some fun. I've got some whips and chains I've wanted to test out."

"I'm game," she said sweetly before the two of them headed for the stairs.

As Sierra followed their every move with her eyes, she was jolted back to reality when she noticed Luke coming the opposite way down the stairs. He seemed oblivious to the two people groping each other as they went up the stairs. Maybe he was used to it. Yep, that had to be it.

Good grief. She was pathetic.

Trying to shake off what she had just seen, more importantly what she had heard, Sierra pasted on a smile and took in the sexy, brooding man coming her way.

Just like every time Luke had greeted her over the past week, he walked right up to her, tilted her chin up before planting a sweet peck on her lips. "How was your day?" He asked, smiling down on her.

"Hopefully getting better," Sierra said, still remembering what the man had said. Whips and chains? Seriously? Maybe she wasn't as ready to see the club as she originally thought. Or, based on the fact that her skin was beginning to tingle, maybe she was more than ready.

"Let's take a look at my office," Luke told her before turning to look at Kane. "I'll be busy for the rest of the afternoon, so don't send anyone my way."

"No problem, boss." Kane said, smiling.

Sierra couldn't hide the blush that crept up her neck and heated her face. What would Kane think they were going to do? Did he know she was only there to look at Luke's office so she could redecorate it? Based on his wicked grin, he wasn't thinking about pictures and upholstery.

Luke took her hand and led her up the stairs. Butterflies erupted in her belly when he punched in a code before turning the handle. Here she was. Walking into the infamous Club Destiny's private section. When the door clicked shut behind her, the lock reengaging automatically, Sierra nearly jumped.

The first thing she saw startled the hell out of her.

There was a long hallway that disappeared in two different directions. But it wasn't the sterile white, with bright fluorescent lighting like she had expected. Oh, she had no idea why she had pictured hospital quality décor when she thought of what was behind those doors, but she had. Instead, she was greeted by soothing colors and dim lighting. The walls were a light brown, accentuated with a faux leather paint technique, with intimate sconces scattered about on each side all the way in both directions. The floor was made of an expensive tile, a dark, gray and brown slate that was immaculately clean.

"Surprised?" Luke asked, obviously picking up on her reaction.

"A little," she answered truthfully.

"What did you expect?"

"I... I really don't know." Oh, she knew all right, but she definitely wasn't going to insult him by telling him. Luke obviously invested a lot of money into the club and based on what she had seen so far, she was highly impressed.

"My office is down that way." Luke pointed to the left. "And down here, we've got the playrooms."

When Luke took her hand, leading her in the direction of the so called playrooms, Sierra had a hard time getting her feet to move. Where were they going? "Playrooms?"

"Yep. You know. Where our members go to *hang out.*"

What was he saying? Too overwhelmed to ask, she focused on putting one foot in front of the other as they moved farther down the hall to where it split off once more.

"There are twenty private rooms, and as of right now, a little over half of them are rented," Luke said as they turned the corner.

The hallway looked just like the one they had just left, but there were doors on both sides, along with a few tables holding massive vases of flowers in various places. "Rented? Like a hotel room?"

"Not exactly. And no, we don't rent by the hour, honey," Luke chuckled. "Members have an option of renting a room, and it functions just like any apartment would. They all have a kitchen, bathroom, small living area, and a monstrous bedroom. Members are required to furnish and pay utilities though."

"I'm assuming the rentals are like the memberships? Not cheap?"

"Correct," he told her, still holding her hand as they made their way farther down the hall. "We've got several open rooms where our members can congregate if they feel the need to. But you won't find any themed rooms here. That's not what we're about."

Sierra stopped short, staring up at him. Obviously she'd had some major misconceptions about the place because she had expected exactly that. Maybe a room with various swings and slings, maybe a couple of whips and paddles, or one of those restraint systems right in the middle. Ok, so maybe she was getting too many ideas from her late night reading.

"So, it's just like a normal place for adults to go and hang out?" Sierra asked, bewildered by the fact her imagination had gotten the best of her.

"I wouldn't say normal," Luke said. "You sure you want to go farther?"

Sierra glanced down the hall, noticing an open doorway and immediately wondered what was in there. "Yes." Although it sounded more like a question than an affirmation, Luke took her by the hand once more and led the way.

Before they entered the room, Sierra heard the sounds. Intimate sounds. A woman moaning. Instead of wanting to turn and run the other way, she was anxious to see what was just around the corner. When Luke would have stopped, Sierra continued going, pulling him along behind her.

When she turned the corner, she saw a tame version of what she expected to see originally. The room was all wrong, but what the two people were doing in the room was accurate. Surprisingly, the man and woman she had seen downstairs were not the two who were fucking like rabbits on a large couch in the center of the room. Nor were they the two people who were sitting on another couch, watching intently.

Luke pressed up against Sierra's back, his erection poking into her. "Do you like this sort of thing?" she asked him as she watched the man and the woman.

"I like watching you," Luke said, whispering quietly in her ear, so she was the only one who heard him. "I want to watch you right now."

That brought Sierra up short. *Did he mean…?*

"Not here, baby," Luke assured her and she felt a smidgen of relief course through her. She wasn't ready for any public displays to this extreme. "But first, let's take a look at my office."

The way he said the words, he could have been telling her in intimate detail all of the things he wanted to do to her. His deep baritone caressed her senses and made her sex throb. What was he waiting for? Sierra turned away from the erotic scene in front of her and led him from the room.

"Was it what you thought it would be?"

"Not entirely, no," she admitted. "I expected more… sex. You know, the way they tell it in books. All of the sexy people, plastered against one another, using toys and all of those things they learned in the Kama Sutra books."

Luke laughed, and the sexy rumble warmed her. Less than a minute later, they were approaching the door to his office and when she entered, she was stunned by the normality of the room. In fact, she was a little surprised.

For Luke's house to be so tastefully designed, masculine and inviting, it was hard to associate the man with this type of office. The furniture was bland; the rug was expensive but repulsive and the monstrosity of a desk overwhelmed the entire space. And there weren't any windows. At all.

Taking a look around, Sierra ventured farther into the room, noting the various objects – nothing at all personal – sitting around and wondered who he had hired to do this. Obviously not the same person who designed the hallway or the "playroom" they had just visited. The image of those two people going at it flittered through her mind and heated her skin.

"So, where should we start?" she asked as she tried to focus on the reason she was there.

"Let's start with the couch," Luke said, his voice moving closer.

"The couch?" She could go on and on about the couch, but she wouldn't. Although it appeared the designer intended to do something similar to what Luke's living room looked like, she'd missed the mark entirely.

"Yes. Let's start with you *sitting* on the couch."

Sierra jerked around to look at him, the raspy tone of his voice sending chills – the good kind – down her spine. He definitely wasn't talking about sitting down to talk, and the intent expression on his face confirmed it. When she didn't move, he did. Closer. Until he was almost touching her.

"You wanted to see the club. You saw it. Now I want to see you, Sierra."

Sierra nodded her head, not knowing what she was nodding for. Apparently her body agreed with where this was going, but her mind was still confused.

"I've never liked that couch, so I figure if you get naked and sit on it, I'll start to like it immensely."

Strip? Here? But…

Anyone could walk in at any moment. The thought startled her, but it didn't turn her off like she expected. Knowing that anyone could walk through that door at any time and find her naked in Luke's office was actually erotic as hell. Which explained her sudden embarrassment. How in the world would she explain a fantasy like that?

"I'm not going to tell you again." Luke's voice deepened and his eyes smoldered.

With fumbling fingers, Sierra managed to unbutton the tiny buttons on her blouse, alternating between looking down to see what she was doing and back up into those sexy bedroom eyes peering back at her. The heated look in Luke's eyes had a way of erasing her inhibitions and making her feel bold. Something she was not used to.

She slipped her shirt down her arms, letting it fall to the floor only because her fingers weren't working and she wasn't able to catch it in time. When Luke pulled up a chair, sitting it opposite of the couch, her breath hitched in her chest. He was actually going to watch her.

"Take off your bra," he ordered as he sat down.

Sierra managed to unclasp the hook, ridding herself of her bra. Her nipples pebbled from the cool air and Luke's hot glare. Again she fumbled as she unhooked her belt, then moved onto the button and zipper of her slacks. Stepping out of her shoes, she wiggled the slacks down over her hips and then stepped out of them.

Clad only in her panties, Sierra suddenly felt modest standing in Luke's office, his gaze holding fast on her nearly naked body. If only she could read his mind, she might have some idea of what was in store for her next.

Chapter Twenty Nine

Standing before him in only a pair of lacey boy short panties, Sierra was utter perfection. It didn't matter if the woman was fully clothed, or completely naked, she was the sexiest thing he'd ever seen. He would be content just to sit there and stare at her, but she was beginning to fidget and he knew she was nervous. She ought to be.

"Turn around," Luke told her, watching as her eyes widened. "Now remove the panties. Very slowly."

Damn that was hot. She did exactly as he told her, turning slowly, then bending at the waist as she slipped the lace down, her ass bared to his hungry gaze. As she bent over farther, he got a peek at her soft, pink pussy. His tongue ached to sweep over those smooth, silky lips, to taste the sweet, warmth between her thighs. But before he got too distracted, he needed to move on with it.

"Now sit on the couch, facing me." Luke watched the graceful way she moved, the soft sway of her hips as she approached the couch. She didn't rush her movements and Luke appreciated every luscious curve nearly hidden by the curtain of her hair. The overhead lighting was directed down on her, giving all of those long black strands a blue tint.

She sat on the couch looking prim and proper although she was completely nude, her perfect nipples pebbled and begging to be sucked. Once she was comfortable, Luke stood up and walked over to her.

He slipped onto his knees before her, her gaze following his every movement, her lips trembling ever so slightly from her excitement. And Luke knew she was excited. He could smell her. Her arousal was a potent thing, the sweet intoxicating scent of her filling his senses and making him long to touch her.

That wasn't going to happen. Not yet.

But, in order to get to the next phase of this little experiment he needed to situate her the way he wanted her. So touching her was necessary, and for the brief moment he was allowed, he was going to enjoy it.

He bent his head, placing his lips on her left knee, kissing lightly while running his hands up her calf, then under her thigh. Lifting her leg, he situated her foot on the couch, her knee bent. He proceeded to do the same with her other leg, the soft, wet folds of her pussy separating, tempting him to take what he wanted, experiment be damned. Taking her hands, he placed them on her knees, forcing her to hold her legs open.

"Damn that's pretty," Luke said, damn near choking on the words. He wanted to bury his face between those smooth, silky thighs and feast on the heart of her. Instead, he wrangled in his self-control and pushed up from the floor. Taking three steps back, he resumed his position in his chair.

He didn't speak, just watched as she swallowed hard, the long column of her neck contracting as she did. Nervous. He liked that about her. She was willing to try almost anything, but she maintained a level of uncertainty that only turned him on more.

The sudden click of the door knob turning had her eyes darting away from him to the area he couldn't see behind him. That would be Cole. Right on time. There was a measure of relief that flashed in those brilliant blue irises right before she directed those ice blue eyes on him. Her gaze darted between the two of them, but she didn't move.

Luke was impressed.

"That's the prettiest thing I've ever seen," Cole said, breaking the silence. "But I'd like to see a little more."

Sierra's eyes landed on Cole as she waited for him to elaborate. Her hands were trembling, but she managed to keep her knees up and her legs open, her pussy on full display. Before he approached, Cole stopped at Luke's desk, opened the top drawer and retrieved the pink vibrator Luke had bought Sierra. She probably didn't recognize it because the last time they used it on her, she had been blindfolded.

Her eye lids lowered and she straightened her spine, ever so slightly, but again, she didn't move from the position Luke had placed her in. Cole pulled another chair beside Luke's before moving toward her and holding out the large pink toy. Sierra reached for it, wrapping her hand around it, but not doing anything more. Cole made his way back to the chair, sliding down slowly as though he didn't have a care in the world. Luke knew Cole was hard enough to pound nails, but he was doing his best not to show it.

"Spread your legs just a little bit more," Cole told her, taking complete control and demanding Sierra's full attention. "Then I want you to turn on that vibrator and play with yourself."

"If we came into your bedroom at night, baby, what would you be doing to yourself with that toy?" Luke chimed in, keeping his voice low and controlled. It took Herculean effort just to stay in his seat.

Engrossed in the highly erotic scene before him, Luke managed to breathe as Sierra slipped the very tip of the pink silicone toy into her mouth and proceeded to damn near blow his mind. Her tongue laved the end before she eased it down between her legs, skillfully turning on the vibration with one hand.

"Spread your pussy lips open, baby," Cole said, his voice sounded choppy and not at all composed like he pretended to be. "Use your other hand."

Sierra did as instructed, using her index and middle finger to separate the soft, swollen lips so they had a better view of the delicate pink folds, wet with her juices. Damn she was hot. Luke caught the daringly bold gleam in her eye and he fought back a smile. Somehow she thought the tables had turned, and she was in control now. He'd have to make sure she realized who was really in control.

"Show me, Sierra. Show me how you play with yourself when we aren't there. What do you do with your toys? Do you slide them deep inside your cunt and fuck yourself until you come? Or do you rub it on your clit, pretending it's a hot, wet tongue?"

He wasn't seeing things. Sierra's thighs tightened, and her eyes widened as she nearly fumbled the vibrator. With his eyes locked with hers, he made sure she saw the heat in his gaze before her said, "Do it, baby. Fuck yourself."

Sierra stopped looking at them, fully immersing herself in the moment as she brushed the pink vibrating tip across her clit, a soft cry escaping her lips as she did. Luke felt more than saw Cole's body tighten next to him, his cock rock hard against his zipper as he watched in awe. Sierra used her own juices to lubricate the tip of the dildo before plunging it into herself, moaning her pleasure. As she continued to drive deep, faster, she used her other hand to rub her clit. Dropping her legs open wider, Luke watched, wondering if he was going to come in his jeans just from the sight.

Then the door clicked, and Sierra's hand froze, her eyes jerked up to the door and widened to the size of saucers. Neither Luke nor Cole turned around.

"Keep going," Cole told her, his voice stern. "Let us watch you fuck yourself."

Tag Murphy approached, pulling up a chair and taking a seat on Luke's other side. Sierra did fumble this time, her gaze landing on Luke's. "Fuck yourself, Sierra. He's here to watch. It's the hottest thing I've ever seen," Luke leaned forward and though he was way too far away to touch her, he tried to ease her mind. "You like being watched, don't you, Sierra?"

When she didn't move, clearly shocked, Cole stood from his chair and made his way over. With quick, easy movements, he managed to get underneath her, placing her feet apart on either side of his thick thighs and taking the toy from her. He eased her to the side so he could watch between her legs, using the vibrator on her clit. At first, Luke thought they had pushed her too far, freaked her out to the point of no return, but then she moaned. Louder this time. Cole continued to fondle her clit for a moment before plunging the toy deep inside of her, eliciting another moan.

Sierra began driving her hips forward, thrusting herself onto the toy as Cole fucked her harder, deeper until she was moaning constantly, hovering on the edge of her orgasm. Before he sent her over, Cole stilled his hand, making Sierra turn to look at him, giving him a *what the hell* look.

Flipping off the vibrator, Cole tossed the toy beside them before using the fingers of one big hand to splay her open, while driving two fingers of the other hand inside of her.

"Fuck my fingers, Sierra," Cole urged her on, kissing the juncture between her neck and shoulder. "Damn you're wet, baby. Do you like being watched? Do you like knowing that another man gets hard watching you get fucked?"

Luke couldn't play the role of bystander any longer. He left Tag sitting in the seat beside him while he maneuvered to the floor in front of Sierra, getting an up close and personal view of Cole finger fucking Sierra, her wet pussy gripping him, slicking his fingers as he drove inside of her. Then Luke took his turn, inserting one finger alongside Cole's, Sierra's moans getting louder and more desperate.

"That's it, baby. Come for us," Luke groaned, driving his finger in before retreating, over and over, in time with Cole's forceful thrusts.

Sierra gripped Luke's hair, pulling tighter as she screamed, an orgasm plowing through her, damn near making Luke come.

~~*~~

Cole nodded his head, letting Tag know it was ok for him to go. The other man knew to lock the door behind him because what they had planned for Sierra next didn't include an audience. Holding her against him, Cole let her have a moment to catch her breath and collect her bearings before he eased out from underneath her.

While Luke helped her up, Cole made quick work of removing his clothes, before planting his ass in the chair once more. His dick was spike hard and throbbing relentlessly. It didn't help that he couldn't stop thinking about how he wanted her mouth on him.

"Come here, Sierra," Cole told her, holding out his hand until her fingers met his. He pulled her forward gently. Placing his hands on her shoulders, he eased her down onto her knees between his legs. "I want to feel your mouth on my cock."

Over the course of the last week, Cole had allowed his more aggressive side to come out, realizing Sierra actually liked it. Oh, there were still times when he would rock her body slow and gentle, making love to her for hours. Then there were times when he allowed himself to be a little rough with her.

Like now.

"Suck harder," Cole encouraged her, holding her hair gently as he guided his cock deep into her mouth, watching the way her cheeks hollowed around him. "Damn that's good. Use your tongue."

Another thing he had figured out about Sierra. She liked to be told what to do. Hell, she thrived on it.

Cole caught sight of Luke in his peripheral vision, removing his clothes and exposing all of that gloriously hard muscle. Cole's cock throbbed again, this time for an entirely different reason.

During the last week, the three of them managed to get to know each other on so many different levels, not just sex, and Cole found himself that much more attracted to Luke. The man was physical perfection, long and lean, outlined with thick, hard muscle. And despite his brooding attitude, Luke could only be described as intense.

Although Cole and Luke hadn't been intimate alone, Cole knew the time would come. Until then, he had the best of both worlds, being with Luke and Sierra at the same time. Like right now, while Sierra continued to use her skillful tongue to paint his cock. Gripping her hair firmly, Cole pulled her closer, watching her expression, one of pure unadulterated enjoyment to one of sheer rapture. The woman definitely liked the more aggressive touch.

"That's it, baby. Just like that," Cole encouraged, thrusting his hips gently, pushing the head of his cock deeper into her mouth. Completely engrossed in the moment, Cole nearly came before he was ready. Easing her off of him, Cole pulled her up, until she was standing before him.

Gripping the base of his cock firmly, Cole stemmed off his release, not ready to come just yet. Not until he was buried to the hilt inside this woman.

"Turn around." He wasn't going to be able to hold off much longer. "Now sit on my cock and ride me."

Sierra faced away from Cole, looking directly at Luke who now stood in front of both of them, stroking his cock. Cole lowered her onto his lap, guiding his cock to the wet entrance of her pussy, biting his tongue as her body slowly consumed him. She was so tight, so fucking hot, and Cole knew he would never tire of being immersed inside her lovely body. Sierra didn't hold back as she ground her ass into his lap, gyrating her hips and successfully pushing him to the edge.

"Ride my cock," Cole grit out between clenched teeth.

She managed to fall into a rhythm, using her thigh muscles to lift and lower herself over his steel hard cock while Cole held her hips in place. He was barely cognizant of what Luke was doing, until the man lowered to his knees in front of them.

"Be still," Luke demanded; the complete opposite of what Cole needed at that moment. He wanted Sierra to impale herself on him, to fuck him so completely that he exploded deep inside of her. Instead, she stopped her movement, Cole's impatient dick throbbing insistently inside the warm depths of her body.

He couldn't see Luke or what he was doing, but he had an idea when Sierra began moaning his name. Cole could feel the gentle scrape of Luke's beard stubble against his thighs, the sensation damn near destroying the last threads of his control. When Luke's callused hand gripped his balls, lightly squeezing, his breath lodged in his chest.

He was going to come. Having Luke's hands on him while lodged to the hilt inside of Sierra was more than he could take. He knew he had to hold on because he needed Sierra to come before he did, but between the light stroke of Luke's jaw between Cole's legs as the man skillfully ate Sierra's pussy and the not so gentle way her body clamped down on his cock, he was 0 for 2 in the *I must hang on* department.

"Fuck," Cole bit out the word, gripping Sierra's hips tighter, digging his fingers into her soft flesh as her body rippled around him, attempting to milk him dry.

Stars began to dance behind Cole's lids, and when something fiercely hot latched onto his balls, Cole's entire body tensed. Luke. The man was using his mouth to torment him, something Luke had never done before, and the brutal way his tongue lapped at him, coaxing him closer and closer to the verge of imploding, was the spark that lit the fuse.

"Fuck me, Sierra," Cole demanded. "Fuck me now!"

Luke continued to stroke and suck while Sierra's wicked hot body consumed him, and Cole held on by the skin of his teeth until he knew he could wait no more. He gripped Sierra's hips, stilling her motion as he managed to thrust upward into her, retreating and slamming home again. Over and over until she latched onto his hands, her body exploding around him, the sweet depths of her body like a velvet vice that clamped down on his cock until his orgasm roared through him like a runaway freight train. Cole's harsh groan echoed in the room as his body stilled, while Luke's wicked tongue bathed his balls one last time.

~~*~~

Sierra hadn't wanted to come. She wanted to hang on to that sensation of floating, while Cole's thick cock glided over every nerve, touching that one spot that sent sparks shooting up her spine and into her hair, before pulling back and repeating the process. But when Luke had knelt in front of them, his dark head disappearing between their legs, his tongue flicking across her clit before he switched his attention to Cole, she hadn't been able to hang on.

Then Cole had taken the reins, fucking her with wild abandon, so deeply, his harsh groans and intoxicating words sent her careening over the edge.

But her body was primed for more.

This was one of those times when she wondered why every woman didn't have two men to focus their attentions on her. While Cole stole a minute to catch his breath, Luke pulled her from her perch on Cole's lap before rearranging her so she was leaning over his desk. The smooth, varnished top was cool against her overheated body, making her nipples stand up and take notice.

"Sexy." The single word sent a shiver down her spine as she waited impatiently for Luke to get on with it. She was done with the foreplay; she wanted to feel him inside of her. The thought of what had happened only minutes earlier when that sexy stranger had walked into the room, his eyes locked on her pussy as she tried desperately to reach the release that had eluded her only seconds before had been the icing on the cake.

The first time the door had opened, Sierra had been shocked, but seeing Cole's handsome face staring back at her had soothed her frazzled nerves. But when the sexy stranger walked through the door, her brain had been on overload, unsure of what to do next. Yes, she might have had some voyeuristic urges in the past, but to have an onlooker watch as she tried to bring herself to orgasm, while two other men – her men – looked on, had been too much.

She had lost her nerve, her brain working too hard to determine what was going on and what she was supposed to be doing. Instinct had told her that it was wrong, so very wrong, but her traitorous body had been turned up a notch, the heat in those unfamiliar gray eyes making her pussy spasm. Then Cole had come to her rescue, and the only thing she had to do was feel.

The way he expertly touched her, knowing exactly what to do to make her squirm with pleasure, combined with the heated stares of Luke and the stranger was enough to send her careening into the abyss. And then as if having Cole in her mouth, his heated words spurring her on, wasn't enough, now Sierra was splayed across Luke's desk, waiting for what was next.

"I won't last," Luke stated matter-of-factly. "I'm going to fuck you hard and fast." It was a warning laced with a promise and Sierra was more than ready to feel the way Luke confidently played her body like a finely tuned instrument.

Her words were lodged in her throat, and when he rammed into her in one well timed motion, Sierra nearly came again. The angle was exquisite, his cock filling her, pressing against her g-spot with every deep thrust. He began pounding into her, the desk rocking with the momentum as Sierra's body began to hum once again.

"Fuck!" Luke's animalistic growl shattered the sexual tension coursing through her, and Sierra gave herself over to the feelings that were igniting in her core. That first tingle of her orgasm building, growing stronger with each powerful thrust until her body spasmed, her muscles locked and her release took her with such powerful force, she wondered if she would literally break apart.

The roar that followed wasn't just the blood pounding in her ears, but Luke's release as he filled her even more completely than she had ever been before.

Chapter Thirty

"Can you meet me at my apartment after work today?" Lucie asked Cole as she dropped off another shot of whiskey. It'd been a long day, and Cole had stopped by Club Destiny, agreeing to meet Alex when the man had called that afternoon.

"Is everything ok?" he asked, noting the dark circles under Lucie's pretty brown eyes.

"Not really," she admitted, turning to go before Cole latched onto her arm, gently stopping her.

"Is it Haley?" He was worried. After they had gone to the doctor a couple of weeks before, Lucie had been a nervous wreck.

The doctor had informed her he definitely needed to remove Haley's tonsils to ease the constant strep and put tubes in her ears to help with the ear infections. Routine surgeries, he had informed them.

Cole didn't know much when it came to kids, but he knew something had to be done to help Haley. They had taken the little girl to McDonald's after the appointment, letting her burn off some energy on the playscape while Cole and Lucie hashed out her next steps. Thankfully Lucie agreed to the surgeries which were scheduled for two weeks from now.

"No. She's fine." Lucie told him, easing some of the tension that had been building over the course of the last two days.

"All right. I'll stop by," Cole conceded, knowing Lucie didn't want to go into detail at the club, and he couldn't necessarily blame her.

"Thanks." With that Lucie walked off, leaving Cole with his drink and a ton of worries.

The things he had on his mind weren't anything out of the norm. At least not for him, but Cole couldn't seem to get past them. One would think that with as much sex as he was getting, he wouldn't have a care in the world, but apparently that wasn't the case. Although he'd spent almost every single night for the past couple of weeks with Sierra and Luke, he couldn't help but think they had come to the point in this so called arrangement that required them to determine what the next steps were.

The fact that he had told both Sierra and Luke that he loved them, and they hadn't returned the sentiment bothered him more than he wanted to admit. Even though he had told them both only once, and during the heat of the moment, he wondered if they knew how hard it had been for him to share that much of himself. To not get anything in return left him wanting more. He only wondered whether they wanted the same thing he did.

Thankfully Alex McDermott chose that moment to intrude on his wandering thoughts as he pulled back a chair at the table and sat down with the same grace and style the man did everything else with.

"Thanks for meeting me." Alex said, turning toward the bar, catching Lucie's attention.

Alex was a regular at the club, both of them in fact, but no one knew much about him other than he had become more and more irritated over the last few weeks. Cole had an idea as to what was causing that irritation, but it was none of his business, and he and Alex weren't what he would consider friends, so he wasn't about to broach the subject.

"No problem. What's up?" Cole knew this had to be about business because that was the only time Alex ever approached him, and since he needed something to help get his mind off of things better left alone, he was anxiously awaiting the reason for the impromptu meeting.

"I need your help." Alex admitted, suddenly looking tired.

"All right," Cole hesitated.

"I want to hire you."

Assuming Alex meant as a contractor, he nodded his head, encouraging Alex to continue. The last time he'd worked for Alex had been at the conference in Vegas and based on the feedback he'd received, they had drummed up some business out of the deal. Which was good for Alex and the man had compensated Cole nicely.

"Permanently." Alex added then paused for Lucie to set the drink on the table. "Thanks," he told her before turning back to Cole.

"Permanently?" Cole wasn't looking for anything permanent. That didn't explain why the idea intrigued him.

"Yes. We've just gotten too busy, and I can't seem to keep up. Even with Dylan onboard and Sam working double to try and fulfill her contract with XTX while helping out with a couple of other big clients we've recently taken on, I'm quickly losing my mind. I can't do everything, and since Dylan has continued to be reclusive, I'm unable to convince him to handle any of the PR work that we need."

"Why me?"

"Because you know the ins and outs of CISS and you're good at what you do. So, before you say no, let me tell you what I need you to do." Alex hurried through the statement, obviously anticipating Cole's immediate rejection.

For the next half hour Cole listened to Alex's spiel. The man had obviously given this some serious thought before approaching him. And although Alex was looking to hire Cole as the front man for their public relations work, he didn't realize how much better he would be at the job if he just handled it himself. But, that didn't mean Cole wasn't interested. For the first time in as long as he could remember, he apparently was ready for something more permanent. Something that he could look forward to day in and day out.

That longing had spilled over into his personal as well as his professional life and Cole figured this wasn't necessarily a bad place to start.

"I'm in," he said, stunning Alex into complete silence.

After a few tension filled seconds passed, Alex blurted, "You're in? Just like that?"

"Just like that."

"Well hell. I thought it would be a harder sell than that. You should've seen the hoops I had to jump through to get Sam onboard."

Cole laughed, remembering the story Logan had shared with him several months back. After some highly escalated HR violations, Alex had come up with a plan to salvage Sam's job while still allowing XTX to benefit from her employment. In the end, it had all worked out, so obviously Alex was a better salesman than he thought.

"So are you still officing out of XTX?" Cole asked.

"No. With Dylan coming on, he wanted to put a little distance between himself and his grandfather, so we took up residence in a building not too far from them. XTX is still our biggest client, and Xavier is a very demanding man." Alex smiled.

"Well, just let me know what the next steps are, and I'm game. I don't have much going on right now, so I just need a week or so to tie up some loose ends."

Alex downed the rest of his drink in one quick swallow. "I'll set up a meeting for you, me, Dylan and Sam so we can discuss what our strategy is. Big things are coming for CISS, and if I don't get ahead of this now, we might have some big *problems* on our hands."

The two men shook hands, both standing from their seats. Cole had a couple of things he needed to get done before he stopped by Lucie's. Once Alex disappeared out the back doors, Cole stopped by the bar, acknowledging Luke as he passed him.

"I'll see you tonight," Cole said to Lucie before turning to leave.

"All right," she whispered, obviously aware of her audience. With both Luke and Kane looking on, she had every right to be nervous.

~~*~~

When Susan opened the front door, looking both elegant and highly pissed off, Sierra knew she was not going to enjoy this meeting. Not that she had enjoyed any of their meetings, especially the last one Susan had insisted on. Sierra had to walk away from Luke and Cole that day just so her work could be questioned yet again. Although that day something seemed off about Susan, and if Sierra wasn't mistaken, the woman was trying to ask about her personal life.

However, being the professional that she was, she'd agreed to meet Susan when she had called that morning. Her inner bitch hadn't been so excited about the deal, but Sierra had repressed that part of her, gotten ready and high tailed it over to Susan's house.

"It's about time."

Well, how the fuck are you too? Sierra had grown accustomed to Susan's bitchiness, but she had to bite her tongue repeatedly to keep from telling the woman exactly what she thought of her. Knowing this woman had been with both Luke and Cole had set off something dark and possessive inside of her, making each and every meeting they had nearly unbearable.

Following Susan into the kitchen, not her office like she expected, Sierra began to get a little nervous. Had something gone wrong? Did one of the contractors screw something up?

"Can I get you something to drink?" Susan was ever the hostess, never missing a beat, but Sierra wasn't going to drag this out any longer than she had to.

"No, I'm good, thank you." When Susan took a seat at the kitchen table, Sierra stopped abruptly.

"Sit." Susan stated firmly, followed by a reluctant, "Please."

Sierra sat.

"We need to talk."

That's the one thing, and probably the only thing, they both agreed on. Getting up each morning was beginning to be a difficult chore just knowing she might have to face Susan again. Although they had agreed on a design, and Sierra had subcontracted out the work, Susan still nitpicked over every little detail, often causing the contractor to insist Sierra come over to smooth the waters so to speak. Not that it had ever done any good.

"There's a rumor going around that has me concerned." Susan started, glancing down at her hands and then back up at Sierra.

Unsure of where this was going, Sierra remained silent.

"It's been brought to my attention that you are in a relationship with two men."

Susan was doing her best to sound disgusted with the notion, but Sierra's hackles immediately rose. Susan was a member of the club. She had been a willing participant in some sexual exploits that would likely blow Sierra's mind, and here she was trying to pretend that the idea of being with two men disgusted her. Did Susan not realize Sierra knew who she was? Or at least who Susie Mackendrick was. They apparently were two very different people, housed in the same body.

Deciding that this might just be the blessing she had been hoping for, Sierra opted for the truth. "I am."

"And you don't see the problem with that?" Susan asked, clearly startled by Sierra's honesty.

"I don't." Keeping her answers simple was the only way Sierra was going to manage to get through this awkward conversation. She only hoped Susan would fire her and get it over with. Never in her life had she wanted to take the easy way out, but that was before she met this overbearing, impossible to please woman.

For a lawyer, used to arguing her case, Susan faltered more than Sierra expected. Or maybe Sierra's answers hadn't been simple enough for her to understand.

"Well." Exasperation tinged the word, and Susan locked her eyes with Sierra's. "I've had to come to a hard decision after learning this information. I wanted to talk to you first, make sure the rumor was actually true. Now that I know it is, I need to tell you I'm concerned about your employment."

Thank goodness. Sierra didn't speak out loud, although she wouldn't have been more surprised if the words had burst from her chest with pride. "Ok."

"I think it is in your best interest for you to quit."

Ok. There was the *more* surprise.

Being fired was one thing. Quitting was something entirely different. She couldn't control the actions of others, and if Susan wanted to fire her because she wanted to feign concern over Sierra's personal life, that was her prerogative. But quitting. That wasn't in Sierra's nature.

"I'm not the one with the problem," Sierra said, shocking herself with the anger seeping into her blood.

"You're in a relationship with two men, and I can't subject myself to that sort of association. You should be ashamed of yourself first of all."

O – K. Now the anger was coursing fast and hot. Did the woman really have the audacity to project her own personal opinion on Sierra's personal life when it in no way affected her ability to do her job? "Well, I assure you that I am not ashamed."

"I thought you might say that which is why I had to come up with a second option if you chose to be bullheaded."

Bullheaded? *What the fuck?*

"I insist that you quit, or I am going to have to proceed with a civil suit against you for misrepresentation."

"Excuse me, *what*?" Sierra was dumbfounded. This woman was actually blackmailing her.

"You heard me. You clearly misrepresented yourself, and in order to protect myself, I am going to file a civil suit. I will make sure you never work in Dallas or any of its surrounding areas ever again." The full bitch was back, a sneer on Susan's face told Sierra she wasn't kidding.

Pushing back her chair, Sierra stood abruptly. She'd heard enough of this. Her anger had reached maximum capacity, and if she wasn't careful she was going to make this bad situation even worse.

She didn't speak as she exited the kitchen, walking as calmly as she could manage down the long hallway to the front door. She heard the click of Susan's heels behind her, and she prayed she could reach the door before the other woman said another word.

"Your slutty behavior has no place in a professional environment. You should seriously consider making adjustments before you even think about working for anyone else. I'll make sure this rumor circulates."

Temptation

Her blood pressure spiked and a red haze clouded Sierra's vision. For the last couple of months she had put up with more abuse from this one woman than she had anyone else in her entire life. Turning abruptly, she came face to face, although Susan was quite a bit taller, with the woman. Keeping her hands at her side, not wrapped around Susan's neck like she wanted, was harder than she imagined.

"I don't have many regrets in my life, Ms. Toulmin. Or is it Ms. *Mackendrick?*" Keeping her voice level, Sierra stared back at the woman noting the flash of fear in her eyes. "I definitely don't regret the actions I take in my personal life. If I want to be in a relationship, that is my choice. Not yours. Who I do that with is also my choice. Not yours. And if I choose to live my life out in the open, instead of hiding behind another name, or the closed doors of a sex club, that's my choice as well."

Apparently the comment hit home, and Susan must have realized Sierra knew more than she thought. That didn't stop Sierra speaking her mind.

"And being the jilted ex-lover is not a good look for you. If you can't handle rejection then I suggest you keep your snooty ass in the house, and limit who you interact with. I'm not naïve enough to think that you won't do what you said you would and by all means, go ahead and try. But just remember one thing. When it comes to secrets, I'm not the one who has any."

With that Sierra turned and walked gracefully out of Susan's front door, not looking back. She didn't have to. The woman's eyes had nearly bugged out of her head, and her audible gasp told Sierra that she had hit her mark.

If Susan thought Sierra was going to sit back and take any sort of threat from the likes of her, she was sadly mistaken. Accepting who she was hadn't come easily for Sierra, but once she had made that decision, her life had taken a turn. And the only direction she was willing to go from here on out was forward.

~~*~~

Luke had missed Sierra's call. He'd been too wrapped up in what he had just heard to answer the phone. Was Cole really going to see Lucie tonight? After everything that the three of them had developed over the last couple of weeks, was he really going to flaunt his involvement with another woman? After blatantly lying to Luke's face and telling him they were nothing more than friends? Right. But he had believed him.

Luke couldn't imagine the devastation this would have on Sierra. Which was partly the reason he had let her call go to voicemail. He damn sure wasn't going to be the one to break the news to her, and at the time she had called, he wouldn't have been able to keep from mouthing off about it. That slow burning rage that he thought he had under control was surfacing once more, this time boiling hot and fiery as hell. The bastard.

He thought about asking Lucie what the hell that was all about, but decided against it. She worked for him. Besides she had been acting really strange around him for a while now, but Luke chalked it up to the fact that she had been caught stealing. They had set up a payment plan, and she was having the money deducted from her payroll, though Luke hadn't felt good about the idea. When he tried to talk to her about it, she clammed up, insisting that it was her punishment, and the right thing to do.

So here they were. Lucie was paying him back for stealing and apparently Cole was paying him back as well. For what, he didn't know. And he damn sure didn't like it. He just wasn't sure how to go about approaching Cole about it. Part of him wanted to go to Lucie's and wait for Cole to show up, just so he could beat the shit out of him for hurting Sierra that way.

Oh, who was he kidding? He wanted to beat the shit out of Cole for hurting *him* that way too.

When his phone rang, Luke grabbed it from his pocket and glanced at the caller id.

Sierra.

He very well couldn't ignore her. Especially since she had called twice in the last thirty minutes.

"What's wrong?" he asked immediately when he hit the talk button.

"Can you come over?" Her voice sounded strange, a little shaky.

"Now?" Luke headed to his office, fully intending to leave, regardless of what her answer was.

"Whenever you get a chance," she told him, sounding very unsure of herself.

"I'll be there in a few minutes. Are you sure everything's ok?" he asked, needing her reassurance.

"It will be."

And what the hell was that supposed to mean? Was there a full moon or something?

Luke was beginning to wonder what the hell was going on. Both Cole and Sierra were acting strange. And here he had been getting comfortable, the one thing he had warned himself not to do. Yes, that likely made him a pessimist, but damn it, if Logan could make a relationship work, Luke was bound and determined that he could too.

With a renewed sense of vigor, Luke grabbed a small box out of his desk drawer before stopping at the bar to let Kane know he'd be gone for a while. Luke made a mental note to talk to Kane first thing tomorrow, because the man definitely deserved a raise.

The drive to Sierra's took longer than Luke wanted it to, but the afternoon traffic was a bitch. That was the one thing Luke hated about Dallas. No matter what time of day, or what day it was, traffic sucked. With his irritation level already reaching epic proportions, the added frustration hadn't helped his mood any. Thankfully he pulled into Sierra's drive, which helped him relax just a bit. Seeing her tended to do that to him.

Luke might be an irate asshole most of the time, but when it came to Sierra, she was the only person who could soothe his frazzled nerves. Just seeing her was like a salve to what seemed to be a constant ache inside of him. Since the moment he met her, and despite some of his more ignorant reactions, Luke knew that he lived for this woman.

Before he exited the truck, he grabbed the small box he had tossed in the center console and removed the tiny object inside. Slipping it into his pocket, he was overcome with an emotion he wasn't all that familiar with. Nervousness.

And he had every right to be. He didn't know what he was walking into, but heaven help him, it was time that he set this woman straight. Not knowing what it was she needed to talk to him about was eating away at him, and he prayed she hadn't gone back to thinking she was moving back to Nashville. The thought almost leveled him.

When he reached the front porch, he took a calming breath – it didn't help one bit – and rapped his knuckles against the door. A few seconds later, the door opened, and the most beautiful woman in the world stood before him. That's when his heart plummeted into his stomach. She had been crying.

"What's the matter?" he asked, stepping inside and pulling her up against him, not wasting a single second before touching her. When she wrapped her arms around him, pressed her face against his chest and began sobbing, he experienced that same killing rage he'd felt once before. Whoever had made her cry would be sorry.

Instead of pushing her to talk, he held her against him, soaking up the feel of her, running his hand down her spine, through the long, glossy tresses flowing like satin down her back. When her body stopped shaking, he eased back a step, cupping her face in his hands, forcing her to look up at him.

"She wants me to quit."

Huh?

Leading her to the couch, Luke sat beside her, still holding her close. Who wanted her to quit? Before he could ask the question, Sierra exploded into words and motion, pushing up from her seat and pacing back and forth across the room.

"Susan called me to her house, and when I got there, she proceeded to tell me that I needed to quit." Sierra kept pacing, not looking at him. "If she was going to fire me, I was going to be ecstatic, but the bitch said I needed to quit. I'm not going to quit. I'm not a quitter."

Luke hadn't seen this side of Sierra. She was fiercely adamant, and the use of the B word nearly made him smile. He still wasn't sure what she was talking about, but he didn't interrupt.

"She, of all people, wants to tell me that it's wrong to be in a relationship with two men. But how would she know anyway? The hypocrite. She didn't give me a choice, telling me that it's wrong, and I should be embarrassed." Then she did turn and look at him. "But I'm not embarrassed, Luke. That's the problem."

He definitely didn't see a problem with that.

"I'm happy being who I am and going after what I want. I've spent my entire life wondering what was wrong with me. Then she all but tells me that if I ever plan to work in this town again, I needed to quit, or she was going to sue me. Sue. Me. Can you believe that?"

Ok hold up just a minute. All of the pieces clicked into place and Luke prayed that it wasn't true. "Are you telling me Susie told you that you needed to quit because of me and Cole?"

"Yes," Sierra said before stopping and tossing her hair back over her shoulder. "She implied that I'm not normal and that I'm an embarrassment for being in a relationship with two men and that if I didn't quit, she would sue me for misrepresentation. How could she?"

Luke couldn't sit still any longer. He made his way over to Sierra, standing in her path so that the next time she paced, she came in direct contact with him. He reached out and held her in place, smiling down at the woman. His woman. "What did you tell her?"

"Everything that was on my mind." Sierra smiled, and Luke's heart turned over. God he loved this woman.

"Which was?"

"I told her that I wasn't going to quit. That I wasn't going to end my relationships because this is my life, damn it, and I can do whatever I choose to do. She doesn't have any say in the matter." Taking a deep breath, Sierra closed her eyes, then opened them once more. "Then I told her to remember that I wasn't the one keeping secrets."

Chapter Thirty One

Good girl.

Standing there, staring down at her, Luke was beaming with pride. This woman had stood up for him. For Cole. So their relationship wasn't normal. It would never be normal in the eyes of most people, but he didn't care. What he felt for both Sierra and Cole couldn't be changed by the harsh stares of others, or their ignorant comments. And to know that Sierra stood up for them had his heart swelling in his chest.

"I love you," he blurted the words out.

Sierra stumbled back a step, still staring up at him. "What?"

"You heard me," he said, stalking her as he moved forward and she took another step back.

"Say it again."

"I. Love. You," he told her before he pulled her up against him and crushed his mouth to hers. He filled his hands with her luscious body, while letting his tongue tease hers. When she tried to pull away, he kept her close, a little worried about what she would say. And yes, maybe he was a little insecure. But, Luke knew one thing beyond a shadow of a doubt. He loved this woman fiercely and with everything that he was made of.

Sure, it took him longer than it should have to say it, almost as long for him to accept it, but now that the words were out there, he felt an overwhelming sense of relief.

To think that his own actions could have very well pushed away this woman because he was too insecure to have something of his own, scared that she would be taken away from him and he would be left with another empty space inside of him had been too much to bare. It had happened with his parents. They had been torn from his life so easily and Luke had vowed, even as a young kid, that he would never have something stolen from him again. Yet he had almost done that to himself.

"Luke." Sierra managed to push back from him, breaking the kiss, but not letting go of him. He stared down at her, holding his breath as he waited to hear what she had to say. God, please don't let her reject him. He didn't think she would, but with the way his luck seemed to run lately, there were no guarantees.

"I love you," she whispered the words and they went straight through him, piercing his heart.

When she kissed him, he poured every ounce of what he was feeling into the kiss, lifting her in his arms and carrying her to the bedroom.

"Where are we going?" she asked, grinning.

"To get you naked." Plain and simple.

Luke didn't waste any time getting them both out of their clothes and then climbing on top of her. "Wait, I forgot something," he said and rushed off the bed, nearly face planting off the side.

"We don't need a condom," she told him, laughing as she watched from where she lay, naked and beautiful, sprawled out like a goddess before him.

No. They didn't need a condom. But that wasn't what he was looking for. As he searched through his pockets, finally finding it, he crawled back over her once more.

Staring down at her, seeing the light in her eyes, the soft smile on her lips had his heart rate increasing. The fact that she was naked already spiked his blood pressure, but the way she looked at him so sweetly, had him grinning like an idiot.

"What are you waiting for?" she asked, looping her arms around his neck and pulling him closer.

What *was* he waiting for? He didn't know.

"Marry me." For the second time that day, his mouth got ahead of his brain. Since he wasn't the romantic, gushy type, he knew it was the best he could do, even if he had spent the better part of the day trying to come up with poems and sonnets to express how much he loved this woman. "Marry me, Sierra."

She didn't immediately say no, and she didn't try to pull away, so he took that as a good sign, but he was frozen in place, staring down at her as he aligned their bodies, wanting to lose himself in her warmth, needing to make love to her. Holding on to his sanity by a very fine thread, he held back, sliding his cock through her slit, but not penetrating her.

"Please." Hoping that was the magic word, definitely not one of the most used from his vocabulary, Luke continued to look at her.

"Yes," Sierra whispered the word, but that didn't matter because she had said it. She said yes!

Luke drove himself inside of her, overwhelmed by the emotions that lit him up like the Rockefeller Center Christmas tree. When Sierra pulled him down, crushing her soft, sweet lips to his, he could barely move. Her pussy clamped down on his cock, sending shockwaves through him and making his balls draw up tight.

He pulled back, slid his hands into hers, their fingers twining together as he pulled her arms above her head. Holding himself above her, their bodies touching from chest to ankle, Luke lurched forward, then pulled back. Over and over he slid into the wet, warm depths of her body and let her consume him. Mind, body, and soul.

A few minutes later when their bodies were coated in perspiration, the velvet walls of her pussy tightened around him, milking him until he couldn't hold back. "Come with me, baby."

Her fingers tightened around his as her body tensed, those blue, quicksilver eyes lit up like a flame as she came, sending his body skyrocketing into paradise.

~~*~~

Sierra couldn't move. She couldn't breathe. And it had nothing to do with the two hundred plus pounds on top of her. Her orgasm had registered a 10+ on the Richter scale.

When Luke moved, falling to his side and pulling her against him, she didn't let go of him. Wanting to keep him close, praying this wasn't a dream, Sierra kept her eyes open although exhaustion was closing in on her.

Luke took her left hand and lifted it, placing a kiss to the tips of each finger before something cool slid down her finger. It was real. He had really asked her to marry him, and now he had…

"Oh my goodness! Luke!" Sierra pushed up, staring at the ring on her finger, wondering how she was going to carry it around on her hand every day. The one single diamond sparkled radiantly, a very simple, yet elegant – although enormous – setting that made her head spin.

"Do you like it?" he asked. If she wasn't mistaken, there was a hint of uncertainty in his tone.

"I love it," she answered, then looked at him. "I love you."

He kissed her once more, warming her body from the inside out, a tender, heart wrenching press of his lips against hers. She needed to get out of that bed, or they would end up there for the rest of the day. Not that she minded at all, but she had people she wanted to tell. Her mother. Samantha. Cole

Oh God. Cole.

Sierra shot up off the bed, unsure of what to do or where to go – feeling the same way she imagined Luke had when they hadn't used a condom that first time. She grabbed her robe from the back of the door, slipping it on while Luke merely sat up, watching her intently.

"What's wrong?" he asked, apparently picking up on her panic attack.

"What's wrong? What's *wrong*?" Broken record that she was, Sierra couldn't think of anything else to say. How could they have not thought about Cole in all of this? This wasn't a relationship of just two people, no matter how strange that sounded. The three of them were in this together. At least Sierra thought they were. She loved Luke. She also loved Cole. Equally. She wasn't complete without either one of them, yet she had just agreed to marry Luke without even thinking about Cole. How could she?

Sierra stormed from the room, trying to get her brain to settle down, and her heart rate to follow along. When Luke appeared moments later, he was wearing his jeans but not his shirt, and his feet were bare and holy cow, he looked amazing.

"We didn't even think about Cole," she blurted out, turning to face him. The look on his face was not one she recognized, but when he didn't say anything, she knew there was trouble brewing. "What's wrong?"

Luke shook his head but didn't move. Sierra wanted to scream at him, but she didn't. She'd already lost her head once today, and that might have ruined her career.

"We need to talk to him," Sierra said, dropping into a chair, resting her head in her hands. Luke might not be talking, but they needed to.

This was big.

Huge.

~~*~~

Cole rapped his knuckles against the door, waiting patiently for Lucie to answer. His patience was running thin, so he wasn't sure how he managed. He'd received a call from Sierra earlier, asking him to stop by. Her message had been cryptic and she sounded worried which made Cole worry. Two attempts to call her back had failed, so he opted to go over to Lucie's before he went to Sierra's.

"Thanks for coming." Lucie said when she opened the door. She had changed out of her work uniform into a pair of jeans and a t-shirt. She looked tired. Her eyes were puffy like she had been crying.

"Sure," he replied, walking in and shutting the door behind him. "Is Haley here?"

"No. She's at my mom's. I didn't want to take a chance that she would overhear our conversation, so I asked my mom to keep her for the night."

Cole knew where this conversation was going to go, especially if Lucie made a point to keep Haley away.

"Can I get you something to drink?" she asked politely, but without heart.

"I'm good." He took a seat on the sofa, waiting for her to join him. When she didn't, he waited. He didn't have to wait long though.

"I have to tell him."

That was a good start. At least Cole thought it was. "What made you decide that?"

"Haley deserves to know who her father is."

Cole didn't know if she was telling him the reason, or trying to convince herself that this was the right thing to do.

"You know how I feel about this." They'd talked about it numerous times and Lucie never agreed with him, but he hadn't held back how he felt. Having grown up without a father, not knowing who the man was, Cole had firsthand knowledge of what that felt like. Although his situation was different. Cole's father knew about him, he just chose not to be a part of his life. Haley's father didn't even know.

"When are you going to tell him?" Cole asked, hoping to get her to open up a little.

"I don't know."

"Lucie. Sit down," Cole told her, letting her hear the insistence in his words. She had asked him to come over, and he would never turn his back on a friend, but he needed to check on Sierra, which meant Lucie had to get on with it. "Talk to me."

Her feet moved albeit reluctantly, and she made her way to the couch, sitting down beside him and putting her head in her hands as she spoke. "Haley deserves to know him. And he deserves to know her. It's not her fault that he doesn't remember what happened."

"It's not your fault either, honey," Cole assured her.

"I know it's not. But I could have brought it up to him. I could have told him what happened. I mean we had sex. And it was amazing," she sighed. "How can he not remember?"

Cole didn't have an answer for that. He'd never had an answer for that.

"This is going to turn his world upside down." Lucie continued. "He seems happy. Truly happy right now. How can I just unleash this on him? He's going to hate me. And probably fire me."

"He's not going to fire you." That he was sure of. "Look, honey." Cole took her hand and turned her to face him. "This isn't going to be easy, but it's the right thing to do. Haley needs to know her father. He needs to know about her. Hell, we don't even know how he'll react until you tell him."

Lucie nodded her head.

"I think you should call him. Tonight."

That had Lucie's head jerking back in surprise. "Tonight?"

"Yes. Call him. Ask him to come over so you can talk to him. He's a reasonable man." Granted, he might not be reasonable once he realizes he slept with one of his bartenders, getting her pregnant and having absolutely no recollection of the night in question. But, that didn't change the fact that the man was a father.

Cole couldn't sit any longer. He hated to leave Lucie, hated that she would have to go through this alone, but he needed to get to Sierra. "I hate to run, but I've got somewhere I need to be. Call me tomorrow and let me know how things went tonight," he told her as he walked toward the door. "You can do this, Luce. Just remember, it's best for all three of you."

Cole left Lucie nodding her head, whether she was placating him or agreeing with him, he didn't know. As much as he wanted to see the man's reaction when she sprang the news on him, Cole couldn't stick around.

He quickened his pace on his way to his truck, pulling out his cell phone. He fumbled through the numbers, but managed to dial Sierra's phone, listening to it ring as he started up his truck. When Luke answered, Cole glanced down at the screen, wondering if he'd misdialed.

"Where are you?" Luke asked.

"On my way to Sierra's," he told him as he put the truck in Drive and tore out of the parking lot.

"That wasn't the question."

Well, fuck. Luke knew exactly where Cole was because he heard him tell Lucie he would see her tonight. Apparently Luke wasn't happy with the idea. Was he jealous? The thought made Cole smile. Luke McCoy. Jealous. Ha. "I'm leaving Lucie's."

"What the fuck are you doing with her?" Luke's voice lowered, and Cole realized he was trying to hide his conversation from Sierra. Not that there was any reason to. He was sure once he told Sierra exactly what was going on with Lucie, she'd understand. Not that he could. At least until Lucie shared her news. Cole damn sure wasn't going to be the one to spread that little rumor. He'd never be forgiven. Not to mention, too many people could get hurt.

"She just needed someone to talk to," Cole assured him as he pulled onto the highway. Traffic was light, so Cole floored it, gaining speed and getting closer to his destination. "I'll be there in ten. We'll talk then." With that Cole disconnected the call.

~~*~~

Luke wanted to throw the phone, and he might have if it had been his own. Instead he dropped Sierra's cell phone on the coffee table, staring at it in disbelief. Thankfully Sierra had gone to take a shower because Luke would have hated for her to talk to Cole. Knowing that he was coming straight from Lucie's to see Sierra actually made Luke's stomach hurt. Dropping his head into his hands, he closed his eyes.

Temptation

What the hell had happened? Just yesterday the three of them had been happy. Or so Luke thought. They'd spent nearly every night for the past week together, at one of their houses. And in the matter of just a few hours, each one of them had done something to change the entire dynamic of their relationship. Luke had asked Sierra to marry him. Sierra had said yes. And Cole had been doing God knows what at Lucie's during that time.

Should he have consulted Cole before he proposed to Sierra? Probably. Was the man going to be pissed? More than likely. Did Luke actually give a shit? The answer should be a resounding no, but it wasn't. Luke did care. He cared about Cole. Hell, he loved the man.

Yes. Love.

Not a feeling he thought he would ever feel for another man. At least not that way. But he did. Since the day he met Cole all those years ago when he waltzed into the club, fully intending to make it his own, Luke had been fascinated by Cole. Then over the years they'd become friends, sharing women.

Then that one October night... Logan's bright idea to shock some sense into Sam had turned out to be Luke's nightmare. He had been so taken with Cole that night, the intensity of being close to him, having Cole touch him, put his mouth on him, surrendering to him in every way. It had been too much. So much that Luke had lost all common sense and had fucked Cole three ways to Sunday. Rightfully so, that had been the most erotic night of Luke's life. Which was saying something because Luke had done some crazy things before then.

And somehow being with Cole had changed him. The two of them, when they took Sierra for the first time - that had altered him as well. And now, here he was, engaged to the one and only woman he had ever loved, and feeling as though he had just betrayed Cole. Hell, he *had* betrayed Cole.

Even with all of that, Luke still wanted the man. Desperately. They had yet to be together, just the two of them. Except for that morning in the shower in Vegas. That was the closest the two of them had ever been. Yet Luke wanted more. He wanted Cole to give himself completely. And Luke wanted to give back.

And maybe that's what bothered him the most about Cole being with Lucie. He said they were just friends, and he had no reason to believe otherwise. Was it his way of pushing Cole away? Still?

Pushing to his feet, Luke looked around. Sierra was still in the shower. Knowing he couldn't leave, nor did he want to, Luke resigned himself to figuring out the next step. It was time the three of them hashed this out. Cole would probably be pissed, but that couldn't be helped. Come hell or high water, they were going to make this permanent. Tonight.

Twenty minutes later, when Cole walked through the front door, Luke was sitting on the couch, and Sierra was in the kitchen. Making tea.

Seriously. Tea.

Luke had turned down her offer. He'd prefer a shot of whiskey, but since she didn't have it, he opted for nothing.

Keeping his eyes on Cole as he shut the door behind him, Luke felt his muscles tense, gearing up for a fight. He'd told himself they wouldn't do this. They could talk this out like rational adults and figure out what they were going to do next. Sierra didn't think it would be that simple. Or so she said while they waited for Cole to show up.

Luke had been surprised when she didn't take the ring off of her finger. That little gesture lifted four tons of bricks from Luke's chest. She wasn't going to hide it. That said more than words ever could, although they both knew it could very well be the final shove in pushing Cole away. At the moment, thinking about where the man had just come from, Luke didn't know if that was necessarily a bad thing.

"Where have you been?" Sierra asked when she walked in the room carrying a coffee mug.

Cole glanced at Luke, then back to Sierra. "I had to go talk to a friend. Sorry I missed your call earlier. Is everything ok?"

"No," she said honestly.

"What's the matter?" Once again Cole was looking back and forth between the two of them, but Luke didn't say anything. He didn't know what to say.

"I had a run in with Susan Toulmin – sorry, you know her as Susie Mackendrick. The woman had the audacity to blackmail me. She told me I had to quit, or she was going to sue me for misrepresentation," Sierra rambled quickly. "But the thing is, she wasn't worried about my professional abilities. She was pissed off that I'm in a relationship with the two of you."

Sierra sat her mug on the table before sitting in the chair opposite of Luke. He wanted her to come over beside him, but he didn't move from where he was. He was waiting for Cole to elaborate on just what the hell he had been doing at Lucie's.

"Is your friend all right?" Sierra asked.

"She will be," Cole said before taking a seat on the couch beside Luke. It was the only other place to sit after all.

"She? Do I know her?"

Luke didn't have to say a word; apparently Sierra's curiosity was going to get him the answers he wanted.

"Lucie Werner. She's a bartender at Club Destiny."

"Oh. The one who was caught stealing?"

"Yes."

Chapter Thirty Two

For a moment the room was silent, no one was looking in any one direction and the tension was slowly increasing. This was the awkwardness that Luke tried to avoid. It was so much easier to sleep with a woman, or participate in a hot, steamy ménage, and disappear in the middle of the night. Instead, they had to work out their differences, after figuring out what they even were. When it finally got too uncomfortable for Luke, he turned his attention to Cole.

"Why were you at Lucie's?"

"I told you. She needed to talk," Cole said, his tone reflecting his sudden irritation.

"About what?"

"If that was your business, she would have called you."

Luke had to hold back his anger. His first instinct was to walk out the front door and not look back. He'd gotten so used to avoiding confrontation that it was second nature just to walk away. He couldn't this time. He had something to prove. And not so much to Sierra and Cole, but to himself. This was what he wanted. These two people. Relationships weren't always wine and roses and Luke had to figure out a way to cope with it.

He couldn't sit still though, so he stood and paced toward the front door. Before he reached it, Cole's voice resounded from the other side of the room. "Don't you dare walk away."

That brought Luke up short. He wasn't planning to walk away, but obviously that was Cole's first assumption. Apparently Luke had burned the man one too many times. And if that thought didn't just piss him the fuck off.

"Or what?" Luke retorted, turning toward the man. "What the fuck do you care?"

Great. Now he was going to taunt him. So much for acting like a rational adult.

"See. That's what you've never seemed to understand, Luke." Cole's voice was calm, and he remained sitting which only pissed Luke off more. "I do care. I've always cared. It's you who doesn't seem to give a shit about anyone but yourself."

"Is that right?" Luke asked, taking a step closer to Cole.

Obviously feeling the need to get on a level playing field, Cole stood; his large body now only inches away.

"I've never heard you say it," Cole stated, his dark blue eyes glimmering with anger.

"Say what?"

"How you feel. You've insisted that I say it, but you've never been man enough to tell me how you feel."

Luke took another step closer, bringing them almost nose to nose. "You don't need me to say it."

Cole's eyes were suddenly somber. "That's where you're wrong."

And if that wasn't a punch to the gut. Luke faltered for a moment, his eyes glancing down at Cole's mouth, then back up to his eyes. He'd never told Cole how he felt, but he had expected him to figure it out.

"Tell me, Luke," Cole said, moving closer, their chests touching, and a fire sparked in Luke's gut. Damn this man could make him feel things he'd never imagined he'd feel. "Tell me how you feel."

Luke reached up and slid his hand into Cole's hair, pulling firmly, his mouth hovering a breath away.

"Tell me."

Luke wanted to say the words that would assure Cole this was more than just chemistry between them, more than just explosive sex, more than just… "I love you." *Holy fuck!* The words slipped out and the heat he saw in Cole's eyes fanned the flame that had sparked seconds before. Before Luke could move, Cole crushed his mouth down on his and Luke was lost for a moment.

Cole gripped his hair, pulling him closer as their mouths ate at one another, Cole's firm, warm lips gliding against his until Luke was damn close to ripping his clothes from his body.

"Easy." Cole's voice broke through the maelstrom of emotion churning inside of him, his lips pulling back, gently brushing against Luke's. Damn it felt good. Too good.

And then Sierra was behind him, her slender arms wrapping around his waist, her lips pressing against his back, sending a chill down his spine. He wouldn't survive this. He needed the heat, the flames, not this sweet seduction. Luke didn't do sweet. His need was too strong.

Cole's fingers went to the waistband of Luke's jeans and his stomach muscles tightened. Those rough fingers scraped his lower stomach as they eased open the button, then slid down the zipper with practiced movements. When Cole trailed his mouth down Luke's neck, across his pectoral muscle, and then farther down the center of his stomach, lowering himself to his knees in the process, Luke thought he would explode. Sierra was behind him, but she wasn't doing anything more than kissing his back, sending tingling sensations over his skin.

Somehow Luke ended up on the couch, sitting with Sierra behind him. He didn't want to crush her, so he tried to move forward, only to have her pull him back against her. His jeans were around his ankles, and Cole was kneeling between his legs, his big fist wrapped firmly around his iron hard cock. Luke wanted rough. He wanted hard and fast, but he knew by the look in Cole's eyes that he wasn't going to get it. Not tonight.

Sierra wrapped her arms around Luke, using her hand to tilt his head as she placed heated kisses along his neck, his shoulder. Torn between Sierra's bewitching kisses and the feel of Cole's mouth as he took Luke's cock in deep, he was pretty damn sure his head would explode. Cole expertly sucked him, using his tongue to torture his shaft, then lapping at the engorged head, before sucking harder.

"Fuck," Luke growled, wanting to move, but trapped by Cole's firm grip on his thighs and Sierra's arms holding him back against her.

"Let him love you," Sierra whispered in his ear, and Luke's cock jumped.

Cole's eyes darted up to his as he continued to take him deeper, feeling the back of his throat as it hit the swollen head of his dick. There was heat. There was intensity. But it was unlike anything Luke had ever known.

When Cole moved down, sucking Luke's balls into his mouth, laving them one at a time, before sucking them inside the hot, moist cavern of his mouth again, Luke groaned. He was going to come. He needed to come.

"I want to watch you make love to him." Sierra's words had the impact of a two by four, and suddenly Luke wanted the same thing. He wanted to bury himself to the hilt inside of Cole, holding on for dear life. He wanted to love him.

"Naked. Now," Luke said, managing to gain back some of his equilibrium, although Cole still had Luke's cock buried deep in his mouth, sucking vigorously while Sierra nipped at his neck.

"Now," Luke growled, pulling out of Cole's mouth and pushing his jeans from his ankles, needing to be able to move.

When he would have stood, Sierra held him back once more, and Luke turned his head. "I need to fuck him."

"Stay right where you are," she told him, holding him although he could have easily pulled away if he wanted to.

Within seconds Luke realized what their intentions were. Cole disrobed quickly, baring his exquisite body to Luke's gaze before he disappeared from the room for a moment. Returning with a tube of lubrication in his hand, he handed it off to Sierra. She had to maneuver around Luke, but somehow she managed, and when she gripped his cock in her small hand, he damn near lost it again. They were going to kill him.

But before he knew it, Cole was lowering himself onto Luke's cock, his back against Luke's chest, riding him. It was the most exquisite feeling he'd ever known. Lifting and lowering himself on Luke's cock, Cole rode him slow and easy, taking him deeper until Luke had no choice but to grip Cole's hips.

Holding him still, he thrust his hips upward, burying his cock deeper, the tight ring of muscles gripping him so intensely, white sparks shot off behind his eyelids.

"I can't... Oh, fuck! I'm going to come, Cole," Luke groaned, the words torn from his chest as they both began to move in unison, Cole dropping down on Luke's cock while Luke thrust upward. Luke leaned forward, slipping his hand around Cole's waist and gripping his cock while the man continued to ride him. And then he did explode – in a blur of light and heat so powerful, Luke barely managed to remain upright as Cole's cock pulsed in his hand.

~~*~~

"So when were you going to tell me?" Cole asked Sierra when they were lying in her bed a little while later. Luke had disappeared to the bathroom and had yet to return. She knew he needed a minute, so they opted to wait for him.

"Tell you what?"

"That Luke proposed to you."

Sierra jerked, pulling away, feeling an overwhelming sense of guilt.

"Come here." Cole pulled her back into his arms, flipping her onto her back before pressing his huge body into her. He was hard. His erection pressed into her belly, and her clit pulsed in response.

"It's ok," Cole said, pressing his lips against hers.

She was crying. Unable to hold back the tears any longer. The last thing she ever wanted to do was hurt Cole.

"I love you," Cole said the words, but the emotion she saw in his eyes drove them home.

"I love you too. More than you will ever know."

"See, that's where you're wrong. I do know."

"But…"

"You can't marry us both, baby," Cole told her, cupping her cheek with his hand. "As much as I'd like to be the one, I'm ok with it."

Luke chose that moment to walk in the room, and Sierra felt another flood of guilt. How was she ever going to get used to this? How would they ever make it work?

Luke crawled into bed, easing up to her other side and holding her close, his hand resting on her lower stomach.

"I was thinking." Luke kissed her sweetly, all three of their heads close together. "What if we don't get married?"

"What?" She tried to pull away, but the two men were so much bigger than her and she was held down by them both. "You don't want…"

She couldn't get the words out.

"Oh, baby, I definitely want." Trailing his hands down between her thighs, he lingered there for a moment. "Definitely want."

"What are you saying?"

"I'm saying we don't have to get married. This isn't a traditional relationship, Sierra. I don't expect it to be." Luke glanced over at Cole and Sierra saw something pass between them. "I was being selfish."

"Surprising," Cole muttered, but he had a smile on his face.

"I'd like you to wear both of our rings. No, we can't both marry you, but we can make this work."

"He's right, you know," Cole said, kissing the side of her mouth. Then Luke kissed the other side and Sierra had to fight to remember what they were talking about.

Temptation

"I love you. Both of you," Luke said the words they had both longed to hear. "I don't care how we do this, just as long as I know I have you both with me. Forever."

Forever sounded amazing to her. More amazing than that was the way both men proceeded to love her.

And as long as they loved her, she didn't mind being the filling in their carnal delight sandwich.

Epilogue

Sierra sat at the table, glancing around at the couples they had invited to celebrate their announcement. She hadn't known what to expect, possibly awkwardness, weird glances maybe. Definitely not this outpouring of support from all of their friends and family.

Luke closed the club to the public and they invited everyone they knew. The turnout had been phenomenal. Across from her, Logan and Sam were making eyes at one another, a sweet reminder that the two of them were going strong, even if they hadn't yet chosen a third to join them – a frequent reminder from Sam. Apparently the woman enjoyed the attention of having two men in her bed, her husband ordering her pleasure. Sierra knew how she felt, although she didn't have a husband.

At least not on paper anyway.

She and Luke and Cole had come to a decision, the three of them wanting to make their relationship permanent, and they had done just that. Breaking the news to her mother had been her biggest fear, but Veronica quickly eased her mind. As always, her mother was supportive of her and her decisions, which had brought tears to Sierra's eyes. Knowing her mother loved her, unconditionally, was the greatest gift in the world.

In fact, Veronica insisted on playing a critical role in the planning of this celebration. She was now sitting, thanks to a very persuasive Cole, at one of the tables enjoying a glass of wine and conversation with none other than Xavier Thomas.

Ashleigh Thomas had also come, sitting at the same table as Sierra. In recent weeks, Sam and Sierra and Ashleigh had forged a bond unlike any friendship Sierra had ever known. The three women spent many a day having lunch and hanging out, laughing and joking with one another.

Although Ashleigh was still reluctant when it came to Alex McDermott, the woman seemed to be opening up. The way Alex watched her, like she was the only woman in the room, made Sierra smile. If only Ashleigh saw what everyone else did when they looked at the two of them. Only time would tell how that one would work out, but Sierra was hoping for the best.

Lucie Werner had come, under the pretense that she was going to be a bartender. As if Cole would have any of that. Lucie was going through a rough time, having just revealed a secret that had rocked the house. Apparently the woman had kept her daughter's paternity a secret until recently. Having broken the news to Kane Steele, Club Destiny's uber sexy bar manager couldn't have been an easy task. To everyone's surprise, Kane had been supportive, immediately taking interest in the little girl he'd lost so much time with.

Dylan Thomas, Ashleigh's brother and Alex's business partner, was sitting at a table by himself, knocking back champagne like nobody's business. That was amusing in itself because watching Dylan drink from a small, dainty glass was similar to watching Luke try to do the same.

The man would never be accused of being average. He stood at least six feet tall, and his broad shoulders and muscular arms spoke to the years he'd spent on the ranch he had recently sold in favor of moving closer to his daughter. He was a very quiet man, and although Sierra had only gotten a few details from Ashleigh, he was apparently still heartbroken over losing his wife.

"Care to dance," Cole asked, capturing Sierra's immediate attention. The man was so freaking hot, Sierra thought she might simultaneously combust the moment they touched.

"I'd love to," she answered with a smile, taking his hand.

Luke was across the room, talking with Tag Murphy, the stranger who had walked in on their last romp in Luke's office – the same one who had been put up to that little scene Sierra had witnessed at the bar. So Club Destiny wasn't as blatantly obvious as Sierra expected. Apparently that had been planned, by both Luke and Cole. According to them, they had been playing up her voyeuristic fascination which had definitely paid off tenfold.

Turns out, which no one knew this except for Luke and Logan, Tag is Cole's stepbrother. Cole's mother married Tag's father after Cole graduated from high school. Since the two men hadn't been living at home, they had never been close. That had changed recently, after Tag joined the club. Apparently they had more in common than they thought, and just like most people, Tag was drawn into Cole's orbit. Never had there been a better friend to anyone than Cole.

Sierra pressed up against him, relishing in the sexy, musky scent of his expensive cologne and the warmth of his hands on her back. She'd gotten quite used to his touch, being blessed to have him in her bed each and every night. She and Cole had both moved in with Luke, all of them deciding this was it for them. They'd finally found what they had been missing all of their lives, and they wanted to move forward.

"I've missed you," Cole whispered sweetly.

Sierra turned her head up to look at him. "Missed me?" She smiled. "But I've been right here."

"I know. That's the problem."

When Cole pulled her closer, she felt the evidence of his reasoning. "Ah."

"Yep. It's taken a tremendous amount of willpower not to sneak you upstairs and fuck you repeatedly while you scream my name."

Sierra's pussy spasmed, and her tummy tumbled. The man had come out of his shell recently, offering up those same seductive comments whenever he saw fit. He'd even taken charge on more than one occasion, his sexual appetite waylaying many of their attempted outings. Not that Sierra minded. Having him and Luke naked was still an overwhelming sight to see.

When the song ended, and a loud *click click click* resounded, Sierra turned to see Luke standing at the head of their table, his eyes directed at her. Oh boy. She wasn't sure she was ready for this part.

~~*~~

"First let me thank each of you for coming today," Luke said, staring out at the faces of his friends and family. He'd never been one to enjoy making a speech, but he had some things he wanted to share.

When Sierra walked over to him, wrapping her arm around his waist and cuddling up to his side, Luke felt like he could conquer the world. And then when Cole came and stood beside her, Luke finally felt complete. Cole's hand grazed Luke's back, reassuring him that yes, he was there for him.

"I know this might have come as a shock to some of you, but I've always considered myself blessed to be in the company of so many open minded people. Unfortunately, as many of you know, not everyone has welcomed our relationship with open arms," Luke said, referring to Susie Mackendrick who had made good on her word.

She had filed a lawsuit against Sierra, which was still underway despite Luke and Cole's attempted conversation with the woman. "I've never tried to hide who I was, never been ashamed of myself, and I'm still not. But that doesn't mean my lifestyle hasn't come under scrutiny in recent weeks."

That was an understatement. Although Susie decided to go public with her accusations, then bringing Club Destiny, and Luke, directly into the spotlight, her plot had backfired. She had been in direct violation of her contract with the club, and the penalties were steep.

In Sierra's defense, despite her request to just let it go, Luke had filed suit against Susie, and his case was solid according to his lawyer. It didn't hurt that his lawyer happened to be Tag Murphy. And just like Luke, Tag had zero tolerance for bullshit. Susie had basically signed her professional reputations death certificate after the debacle she caused. Although she was still pursuing the lawsuit against Sierra, Tag was adamant that Susan wouldn't win.

"I've heard the whispered comments, calling me a world class asshole, and I've accepted the truth in them." Chuckles filled the room. "But, for those of you who know me best, you know my life has changed in dramatic ways recently. It might've taken a couple of two by fours to the head to make me open my eyes, but I can tell you, standing here with Sierra and Cole, I've never been happier."

A round of applause broke out, and Luke swallowed hard. The emotions still seemed to get the best of him at times he least expected it.

"Our intentions here today were to share with the world the fact that the three of us will be spending the rest of our lives together. It won't always be easy, I'd never expect it to be, but no matter what obstacles we come across, in the end, it will always be worth it."

Luke couldn't say anymore because Sierra leaned into him, lifting her hand up to his cheek and turning his head down toward her. When she pulled him down for a kiss, Luke willing went into her arms, letting loose the swell of emotions that had ignited in his very soul. And then, because his life wouldn't be complete without him, when Sierra pulled back, Luke pulled Cole in close, their mouths meeting. A gasp could be heard from the audience, immediately followed by whistles and more clapping.

Luke would have never believed he would be at this point in his life, in love with one woman and one man. But he was. Irrevocably. The two of them had altered him in ways that he'd never imagined.

"I love you," Luke said to both of them.

"I love you, too," Sierra whispered, pulling him down once again, and then doing the same to Cole until their mouths met together. And there, in front of their friends and family, Luke gave himself over to these two people, for better or worse, as long as they all three shall live.

"It's about damn time!" Logan's deep voice pierced the air.

"I second that," Alex called out, causing the room to erupt in more laughter.

Luke turned his gaze on Alex. "Be careful what you wish for, man. For some reason, I get this feeling that you're next."

The End

Additional Books by Nicole Edwards

The Club Destiny Series:
Conviction
Temptation
Addicted
Seduction
Infatuation
Captivated
Devotion
Perception
Entrusted

The Alluring Indulgence Series:
Kaleb
Zane
Travis
Holidays with the Walker Brothers
Ethan

The Devil's Bend Series:
Chasing Dreams

The Dead Heat Ranch Series:
Boots Optional

Nicole would love to hear from you:

Twitter: https://twitter.com/NicoleEAuthor

Facebook: https://www.facebook.com/Author.Nicole.Edwards

Website: www.nicoleedwardsauthor.com

And don't forget to sign up for Nicole's monthly newsletter on her website or on Facebook.

34488286R00176

Made in the USA
Lexington, KY
07 August 2014